Nickolaus Albert PACIONE delivers

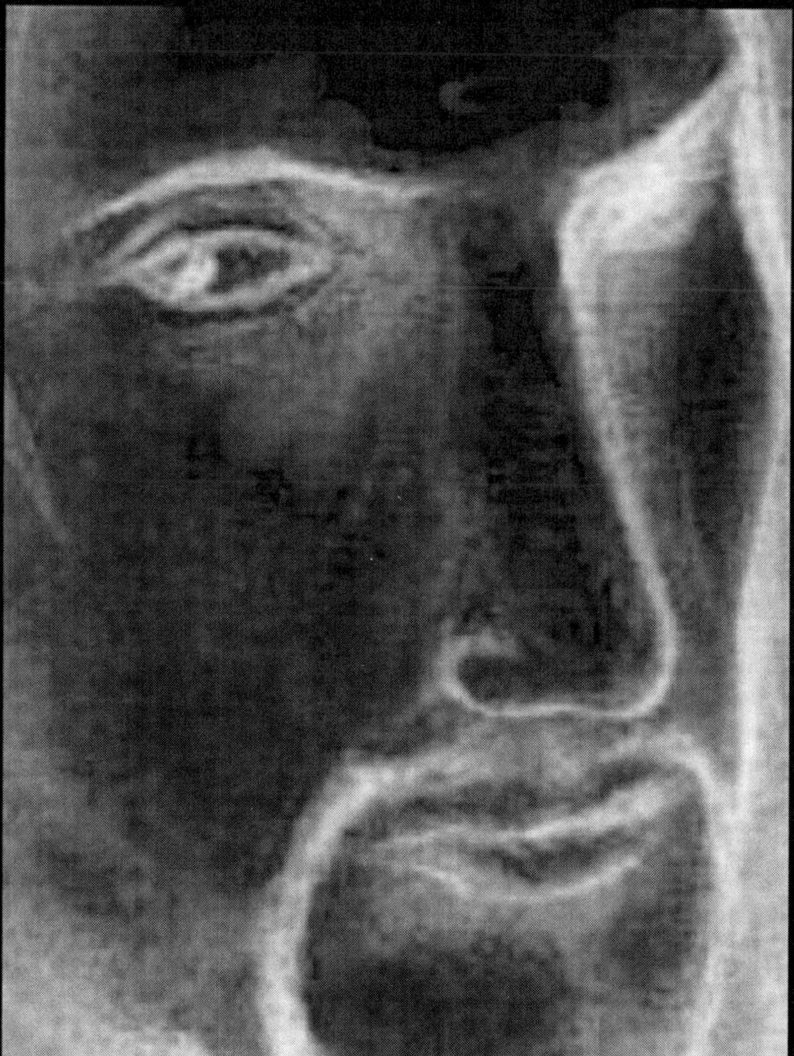

A Library Of Unknown Horrors

NICKOLAUS ALBERT PACIONE DELIVERS:
A Library Of Unknown Horrors

Pacione, Nickolaus Albert (August 3, 1976 -- Present)

The editor's short story, *Ghosts In The Tornado,* was published on Insomnia Magazine July/August 2006, the last issue to feature fiction. The story was written during the **Tabloid Purposes 3** sessions while at the apartment in Justice, Illinois. As of this edition, Insomnia Magazine folded and the site went black. This anthology is the second revised edition that Lake Fossil Press as a 6 x 9 Trade Paperback and possible 6.21 x 9.14 on CreateSpace.com Future editions will not carry *Electrocuting the Clowns* because it was plagiarized by David Boyer. All the current era contributors retain all their original copyrights. This book is designed to be a museum of horror short stories, and all the authors sent me their stories in donation to the project.

PAPERBACK ISBN: 978-0-557-83014-5

HARDCOVER ISBN: 978-0-557-07055-8

6.13 X 9.21 TRADE: 978-0-557-85096-9

The Premature Burial by Edgar Allan Poe, How He Left The Hotel By Louisa Baldwin, Valley of the Spiders by H.G. Wells, Ancient Lights by Algernon Blackwood, The Seer By Bram Stoker, The Derilict by William Hope Hodgson, A Thousand Deaths by Jack London, Legend Of Sleepy Hollow by Washington Irving, The Damned Thing By Ambrose Bierce, The Temple By H.P. Lovecraft, The Mortal Immortal by Mary Shelley, and The Monkey's Paw by W.W. Jacobs along with the other obscure short stories are hearby released into public domain.

These stories were all previously published between 1825-1925, for the first time they are collected in this volume mixed with newer authors. Some of the stories here are more obscure while others are better known than others.

COVER CREDITS ON LULU.COM EDITION

The about the editor photo was done by I.Gor Never of Biocarbon 13 during GOTHICFEST 2007. Artwork on the title page is done by Alexander Rivera, more information about his work can be seen on the following website, http://xenshin.deviantart.com/.

It caries a copyright of 2007 and originally appeared on the original website. If you want to comment on the anthology after purchase or got it from an event (these anthologies are done namely for different events and carry them for the giveaway item.)

Credits on the Lulu.com Version – Alex Rivera, Tiffany Proctor, I.Gor Never & Nickolaus Pacione provided the visuals. In it's paperback form you're welcome to loan this out how you wish, but only after you've purchased the book. But the e-book version – distribution of the book by any means are entirely forbidden. Proctor can be reached via email, darkandalusian@gmail.com. Front cover art b Alex Rivera, and the back cover art carries a copyright of 1998 by Nickolaus Pacione. These editions are signed. The TOC photo was done in 2002 and was used on Collectives.

Myspace Profiles for I.Gor Never and Nickolaus Pacione

Ig; http://myspace.com/biocarbon13

Nickolaus: http://myspace.com/nickolauspacione

e-mail: npacione@gmail.com

Layout Design and Arranged By Nickolaus Pacione

http://stores.lulu.com/lakefossilpress

http://npacione.ulmb.com — Pacione's official website.

Special Acknowledgements

First off, reworking an anthology is never easy when it's having to be done from a pdf. Due to the recent events of the plagiarism of David "Doc" Byron's entry "Electrocuting The Clowns" is one of the reasons this book commanded to be reworked. I included some more current writers in this volume as well as some more from the public domain. I want to thank the people at Wikipedia for giving me the research about the H.P. Lovecraft stories being in the public domain, as in the stories before 1923. I was talking about this to Kevin Olsen about when I was reworking this book, I wanted to include some more current authors too.

I want to thank one of my standbys from Tabloid Purposes, Everette Bell and all at Wild Cat Books for teaching me how to be a historian in the horror genre. I also want to thank Donna Burgess at Naked Snake Press for believing in the Tabloid Purposes banter, and this would be the second book published under my official website Writings From The Grave. All who contributed to my magazine, The Ethereal Gazette over the history since it established in 2005 and the friends I have in the business. I am very blessed to have talented authors coming out each issue and showing the world they can scare the hell out of everyone.

Some people might not know this, but I've been at this in the horror genre for 13 years online - since the ripe age of 20. I've been discovering writers since the age of 20 years old and always wanted to do a vehicle for this kind of project. Tabloid Purposes was the first, and I want to thank S.G. Cardin, Ken Goldman, and Casey Gordon for hanging around for as long as they have. The rework of this anthology I have to thank Ferrel "Rick" Moore for his patience in getting the situation with David "Doc" Byron squared away. I wanted him to join me in the revision with the proper ownership. Having a plagiarism in a publication is a real embarassment and a frustration in every editor's life.

It's hard to keep track of everyone I worked with over the years having five Tabloid Purposes books, and ten issues up to this point of The Ethereal Gazette. I would like to really thank the owner of the H.P. Lovecraft Cult on VampireFreaks.com for giving Writings From The Grave a second home to really get it's wings emerged.

In the age of places like Facebook.com, LiveJournal.com, Myspace.com, VampireFreaks.com and other blog / social networking sites the art of designing a website from the ground up is a dying art.

Writings From The Grave deserves it's iconic status in the era where everyone was getting a website - and I want to thank all the friends who hung around for the evolution of my website to become the monster it is once again. I want to thank the long time friends Bruce Swift, Rey Perra, Tony, David Delamancha, and the rest of the friends from Wheaton and Glendale Heights - the original Grave Diggers from College of DuPage when Writings From The Grave was a copyright name I came up with to coin my own work in 1996, had no idea it would become the website it would become.

Forgive me for my profanity at times, but I am a horror writer at the root and one that does use the strong language. I also want to thank Voltaire for letting me share a billing with him back in 2009, and Skot for letting me crash at his place when the ex-room mate had some of her lust filled parties. Then the chance to hang out with Scot Savage and Tiffany Proctor before becoming part of the maiden line up of my namesake. I hate doing long lists to say thanx, they're fucking boring.

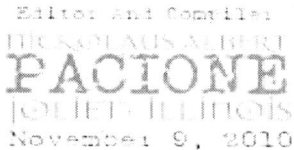

Editor And Compiler
NICHOLAUS ALBERT
PACIONE
JOLIET - ILLINOIS
November 9, 2010

The Contents In The
Museum Of Horror Fiction

INTRODUCTION

With the escalation of technology, the written word seems to have taken a back seat to a generation of internet surfers, game fanatics, and DVD mongers. Nickolaus Pacione being from the "game generation," has proven that the imagination still remains strong and the passion for the word an obsession. His attraction to the paranormal keeps him producing such classic collections as Tabloid Purposes and Quakes and Storms.

I am content to be a part of Tabloid Purposes II and IV and the charity collection, Quakes and Storms.

Unfortunately, there will always be critics. Whether or not a story passes the test of time, I believe, does not depend on what critics say, but on the originality of the story and the relevance to its contemporariness. There has been dozens of writers who have been raped by critics for the last thousand years. Oddly enough, the same writers have gone on to become the greatest contributors to the written word. I can remember reading many bad write-ups about Philip K. Dick. The adaptations of Philip K. Dick books (Blade Runner, Minority Report, Next, etc) are being produced with the top actors in Hollywood. So what am I saying? Read the story; don't rely on what someone else says.

Let's talk briefly about perception. I've had the honor for three colleagues to read my first published story Death Stop 13. It was published in The Horror Express #2, 2004.

Anyway, to my astonishment, I found that each reader had perceived the story in a completely different way. One said it had to do with a man's fear of the unknown, another said it had to do with the deception of time, and another said it had to do with "dog-eat-dog" New York City. They were all correct. They were all correct for the simple reason that everyone has a unique and different perception. Who's to tell another they are right or wrong? Why bother! Their perceptions are their realities.

What I enjoyed about this collection, was the fact that the stories could take you on different perceptive journeys. I frequently get tired of reading themed anthologies about zombies and werewolves. Usually, the plot skeletons are frozen with very little left for the imagination. Zombie kills man, werewolf attacks woman . . . then the death of the monster. Although tales of this nature are enjoyable, sometimes the imagination needs to be swept into an analytical frenzy. And this anthology does just that. Theodore Sturgeon had the talent as a writer to get the reader to think. No matter what the subject, no matter what the plot entailed, he would make the reader think about himself, his society, his actions. Yes, there are many writers today that emphasize important issues, (some as well as Mr. Sturgeon) but because of commercialism, they rarely see their work in print. This is a shame.

So before I get indignant and bore you, I'll stop and talk about the anthology.

Nickolaus has assembled and edited a collection of horror stories that will make your skin crawl and your hands tremble. He has edited and compiled many anthologies of demented tales and horrendous horrors. So prepare yourself for a frightening journey into the realms of lost souls, vampires, premature burials, giant spiders, and twisted nightmares. Here we have twenty-seven tales of horror. Some are new, some are old, but all are superbly written. They are all, indeed, great examples of traditional horror. I will talk about only a few, because, as I have stated earlier, my perception is my perception, and your perception is your perception. Also, I hate long introductions.

In the days of Edgar Allan Poe, terror lurked behind corners, behind minds, and behind doors. There were no televisions, no video games, and no internet services.

There was only the grip of the written world. In the classic tale The Premature Burial, the protagonist s catalepsy is the extreme horror. One of the finest ' horror stories ever written -- which proves, beyond a doubt, that truth is, indeed, stranger than fiction. I can remember at the age of seven, my aunt reading me The Derelict by William Hope Hodgson. The fear of the unknown and his dark style always scared the daylights out of me. In A Night in the Unlife of Roger Sparks, we find the truth about vampires in a humorous and original piece by Scot Savage. After reading the story, I couldn't help to wonder if the author might actually be a vampire. I think you might too.

Nickolaus brings us to a realization that catastrophes are more insidious than we might imagine. In Ghosts in the Tornado, an original concept, the protagonist is haunted by a ghostly victim of a tornado. A twisted tale of the supernatural, one guaranteed to cause goose bumps. The essential element of fear is the unknown and the incomprehensible.

In the lyrical prose of The Valley of Spiders, H. G. Wells brings us grotesque airborne spiders. It is a story of a knight's bravery, understanding, and limits. Jack London was an American writer and author of The Call of the Wild. His memorable tale, A Thousand Deaths, is a dark science fiction story of a father who uses his son for experiments. He uses an apparatus that can bring him back and forth from the dead. But his son has his own apparatus -- one that might just free him forever. It is an enjoyable and humorous tale.

No other author has the perfection of background and detail than Bram Stoker. In the tale The Seer, you can see a great amount of study before his pen hit the paper. In this story we have a drowned child, a gaunt old woman, a sear, and conversations of Second Sight, death and doom, and other mysteries. Andrew Jones brings us on a journey of terror in an eerie tale titled: Wolf in Sheep's Clothing. The power of suggestion has always been the greatest tool for the horror writer -- the power to take the reader into an atmosphere where the incredible seems credible.

Algernon Blackwood used the power of suggestion to broaden the horizons of his stories. Being an avid reader and collector of Weird Tales, I'm always elated to run into one of his stories. In the classic tale, Ancient Lights, Mr. Blackwood takes us on a surveyor clerk's journey. On his quest, the clerk is plunged into illusions of eerie fantasy and bizarre incidents.

Alistair Canlin's Bathtime is an extremely creepy tale -- a memorable story, very suspenseful and entrancing.

There are a host of other great stories in this volume: The Legend of Sleep Hollow, The Monkey's Paw, The Great Morgan Family Reunion and Snipe Hunt, Night of the Black Malkin, 18 Miles From Pittsburg, How He Left The Hotel, The Shadow of the Plain, Scarlet frost, and The Dark Lagoon. I'd like to have commented on all the stories, but I have to get back to my dungeon. I have built a dungeon in my mind, a place where I seek strange ideas. Where does a story come from? All writers have been asked the question: "Where do you get your ideas?" It is the type of question which makes you want to hide under a bridge. I believe a chronic reader, or bookworm, becomes a writer because he has exercised his imagination. I believe the imagination is located in a space between the subconscious and the conscious mind. It is a creative wave, or state, that drifts the writer into other worlds. The famous gurus call this state The Alpha Wave. The waves are related primarily to a relaxed, passive, and tensionless state. So during periods of creativity, the alpha waves are freely admitted.

And other times we pull the hair out of our heads. Enough said!

So it is time to surrender unconditionally to the darkness. I advise you to keep your doors locked, and whatever you do, DO NOT turn off the lights. You may find yourself forming posthumously as the protagonist in this terror-binding collection. You may hear creaks and moans coming from the walls and floorboards. You may witness strange apparitions and demented creatures. You may scream at the top of your lungs and strangle your friend. But no matter what you do, I repeat, keep your doors locked!

At any rate, here's a collection of spine gripping tales, scrapping nerves, and hair raisings to you!

Jeff Skinner
Bloomington Indiana.
December 6, 2007

iii

A NIGHT IN THE UNLIFE OF ROGER SPARKS
BY SCOT J. SAVAGE

The sun has finally set.

I have not actually seen it with my own eyes; as a matter of act, I haven't seen the light of day for over forty years. All that matters is that I know it is night... I can feel that it is night. And so... I awaken!

The night belongs to me and all my kind. It is ours to rule! The city belongs to us as well as the human sheep that live in it.

It's time for me to come out and play.

The night is my time. The city is my playground. Since I have sensed that night has fallen, I open my coffin to embrace the start of a new evening. And with that darkness, I know it is safe for me to come out.

I push aside the window curtains and gaze at the half moon that is somewhat obscured by the dark clouds. Even after forty years, every night I wake up gives me a sense of excitement... invigoration... I still get a kick. I look down from my apartment window and watch the denizens of the city scurry about and tending to their petty human and mundane concerns. I laugh to myself at the fact that these mortals think that the run the show, when in actuality, it is my brood that are the real rulers. We are the true predators... the top of the food chains.

And what exactly am I a part of? Well... then let me explain it this way: It is 2005 and I am sixty-five years old, but I have the physical appearance and same fitness of body as I had since I was nineteen years old. As a matter of fact, I stopped aging at nineteen when I was "taken" into "the fold." Despite my years, I am but a child in the eyes of most of my "family."

My name is Roger Sparks... and I am a vampire.

Now, don't get all hyper when you hear that. I'm not some blood sucking psycho that goes around ripping apart innocent people's throats. Just because some asshole from Transylvania and a few other bad apples went on a murdering spree, doesn't mean that the rest of us have to take a bad rap.

Sure, we feed on human blood, but most of us don't have to kill the poor bastard in the process. We only need to drink a portion of their blood... not all of it. We vampires have to keep a low profile. If too many dead bodies show up, totally drained of blood, it would bring too much attention on us. Then we would tip off the humans and they would be hunting us down left and right. Humans may be sheep, but they're pretty determined sheep when they band together to fight a common enemy.

To remedy that situation, we mentally dominate a dozen or so humans to use as permanent feeding vessels. Now, if we get "hungry," we give one of our vessels a call and tell them to come over. We'll suck only a pint, and afterwards we make sure to give our vessels lots of liquids and foods with plenty of sugar in them. I lick the two puncture marks which instantly seal the wound and make it undetectable. Then, when they replenish their lost blood, we send them home and no one's the wiser. We give them strict instructions not to do any heavy exertion for the next twenty-four hours.

In exchange for allowing us to feed, we, in turn, look out for the human vessel and see that nothing or no one harms them. We even manipulate things from behind the scene so that they have a few advantages in life. In other words, we protect our feeding stock. Some say that we treat our vessels as pets... but we consider them beloved pets. This may sound crazy, but I know this old bastard that lived a few houses down from me that treated his mangy German Sheppard better than he did his own wife. Occasionally, we'll even let our vessels drink a drop of our own blood, thereby preserving their youth and vitality for a few extra years. That explains why you see some people that still look youthful despite being in their forties or fifties.

I, too, am very protective of my vessels. And I am proud to say that I never killed anyone that didn't deserve it.

Being a vampire has its advantages. For starters, you don't age. And since the blood in my body isn't burdened by keeping me "alive," I can use the blood for other purposes, such as increasing my strength, sharpening my reflexes, and healing my wounds in a matter of seconds. You see, vampires are not invulnerable and impervious to injury like it is portrayed in the movies. Ever see a flick where a vampire takes a shot to the chest with a .357 magnum and doesn't even bat an eye? That's a load of crap. I've been shot in the chest and it friggin' hurts like hell. I'm only able to use the blood in my system to heal myself so quickly that it only appears that I'm immune to the bullet. When a human sees this, they usually get so distraught that they give up shooting (lucky for us). Think of it as something similar to a certain claw-retracting super-hero's healing factor. Hey, if it works for a comic book hero, it works for vampires. Of course, if my system is low on blood, I can't heal as effectively. So if some guy has a sub-machine gun, I better have access to a few vessels for later on.

That's only one of the many misconceptions about vampires. While I'm on the subject, I'll clear up a few more...

Since vampires need to keep a low profile, humans tend to make up a lot of superstitious mumbo-jumbo to make up for things they don't understand due to lack of information. Let's start with the crap about vampires not being able to see their own refection in a mirror.

Yeah... right. I am so sure! Some ignorant gypsy woman came up with that one. Since we no longer have a soul, we are unable to cast a reflection. What a crock! I'm a vampire for crying out loud... not a ghost. I'm still a creature of physical substance. Of course, I'm going to cast a reflection. A rock doesn't have a soul either, but even an inanimate object casts a reflection.

Sure, we don't see mirrors in a vampire's home... but get real. Since we don't age, we never change in our physical appearance... so what's the point of having a mirror? We already know what we look like. You could shave my head and my hair will totally grow back by the next evening. I could even do it in a matter of seconds if I use my blood reserves.

Then there's that crap about silver. Where do humans get off thinking that silver is going to hurt us more than any other metal? I'm not a freakin' werewolf (and you don't want to get me started on those jerks right now... but I could tell you some stories).

Anyway, a silver bullet or a silver knife won't hurt anymore than any other bullet or knife.

How about the fact that vampires can't enter someone's home unless they are invited to come in by the legal owner? That piece of shit is my favorite. That's about as lame as the mirrors. Like... I'm so sure that some old geezer shouting "you can't come in" is really going to stop some blood-thirsty vampire from feeding off the poor old bastard. Of course, we prefer to be invited in by the potential victim. It attracts less attention than breaking in. It's also our own little inside joke of mocking a human's intelligence.

Next, we are supposed to be repealed by the smell of garlic. Bogus! Bogus! Bogus! This one goes back to the Transylvanian twit that screwed it up for the rest of us vampires. It seemed that ol' Vladimir, back in his human days, was allergic to garlic and became ill when he ate or smelled the stuff. To make it worse, a vampire's senses are keener than a human's due to the fact that we are predatory. And since Drac's sense of smell was more sensitive after his transformation, his allergy to garlic intensified as well. So, just keep in mind, that the garlic problem was a unique quirk to one specific vampire.

A vampire is not supposed to be able to cross running water. I'll make this one simple: Bullshit. A vampire can only "rest" on his/her native soil. If a vampire leaves his/her homeland, they must put their native soil in the coffin. Again, I say bullshit. We can rest anywhere we want. But to be fair... since vampires exist for centuries upon centuries, we tend to become set in our ways. Long distance traveling requires resting during the day in an unfamiliar place which would make us very vulnerable. It's very difficult to find a trustworthy human to guard us during the daylight. Why take the risk? I love this Windy City playground and I have no intention of existing anywhere else... so I might as well rest here.

Then again, some of the stuff you have read about vampires is true. I'll give humans some credit. You can be right some of the time... and I only mean "some."

Yes, it's true that beheading a vampire will do him/her in. With great effort, and lots of blood, we can regenerate lost limbs such as ears, arms, or legs... but we cannot regrow a new head. No vampire I know, no matter how ancient or powerful, can pull that off.

A stake through the heart will definitely immobilize a vampire, but make sure you finish the job... and I'm not telling you the rest of the work to be done. I'm not stupid. Once the stake is removed, we are up and about and ready to party once again... and hopefully to get back at the jerk that put the stake there in the first place.

Fire is especially nasty, since we are unable to immediately regenerate burn wounds. Any vampire unfortunate enough to get engulfed in flames is sure to be dead meat. If a vampire can put out the flames and remain in hiding for a very long time, recovery is possible. Even with our great healing powers, third degree burns take weeks to regenerate. Usually, after being burned with fire, the psychological scars linger long after the physical scars have healed. Even vampires can have traumatic experiences.

It is true that vampires can't go out during the light of day. The fact that the sun is the giver of life and that its pureness cannot be tolerated by the undead is more superstitious crap. The real reason is that once we undergo our vampiric transformation, one of the physical changes that our body endures is that our skin loses that special what-ever-it-is that filters out the ultraviolet radiation of the sun; henceforth, we begin to smoke, sizzle, and pop. You might think that being denied the light of day is a curse, but... hey... immortality has its price and no one said it was going to be cheap.

Finally, there is "faith." This one I can't back up with any scientific facts because it is something that can't be explained away. It is a human's greatest strength and most powerful weapon against us. Fortunately, most humans don't have a lot of faith and don't know how to summon it when they really need it. Once a human believes in something so strongly, their power is unshakable... but not too many have that kind of willpower. Our vulnerability to faith is the only mystical phenomenon to our existence. It is not the cross that is flashed in our face, but the belief that is channeled through it. The channeling holy symbol doesn't have to be a cross either. It could be the Star of David, an Ankh, or even a pocket-sized statue of Buddha. Some humans have such create faith that that don't even need an item to use as a channel. The actual existence of a Supreme Being or Higher Power is not the point. The mere fact that the human believes in that being is more than enough.

So I shouldn't mock the human population too much. After all, I use to be one myself.

Some vampires don't like to be reminded of that... but, hey... I can't deny my own past.

Yes, indeed, I was a human. And if you were to take a trip to the hall of records, you could find my birth certificate which easily proves my claim. Of course, you would have to go back as far as June of 1940.

To be blunt, the first sixteen years of my life sucked big time. My father knocked up my mother just after he graduated from high school so they "had" to get married (things were very different back then). Since Pop had to blow his college fund to raise a family, the best job that he could find was that of a janitor. The pressure of being a family man at age eighteen drove him to drink. He couldn't deal with the fact that he was a loser that had tossed away his golden years. His drunken frustrations caused him to take his anger out on my mother and me. I hated the son-of-a-bitch for that! Still worse, I hated my worthless mother for taking his abuse. Maybe if my mom had the guts to leave my dad and take me with her, I could have turned out better. Because I lived in a dysfunctional family environment, I didn't do well in school and soon became a teenage delinquent. Half way into my junior year, I was old enough to be kicked out of school. I could have fought it, but why should I stick at something I was failing at? This news drove my old man through the roof.

He called me a loser. Loser? I had a plan. Losers don't have plans. My summer, part-time job at the gas station was offered to me full-time. Even better, Chuck, the owner, had taken me

in under his wing and offered to train me as an auto and motorcycle mechanic. I was going to pull in eighty bucks a week (and back in the 50s, that was great money for a teenager with no family obligations). Pop said that I was still a loser and a bum. I argued back, thinking I had a point, and that he would actually listen to me for once. I reminded Pop that I was earning money… and legally at that. Bums don't have a job and a steady income… but I did! I even offered to pay my fair share of the bills. This wasn't good enough for the stubborn old bastard. He threw me out of the house.

Luckily, Chuck let me live in the back room at the gas station. I loved that old man. And so, for the next three years, I busted my tail. I did everything from pumping gas, changing oil, and over-hauling engines. I loved every minute of it! I scrimped and saved, and after three years, I bought something for myself that I always wanted… a motorcycle. It was 1959 and I was a big fan of the late James Dean. I had it all: leather jacket, leather riding hat, black sunglasses, t-shirt, blue jeans, and black leather riding boots. I had my hair slicked all back with grease… duck tail and all. I was one bad ass!

The summer of '59 and my very first bike was one that I'll never forget. It was the twilight of my eighteenth birthday. I was a mechanic by day and a self-proclaimed rebel by night. The fact that I worked in a garage enabled me to purchase accessories for my bike at wholesale. My machine was an ensemble of leather seats and chrome pipes. I finally learned how to smoke Marlboros without choking all over myself. I was the king of cool. I even earned a spot to ride with the local biker club. I was on top of the world. I had my whole life ahead of me… or so I thought.

It was two weeks after I joined the club that things took a turn.

It was on a Friday night when a certain female biker in the club had taken notice of me.

Her name was Jeannie… just Jeannie. To this day, I never learned what her last name was. She liked to wear leather and tight blue jeans. At first, I kept my distance from her because she didn't like it when the other guys in the club made passes at her. Those that insisted on touching her without her permission ended up getting the shit knocked out of them. I never would have believed it if I hadn't seen it with my own eyes. This chick could kick any guy's ass without working up a sweat. She could also ride circles around the rest of us... almost as if she was riding motorcycles for many years. I never paid much attention to her at first because I thought I preferred my women to be more... well... like a lady. I liked the Peggy-

Sue, pony-tail, poodle skirt, angora sweater, sweet and innocent type. Not to say that Jeannie wasn't a blond bombshell babe in her own right. As a matter of fact, she was hot... but I stayed away because I saw that the more these other idiots forced their attentions on her, the harsher that she inflicted punishment. Not that I was afraid to take a shot at her, but I'd feel kind of stupid if I had to swap punches with a girl. Maybe, she was one of those strange chicks that preferred other chicks over men... or maybe a little of both. Boy, was I ever wrong.

It was on that Friday night that I was with my fellow bikers in our usual abandoned back lot hangout. I was innocently sitting around stuffing my face with hotdogs, fries and beer, when all of a sudden, out of nowhere, Jeannie walks right up to me, and sits on my lap. She takes off my hat and starts running her fingers through my hair and blows in my ear. She starts telling me how she's been watching me for the past few weeks and how much she likes me. She says I'm real cool because I was the only member of the pack that didn't make a move on her. She also said I was the second best rider in the group. She was number one, of course. She tells me that she pushed the other guys away because she'll only be with a guy that can win her over.

"Why the sudden attention?" I asked. "You never paid attention to me before."

"I'm paying attention to you now," she said back. Then she puts this massive lip-lock on me that sends my teenage hormones into over drive. All I want is more of her. "Win me over, Roger."

"How do I do that?"

"Do something crazy," she whispered in my ear.

Crazy? Wasn't the fact that the babe who would let no one else go down her pants was now coming on to me crazy enough? Not knowing what else to do, I got the boys to set up the jumping ramp and lined up twelve garbage cans. That should be crazy enough to impress her. I practiced all month to get up to twelve.

I hit the throttle and cleared the last garbage can with ease. The rest of the gang cheered.

For a few seconds, I was proud of myself.

"Not bad," she grinned. She gave a nod of her head and had the boys set up two more cans.

Before any more could be said, she jumped the fourteen cans as easily as I did the twelve.

She pulled up to me and said, "Your turn, Roger."

Was she nuts? Fourteen cans? I damn near killed myself attempting thirteen for few days ago. I tried to explain my hesitation, but the guys kept cheering me on. They wanted me to put the "untouchable babe" in her place.

"C'mon, Jeannie. You don't really expect me to jump fourteen cans?"

"Of course not, Roger," she winked. "You're going to jump fifteen. No one else in this club, except me, can jump fourteen. I could never do fifteen… and if you can do fifteen… then you'll have beaten me. When you beat me, you get the grand prize: I get to be your girlfriend."

I was about to tell her that this was going too far. As gorgeous as she was, it wasn't worth breaking my neck. Fifteen cans! That's not crazy… it's just plain insane!

"Look, Jeannie. I like you and all, but this is not my idea of…."

Then the first warning sign came. She stared into my eyes. I could feel her gaze touch my soul. She smirks and licks her upper lip. "Don't be such a spoil sport, Roger, darling. You can do this. I know you can. I'll even let you use my bike. It'll give you more lift."

Suddenly, within her stare, I felt my fear fade away. All that mattered at that moment was winning her over. It was the most important thing I had to do. I didn't realize then, but she was using her mental domination to give me a boost of confidence. At that moment, I felt like I could do anything.

Minutes later, I gave the throttle all it had and I was flying over those cans like I never did before. Just as I was about to think that I was going to pull this suicide mission off, I felt the back tire hit the edge of the last garbage can. Jeannie's bike surged ahead of me. I bounced and slid across the pavement. Luckily, I only managed to knock the wind out of myself and get away with only a few bruises and scratches. The bike, on the other hand, didn't get off so lucky. It got all banged up when it crashed in the nearby fence.

As I lay on my back gasping for air, I heard my pals screaming and shouting. They thought

I was awesome but I only thought about how stupid this stunt really was. As I was about to give up, Jeannie puts her foot on my chest and keeps me pinned down.

"You hit the last can, Roger!"

"I'm so sorry, Jeannie. I didn't mean to mess up your bike. I'll take it back to the garbage and fix it up as good as new. I swear."

"I guess you did well enough," she muttered as she suddenly yanked me up and planted another hard kiss on me. I was too dazed at that time to realize the second warning sign: a 110 pound woman had just effortlessly lifted a 175 pound man six inches off the ground in order to give me that kiss. My friends were just as excited as I was. Someone had finally melted the cold heart of the Ice Queen.

After that, we crawled off to a private spot and we screwed each other's brains out. I ignored the third warning sign: she refused my offer to stop by the drug store so I could pick up a condom. I would later find out that her "kind" didn't get pregnant. They reproduced in a non-conventional way.

For the next few weeks, Jeannie and I were always together. I could never get enough of her. I was compelled to always be by her side. We always rode our bikes together.

Sometimes, we rode side to side. Sometimes, she rode on the back of my bike, while at others, I rode on the back of hers. I guess you could say that I was in love with her.

It was on my nineteenth birthday that she said that she had a "special surprise" for me. So, we went to our favorite make-out spot and sat on the grass. She put something in my hand. I couldn't believe my eyes! It was a necklace with a medallion... made of solid gold! I took a closer look and there was an engraving of some kind of French Musketeer on it. I'm no history scholar, but this thing looked like it had to be three or four hundred years old. I told Jeannie that it was great and that I loved it... but where did she ever get something like this?

"I got it as a present from Nigel Shermlock... back in 1885. He was a freelance detective who lived in Victorian England. He's the one that Sir Arthur Conan Doyle adapted into his

Sherlock Holmes stories. This medallion was Nigel's way of thanking me for all my help on his cases. You see, I assisted him from time to time. Now, I want to give it to you, as a show of appreciation for all the good times that you have shown me."

"1885, huh?" I laughed at her little joke. "That would make you older than my grandmother."

"Actually, I'm two hundred and fifty-six years old, Roger, dear."

"Ooookay," I played along with her little game. "You don't look a day over two hundred."

"You'll und on you."

As she slipped the necklace over my head, she kissed me. Then she started to move her lips down to my neck. There I was, thinking that she's about to give me the grand-daddy of all hickeys... when in fact, it was a prelude to the biggest change in my existence.

I glanced over to see hat her gorgeous baby blue eyes suddenly turned to blood red. When she opened her mouth, I didn't see her pearly white teeth... I saw fangs! She had friggin' fangs! Before I could ask about her dental work, she sank her fangs right into my neck and bit down hard. I should have screamed my head off, but something in my mind compelled me to let her my precious life force dwindle away, it all made sense. It all added up. It became all too clear as to why I never saw Jeannie during the day. I now understood how she could out-muscle all the neighborhood toughs. I knew why she was compelled to do her every whim. That's the reason when we made love that she didn't insist on birth control. It was because she was unable to get pregnant. Jeannie was a friggin' vampire! And I fell right into her dangled web!

I was going to be her next victim... all because of my raging hormones!

I cursed myself because I couldn't fight back. She had me under her blasted mental hold!

All I could do was to mutter to her not to take all my blood. As I was on the brink of death,

I experienced a sort of personal ecstasy. I was going to die, but I was going to die on a happy mental high note. Why the hell was I so happy to be her victim?

Just as I felt the last of my life-force waste away, Jeannie slashed her wrist with her now massive fingernails that she had suddenly grown. She shoved her wrist into my mouth and forced me to drink her blood. As I drank, I felt a new sort of energy fill me. I no longer felt weak. I no longer felt human. I felt as if I could have ruled the world!

After I fully waked up, Jeannie told me that I was now the same as her. I was now a vampire... a predator of the night. She told me that we would have to leave town for a while.

She wanted to take me to some old farm that she owned in Wisconsin so that she could properly show me "the ropes." She said that I had to leave my family and all my friends behind because there was no turning back at this point. It was no problem for me since my family had disowned me, and I had no real friends... except for Jeannie and Chuck. It was hard to leave him behind. Against her advice, I snuck away to see Chuck one last time. At the very least, I owed him a goodbye. I couldn't just disappear on him. I told Chuck that I was going away for good in order to start a new "life" with Jeannie. Chuck hugged me and wished me all the best. He said he'd miss me and that he loved me like a son. It was the first time in my life that I remembered crying.

For the next ten years, Jeannie taught me how to hunt and feed. She showed me how to suck blood without leaving a noticeable mark by licking the puncture with my tongue. She taught me how to dominate a human's will and make them my permanent feeding vessel. And most of all, she showed me how to use my newly acquired blood to increase my strength and stamina... something I was quite good at. The only drawback was that I found it impossible to break the domination Jeannie seemed to impose on me. Any thought of betrayal on my part would be instantly sucked away. Jeannie explained that in my early vampire days, I had to drink her blood until I learned to hunt on my own. In a way, I was an extension of Jeannie. I would later learn that this blood bond was a show of love of sorts between two vampires. Of course, when I asked her to bond to me, Jeannie said I had to prove myself worthy of that honor.

So that's where I'm at today. After ten years, she told me that it was time to let me go off on my own and make a reputation for myself so that I could prove myself worthy. And for the past thirty-plus years, that's exactly what I've been trying to do. Jeannie stops by to see me every now and then to see how I'm doing. Every time I see her, I still become putty in her hands. The last time I heard from her was six months ago. She's a nurse at Northwestern Hospital. I guess I can't blame her for wanting to be near by a steady supply of blood. Every time I see her, I ask her, yet again, if I'm worthy. Every time she tells me that I need more time. She keeps reminding me that I am still a young vampire. She keeps telling me that it'll be worth the wait. What's a few more decades to have eternal bliss between us? She insists that she can't wait to be bonded to me, but the time is still not right. I play along with it because... damn it... I love her... that's why... okay!

Thirty-plus years is nothing to a vampire. No fledgling could prove worthiness in so short a period of time. So I must endure. In all these years, I had to endure hippies, beatniks, flower children, Vietnam... and disco. Horrible disco! The changes in music is the worst thing that I had to go through. Music has gone to hell. Now some jerks want to revive disco. Heads will roll for this. How I hate it when certain annoying things make a comeback... but then again... I don't mind the fact that mini-skirts came back so I could have twice the fun.

As all the crap passed me by, I tried to build up my reputation... but as of late... I have been slipping. For all my superior strength, dexterity, and stamina, these blasted humans have been getting the better of me. They've been mocking me and making me look like a chump.

It seems that the harder I try, the more trouble I get into. When the humans mock me, the other vampires accuse me of being all brawn and no brains. They call me a Neanderthal that thinks with his biceps. But I'll show them. I'll show them all!

Tonight I'm going to redeem myself. Tonight, I'm going to see a certain human that made me look like a fool. Tonight, I'm going to get even with a certain bastard bartender. That human sheep caused me undo embarrassment. He made me a laughing-stock... and I will get even. I will regain my honor. I will get one step closer to proving my worthiness to Jeannie. I will make that human pay for the indignity he has made me suffer.

It all started last night. I decided to check out this new bar to see what the atmosphere was like. Most of the patrons were former bikers, would-be bikers and those chicks that liked to dress in the gothic look... all in black and dark make-up. I had no trouble blending in with the sea of leather jackets.

Anyway, this yuppie comes stumbling in and parks his butt in the stool next to mine. He's drunk as a skunk and doesn't have a clue at to where he's ended up. He sticks out like a sore thumb. I figure that he's an easy mark for a quick taste of blood. So, I start up a conversation with the chump and we get pretty friendly. I take out the dice I have in my pocket and casually mention into our conversation if he has ever played craps before. He says he never heard of the game so I offer to show him the basics and he accepts. This trick never fails.

After rolling the dice a few times for fun, I start to make nickel, dime and quarter wagers just to make rolling the dice more interesting. I'm letting him win on purpose so I can get his guard down. Eventually, he's up twenty bucks. Just as I planned. Mr. Yuppie gets cocky and wants to let the whole twenty ride. I see my opportunity to throw the hook. I mention that we're bringing to much attention to ourselves and that the management frowns on heavy gambling. So I suggest that we slip out into the alley and finish the game. The idiot agrees. If there's one thing that you can depend on from mortals, it's greed. He keeps rolling the dice, as I keep an eye out to make sure that no one is watching. By now, the jerk is up fifty bucks.

Finally, the guy rolls snake eyes. As I see that the coast is clear, I tell him that he loses big time. Just as I am about to stick my fangs into his neck, I feel someone grab my shirt and pull me back.

I look to see that it's another vampire by the name of Antonio. He's one of those "sophisticated" Barnibus Collins, Dark Shadows type. He's the kind of vampire that thinks his own shit doesn't stink. There he was, just standing there in his fancy velvet jacket and ruffled shirt. He looked like he fell out of an Ann Rice novel. This guy really irritates me.

"Naughty, naughty, Mr. Rebel-without-a-clue," he taunts me. "You must learn to keep a lower profile."

I get up and tell Antonio to mind his own business. He has no right to interfere with my feeding. He argues back that I'm not discrete. I remind the pansy that just a week earlier in this very area, a girl was assaulted and beaten up by her deranged boyfriend in front of twenty other patrons and no one lifted a finger to help her. No one even bothered to make an anonymous call to the police. Now, someone's supposed to notice a biker "kissing" a yuppie's neck in a dark alley. He should see what's going down on Rush Street. Antonio calls me a barbaric swine. I call him a panty-waist. By this time, the yuppie has staggered back into the bar along with my fifty bucks. Antonio laughs at me for that. I had to get my money back. It wasn't so much the fifty bucks, but it was the fact that this human got the better of me.

I rushed into the bar and found the guy passed out on a stool. I was just about to pick him up and carry him over my shoulder so that I can finish my "business" elsewhere. That's when that stupid bartender suddenly enters the picture.

He asks me where I'm taking him and I tell the nosey bartender that I'm taking my "pal" home. The bartender says not to bother. He'll call the guy a cab instead. I tell the bartender that I'm still taking my pal home, but I didn't give the bar creep enough credit. The bartender knew that this guy came in here alone and was probably figuring that I'd roll the guy. He insisted that he was going to call a cab for the guy. I re-insist on taking the guy home myself.

Who the hell did this bartender think he was anyway? I didn't have time for this, so I ignored this self-appointed guardian. I grab the yuppie and start carrying him toward the door.

It was then that the big, hairy bouncer blocked my way and told me that I wasn't taking my new pal anywhere. I easily pushed the muscle bound jerk out of the way. Just as I take my first step, that weasel bartender snuck up on me and let me have it in the back of the head with a baseball bat. I keeled over and now I'm forced to dip into my blood reserve to heal my broken collar bone. While I'm doing that, the bouncer picks me up and puts me in a full nelson. Little does this half-wit know that his strength is no match for mine so I break his lousy hold and send a fist right into the goon's lower chest. My would-be conqueror drops to the floor like a rock and assumes a fetal position as he wheezes for breath.

Unfortunately, a mob of his angry pals rushes me. I punch, kick, and head-butt at everyone within my reach. The annoying bartender uses the distraction to pop me in the back of the head once again with that friggin' bat of his and then he slithers to the safety behind his bar.

I'm really pissed off by now. I managed to dispatch the mob and was just about to enact my vengeance on the bartender when I hear the police sirens. I wasn't in any condition to take on armed cops. I exited that bar and hopped on my bike in order to make a tactful retreat. I had to circle and cut down side streets because they had three squad cars looking for me. It took two hours to get home and all I had to show for it was a wallet fifty bucks lighter and no blood.

Now, the other vampires are pissed off at me because that was a popular feeding ground and all the commotion I caused will screw up the feeding for at least two weeks unless I settle the score. Rebel-without-a-clue, indeed! I'll show those creeps like Antonio that I have what it takes. They'll see that I'm every bit as good as they are. I'm not a muscle-head! The bartender only caught me off guard... nothing more. I'll get him and I'll make Jeannie proud of me.

The more I think about the incident, the madder I get. I just want to get my hands on that little twerp. It's sneaky little weasel runts like him that cause my sorrow. The same kind of runt as last year. One little mistake and I still don't hear the end of it... and now this bar incident is on my shoulders. How did I know that drug dealer I was going to rip off was an undercover cop? I just wanted some money to fix my bike... and who would complain if a lousy drug dealer got mugged? So what if he called for his hidden back up. I got away. Sure, I had to take three bullets and jump over a fifteen foot fence to get away. I didn't get caught, and the secret existence of vampires was not violated. What's the big deal? What's the harm?

Antonio kept saying that the fact that I got away was inconsequential. I shouldn't have placed myself in that situation in the first place. But if I kept a low profile like Antonio keeps insisting, then how the hell do I build my reputation and prove myself to Jeannie?

I must not dwell in the past. Last year's mistake has blown over... but my little screw up may make it re-surface. I need to teach that bartender not to butt into my business. Now what should I do? Killing him would be too extreme and wouldn't be low profile. I need to be subtle just like Antonio says. I want him alive so he can tell everyone not to mess with Roger Sparks. I'll just rough him up a little. I'll just scare the living shit out of him. I'll have him crying and begging for me not to snap his scrawny little neck. Then I'll demand he pay me the fifty bucks he caused me to lose. Yeah, that's right... still... I'll need a little help. It's too dangerous to go back to that bar myself. Time to call Snake and cash in on one of the favors that he owes me.

About an hour and a half later at the neighborhood Mickey D's, I meet up with Snake, a lieutenant in a Latino gang known as the Cobras. Good ol' Snake. I can always rely on him. I guess you can say that he's one of my allies. Of course, he doesn't actually know that I'm a vampire, but he does know that I'm not an ordinary person. I used my "muscle" to help him out during a "territorial dispute" and, in return, Snakes helps me out when I'm faced with personal dilemmas such as now.

"Don't look so glum, man," Snake keeps insisting. "I'll take care of everything. I had it all planned out as I was driving here."

"Go on," I answered as I puffed down on my Marlboro. It's obvious that I don't have to worry about my health being ruined.

"Okay, it's like this, man... I pull my car into that dark alley right next to the bar and pop my hood. I send my girlfriend, Juanita, inside. You've seen Juanita... she's real fine."

"Yeah, I've seen her," I answer again anxious to hear the rest.

"She'll start pouring on the old charm on this bartender. She'll tell him that she has car trouble and she needs a nice, strong man to help her out. She'll lead him into the alley, where you'll be hiding in the shadows. She'll point to the battery... and while the asshole is distracting looking under the hood... you rush in and... Whammo! You do whatever you need to do... got it?"

Boy, that Snake is such a sneaky little cockroach. What a manipulative mind. Guess that's why I like to have him around.

"Do you really think Juanita can actually get this jerk to come outside?"

"You kiddin', man? I'll have her wear that tight light blue mini-dress... the one that shows almost all of her cleavage. She'll have that creep drooling all over her, unless of course, unless he's one of those guys that likes guys."

"That's a chance we'll have to take. Will she go along with this even knowing things might get... violent?"

"Of course she will, man. She's my woman and she'll do what I tell her."

"And she knows who to bring out?"

"They only have one bartender work at a time. This guy you want works every weeknight.

There's no way that she could screw this up."

"Good," I put out my cigarette. "I'll meet up with you both at 11:30 tonight…"

At twenty-five after eleven, Snake pulls up in the alley with his Cadillac and pops the hood. He sees me stick my head out from the dark corner and awaits my signal. I give him the thumbs up. Snake nods his acknowledging my signal, as he opens the passenger door for

Juanita. I watch her strut in those high heels. I laugh to myself as I watch her little ass swing back and forth. I've never seen Snake's woman look finer. The poor bastard doesn't stand a chance.

Snake walks over and joins me in the shadows. "Don't worry, man. She'll have that guy running out her any second."

"You did real good, Snake," I smiled. "Wait until I get this guy…"

I almost jumped out of my socks as I felt a hand touch my shoulder. Only another vampire could sneak up on me like that… and I had a bad feeling that I knew who that vampire was…

"Roger, you ruffian thug," said Antonio. "Returning to the scene of the crime? Have you suffered enough embarrassment already?"

Just what I need… some out-of-the-closet Jiminy Cricket.

"Antonio, what are you doing here? Don't you have more important things to do? Like shopping for a matching pair of tassels for your shoes?"

Snake began to laugh. "Is this guy a friend of yours, man?"

"Silence insect!" Antonio snarled.

"Don't tell me to…" was all Snake was able to get out before Antonio puts his typical vampire gaze that causes my ally to stand around with a blank look on his face. I didn't get excited about it as Snake should be able to shake it off once Antonio leaves.

"What are you up to, Roger, dear?"

"If you must know, 'dear,' I'm getting my honor back by getting even with that bartender for making a fool out of me last night."

Antonio started shaking his head and starts to make that annoying "tsk, tsk" sound between his teeth. "Oh, Sparkie, how you disappoint me. Revenge is such an empty endeavor.

Being a vampire, you are supposed to be above such petty 'human' motives. Why even trouble yourself by going through with this? The incident will blow over eventually. Your screw-up will be forgotten when the next idiot makes a screw-up."

"Right," I snarl. "But until that time, I'd have to listen to everyone else's wisecracks…"

"But Roger, darling, you get yourself into trouble without even trying. It's bad enough that you mess up naturally without forcing it on yourself like you're trying to do now. We expect natural foolish incidents from you. I even started a pool with the other vampires on what day of the month that you stumble into your next bit of trouble. You make us laugh and feel better about ourselves. No matter what mistakes the rest of us make, you always manage to come up with something better. Why... you set the perfect examples that the rest of the vampires should not follow. That's one of the many reasons that I love you."

The only intelligent comeback I had was, "Says you, Antonio. You won't get me to mess up this time. No way! This is one time that Roger Sparks comes up smelling like a rose. You just sit back and watch. As soon as that jerk puts his head under that hood, you'll see what

being cool is all about."

"Then I suggest you hurry because here he comes...."

I see a male figure under the hood as Juanita slowly backs away from the car looking in all directions and not knowing what's supposed to happen next. I was so busy letting this male vampire queen get my goat that I almost missed my opportunity. I rushed out of the dark corner leaving Antonio to choke on the trail of my dust. I swooped in for the kill like I never swooped before. By the time that my prey got out from under the hood to see what was coming, I'm already on top of him.

In one motion, I grabbed him by his jacket collar and throw him into the wall... hard... but only hard enough to stun him. I don't want to break anything just yet. Before that little weasel can utter a word, I got him raised a few feet off the ground and staring into my furyred eyes.

Now I got him where I want him. My days of ridicule will soon be over. No longer will I be mocked by Antonio and his cronies. Now it's only a question of what to do with this creep.

I can hear his heart pounding over his whimpering. I got him scared to death. Good! I will make him beg like a dog to spare his worthless human life. I want to hear him cry. I laugh as I watch the sweat drip down his forehead... down past his beady little eyes... past his cheeks... and finally drenching his stupid little moustache and... Did I say moustache?

Moustache? Moustache!

This guy isn't supposed to have a moustache! What the hell is going on? This isn't the bartender!

"What are you trying to pull here?"

"I'm not trying to pull anything, mister," he whimpers. "Don't hurt me. Take my wallet!"

"Who the hell are you?"

"I'm just a lousy bartender. I don't have a lot of money... but take it... What have I ever done to you?"

My first response was denial. "You're not the bartender. I saw the bartender last night from this very place, and you're not him. Don't lie to me! Don't try to protect him. I know that he works here every weeknight. Where is he?"

"T-T-That's my brother. I'm stepping in for him tonight. He couldn't make it today.

Some guy tried to beat him up yesterday. Oh Lord... it was you. Please... put me down. I won't say anything. Please, don't hurt me."

I stood there looking at him frozen with self-embarrassment. In my haste for revenge, I rushed out blindly. I automatically assumed that it would be the same guy without even making sure beforehand. I never even bothered to take a good look at this poor schmuck when I rushed out. The whole situation could have been avoided if I had taken one crummy second to take a look. I had just scared the shit out of the wrong guy. It was all for nothing!

By now, the poor guy has passed out from fear. As I gently lower this human sheep, which I had no reason to cause grief, I could hear Antonio laughing loudly at me from the shadows. I will never hear the end of this for a long time to come!

I have been mocked!

THE PREMATURE BURIAL

BY EDGAR ALLAN POE

THERE are certain themes of which the interest is all-absorbing, but which are too entirely horrible for the purposes of legitimate fiction. These the mere romanticist must eschew, if he do not wish to offend or to disgust. They are with propriety handled only when the severity and majesty of Truth sanctify and sustain them. We thrill, for example, with the most intense of "pleasurable pain" over the accounts of the Passage of the Beresina, of the Earthquake at Lisbon, of the Plague at London, of the Massacre of St. Bartholomew, or of the stifling of the hundred and twenty-three prisoners in the Black Hole at Calcutta. But in these accounts it is the fact—it is the reality—it is the history which excites. As inventions, we should regard them with simple abhorrence.

I have mentioned some few of the more prominent and august calamities on record; but in these it is the extent, not less than the character of the calamity, which so vividly impresses the fancy. I need not remind the reader that, from the long and weird catalogue of human miseries, I might have selected many individual instances more replete with essential suffering than any of these vast generalities of disaster. The true wretchedness, indeed—the ultimate woe—is particular, not diffuse. That the ghastly extremes of agony are endured by man the unit, and never by man the mass—for this let us thank a merciful God!

To be buried while alive is, beyond question, the most terrific of these extremes which has ever fallen to the lot of mere mortality. That it has frequently, very frequently, so fallen will scarcely be denied by those who think. The boundaries which divide Life from Death are at best shadowy and vague. Who shall say where the one ends, and where the other begins? We know that there are diseases in which occur total cessations of all the apparent functions of vitality, and yet in which these cessations are merely suspensions, properly so called. They are only temporary pauses in the incomprehensible mechanism. A certain period elapses, and some unseen mysterious principle again sets in motion the magic pinions and the wizard wheels. The silver cord was not for ever loosed, nor the golden bowl irreparably broken. But where, meantime, was the soul?

Apart, however, from the inevitable conclusion, a priori that such causes must produce such effects—that the well-known occurrence of such cases of suspended animation must naturally give rise, now and then, to premature interments—apart from this consideration, we have the direct testimony of medical and ordinary experience to prove that a vast number of such interments have actually taken place. I might refer at once, if necessary to a hundred well authenticated instances. One of very remarkable character, and of which the circumstances may be fresh in the memory of some of my readers, occurred, not very long ago, in the neighboring city of Baltimore, where it occasioned a painful, intense, and widelyextended excitement. The wife of one of the most respectable citizens-a lawyer of eminence and a member of Congress—was seized with a sudden and unaccountable illness, which completely baffled the skill of her physicians. After much suffering she died, or was supposed to die. No one suspected, indeed, or had reason to suspect, that she was not actually dead. She presented all the ordinary appearances of death. The face assumed the usual pinched and sunken outline. The lips were of the usual marble pallor. The eyes were lustreless. There was no warmth. Pulsation had ceased. For three days the body was preserved unburied, during which it had acquired a stony rigidity. The funeral, in short, was hastened, on account of the rapid advance of what was supposed to be decomposition.

The lady was deposited in her family vault, which, for three subsequent years, was undisturbed. At the expiration of this term it was opened for the reception of a sarcophagus; —but, alas! how fearful a shock awaited the husband, who, personally, threw open the door!

As its portals swung outwardly back, some white-apparelled object fell rattling within his arms. It was the skeleton of his wife in her yet unmoulded shroud.

A careful investigation rendered it evident that she had revived within two days after her entombment; that her struggles within the coffin had caused it to fall from a ledge, or shelf to the floor, where it was so broken as to permit her escape. A lamp which had been accidentally left, full of oil, within the tomb, was found empty; it might have been exhausted, however, by evaporation. On the uttermost of the steps which led down into the dread chamber was a large fragment of the coffin, with which, it seemed, that she had endeavored to arrest attention by striking the iron door. While thus occupied, she probably swooned, or possibly died, through sheer terror; and, in failing, her shroud became entangled

in some iron—work which projected interiorly. Thus she remained, and thus she rotted, erect.

In the year 1810, a case of living inhumation happened in France, attended with circumstances which go far to warrant the assertion that truth is, indeed, stranger than fiction. The heroine of the story was a Mademoiselle Victorine Lafourcade, a young girl of illustrious family, of wealth, and of great personal beauty. Among her numerous suitors was Julien Bossuet, a poor litterateur, or journalist of Paris. His talents and general amiability had recommended him to the notice of the heiress, by whom he seems to have been truly beloved; but her pride of birth decided her, finally, to reject him, and to wed a Monsieur

Renelle, a banker and a diplomatist of some eminence. After marriage, however, this gentleman neglected, and, perhaps, even more positively ill-treated her. Having passed with him some wretched years, she died,—at least her condition so closely resembled death as to deceive every one who saw her. She was buried—not in a vault, but in an ordinary grave in the village of her nativity. Filled with despair, and still inflamed by the memory of a profound attachment, the lover journeys from the capital to the remote province in which the village lies, with the romantic purpose of disinterring the corpse, and possessing himself of its luxuriant tresses. He reaches the grave. At midnight he unearths the coffin, opens it, and is in the act of detaching the hair, when he is arrested by the unclosing of the beloved eyes. In fact, the lady had been buried alive. Vitality had not altogether departed, and she was aroused by the caresses of her lover from the lethargy which had been mistaken for death.

He bore her frantically to his lodgings in the village. He employed certain powerful restoratives suggested by no little medical learning. In fine, she revived. She recognized her preserver. She remained with him until, by slow degrees, she fully recovered her original health. Her woman's heart was not adamant, and this last lesson of love sufficed to soften it.

She bestowed it upon Bossuet. She returned no more to her husband, but, concealing from him her resurrection, fled with her lover to America. Twenty years afterward, the two returned to France, in the persuasion that time had so greatly altered the lady's appearance that her friends would be unable to recognize her. They were mistaken, however, for, at the first meeting, Monsieur Renelle did actually recognize and make claim to his wife. This claim she resisted, and a judicial tribunal sustained her in her resistance, deciding that the peculiar circumstances, with the long lapse of years, had extinguished, not only equitably, but legally, the authority of the husband.

The "Chirurgical Journal" of Leipsic—a periodical of high authority and merit, which some American bo a very distressing event of the character in question.

An officer of artillery, a man of gigantic stature and of robust health, being thrown from an unmanageable horse, received a very severe contusion upon the head, which rendered him insensible at once; the skull was slightly fractured, but no immediate danger was apprehended. Trepanning was accomplished successfully. He was bled, and many other of the ordinary means of relief were adopted. Gradually, however, he fell into a more and more hopeless state of stupor, and, finally, it was thought that he died.

The weather was warm, and he was buried with indecent haste in one of the public cemeteries. His funeral took place on Thursday. On the Sunday following, the grounds of the cemetery were, as usual, much thronged with visitors, and about noon an intense excitement was created by the declaration of a peasant that, while sitting upon the grave of the officer, he had distinctly felt a commotion of the earth, as if occasioned by some one struggling beneath. At first little attention was paid to the man's asseveration; but his evident terror, and the dogged obstinacy with which he persisted in his story, had at length their natural effect upon the crowd. Spades were hurriedly procured, and the grave, which was shamefully shallow, was in a few minutes so far thrown open that the head of its occupant appeared. He was then seemingly dead; but he sat nearly erect within his coffin, the lid of which, in his furious struggles, he had partially uplifted.

He was forthwith conveyed to the nearest hospital, and there pronounced to be still living, although in an asphytic condition. After some hours he revived, recognized individuals of his acquaintance, and, in broken sentences spoke of his agonies in the grave.

From what he related, it was clear that he must have been conscious of life for more than an hour, while inhumed, before lapsing into insensibility. The grave was carelessly and loosely filled with an exceedingly porous soil; and thus some air was necessarily admitted.

He heard the footsteps of the crowd overhead, and endeavored to make himself heard in turn. It was the tumult within the grounds of the cemetery, he said, which appeared to awaken him from a deep sleep, but no sooner was he awake than he became fully aware of the awful horrors of his position.

This patient, it is recorded, was doing well and seemed to be in a fair way of ultimate recovery, but fell a victim to the quackeries of medical experiment. The galvanic battery was applied, and he suddenly expired in one of those ecstatic paroxysms which, occasionally, it superinduces.

The mention of the galvanic battery, nevertheless, recalls to my memory a well known and very extraordinary case in point, where its action proved the means of restoring to animation a young attorney of London, who had been interred for two days. This occurred in 1831, and created, at the time, a very profound sensation wherever it was made the subject of converse.

The patient, Mr. Edward Stapleton, had died, apparently of typhus fever, accompanied with some anomalous symptoms which had excited the curiosity of his medical attendants.

Upon his seeming decease, his friends were requested to sanction a post-mortem examination but declined to permit it. As often happens, when such refusals are made, the practitioners resolved to disinter the body and dissect it at leisure, in private. Arrangements were easily effected with some of the numerous corps of body-snatchers, with which London abounds; and, upon the third night after the funeral, the supposed corpse was unearthed from a grave eight feet deep, and deposited in the opening chamber of one of the private hospitals.

An incision of some extent had been actually made in the abdomen, when the fresh and undecayed appearance of the subject suggested an application of the battery. One experiment succeeded another, and the customary effects supervened, with nothing to characterize them in any respect, except, upon one or two occasions, a more than ordinary degree of lifelikeness in the convulsive action. It grew late. The day was about to dawn; and it was thought expedient, at length, to proceed at once to the dissection. A student, however, was especially desirous of testing a theory of his own, and insisted upon applying the battery to one of the pectoral muscles. A rough gash was made, and a wire hastily brought in contact, when the patient, with a hurried but quite unconvulsive movement, arose from the table, stepped into the middle of the floor, gazed about him uneasily for a few seconds, and then—spoke. What he said was unintelligible, but words were uttered; the syllabification was distinct. Having spoken, he fell heavily to the floor.

For some moments all were paralyzed with awe—but the urgency of the case soon restored them their presence of mind. It was seen that Mr. Stapleton was alive, although in a swoon. Upon exhibition of ether he revived and was rapidly restored to health, and to the society withheld, until a relapse was no longer to be apprehended. Their wonder—their rapturous astonishment—may be conceived.

The most thrilling peculiarity of this incident, nevertheless, is involved in what Mr. S. himself asserts. He declares that at no period was he altogether insensible—that, dully and confusedly, he was aware of everything which happened to him, from the moment in which he was pronounced dead by his physicians, to that in which he fell swooning to the floor of the hospital. "I am alive," were the uncomprehended words which, upon recognizing the locality of the dissecting-room, he had endeavored, in his extremity, to utter.

It were an easy matter to multiply such histories as these—but I forbear—for, indeed, we have no need of such to establish the fact that premature interments occur. When we reflect how very rarely, from the nature of the case, we have it in our power to detect them, we must admit that they may frequently occur without our cognizance. Scarcely, in truth, is a graveyard ever encroached upon, for any purpose, to any great extent, that skeletons are not found in postures which suggest the most fearful of suspicions.

Fearful indeed the suspicion—but more fearful the doom! It may be asserted, without hesitation, that no event is so terribly well adapted to inspire the supremeness of bodily and of mental distress, as is burial before death. The unendurable oppression of the lungs—the stifling fumes from the damp earth—the clinging to the death garments—the rigid embrace of the narrow house—the blackness of the absolute Night—the silence like a sea that overwhelms—the unseen but palpable presence of the Conqueror Worm—these things, with the thoughts of the air and grass above, with memory of dear friends who would fly to save us if but informed of our fate, and with consciousness that of this fate they can never be informed—that our hopeless portion is that of the really dead—these considerations, I say, carry into the heart, which still palpitates, a degree of appalling and intolerable horror from which the most daring imagination must recoil. We know of nothing so agonizing upon Earth—we can dream of nothing half so hideous in the realms of the nethermost Hell. And thus all narratives upon this topic have an interest profound; an interest, nevertheless, which, through the sacred awe of the topic itself, very properly and very peculiarly depends upon our conviction of the truth of the matter narrated. What I have now to tell is of my own actual knowledge — of my own positive and personal experience.

For several years I had been subject to attacks of the singular disorder which physicians have agreed to term catalepsy, in default of a more definitive title. Although both the immediate and the predisposing causes, and even the actual diagnosis, of this disease are still mysterious, its obvious and apparent character is sufficiently well understood. Its variations seem to be chiefly of degree. Sometimes the patient lies, for a day only, or even for a shorter period, in a species of exaggerated lethargy. He is senseless and externally motionless; but the pulsation of the heart is still faintly perceptible; some traces of warmth remain; a slight color lingers within the centre of the cheek; and, upon application of a mirror to the lips, we can detect a torpid, unequal, and vacillating action of the lungs. Then again the duration of the trance is for weeks — even for months; while the closest scrutiny, and the most rigorous medical tests, fail to establish any material distinction between the state of the sufferer and what we conceive of absolute death. Very usually he is saved from premature interment solely by the knowledge of his friends that he has been previously subject to catalepsy, by the consequent suspicion excited, and, above all, by the non-appearance of decay. The advances of the malady are, luckily, gradual. The first manifestations, although marked, are unequivocal. The fits grow successively more and more distinctive, and endure each for a longer term than the preceding. In this lies the principal security from inhumation. The unfortunate whose first attack should be of the extreme character which is occasionally seen, would almost inevitably be consigned alive to the tomb.

My own case differed in no important particular from those mentioned in medical books. Sometimes, without any apparent cause, I sank, little by little, into a condition of hemisyncope, or half swoon; and, in this condition, without pain, without ability to stir, or, strictly speaking, to think, but with a dull lethargic consciousness of life and of the presence of those who surrounded my bed, I remained, until the crisis of the disease restored me, suddenly, to perfect sensation. At other times I was quickly and impetuously smitten. I grew sick, and numb, and chilly, and dizzy, and so fell prostrate at once. Then, for weeks, all was void, and black, and silent, and Nothing became the universe. Total annihilation could be no more. From the suddenness of the seizure. Just as the day dawns to the friendless and houseless beggar who roams the streets throughout the long desolate winter night — just so tardily — just so wearily — just so cheerily came back the light of the Soul to me.

Apart from the tendency to trance, however, my general health appeared to be good; norcould I perceive that it was at all affected by the one prevalent malady — unless, indeed, an idiosyncrasy in my ordinary sleep may be looked upon as superinduced. Upon awaking from slumber, I could never gain, at once, thorough possession of my senses, and always remained, for many minutes, in much bewilderment and perplexity;—the mental faculties in general,but the memory in especial, being in a condition of absolute abeyance.

In all that I endured there was no physical suffering but of moral distress an infinitude. My fancy grew charnel, I talked "of worms, of tombs, and epitaphs." I was lost in reveries of death, and the idea of premature burial held continual possession of my brain. The ghastly Danger to which I was subjected haunted me day and night. In the former, the torture of meditation was excessive—in the latter, supreme. When the grim Darkness overspread the Earth, then, with every horror of thought, I shook—shook as the quivering plumes upon the hearse. When Nature could endure wakefulness no longer, it was with a struggle that I consented to sleep—for I shuddered to reflect that, upon awaking, I might find myself the tenant of a grave. And when, finally, I sank into slumber, it was only to rush at once into a world of phantasms, above which, with vast, sable, overshadowing wing, hovered, predominant, the one sepulchral Idea.

From the innumerable images of gloom which thus oppressed me in dreams, I select for record but a solitary vision. Methought I was immersed in a cataleptic trance of more than usual duration and profundity. Suddenly there came an icy hand upon my forehead, and an impatient, gibbering voice whispered the word "Arise!" within my ear.

I sat erect. The darkness was total. I could not see the figure of him who had aroused me. I could call to mind neither the period at which I had fallen into the trance, nor the locality in which I then lay. While I remained motionless, and busied in endeavors to collect my thought, the cold hand grasped me fiercely by the wrist, shaking it petulantly, while the gibbering voice said again:

"Arise! did I not bid thee arise?"

"And who," I demanded, "art thou?"

"I have no name in the regions which I inhabit," replied the voice, mournfully; "I was mortal, but am fiend. I was merciless, but am pitiful. Thou dost feel that I shudder.—My teeth chatter as I speak, yet it is not with the chilliness of the night—of the night without end. But this hideousness is insufferable. How canst thou tranquilly sleep? I cannot rest for the cry of these great agonies. These sights are more than I can bear. Get thee up! Come with me into the outer Night, and let me unfold to thee the graves. Is not this a spectacle of woe? —Behold!"

I looked; and the unseen figure, which still grasped me by the wrist, had caused to be thrown open the graves of all mankind, and from each issued the faint phosphoric radiance of decay, so that I could see into the innermost recesses, and there view the shrouded bodies in their sad and solemn slumbers with the worm. But alas! the real sleepers were fewer, by many millions, than those who slumbered not at all; and there was a feeble struggling; and there was a general sad unrest; and from out the depths of the countless pits there came a melancholy rustling from the garments of the buried. And of those who seemed tranquilly to repose, I saw that a vast number had changed, in a greater or less degree, the rigid and uneasy position in which they had originally been entombed. And the voice again said to me as I gazed: "Is it not — oh! is it not a pitiful sight?" — but, before I could find words to reply, the figure had ceased to grasp my wrist, the phosphoric lights expired, and the graves were closed with a sudden violence, while from out them arose a tumult of despairing cries, saying again:

"Is it not — O, God, is it not a very pitiful sight?"

Phantasies such as these, presenting themselves at night, extended their terrific influence far into my waking hours. My nerves became thoroughly unstrung, and I fell a prey to perpetual horror. I hesitated to ride, or to walk, or to indulge in any exercise that would carry me from home. In fact, I no longer dared trust myself out of the immediate presence of those who were aware of my proneness to catalepsy, lest, falling into one of my usual fits, I should be buried before my real condition could be ascertained. I doubted the care, the fidelity of my dearest friends. I dreaded that, in some trance of more than customary duration, they might be prevailed upon to regard me as irrecoverable. I even went so far as to fear that, as I occasioned much trouble, they might be glad to consider any very protracted attack as sufficient excuse for getting rid of me altogether. It was in vain they endeavored to reassure me by the most solemn promises. I exacted the most sacred oaths, that under no circumstances they would bury me until decomposition had so materially advanced as to render farther preservation impossible. And, even then, my mortal terrors would listen to no reason — would accept no consolation. I entered into a series of elaborate precautions. Among other things, I had the family vault so remodelled as to admit of being readily opened from within. The slightest pressure upon a long lever that extended far into the tomb would cause the iron portal to fly back. There were arrangements also for the free admission of air and light, and convenient receptacles for food and water, within immediate reach of the coffin intended for my reception. This coffin was warmly and softly padded, and was provided with a lid, fashioned upon the principle of the vault-door, with the addition of springs so contrived that the feeblest movement of the body would be sufficient to set it at liberty.

Besides all this, there was suspended from the roof of the tomb, a large bell, the rope of which, it was designed, should extend through a hole in the coffin, and so be fastened to one of the hands of the corpse. But, alas? what avails the vigilance against the Destiny of man?

Not even these well-contrived securities sufficed to save from the uttermost agonies of living inhumation, a wretch to these agonies foredoomed!

There arrived an epoch — as often before there had arrived — in which I found myself emerging from total unconsciousness into the first feeble and indefinite sense of existence.

Slowly — with a tortoise gradation — approached the faint gray dawn of the psychal day. A torpid uneasiness. An apathetic endurance of dull pain. No care — no hope — no effort. Then, after a long interval, a ringing in the ears; then, after a lapse still longer, a prickling or tingling sensation in the extremities; then a seemingly eternal period of pleasurable quiescence, during which the awakening feelings are struggling into thought; then a brief resinking into non-entity; then a sudden recovery. At length the slight quivering of an eyelid, and immediately thereupon, an electric shock of a terror, deadly and indefinite, which sends the blood in torrents from the temples to the heart. And now the first positive effort to think. And now the first endeavor to remember. And now a partial and evanescent success.

And now the memory has so far regained its dominion, that, in some measure, I am cognizant of my state. I feel that I am not awaking from ordinary sleep. I recollect that I have been subject to catalepsy. And n overwhelmed by the one grim Danger — by the one spectral and ever-prevalent idea.

For some minutes after this fancy possessed me, I remained without motion. And why? I could not summon courage to move. I dared not make the effort which was to satisfy me of my fate — and yet there was something at my heart which whispered me it was sure. Despair — such as no other species of wretchedness ever calls into being — despair alone urged me, after long irresolution, to uplift the heavy lids of my eyes. I uplifted them. It was dark — all dark. I knew that the fit was over. I knew that the crisis of my disorder had long passed. I knew that I had now fully recovered the use of my visual faculties — and yet it was dark — all dark — the intense and utter raylessness of the Night that endureth for evermore.

I endeavored to shriek-, and my lips and my parched tongue moved convulsively together in the attempt — but no voice issued from the cavernous lungs, which oppressed as if by the weight of some incumbent mountain, gasped and palpitated, with the heart, at every elaborate and struggling inspiration.

The movement of the jaws, in this effort to cry aloud, showed me that they were bound up, as is usual with the dead. I felt, too, that I lay upon some hard substance, and by something similar my sides were, also, closely compressed. So far, I had not ventured to stir any of my limbs — but now I violently threw up my arms, which had been lying at length, with the wrists crossed. They struck a solid wooden substance, which extended above my person at an elevation of not more than six inches from my face. I could no longer doubt that I reposed within a coffin at last.

And now, amid all my infinite miseries, came sweetly the cherub Hope — for I thought of my precautions. I writhed, and made spasmodic exertions to force open the lid: it would not move. I felt my wrists for the bell-rope: it was not to be found. And now the Comforter fled for ever, and a still sterner Despair reigned triumphant; for I could not help perceiving the absence of the paddings which I had so carefully prepared — and then, too, there came suddenly to my nostrils the strong peculiar odor of moist earth. The conclusion was irresistible. I was not within the vault. I had fallen into a trance while absent from homewhile among strangers — when, or how, I could not remember — and it was they who had buried me as a dog — nailed up in some common coffin — and thrust deep, deep, and for ever, into some ordinary and nameless grave.

As this awful conviction forced itself, thus, into the innermost chambers of my soul, I once again struggled to cry aloud. And in this second endeavor I succeeded. A long, wild, and continuous shriek, or yell of agony, resounded through the realms of the subterranean Night.

"Hillo! hillo, there!" said a gruff voice, in reply.

"What the devil's the matter now!" said a second.

"Get out o' that!" said a third.

"What do you mean by yowling in that ere kind of style, like a cattymount?" said a fourth; and hereupon I was seized and shaken without ceremony, for several minutes, by a junto of very rough-looking individuals. They did not arouse me from my slumber — for I was wide awake when I screamed — but they restored me to the full possession of my memory.

This adventure occurred near Richmond, in Virginia. Accompanied by a friend, I had proceeded, upon a gunning expedition, some miles down the banks of the James River. Night approached, and we were overtaken by a storm. The cabin of a small sloop lying at anchor in the stream, and laden with garden mould, afforded us the only available shelter. We made the best of it, and passed the night on board. I slept in one of the only two berths in the vessel — and the berths of a sloop of sixty or twenty tons need scarcely be described. That which I occupied had no bedding of any kind. Its extreme width was eighteen inches. The distance of its bottom from the deck overhead was precisely the same. I found it a matter of exceeding difficulty to squeeze myself in. Nevertheless, I slept soundly, and the whole of my vision — for it was no dream, and no nightmare — arose naturally from the circumstances of my position — from my ordinary bias of thought — and from the difficulty, to which I have alluded, of collecting my senses, and especially of regaining my memory, for a long time after awaking from slumber. The men who shook me were the crew of the sloop, and some laborers engaged to unload it. From the load itself came the earthly smell. The bandage about the jaws was a silk handkerchief in which I had bound up my head, in default of my customary nightcap.

The tortures endured, however, were indubitably quite equal for the time, to those of actual sepulture. They were fearfully — they were inconceivably hideous; but out of Evil proceeded Good; for their very excess wrought in my spirit an inevitable revulsion. My soul acquired tone — acquired temper. I went abroad. I took vigorous exercise. I breathed the free air of Heaven. I thought upon other subjects than Death. I discarded my medical books.

"Buchan" I burned. I read no "Night Thoughts" — no fustian about churchyards — no bugaboo tales — such as this. In short, I became a new man, and lived a man's life. From that memorable night, I dismissed forever my charnel apprehensions, and with them vanished the cataleptic disorder, of which, perhaps, they had been less the consequence than the cause.

There are moments when, even to the sober eye of Reason, the world of our sad Humanity may assume the semblance of a Hell—but the imagination of man is no Carathis, to explore with impunity its every cavern. Alas! the grim legion of sepulchral terrors cannot be regarded as altogether fanciful—but, like the Demons in whose company Afrasiab made his voyage down the Oxus, they must sleep, or they will devour us—they must be suffered to slumber, or we perish.

HOW HE LEFT THE HOTEL

BY LOUISA BALDWIN

FROM ARGOSY (1894—SEPT)

I USED to work the passenger-lift in the Empire Hotel, that big block of building in lines of red and white brick like streaky bacon, that stands at the corner of − − Street. I'd served my time in the army, and got my discharge with good-conduct stripes; and how I got the job was in this way. The hotel was a big company affair with a managing committee of retired officers and such-like; gentlemen with a bit o' money in the concern, and nothing to do but fidget about it, and my late Colonel was one of 'em. He was as good-tempered a man as ever stepped when his will wasn't crossed, and when I asked him for a job, "Mole," says he, "you're the very man to work the lift at our big hotel. Soldiers are civil and businesslike, and the public like 'em only second best to sailors. We've had to give our last man the sack, and you can take his place."

I liked my work well enough and my pay, and kept my place a year, and I should have been there still if it hadn't been for a circumstance − − But don't let me anticipate. Ours was a hydraulic lift. None o' them rickety things swung up like a poll parrot's cage in a well staircase that I shouldn't care to trust my neck to. It ran as smooth as oil, a child might have worked it, and safe as standing on the ground. Instead of being stuck full of advertisements like an omnibus, we'd mirrors in it, and the ladies would look at themselves, and pat their hair, and set their mouths when I was taking 'em downstairs dressed of an evening. It was a little sitting-room, with red velvet cushions to sit down on, and you'd nothing to do but get into it, and it 'ud float you up or float you down light as a bird.

All the visitors used the lift one time or another, going up or coming down. Some of them was French, and they called the lift the "assenser," and good enough for them in their language, no doubt; but why the Americans, that can speak English when they choose, and are always finding out ways of doing things quicker than other folks, should waste time and breath calling a lift an elevator, I can't make out.

I was in charge of the lift from noon till midnight. By that time the theatre and diningout folks had come in, and anyone returning late walked upstairs, for my day's work was done. One of the porters worked the lift till I come on duty in the morning; but before twelve there was nothing particular going on, and not much till after two o'clock. Then it was pretty hot work with visitors going up and down constant, and the electric bell ringing you from one floor to another like a house on fire. Then came a quiet spell while dinner was on, and I'd sit down comfortable in the lift and read my paper, only I mightn't smoke.

But nobody else might neither, and I had to ask furren gentlemen to please not smoke in it, it was against the rule. I hadn't so often to tell English gentlemen, they're not like furreners that seem as if their cigars was glued to their lips.

I always noticed faces as folks got into the lift, for I've sharp sight and a good memory, and none of the visitors needed to tell me twice where to take them. I knew them and I knew their floor as well as they did themselves.

It was in November that Colonel Saxby came to the Empire Hotel. I noticed him particularly, because you could see at once that he was a soldier. He was a tall, thin man about fifty, with a hawk nose, keen eyes, and a grey moustache, and walked stiff from a gun-shot wound in the knee. But what I noticed most was the scar of a sabrecut across the right side of the face. As he got into the lift to go to his room on the fourth floor, I thought what a difference there is among officers. Colonel Saxby put me in mind of a telegraph-post for height and thinness; and my old Colonel was like a barrel in uniform, but a brave soldier and a gentleman all the same. Colonel Saxby's room was number 210, just opposite the glass door leading to the lift, and every time I stopped on the fourth floor number 210 stared me in the face. The Colonel used to go up in the lift every day regular, though he never came down in it till − − But I'm coming to that presently. Sometimes, when he was alone in the lift, he'd speak to me. He asked me in what regiment I'd served, and said he knew the officers in it.

But I can't say he was comfortable to talk to. There was something stand-off about him, and he always seemed deep in his own thoughts. He never sat down in the lift. Whether it was empty or full he stood bolt upright under the lamp, where the light fell on his pale face and scarred cheek.

One day in February I didn't take the Colonel up in the lift, and as he was regular as clockwork I noticed it, but I supposed he'd gone away for a few days, and I thought no more

about it. Whenever I stopped on the fourth floor the door of 210 was shut, and as he often left it open, I made sure the Colonel was away. At the end of a week I heard a chambermaid say that Colonel Saxby was ill; so, thinks I, that's why he hasn't been in the lift lately.

It was a Tuesday night, and I'd had an uncommonly busy time of it. It was one stream of traffic up and down, and so it went on the whole evening. It was on the strike of midnight, and I was about to put out the light in the lift, lock the door, and leave the key in the office for the man in the morning, when the electric bell rang out sharp; I looked at the dial, and saw I was wanted on the fourth floor. It struck twelve as I stepped into the lift. As I passed the second and third floors, I wondered who it was that had rung so late, and thought it must be a stranger that didn't know the rule of the house. But when I stopped at the fourth floor and flung open the door of the lift, Colonel Saxby was standing there wrapped in a military cloak. The door of his room was shut behind him, for I read the number on it. I thought he was ill in his bed, and ill enough he looked, but he had his hat on, and what could a man that had been in bed ten days want with going out on a winter midnight? I don't think he saw me, but when I'd set the lift in motion, I looked at him standing under the lamp, with the shadow of his hat hiding his eyes, and the light full on the lower part of his face, that was deadly pale, the scar on his cheek showing still paler.

"Glad to see you're better, sir," said I; but he said nothing, and I didn't like to look at him again. He stood like a statue with his cloak about him, and I was downright glad when I opened the door of the lift for him to step out in the hall. I saluted as he got out, and he went past me towards the front door.

"The Colonel wants to go out," I said to the porter who stood staring, and he opened the door and Colonel Saxby walked out into the snow.

"That's a queer go!" he said.

"It is," said I. "I don't like the Colonel's looks, he doesn't seem himself at all. He's ill enough to be in his bed, and there he is gone out on a night like this."

"Anyhow he's got a famous cloak to keep him warm. I say, supposing he's gone to a fancy ball, and got that cloak on to hide his dress," said the porter, laughing uneasily, for we both felt queerer than we cared to say, and as we spoke there came a loud ring at the door-bell.

"No more passengers for me!" I said; and I was really putting the light out this time, when Joe opened the door, and two gentlemen entered that I knew at a glance were doctors. One was tall, and the other was short and stout, and they both came to the lift.

"Sorry, gentlemen, but it's against the rule for the lift to go up after, midnight."

"Nonsense!" said the stout gentleman; "it's only just past twelve, and a matter of life and death. Take us up at once to the fourth floor," and they were in the lift like a shot; so up we went, and when I opened the door, they walked straight to number 10. A nurse came out to meet them, and the stout doctor said: "No change for the worse, I hope?"

And I heard her reply: "The patient died five minutes ago, sir."

Though I'd no business to speak, that was more than I could stand. I followed the doctors to the door and said: "There's some mistake here, gentlemen, I took the Colonel down in the lift since the clock struck twelve, and he went out."

The stout doctor said sharply: "A case of mistaken identity. It was someone else you took for the Colonel."

"Begging your pardon, gentlemen, it was the Colonel himself, and the night porter that opened the front door for him knew him as well as me. He was dressed for a night like this, with his military cloak wrapped round him."

"Step in and see for yourself," said the nurse.

I followed the doctor into the room, and there lay Colonel Saxby looking just as I had seen him a few minutes before. There he lay, dead as his forefathers, and the great cloak spread over the bed to keep him warm that would feel heat and cold no more. I never slept that night. I sat up with Joe, expecting every minute to hear the Colonel ring the front door bell. Next day, every time the bell for the lift rang sharp and sudden, the sweat broke out on me and I shook again. I felt as bad as I did the first time I was in action. Me and Joe told the manager all about it, and he said we'd been dreaming; but, said he, "Mind you don't talk about it, or the house'll be empty in a week."

The Colonel's coffin was smuggled into the house the next night. Me and the manager and the undertaker's men took it up in the lift, and it lay right across it, and not an inch to spare. They carried it into number 210, and while I waited for them to come out again, a queer feeling came over me. Then the door opened softly, and four men carried out the long coffin straight across the passage, and set it down with its foot towards the door of the lift, and the manager looked round for me.

"I can't do it, sir," I said. "I can't take the Colonel down again. I took him down at midnight yesterday, and that was enough for me."

"Push it in," said the manager, speaking short and sharp, and they ran the coffin into the lift without a sound. The manager got in last, and before he closed the door he said, "Mole, you've worked this lift for the last time, it strikes me." And I had, for I wouldn't have stayed on at the Empire Hotel after what had happened, not if they'd doubled my wages; and me and the night porter left together.

THE DARK LAGOON

BY DOUGLAS T. ARAUJO

Justin was sitting on the hood of his car, his back against the windshield and his arms resting on his lap, a half-empty beer can on his right hand. During the last few hours, an army of empty cans had pilled around the car like bodies on a battlefield, and during all that time his eyes never left the lagoon, not even when he groped for another beer in the Styrofoam box beside him. He seemed hypnotized by the perfect reflection of the full moon on the dark and still surface ahead of him.

But he wasn't. He had barely seen the reflection, because his sight was blurred with tears that didn't cease running down his cheeks. And the same way as he didn't notice the full moon, he also didn't notice the stillness that seemed to spread over that warm night, or the way the air had become still, or the shadows of the pine trees that stopped dancing on the ground and seemed to cover him like a shroud. He didn't even notice the way a cricket somewhere nearby filled the silence with its melancholic song, almost as if it were a requiem.

All Justin had been aware of during that last hour was the beer can in his right hand. That, and his memories of Claire.

"I miss you", he whispered, and his voice sounded solemn in the silence. "I miss you so much."

Justin knew he shouldn't be here. He had seen the way his friends and relatives looked at him. He had heard the words "depressed" and "suicidal" whispered at his back when they thought he couldn't hear them; he had noticed the expression of concern on his parents' faces.

Fresh tears ran down his face while a memory from no more than three months ago again popped into his mind, as vivid as if it were happening at that very moment:

"You need to let her go", his grandmother said to him on a Sunday afternoon, taking advantage of a moment when his parents had left the living room. "You have already mourned her enough. Just let her go."

He had looked at the old woman, turning his wet eyes from the television he had pretended to be watching, and feeling her fierce gaze on him. For an instant he felt the urge to explain to her how he was feeling, to say to her that he knew it wasn't normal to go back night after night to the place where his wife had drowned, but he just couldn't keep himself from it. He wanted to say to her that the lagoon was the only place where he still felt alive.

That it was the only place where he still could feel her presence.

But he said nothing. Instead, another tear ran down his cheek.

"That lagoon is haunted", his grandmother whispered, as if she had read his thoughts. "It has been since the Indians lived at this place. There is something evil living there, and you are letting it dominate you." She looked over her shoulder at the place where they could hear his father's voice approaching. "Let her go", she repeated, and then his parents entered the room again.

His grandmother smiled and began started talking about the weather, while Justin stared at the television again.

As suddenly as it had came, this memory faded.

Justin drank the rest of the beer in his hand in a single gulp, smashed the can and threw it over his shoulder. It hit the ground some feet away and rolled over twice before stopping.

Another body in the battlefield.

Justin groped for another beer. He opened it quickly, almost violently.

The sound of the can opening reverberated like thunder, echoed on the pine trees and spread over the dark surface of the lagoon like a death threat until it finally died in the distance.

The cricket stopped singing.

Complete silence fell over the lagoon, covering everything like a mantle.

But Justin didn't notice the silence, as he hadn't noticed the cricket before. He had already been taken away by the stream of his thoughts, the same way Claire had been taken from him one year ago.

Of course, Justin knew the legends about the lagoon. He had been hearing them since he was a boy, years before he first met Claire and the older children had told him everything about the ghastly creature that lived in the lagoon's deep water.

"It makes you see things ," a ten year-old boy named Clement, who lived in a house in the next block, told him one summer morning. "Then it makes you go to the deep and drowns you. And then," he added, lowering his voice to improve the scary effect he was trying to put in it, "it eats you."

And after that he had told Justin everything about the dozens of people that had drowned there, those whose bodies had been found half-eaten or had never been found at all.

Yes, Justin knew everything about the Dark Lagoon.

As a kid, Justin had believed everything he had heard, and he'd avoided the place like all the other children. But when he became a teenager and started dating, he soon discovered that a haunted place had its advantages. It was alone and dark, the forest and the sky created a romantic mood, and most of the girls became pretty excited when they were scared.

Besides, he had never seen a single hint of the creature that was supposed to live in those waters. Justin had always thought it was no more than an urban legend, a story created to keep the kids away from that area.

But now he wasn't so sure of that.

He and Claire had come to the lagoon several times when they were dating. He remembered very well the moments they had spent there together: their first kiss, the first time they made love on the back seat of his father's car, the love promises they whispered to each other.

"This lagoon is so beautiful", Justin remembered her saying one night, her eyes fixed on the dark water. "It's hard to believe so many people died here ." She paused for a moment, a thoughtful expression on her beautiful face. "Do you believe it is really haunted, Justin?"

"The only thing I believe at this moment", he had answered, "is that I love you."

She turned her gaze from the lagoon and looked right inside his eyes. Then she smiled, and a fire seemed to burn inside Justin's heart.

"I love you too", she said, and kissed him. Less than one month after that, at the margins of that same lagoon, he asked her to marry him.

The funniest thing of it all is that, after their marriage, he and Claire had stopped going to the Dark Lagoon. It wasn't a thing they had decided or that they had even talked about. It just happened. For three years, they just didn't go there.

Then, on a night one year ago, when they were going back home from a birthday party at a friend's house, Claire asked him to go there.

"Why don't we go to the Dark Lagoon now?" She had said. "It's still early, and we could spend some time there looking at the stars."

Justin glanced at her from his place at the driver's seat, and knew immediately by the smile on her face and by the way her nipples were showing through the red fabric of her blouse what she really meant by "looking at the stars".

So they went to the Dark Lagoon, and they made love in the back seat as if they were teenagers, and after that they made love again right on the ground. When they finished, their bodies were covered by earth, dead leaves and pine needles.

"Let's bathe in the lagoon," she said, taking away a pine needle from her hair, and started walking toward the water.

"I don't think we should do that ," Justin said, not knowing exactly why. "We never did this before."

"Well, there is always a first time," she answered. "Besides, we never made love on the ground, either."

Then she smiled and stepped into the water.

"It's cold!" she said, giggling through her chattering teeth. Then she dived under the surface and swam away from the margin with steady strokes. She stopped in the middle of the lagoon and turned to look toward the spot where Justin was standing at the edge of the water. A thin mist swirled and coiled around her.

"Won't you come? Are you afraid of the creature?" she teased.

Then she turned and started swimming again away from him until she disappeared from sight inside the mist.

It was the last time Justin saw her alive.

When the police finally found her body hours later, they told him she had drowned.

They told him she must have been caught up in the heavy algae at the bottom of the lagoon when she dived, and that's why she had so many scratches on her body. They also told him that the teeth marks on her flesh had been done by fish.

"There are some really big fish living at this lagoon," a policeman had told him. But Justin wasn't so sure it had been a fish. He had seen the expression of horror on Claire's dead face. He had seen the bewilderment on the policemen faces when they looked at her.

No, he wasn't so sure of it.

A sudden noise broke the sepulchral silence and brought Justin back to the present. He wiped the tears with the back of his hand and looked at the lagoon. He thought the sound seemed to be coming from there.

He jumped from the hood of the car and walked drunkenly toward the lagoon. He stopped at its edge, the cold water touching his feet, and scanned the surface for whatever had caused the noise. The lagoon was now almost completely covered by a thin white mist that seemed to float a few inches above it, hiding the reflection of the full moon, exactly the way he remembered it looked the night Claire died. He shuddered.

At the middle of the lagoon, slightly to the left from where he was, Justin saw a ripple on the otherwise still water, as if somebody had thrown a stone into it.

Or as if something had been pulled out of it.

"Claire?" He called out drunkenly. "Is that you?"

Silence.

Everything was still, except for the ripples in the water and the mist that swirled slowly above it.

"I miss you so much."

The ripples had vanished, and the water becoming still again. "I wish I could be with you once more, Claire. I wish I had gone with you that day. I wish..."

He didn't finish the sentence. Hiding his face in his hands, he let himself fall to the wet ground, crying and sobbing like a child.

But he didn't cry for long.

"Don't cry," a woman's voice filled the night, overwhelming his sobs. "I'm here for you."

Justin jumped to his feet, a chill running down his back when he recognized the voice. He looked around, his heart racing.

Then he saw her.

The whole world turned gray. For a crazy moment, Justin thought he would faint and drown into the dark water at his feet, but at the next instant the feeling disappeared, and the world came back into focus again.

"Claire...," he whispered, and his mouth opened into a smile that illuminated his whole face.

She was waist-deep in the water, as if she was just standing there, not far from the spot where the small waves had appeared before. Her skin and blonde hair were totally dry, as was the red blouse she was wearing, the same one she had on the night she died.

"It is not possible," said a little voice inside his head. "She is dead."

But Justin didn't care about this voice at all. Claire was there, and it was all that mattered to him.

"Come to me," she said, and moved backwards. She began to step back, as if she could touch the bottom of the lagoon with her feet. At each step, the mist swirled and coiled around her like a snake.

"Claire...," Justin repeated, louder this time, "Don't, don't leave me again! Don't go."

He stepped forward toward her, but before he even noticed, he was knee-deep in the cold water.

Claire raised her arms toward him.

"Come to me, sweetheart," she repeated, and her voice was soft and demanding at the same time. And although she was very far from him now, Justin heard her and understood her words as clearly as if they were sounding right inside his head.

Without thinking, he walked further out into the water, finding himself rapidly descending down the sloping bottom. With just three steps, the water reached his neck, its coldness penetrating his skin like pins.

"Come to me, Justin," Claire's voice seemed more distant now.

"Wait for me, Claire! Wait!" He shouted and started swimming as fast as he could toward her.

He stopped, the alcohol affecting his coordination. The water was so cold his body was numb. He looked around, trying to see her, to follow the voice, but there wasn't a sound.

The mist had now turned into a fog that seemed to be swallowing him up completely. He couldn't see anything.

Despair began to wash over him, but he fought it, struggling to see a sign of her, to hear anything but his own labored breathing.

"CLAIRE!" He shouted with all the power left in his lungs. "CLAIRE!"

Then he heard it. A noise. Ahead of him.

Somebody was struggling in the water, fighting a force that seemed to have it in its grip.

"NO!" He shrieked, and started swimming again with all his strength. His whole body ached from the cold and the effort, but he didn't stop.

He wouldn't let her die again.

He couldn't.

Then he saw her. A few yards ahead of him, she sank into the dark water.

Justin filled his lungs with air and dived after her.

The water was totally dark, and it got colder and colder as he got deeper. His body was numb and his heart was racing, the despair and the fear of letting Claire die again overcoming him.

He couldn't see her.

He dived deeper.

Darkness all around him.

Coldness penetrating his skin, his muscles, reaching his bones.

His lungs started to ache. He needed to go back.

No! Not yet! Not without her!

Deeper.

Then he saw something. A glimpse of something red.

His heart jumped in his chest.

Yes, it was her. He could see her red blouse now, her blonde hair floating and swirling around her as the mist had done before.

He swam toward her.

Deeper.

Lungs almost exploding.

Coldness.

Darkness.

He touched her. He reached her arm, pulled her to him, and turned her face toward him to see if she was all right.

It was too late. She was dead.

But in the next moment Claire opened her eyes, her pupils glowing in the dark water with a green light.

"That lagoon is haunted", the voice of Justin's grandmother popped in his mind again.

"There is something evil living there, and you are letting it dominate you."

Claire smiled, and her teeth were as sharp-pointed and as numerous as those of a piranha.

"The lagoon makes you see things," a voice from his childhood came to him through the years. "Then it makes you go to the deep water and drowns you."

The last air escaped from Justin's lungs as realization finally struck him. He tried to get away from her, to go back to the surface, but it was too late. The creature grabbed him with scale-covered hands that were as cold as ice, as strong as steel.

Within seconds, Justin had drowned.

The creature pulled his body deeper into the dark water, to the place where it used to feed.

WOLF IN SHEEP'S CLOTHING

BY AΠDREW JOΠES

Bradley was driving well over the speed limit, but he didn't care. There wasn't anybody else on the road, and besides, he was with his friends, and they all wanted to have a good time. He could hardly be bothered to watch the speedometer with all the commotion in the car anyway.

Stacey and Devon were fighting over their last cigarette in the back. If there was a picture in the dictionary of a bimbo it would have been Stacey's. She had shoulder length blond hair and a large chest. She was always wearing skimpy outfits, especially small shirts that showed off her belly ring.

Devon was more of a tomboy. She had cut her blond hair very short and had several piercings in unmentionable places. She was a bit of a pot head and loved to take a dare.

"Settle down you two," Bradley yelled back at them. "Don't make me come back there."

The two girls laughed loudly at him.

"Come on back here," Stacy said laughing. "We can have a party." Sarah shot her an angry glance.

Sarah was sitting in the passenger seat next to him. She was his girlfriend for the time being. She was the head cheerleader and she fit the bill. She had long blond hair, a skinny figure and a nice rack which was the main reason he was interested in her.

"Oh no," Devon said chuckling. "You've angered he monster. Hey don't worry Sarah, you can come back here to, and we can have a really good time." She laughed louder as she tossed an empty beer can out the open window.

Bradley was a jock, captain of the football team. His dark blond hair was short and curly. He always seemed to be squinting because he spent so much time out partying at night the light hurt his eyes. He was a big guy thanks largely to steroids and he wasn't shy about showing just how tough he was on the occasional freshmen that didn't get out of his way.

They flew down the road to the secret place in the woods where they were meeting their friends. They had been planning this for over a month now, and it was finally spring break.

No more homework or practice, just beer, sex and drugs for the next couple of days. A few hours later Bradley pulled off the road and onto the trail leading into the brush. It wasn't as thick as it had been last year, but it was still as bumpy as ever. Bradley cursed as he heard sticks and twigs scraping against his car. He could only hope it wouldn't leave any permanent marks on his baby.

"Oh for fucks sake, you can wax it when we get back," Sarah said. Bradley shot her an angry look and shook his head. She was a good lay, but she was as annoying as hell.

A few minutes later they came out of the trees and into the clearing where their friends were already waiting for them. At least Eric had the sense to bring his jeep. Judging from the smile on Eric's face, Bradley knew he must have scratched his paint job.

Bradley had met Eric on the football team their freshmen year, but Eric had been kicked off when he tested positive for steroids. It wasn't even to buff him up, Eric's goal in life was to try every drug made by man at east once, and he had tried most of them. He was always the guy to find if you wanted to score some stuff.

He was bigger than Bradley with very short brown hair. His eyes were always squinting as if the lights were too bright like Bradley but for a different reason. Apparently it was a side effect from sniffing too much paint thinner. He thought of himself as a tough guy and liked to push around people smaller than he was, not to be mean, it was just the natural order, or so he said.

Bradley parked his car and the girls all unloaded. He popped the trunk, and Eric pulled out the cooler filled with beer. Stacy got the bag of sandwiches and chips while Devon took out the blanket for their little picnic. Sarah watched with irritation as Bradley got out and looked over his precious car. She hated that he paid more attention to that dumb car than to her.

"My poor baby," he said as he rubbed his hand over a large scratch mark. He sighed and stood up, he would have to take it to the shop and have it fixed up good as new when he got back to the world.

Bradley saw Whitney leaning against the jeep, watching them. She wore a short red skirt and tang top with sunglasses covering her eyes. She had long blond hair and a hot body. She was the newest member of their little group and had fallen in with them her very first day.

Ryan was lying on the jeep's hood. He was the goofball of the bunch. He was scrawny compared to Eric and Bradley, and the two of them always pushed him around. He had shaggy dark blond hair and was always putting on a show for attention. The others kept him around for laughs, but he could be very annoying at times. He and Devon had an unofficial relationship.

Sarah and Devon set up the picnic while the boys pitched the tents for the night. They had come here several times before, and even though they didn't have permission to be here, no one had ever dropped in on them before.

After nightfall, the group of friends sat around a campfire they had made and roasted smores. They had been drinking for hours, and Ryan had just pulled out a bag of weed.

Everyone was laughing and having a good time.

"So who's up for a story?" Bradley asked. Several cheerful hollers egged him on.

"Hey, tell Whitney about the monster," Eric said. The others chuckled amongst themselves while Whitney looked around at them.

"Ok, ok," Bradley said. "For a couple of years now, there have been reports of a big animal in these woods picking off hunters and kids who wander off from their parents."

"You're telling me there is a bear around where we're going to be sleeping tonight?"

Whitney asked with alarm.

"Oh it's not a bear," Bradley continued. "There are no bears that live anywhere near here. People only catch glimpses of it at night, but it's big and covered with bristly hair. Just two weeks ago a kid went missing less than a mile from where we are now, but don't worry. Apparently, it only attacks people when they are alone, so don't go far from camp. Whitney smiled and looked around, but she became worried when she saw the sullen expressions on her friends' faces. "You guys are just messing with me…right?"

"Better tell her about Gwen," Eric said, a hint of warning in his voice. Bradley looked around at his friends with a dark smile on his face. Each of his friends gave their own knowing grin as they remembered what had happened. Whitney waited anxiously for him to continue speaking with a look of excitement in her eyes.

"A few years ago, right around the time it all started, we were out here with a girl named Gwen. We were carrying on, having a good time like we always do; Gwen was sitting right where you are now. She said she had to use the bathroom, so she got up and walked away. A few minutes later, we heard this horrible scream. It was like something out of a horror movie. We all looked, but we couldn't find any trace of her. No one ever saw her again."

Whitney sat quietly, staring wide-eyed with her mouth hanging open in disbelief. The others burst out laughing and Whitney's mood lightened slightly. Ryan laughed so hard he fell over, or it might have been that he was too high to sit up straight. Devon took the joint away from him and took a hit herself.

"Well I guess I'll have to hold it until I get back home," Whitney said. "So what happened to her?"

"Well, nobody knows," Bradley said, trying to sound cryptic. "She was never seen again.

Maybe she was just too embarrassed to show her face again. Or maybe she got eaten by the monster out in these very woods. Either way, it was a long time ago."

They all laughed and chuckled at poor Gwen's misfortune. Eric was about to say something, but he was cut off by a loud howl. Everyone froze to listen to the eerie cry from the dark; there was a wolf nearby. It didn't sound too close, but it didn't sound all that far away either. They were quiet for a long time, even after the sound had died away, but Ryan broke the silence by laughing.

"Man, I always thought she was a dog anyway; maybe that was her," he chuckled. The others laughed nervously, trying to put the creepy experience out of there minds. Devon finished off the joint and threw herself on Ryan. The two of them fell over giggling as the others got up to stretch their legs or find a bush.

Whitney walked over to get a blanket out of the jeep; it was dark and getting cold.

Suddenly, someone grabbed her from behind. She let out a startled scream when she was lifted up off of her feet. The scream turned into laughter as her attacker started to tickle her; she turned around to see Eric smiling at her.

"A little jumpy aren't we?" he asked. He let her go and she weakly punched him on the shoulder.

"That wasn't funny!" she snapped. "What do you want?" Eric smiled at her question and stepped closer.

"Well I just thought you might want a little company on such a nice night," he said, getting even closer to her. Whitney smiled and moved in close as if she would kiss him.

"I see," she said. "Ryan has Devon, Bradley has Sarah, and everybody's had Stacy, so I'm what's left is that it?" She stepped away from Eric when he was just about to make his move.

"Well you'll have to catch me first," she said as she laughed and ran off. Eric smiled and chassed after her; he loved it when they played hard to get.

The two of them ran around to the edge of the tree line where Eric finally caught up with her. He swung her around and grabbed her firmly by both her arms so she couldn't get away.

He pressed his body up against hers, and he could feel her heart racing. The sweat on her face glistened as it dripped down her neck onto her chest. He could see her breath as she panted from there little exercise.

Eric moved in to kiss her but, just before their lips touched, he heard something. He could hear something else breathing, something big and close by. He could see from the look in Whitney's eyes that she heard it to, and it was coming from the bushes right behind her.

"Hey Bradley, is that you?" Eric called out. There was no answer. Eric was about to look for himself when something reached out from the bushes and grabbed Whitney. For one terrible second, Eric looked into Whitney's terrified eyes just before whatever had a hold of her pulled her away from him. Whitney was yanked right off her feet and pulled into the bushes before she could let out a scream. Eric sat there for a moment, trying to figure out what had happened, too dumbfounded to move. Then he heard Whitney start to scream, a horrible scream of deadly terror, a scream he had never heard before in his life.

Eric jumped up and ran back to the camp for the others. He wasn't about to go after whatever that thing was by himself. He ran as fast as he could back to the campsite. He flew open the flaps to one of the tents and stumbled in on a naked Devon and Ryan trying to cover themselves.

"Guys, something got Whitney!" Eric panted. Devon and Ryan looked at each other and started to laugh. Eric wasn't sure if it was because they thought he was joking or because they were too high to care. Either way it wasn't getting him anywhere.

He turned towards the other tent in time to see Bradley and Sarah coming out. Bradley was in his shorts and Sarah had a blanket wrapped around her. Eric looked around in a panic for Stacy, worried that she might have been attacked as well.

"Where's Stacy?" he asked in a panic? Bradley looked at Eric for a moment, trying to figure out if this was all a joke or not. The look of fear in his eyes was no joke. Bradley nodded towards a tree, and Eric turned to see Stacey leaning against it, smoking a cigarette.

Bradley whistled to her and waved her over.

"What's going on man?" Bradley asked. Eric looked at his friends, trying to sort out what to say.

"I was with Whitney, and something attacked her," he said. "It pulled her into the woods, and I lost her. We need to go find her, quick." His friends all gave him a look of disbelief, but Bradley nodded, and they all followed Eric to where he had lost her. Eric pointed to the very bush that Whitney had been pulled into.

"You sure this is the spot?" Bradley asked. Eric nodded, and the two of them stepped through the bush. There was nothing on the other side. Bradley sighed and grabbed a stick; Eric and Ryan did they same, and Bradley got out his flashlight. The three boys started to move through the trees. Bradley was in the middle with the flashlight, Eric was on his left, and Ryan was on the right. The girls had stayed at the campsite where it was safe while the boys went out to play the heroes.

As Bradley and the others searched, they started to see blood in the dirt. They followed the trail until they found Whitney's clothes lying on the ground. They had been torn apart and were stained with blood, but there was no sign of Whitney, or the animal that had attacked her.

"Dude, this is so fucked up," Ryan said. Bloody clothes and a missing girl were a real buzz kill.

"Where the hell is she?" Eric asked. The three boys looked all around, but the blood trail stopped with the torn clothes. The three of them stood scratching their heads, trying to figure out what to do. They couldn't call the police; they weren't supposed to be here, and there wasn't anyone else who could help.

"Alright," Bradley said. "We'll split up and look around. Meet back here in five minutes, and yell if you find anything." The other boys nodded, and they split up in three directions.

Back at the camp, Devon and Sarah had gotten dressed. They sat around the fire with Stacy smoking as they waited for the boys to return. They didn't say a word; they didn't have to since they were all thinking the same thing. They were all wondering if Whitney was alright.

Ryan stumbled though the dark looking for the damn boogieman. One thing was for sure, this had better not be a joke. First Eric interrupts his fun with Devon, and then he had dragged him out into the woods to find a monster, or animal, or something that apparently liked to undress people before eating them.

He wandered around until he realized he couldn't see the light from Bradley's flashlight anymore. He looked around, but there was no sign of him. He called out to Bradley and Eric, but there was no response. He realized that he must have wandered too far away. He sighed to himself and slowly started to backtrack.

He hadn't gone far when he froze. He could hear something moving around him. He looked around, but it was too dark to see anything; even the moonlight was blocked by all the trees. And with no Bradley and no flashlight, Ryan couldn't see two feet in front of him.

Ryan heard a twig snap to his right, then behind him. He tried to stay facing whatever it was, but it kept moving around. Whatever it was, it was circling him, and even Ryan knew that wasn't a good thing.

"Eric…Bradley, is that you?" Ryan whispered at the dark. He started to back up until he bumped into a tree; at least the thing couldn't get him from behind like in the movies. Ryan held his stick like a baseball bat. Whatever came at him was going to be sorry.

Suddenly Ryan felt the tree he was up against move, just a little. It seemed to bulge slightly and then go back to normal. A stream of hot, fogy breath went past Ryan's face.

Then the tree moved again, and again a stream of smelly breath passed Ryan's ear. The boy's blood went cold as he realized that he hadn't been pressed up against a tree at all. Ryan was too petrified to turn around. His mind kept hoping that if he didn't turn around, if he didn't see it, then it would leave him alone. Then whatever it was moved, and every muscle in Ryan's body tensed up. For a moment Ryan dared to think it was leavening. That thought ended when he felt something slam into his back, hard.

Ryan thought he was going to fall forward, but he was caught on something. He could feel something inside his lower back, wrapping around his spine! He was too shocked to even notice the pain at first. Something was grabbing a hold of his spinal cord, and now it was pulling. Now Ryan felt the pain, and he screamed as loud as he could as he felt his back bone being ripped out of his body.

Bradley was just about to give up looking for Whitney when he heard a terrible scream.

It was coming from the direction Ryan was searching. Suddenly the scream was cut off, and then there was silence. Bradley knew that couldn't be good.

He rushed towards the origin of the scream with stick and flashlight in hand. He ran through bushes and over rocks that tried to trip him up, but he didn't let any of that slow him down. He was almost there when Eric caught up with him.

The two reached the spot that the scream seemed to come from. At first they didn't see anything, but then Eric tapped Bradley's arm and pointed towards a tree. Bradley pointed the flashlight, and there was Ryan, standing with his head down and arms folded across his chest.

Bradley felt a wave of relief; Ryan was alright. He lowered the light out of Ryan's face, but Ryan didn't lift his head up. Bradley thought the idiot must have dozed off or something. Eric walked over to him.

"Ryan?" he asked. Bradley was about to yell and scare him awake, when he saw the look on Eric's face. Eric saw something that was scaring him pale, something behind Ryan.

"What is it?" Bradley asked. Eric didn't answer; he just stared with wide eyed horror at something Bradley couldn't see.

Bradley wasn't sure if he really wanted to, but he had to see what Eric saw. He walked over beside his friend and followed his gaze, and he too was frozen with horror.

Ryan wasn't ok at all; his back bone had been ripped out and wedged into a tree to keep him upright. Ryan was dead.

Bradley forced himself to snap out of it. His friend was dead, but why had he been positioned like this? If it had been a trap for them then surely whoever did it would have attacked by now, unless...

"Eric, we need to get back to the girls!" Bradley said urgently, pulling at Eric's arm. Eric followed, but the look of shock did not leave his face.

The only reason anyone would prop Ryan's body up like that, was for a distraction. The killer wanted to buy himself some time to get to the girls before they did.

Back at the campsite, the girls watched the fire as it started to die out. The boys had been gone awhil Stacy looked more bored than anything, but Sarah had her eyes fixed in the direction the boys had gone.

"What do you think's taking them so long?" Sarah asked. The tension was obviously making her nervous.

"Who knows," Stacy said. "Maybe the whole thing was just a trick to get Whitney alone and gangbang her."

"Bradley wouldn't cheat on me!" Sarah snapped defensively. Both Devon and Stacy chuckled; they knew about Bradley's numerous transgressions. Sarah looked at her two friends with a confused look; she didn't see what was so funny.

She shook her head in frustration and got up to go to the jeep. She was out of cigarettes, and she needed a smoke to calm her nerves. As soon as she walked away, she heard Devon and Stacy laughing. They could be so stupid sometimes.

She walked to the jeep and looked in the back with no luck. She decided to head back to camp and check the tents again; maybe she had missed them. She was half way back when she heard something. Even with the full moon out, she couldn't see very well, but she definitely heard a twig snapping close by.

Sarah froze in place, her mind filing with the image of every horror movie she had ever seen. She was a girl alone in the dark, and something was out there. She wasn't sure if she should run for camp or for the car. She didn't think Bradley had locked the door, didn't think but wasn't sure. If she ran to the camp, it wouldn't do much good; there would just be three screaming girls in a tent instead of one inside a car.

Sarah heard another twig snap, and she was just about to run away screaming when she heard another sound. It was Bradley calling for her; the boys must have come back! Sarah ran in the direction of the camp as fast as she could. She wanted to be back in Bradley's arms.

She wanted him to protect her from anything that might hurt her.

Sarah hardly had time to notice the blur of movement. Something swung at her from the right and struck her midsection. Sarah tumbled to the ground, the leaves and dirt soiling her hair as she rolled until she could bring herself to a stop.

Sarah was too disoriented to know what had happened. She looked around in a daze, trying to figure out where she was. She could just barely see the light of the campfire up ahead. She was so close to safety and friends, but what had hit her?

Sarah looked back over her shoulder and saw something standing over her, something big. It had broad shoulders with its head held low. Its arms seemed longer than they should be, and its feet looked too narrow at the bottom. It was too dark for Sarah to see much else, except for its right hand.

Sarah could see it was holding something in its right hand. It looked like torn rags, but they were glistening in the distant fire light. It was wet and red, and the truth slowly dawned on Sarah. She reached down to feel her belly. Her hand stopped where she knew her stomach should be, but there was nothing there. She looked down and wanted to scream but found her breath stolen from her. Her stomach had been torn out and was now a gaping hole with blood oozing out.

The creature moved towards her, but Sarah couldn't take her eyes off of the void in her belly. Her mind couldn't accept what was happening, the pure shock blocked out any sensation of actual pain. She didn't even struggle when the creature grabbed a hold of her ankle and dragged her away. All she could do was watch as the campfire got farther and farther away.

Devon and Stacy had been laughing at Sarah for being so naïve when Eric and Bradley had ran up screaming about needing to leave. They hadn't answered Devon when she had asked where Ryan was. They hadn't even bothered to grab their things. They only asked where Sarah was, and when the girls had told them she had gone off on her own, Bradley had freaked out.

Now they were running towards the vehicles, looking for Sarah. She wasn't answering their calls, and that wasn't helping Bradley at all. He kept screaming her name until they reached the car, and then everyone was silent.

The hood of the car had been pealed back like a sardine can, and the engine had been ripped out. Nothing else on the car had been touched, not the food, or the blankets, just the engine. Whatever had done it had known exactly what it was doing, and it hadn't been too long ago; steam and fluid were still leaking from the wrecked vehicle.

"No, not my car!" Bradley cried. He fell to his knees in tears, mourning his wrecked vehicle. Devon rolled her eyes at him, Sarah was missing, but he was mourning his car.

The girls ran to the jeep, but Eric and Bradley didn't bother. They already knew it would be in the same condition. The hysterical cries from the girls only confirmed it. Eric looked at Bradley, hoping for a suggestion on how to get out of this mess, but he was equally stumped. Stacy and Devon came back, looking like they wanted some answers.

"What the hell is going on?" Stacy asked. "What happened to the cars, and where the hell are the others?"

"I don't know!" Bradley snapped. "I don't know where Whitney and Sarah are. Sarah was with you two." Devon looked at Eric and Bradley expectantly.

"What about Ryan?" she asked. Eric and Bradley looked at each other, unsure whether or not they should answer. Devon having a breakdown was the last thing either of them wanted to deal with.

"What happened to Ryan?" Devon yelled.

"He's dead!" Bradley shot back. "Something killed him and probably Whitney and maybe Sarah too, and it's going to get us if we don't get the hell out of here."

Devon was quiet; she didn't scream or cry like Bradley had been expecting. She just stared at the ground quietly while her mind tried to grasp what she had been told. Ryan was dead and maybe two other friends as well. She had been talking to them just a few minutes ago.

"Ok look," Eric said trying to calm everyone down. "Sarah's probably back at the camp. Lets go back and get our stuff; we can make our way to the road and get some help." The others nodded in agreement, and they started to head back. Stacy had to help Devon get moving and held onto her like a safety blanket.

They didn't notice anything out of place at first, but when they got closer, Eric could see that the tents had been ripped apart. Their stuff had been thrown all over, and their spare blankets and clothes were in the fire.

"What the hell is going on?" Stacy screamed. "We were just here!" Eric looked around franticly trying to find something salvageable while Bradley angrily kicked the cooler over.

"God damn it!" Bradley screamed. Devon didn't make a sound; she just stood quietly with her head down, looking at the ground. She couldn't accept that any of this was real; it was just a bad dream. There was no way Ryan could be dead.

Eric gave up looking for anything they could use; whatever had done it hadn't left anything behind and, he wasn't about to go back to the vehicles. He looked at Bradley for leadership but realized his friend was in no condition to be giving orders now.

"Ok...look, heading for the road and getting help is still our best chance, right?" Eric asked uneasily. He was more used to doing what others told him rather than taking charge, but he didn't seem to have much choice this time.

Stacy nodded, or maybe she was just shaking. She looked at Bradley and Devon for support. Devon didn't seem to be aware of what was going on anymore, and Bradley was crouched down, trying to hold back his tears.

"What about Sarah?" Bradley asked. "We can't just leave her out here." Eric looked to Stacy for help on this one. She nodded and walked over to put her hand on Bradley's shoulder.

"If she isn't here I don't think were going to find her," she said softly. Bradley shot a mean glair at her.

"We don't know that she's dead. She might be lost or something, and whoever's out there could be after her!" he yelled. Stacy stood up, having failed to comfort her friend. Sarah might have been annoying sometimes, but Bradley didn't want her to die.

"Look," Eric said. "We'll come back, and we'll bring help to look for her and Whitney too, and then we'll get the son of a bitch who did all this."

Bradley looked down and nodded, he knew they were right. Staying here wasn't going to do any good. He stood up, and they all started walking in the direction of the road. It was over a mile away, and although it had only taken a few minutes in the car to get through the dense brush, now they were on foot and in the dark.

Devon still wasn't talking but, Stacy made enough noise for the both of them. Every ten seconds she screamed when a stick scratched her leg or a branch hit her face. Eric was beginning to think that if that thing didn't kill her, he would.

Not that he could really blame her; every step he took could be his last. Every shadow hid a monster; every sound was something stalking them. Their only shield against the darkness was the single flashlight that Bradley had. Their only weapons were sticks that

Ryan had already proved were ineffective.

They had been walking for awhile, and the only monsters that had bothered them were the ones they imagined. Bradley was starting to think that they would be ok now. They would get to the road, get help, and find that Sarah had simply gotten lost, maybe that

Whitney had escaped, and the police would hunt down the psycho that had killed Ryan. Then the flashlight started to flicker.

"Oh no," Bradley said, slapping the side of the light. "Come on, don't die on us now!"

But the flashlight didn't obey. It flickered one last time and went dark. Now the four friends stood alone in the dark with someone or something trying to kill them and no one to help.

Before they could even come up with a plan, Stacy heard something. It was the sound of wood cracking. They all looked at each other and all around as the sound grew louder. Then they heard the sound of wood creaking, and they looked in the direction of the noise to see a large tree start to fall towards them.

The four of them scattered as the tree fell right were they had been standing. They all dove for cover, and when the dust settled, Bradley found himself covered by branches and leaves. He picked himself up and made sure he was alright before looking around for his friends.

Eric stood up a few feet away from him, but there was no sign of Devon or Stacy. Then they heard someone moaning from under the tree branches. The boys moved away the debris and found Stacy with her leg pinned under the tree.

Eric and Bradley looked at each other with concern; Stacy's leg was badly broken and bleeding but they knew they couldn't get her loose. Stacy was crying hysterically and staring at her mangled leg. Eric started to look for something they could use as leverage to try and get her loose while Bradley called out to Devon.

Bradley couldn't find any sign of Devon; it was like she had just disappeared. Eric found a large stick, and the two of them tried to lift the tree enough for Stacy to get out. The moment they got the stick in position they heard a deep growl from something close by.

Eric and Bradley gave each other the same scared look. Bradley looked over his shoulder, searching for whatever was out there while Eric looked at Stacy and saw the look of terror in her eyes. Bradley couldn't see anything, so the two of them frantically tried to get their friend free, but the moment they did, they heard another growl, this one even closer than the first.

"Hurry up!" Stacy said as she started to cry, but the boys were loosing their nerve. One more ferocious growl that seemed to come from everywhere, and Bradley took off running for his life. "No!" Stacy pleaded. "Please don't leave me here!" But with Bradley gone, Eric knew he had no chance of getting her free. The thing sounded like it was right on top of him, so, despite Stacie's pleas, he left her and went after Bradley.

Stacy was all alone, abandoned by her friends and left to die pinned under a tree. She desperately tried to free herself, but her leg wouldn't budge. She heard whatever was out there growling and snarling as it circled her. Stacy held her breath and stayed as quiet as she could despite the pain, hoping it wouldn't find her. She didn't even know what it was. Was it a wolf or some kind of monster? She knew no human could have ripped a car open, but what kind of animal would do that?

Then she saw something come out of the bushes. It looked like a huge wolf at first, but then, when it got closer, it stood up on two legs. The thing was enormous with bulging shoulders and dark fur covering its body. Its pointy ears went back, and it opened its muzzle, revealing large and very sharp teeth.

Stacy stared into its golden brown eyes as it looked down at her hungrily. It flexed its clawed hand, and Stacy could see they were still red with blood from whatever or whoever it had killed earlier. She screamed in terror as the creature's sharp teeth came down on her.

Bradley didn't stop when he heard Stacy scream. He didn't even stop when the scream was suddenly cut short. He just wanted to get as far away as he could. He wasn't a coward for running away; there was nothing he could have done to help her. If he had stayed with her, he would have been killed too, and that wouldn't have helped anything.

Bradley didn't hear Eric screaming, so he must have run away too. Bradley ran until he collapsed from exhaustion. He was physically and mentally worn out. His friends were dieing all around him, and he might be next. He sat all alone in the woods, sobbing, but he wasn't crying for his dead friends; he was crying for himself.

Devon wandered aimlessly through the trees; she had gotten separated from the others when the tree had fallen. She had heard Stacy screaming and knew what it probably meant.

She didn't care anymore; Ryan was dead, Stacy was dead, and Sarah and Whitney were probably dead. She realized that none of them were getting out of here alive. Devon walked calmly in the dark until she saw something in front of her. At first she thought it was Eric or Bradley, but when she looked harder she realized it was far too big. It stood still, its hot breath fogging the air. Devon didn't try to run; she didn't cry or scream.

She just didn't care anymore.

The creature slowly walked up to her; she could see it wasn't human. It reached out one massive, clawed hand and took a hold of Devon's head. It almost seemed gentle.

The creature easily lifted Devon into the air with one hand. She almost felt as if she were watching herself as the thing took hold of her legs with its other hand. Then there was a strange disorientation, and Devon felt herself flying through the air. She landed in some leaves and looked up to see the creature slowly walking away from her.

At first Devon didn't understand what had happened, at least not until she tried to stand.

For some reason she couldn't get up, she looked down at her legs and saw they weren't there.

All she saw was a bloody lump of torn flesh were her waist used to be.

Devon's mouth opened and she tried to scream, but nothing came out. She could see her lower half lying in the dirt near where she had been standing a moment ago. The monster had ripped her in half, though she was only partially aware of it in her delirious state; she didn't even notice any pain. Devon felt cold now; her body was becoming numb and tired. She lay down and let out her final breath.

Bradley had been resting for awhile now. He was about to get up when something caught his eye. There was something shining in the moonlight a short distance away. Bradley walked over to see what it was and found something hanging from a tree branch. It was a golden necklace with a cross.

Bradley took it from the branch and started to sob. It was the necklace he had given Sarah for her birthday. He realized she must be dead; the bloodstains were still visible on the shiny metal. That damned thing had killed her.

Bradley wanted the thing dead; he wanted to rip it apart with his bare hands. It had killed Sarah, Ryan, Stacy and even Whitney, and it had wrecked his car. It had to pay, and he would make it pay. He would find a way to kill it, somehow.

Bradley never even wondered why the necklace had been hanging from a tree right were he could find it. Nor did he notice something coming up behind him. However he did notice the large teeth coming at him when he turned around.

Eric had been trying to find Bradley when he heard his friend screaming. He ran to where the sound had come from, but all he found was a bloody mess. Eric found the gold necklace that Bradley had given Sarah for her birthday and knew it meant she was dead to.

Eric wondered if he was the only one left alive, he didn't know what had happened to Devon, but she wouldn't have been much help anyway. He had to try and make it to the road, it was his only hope.

He made his way through the dark while listening for anything that might be a monster hunting him down. He hadn't gone far when he heard what he was listening for: heavy breathing. It was close, just a few feet past some bushes in front of him and to his right.

Eric slowly stepped away from the sound, and it didn't follow. Apparently it hadn't noticed him, and for that, Eric was thankful. He continued on a short way until he again heard the creature. As before it was in front of him and slightly to the side, and as before Eric adjusted his course.Eric felt pretty confident he could avoid the thing. It blocked his path several more times, and each time he avoided it without being noticed. Eric was still roughly headed towards the road, but it was taking longer than he would like.

Before Eric could get to the road, he noticed what appeared to be a well in an open field.

Once again he heard the thing close by, but this time it was behind him. Before Eric could sneak away again he heard the thing growl and charge at him.

Eric ran into the field, trying to get away. He looked over his shoulder and saw a huge animal charging for him on all fours.

Before he could look ahead of him again he ran into something. He fell forward and then down, and down some more. Eric landed hard on a dirt floor. It took him a moment to realize that he had fallen into the well. He collected himself, and then he remembered the monster.

Eric rolled over on his back expecting to see the thing on its way down to meet him, but all he saw was the round opening at the top and the stars beyond. There was no water in the well, and as Eric looked around he saw that it wasn't a well at all.

There was a doorway leading to a tunnel. Eric picked himself up and headed down the passage. It was so dark he could barely see his hand in front of his face. He stumbled down the stone walled hallway until he came to a larger chamber that smelled like dog hair and raw meat.

Suddenly the room was lit up, not brightly, just enough for Eric to see what was left of all his friends. Their heads were lined up on the wall like mounted trophies. Eric recognized all of his friends, except one.

"Nice to see you again, Eric," a familiar voice said. Eric spun around and his eyes rested on the form of someone who should have been dead.

"Whitney?" he asked shocked. She was wearing different clothes, but it was still her. The girl Eric had seen dragged away by a monster now stood before him, smiling at him despite their friends being mounted on a wall only a few feet away.

"Actually if you don't mind I'd prefer it if you called me by my original name," she said.

"Gwen." She could hardly hold back a laugh as she saw the expression on Eric's face.

"It can't be," Eric said with astonishment.

"Can't it?" Gwen asked. "That was a very touching story Bradley told earlier, but it wasn't the whole story, was it? He left out how you bastards dragged me out here and then ditched me as a cruel joke. When you and your little friends left me out here, I was lost. I was hunted, much the same way you all have been tonight, hunted by something inhuman.

But it worked out rather nicely. The thing I had been running from actually turned out to be rather nice."

"Nice?" Eric asked. "That thing killed everyone and mounted their heads on a wall!"

Gwen smiled at him.

"Actually that was me," she said. "Being bitten by a werewolf has a lot of fringe benefits.

My appearance changed, and after some hair dye and a makeover, I was ready for my revenge.

I simply joined your little group and waited until you came out here again.

Once you did, well you know the rest."

"But I saw you attacked and taken away," Eric exclaimed. "We found your clothes covered in blood." His mind still couldn't wrap around what was going on.

"I killed a rabbit and set up my clothes so you would think I was dead, just in case any of you actually got away. As for me being taken away, that was my mate; he gets so jealous," she said as a large shape appeared behind Eric. "But you're going to find out about that for yourself I suppose."

Eric heard something growl behind him. He turned around and saw the beast in the light.

He could see its sharp claws, large teeth, and those vicious eyes that looked at him with animalistic rage. Gwen smiled with pleasure as her mate ripped apart the last of her former tormentors. It had been one hell of a vacation.

THE VALLEY OF SPIDERS

BY H· G· WELLS

Towards mid-day the three pursuers came abruptly round a bend in the torrent bed upon the sight of a very broad and spacious valley. The difficult and winding trench of pebbles along which they had tracked the fugitives for so long, expanded to a broad slope, and with a common impulse the three men left the trail, and rode to a little eminence set with olive-dun trees, and there halted, the two others, as became them, a little behind the man with the silver-studded bridle.

For a space they scanned the great expanse below them with eager eyes. It spread remoter and remoter, with only a few clusters of sere thorn bushes here and there, and the dim suggestions of some now waterless ravine, to break its desolation of yellow grass. Its purple distances melted at last into the bluish slopes of the further hills — hills it might be of a greener kind — and above them invisibly supported, and seeming indeed to hang in the blue, were the snowclad summits of mountains that grew larger and bolder to the north-westward as the sides of the valley drew together. And westward the valley opened until a distant darkness under the sky told where the forests began. But the three men looked neither east nor west, but only steadfastly across the valley.

The gaunt man with the scarred lip was the first to speak. "Nowhere," he said, with a sigh of disappointment in his voice. "But after all, they had a full day's start."

"They don't know we are after them," said the little man on the white horse.

"SHE would know," said the leader bitterly, as if speaking to himself.

"Even then they can't go fast. They've got no beast but the mule, and all to-day the girl's foot has been bleeding — -"

The man with the silver bridle flashed a quick intensity of rage on him. "Do you think I haven't seen that?" he snarled.

"It helps, anyhow," whispered the little man to himself.

The gaunt man with the scarred lip stared impassively. "They can't be over the valley," he said. "If we ride hard — "

He glanced at the white horse and paused.

"Curse all white horses!" said the man with the silver bridle, and turned to scan the beast his curse included.

The little man looked down between the mclancholy ears of his steed.

"I did my best," he said.

The two others stared again across the valley for a space. The gaunt man passed the back of his hand across the scarred lip.

"Come up!" said the man who owned the silver bridle, suddenly. The little man started and jerked his rein, and the horse hoofs of the three made a multitudinous faint pattering upon the withered grass as they turned back towards the trail. . . .

They rode cautiously down the long slope before them, and so came through a waste of prickly, twisted bushes and strange dry shapes of horny branches that grew amongst the rocks, into the levels below. And there the trail grew faint, for the soil was scanty, and the only herbage was this scorched dead straw that lay upon the ground. Still, by hard scanning, by leaning beside the horses' necks and pausing ever and again, even these white men could contrive to follow after their prey.

There were trodden places, bent and broken blades of the coarse grass, and ever and again the sufficient intimation of a footmark. And once the leader saw a brown smear of blood where the half-caste girl may have trod. And at that under his breath he cursed her for a fool.

The gaunt man checked his leader's tracking, and the little man on the white horse rode behind, a man lost in a dream. They rode one after another, the man with the silver bridle led the way, and they spoke never a word. After a time it came to the little man on the white horse that the world was very still. He started out of his dream. Besides the little noises of their horses and equipment, the whole great valley kept the brooding quiet of a painted scene.

Before him went his master and his fellow, each intently leaning forward to the left, each impassively moving with the paces of his horse; their shadows went before them — still, noiseless, tapering attendants; and nearer a crouched cool shape was his own. He looked about him. What was it had gone? Then he remembered the reverberation from the banks of the gorge and the perpetual accompaniment of shifting, jostling pebbles. And, moreover — ?

There was no breeze. That was it! What a vast, still place it was, a monotonous afternoon slumber. And the sky open and blank, except for a sombre veil of haze that had gathered in the upper valley.

He straightened his back, fretted with his bridle, puckered his lips to whistle, and simply sighed. He turned in his saddle for a time, and stared at the throat of the mountain gorge out of which they had come. Blank! Blank slopes on either side, with never a sign of a decent beast or tree — much less a man. What a land it was! What a wilderness! He dropped again into his former pose.

It filled him with a mo the form of a snake, and vanish amidst the brown. After all, the infernal valley WAS alive.

And then, to rejoice him still more, came a little breath across his face, a whisper that came and went, the faintest inclination of a stiff black-antlered bush upon a little crest, the first intimations of a possible breeze. Idly he wetted his finger, and held it up.

He pulled up sharply to avoid a collision with the gaunt man, who had stopped at fault upon the trail. Just at that guilty moment he caught his master's eye looking towards him.

For a time he forced an interest in the tracking. Then, as they rode on again, he studied his master's shadow and hat and shoulder, appearing and disappearing behind the gaunt man's nearer contours. They had ridden four days out of the very limits of the world into this desolate place, short of water, with rocks and mountains, where surely none but these fugitives had ever been before — for THAT!

And all this was for a girl, a mere wilful child! And the man had whole cityfuls of people to do his basest bidding — girls, women! Why in the name of passionate folly THIS one in particular? asked the little man, and scowled at the world, and licked his parched lips with a blackened tongue. It was the way of the master, and that was all he knew. Just because she sought to evade him. . . .

His eye caught a whole row of high plumed canes bending in unison, and then the tails of silk that hung before his neck flapped and fell. The breeze was growing stronger. Somehow it took the stiff stillness out of things — and that was well.

"Hullo!" said the gaunt man.

All three stopped abruptly.

"What?" asked the master. "What?"

"Over there," said the gaunt man, pointing up the valley.

"What?"

"Something coming towards us."

And as he spoke a yellow animal crested a rise and came bearing down upon them. It was a big wild dog, coming before the wind, tongue out, at a steady pace, and running with such an intensity of purpose that he did not seem to see the horsemen he approached. He ran with his nose up, following, it was plain, neither scent nor quarry. As he drew nearer the little man felt for his sword. "He's mad," said the gaunt rider.

"Shout!" said the little man, and shouted.

The dog came on. Then when the little man's blade was already out, it swerved aside and went panting by them and past. The eyes of the little man followed its flight. "There was no foam," he said. For a space the man with the silver-studded bridle stared up the valley. "Oh, come on!" he cried at last. "What does it matter?" and jerked his horse into movement again.

The little man left the insoluble mystery of a dog that fled from nothing but the wind, and lapsed into profound musings on human character. "Come on!" he whispered to himself.

"Why should it be given to one man to say 'Come on!' with that stupendous violence of effect. Always, all his life, the man with the silver bridle has been saying that. If I said it — !" thought the little man. But people marvelled when the master was disobeyed even in the wildest things. This half-caste girl seemed to him, seemed to every one, mad — blasphemous almost. The little man, by way of comparison, reflected on the gaunt rider with the scarred lip, as stalwart as his master, as brave and, indeed, perhaps braver, and yet for him there was obedience, nothing but to give obedience duly and stoutly. . .

Certain sensations of the hands and knees called the little man back to more immediate things. He became aware of something. He rode up beside his gaunt fellow. "Do you notice the horses?" he said in an undertone.

The gaunt face looked interrogation.

"They don't like this wind," said the little man, and dropped behind as the man with the silver bridle turned upon him.

"It's all right," said the gaunt-faced man.

They rode on again for a space in silence. The foremost two rode downcast upon the trail, the hindmost man watched the haze that crept down the vastness of the valley, nearer and nearer, and noted how the wind grew in strength moment by moment. Far away on the left he saw a line of dark bulks — wild hog perhaps, galloping down the valley, but of that he said nothing, nor did he remark again upon the uneasiness of the horses.

And then he saw first one like a gigantic head of thistle-down, that drove before the wind athwart the path. These balls soared high in the air, and dropped and rose again and caught for a moment, and hurried on and passed, but at the sight of them the restlessness of the horses increased.

Then presently he saw that more of these drifting globes — and then soon very many more — were hurrying towards him down the valley.

They became aware of a squealing. Athwart the path a huge boar rushed, turning his head but for one instant to glance at them, and then hurling on down the valley again. And at that, all three stopped and sat in their saddles, staring into the thickening haze that was coming upon them.

"If it were not for this thistle-down — " began the leader.

But now a big globe came drifting past within a score of yards of them. It was really not an even sphere at all, but a vast, soft, ragged, filmy thing, a sheet gathered by the corners, an aerial jelly-fish, as it were, but rolling over and over as it advanced, and trailing long, cobwebby threads and streamers that floated in its wake.

"It isn't thistle-down," said the little man.

"I don't like the stuff," said the gaunt man.

And they looked at one another.

"Curse it!" cried the leader. "The air's full of it up there. If it keeps on at this pace long, it will stop us altogether."

An instinctive feeling, such as lines out a herd of deer at the approach of some ambiguous thing, prompted them to turn their horses to the wind, ride forward for a few paces, and stare at that advancing multitude of floating masses. They came on before the wind with a sort of smooth swiftness, rising and falling noiselessly, sinking to earth, rebounding high, soaring — all with a perfect unanimity, with a still, deliberate assurance.

Right and left of the horsemen the pioneers of this strange army passed. At one that rolled along the ground, breaking shapelessly and trailing out reluctantly into long grappling ribbons and bands, all three horses began to shy and dance. The master was seized with a sudden unreasonable impatience. He cursed the drifting globes roundly. "Get on!" he cried; "get on! What do these things matter? How CAN they matter? Back to the trail!" He fell swearing at his horse and sawed the bit across its mouth.

He shouted aloud with rage. "I will follow that trail, I tell you!" he cried. "Where is the trail?"

He gripped the bridle of his prancing horse and searched amidst the grass. A long and clinging thread fell across his face, a grey streamer dropped about his bridle-arm, some big, active thing with many legs ran down the back of his head. He looked up to discover one of those grey masses anchored as it were above him by these things and flapping out ends as a sail flaps when a boat comes, about — but noiselessly.

He had an impression of many eyes, of a dense crew of squat bodies, of long, manyjointed limbs hauling at their mooring ropes to bring the thing down upon him. For a space he stared up, reining in his prancing horse with the instinct born of years of horsemanship.

Then the flat of a sword smote his back, and a blade flashed overhead and cut the drifting balloon of spider-web free, and the whole mass lifted softly and drove clear and away.

"Spiders!" cried the voice of the gaunt man. "The things are full of big spiders! Look, my lord!"

The man with the silver bridle still followed the mass that drove away.

"Look, my lord!"

The master found himself staring down at a red, smashed thing on the ground that, in spite of partial obliteration, could still wriggle unavailing legs. Then when the gaunt man pointed to another mass that bore down upon them, he drew his sword hastily. Up the valley now it was like a fog bank torn to rags. He tried to grasp the situation.

"Ride for it!" the little man was shouting. "Ride for it down the valley."

What happened then was like the confusion of a battle. The man with the silver bridle saw the little man go past him slashing furiously at imaginary cobwebs, saw him cannon into the horse of the gaunt man and hurl it and its rider to earth. His own horse went a dozen paces before he could rein it in. Then he looked up to avoid imaginary dangers, and then back again to see a horse rolling on the ground, the gaunt man standing and slashing over it at a rent and fluttering mass of grey that streamed and wrapped about them both. And thick and fast as thistle-down on waste land on a windy day in July, the cobweb masses were coming on.

The little man had dismounted, but he dared not release his horse. He was endeavouring to lug the struggling brute back with the strength of one arm, while with the other he slashed aimlessly, The tentacles of a second grey mass had entangled themselves with the struggle, and this second grey mass came to its moorings, and slowly sank.

The master set his teeth, gripped his bridle, lowered his head, and spurred his horse forward. The horse on the ground rolled over, there were blood and moving shapes upon the flanks, and the gaunt man, suddenly leaving it, ran forward towards his master, perhaps ten paces. His legs were swathed and encumbered with grey; he made ineffectual movements with his sword. Grey streamers waved from him; there was a thin veil of grey across his face.

With his left hand he beat at something on his body, and suddenly he stumbled and fell. He struggled to rise, and fell again, and suddenly, horribly, began to howl, "Oh — ohoo, ohooh!"

The master could see the great spiders upon him, and others upon the ground.

As he strove to force his horse nearer to this gesticulating, screaming grey object that struggled up and down, there came a clatter of hoofs, and the little man, in act of mounting, swordless, balanced on his belly athwart the white horse, and clutching its mane, whirled past. And again a clinging thread of grey gossamer swept across the master's face. All about him, and over him, it seemed this drifting, noiseless cobweb circled and drew nearer him...."

To the day of his death he never knew just how the event of that moment happened. Did he, indeed, turn his horse, or did it really of its own accord stampede after its fellow? Suffice it that in another second he was galloping full tilt down the valley with his sword whirling furiously overhead. And all about him on the quickening breeze, the spiders' airships, their air bundles and air sheets, seemed to him to hurry in a conscious pursuit.

Clatter, clatter, thud, thud — the man with the silver bridle rode, heedless of his direction, with his fearful face looking up now right, now left, and his sword arm ready to slash. And a few hundred yards ahead of him, with a tail of torn cobweb trailing behind him, ode the little man on the white horse, still but imperfectly in the saddle. The reeds bent before them, the wind blew fresh and strong, over his shoulder the master could see the webs hurrying to overtake. . . .

He was so intent to escape the spiders' webs that only as his horse gathered together for a leap did he realise the ravine ahead. And then he realised it only to misunderstand and interfere. He was leaning forward on his horse's neck and sat up and back all too late.

But if in his excitement he had failed to leap, at any rate he had not forgotten how to fall.

He was horseman again in mid-air. He came off clear with a mere bruise upon his shoulder, and his horse rolled, kicking spasmodic legs, and lay still. But the master's sword drove its point into the hard soil, and snapped clean across, as though Chance refused him any longer as her Knight, and the splintered end missed his face by an inch or so.

He was on his feet in a moment, breathlessly scanning the onrushing spider-webs. For a moment he was minded to run, and then thought of the ravine, and turned back. He ran aside once to dodge one drifting terror, and then he was swiftly clambering down the precipitous sides, and out of the touch of the gale.

There under the lee of the dry torrent's steeper banks he might crouch, and watch these strange, grey masses pass and pass in safety till the wind fell, and it became possible to escape.

And there for a long time he crouched, watching the strange, grey, ragged masses trail their streamers across his narrowed sky.

Once a stray spider fell into the ravine close beside him — a full foot it measured from leg to leg, and its body was half a man's hand — and after he had watched its monstrous alacrity of search and escape for a little while, and tempted it to bite his broken sword, he lifted up his iron-heeled boot and smashed it into a pulp. He swore as he did so, and for a time sought up and down for another.

Then presently, when he was surer these spider swarms could not drop into the ravine, he found a place where he could sit down, and sat and fell into deep thought and began after his manner to gnaw his knuckles and bite his nails. And from this he was moved by the coming of the man with the white horse.

He heard him long before he saw him, as a clattering of hoofs, stumbling footsteps, and a reassuring voice. Then the little man appeared, a rueful figure, still with a tail of white cobweb trailing behind him. They approached each other without speaking, without a salutation. The little man was fatigued and shamed to the pitch of hopeless bitterness, and came to a stop at last, face to face with his seated master. The latter winced a little under his dependant's eye. "Well?" he said at last, with no pretence of authority.

"You left him?"

"My horse bolted."

"I know. So did mine."

He laughed at his master mirthlessly.

"I say my horse bolted," said the man who once had a silver-studded bridle.

"Cowards both," said the little man.

The other gnawed his knuckle through some meditative moments, with his eye on his inferior.

"Don't call me a coward," he said at length.

"You are a coward like myself."

"A coward possibly. There is a limit beyond which every man must fear. That I have learnt at last. But not like yourself. That is where the difference comes in."

"I never could have dreamt you would have left him. He saved your life two minutes before. . . . Why are you our lord?"

The master gnawed his knuckles again, and his countenance was dark.

"No man calls me a coward," he said. "No. A broken sword is better than none. . . . One spavined white horse cannot be expected to carry two men a four days' journey. I hate white horses, but this time it cannot be helped. You begin to understand me? . . . I perceive that you are minded, on the strength of what you have seen and fancy, to taint my reputation. It is men of your sort who unmake kings. Besides which — I never liked you."

"My lord!" said the little man.

"No," said the master. "NO!"

He stood up sharply as the little man moved. For a minute perhaps they faced one another. Overhead the spiders' balls went driving. There was a quick movement among the pebbles; a running of feet, a cry of despair, a gasp and a blow. . . .

Towards nightfall the wind fell. The sun set in a calm serenity, and the man who had once possessed the silver bridle came at last very cautiously and by an easy slope out of the ravine again; but now he led the white horse that once belonged to the little man. He would have gone back to his horse to get his silver-mounted bridle again, but he feared night and a quickening breeze might still find him in the valley, and besides he disliked greatly to think he might discover his horse all swathed in cobwebs and perhaps unpleasantly eaten.

And as he thought of those cobwebs and of all the dangers he had been through, and the manner in which he had been preserved that day, his hand sought a little reliquary that hung about his neck, and he clasped it for a moment with heartfelt gratitude. As he did so his eyes went across the valley.

"I was hot with passion," he said, "and now she has met her reward. They also, no doubt — "

And behold! Far away out of the wooded slopes across the valley, but in the clearness of the sunset distinct and unmistakable, he saw a little spire of smoke.

At that his expression of serene resignation changed to an amazed anger. Smoke? He turned the head of the white horse about, and hesitated. And as he did so a little rustle of air went through the grass about him. Far away upon some reeds swayed a tattered sheet of grey.

He looked at the cobwebs; he looked at the smoke.

"Perhaps, after all, it is not them," he said at last.

But he knew better.

After he had stared at the smoke for some time, he mounted the white horse.

As he rode, he picked his way amidst stranded masses of web. For some reason there were many dead spiders on the ground, and those that lived feasted guiltily on their fellows. At the sound of his horse's hoofs they fled.

Their time had passed. From the ground without either a wind to carry them or a winding sheet ready, these things, for all their poison, could do him little evil. He flicked with his belt at those he fancied came too near. Once, where a number ran together over a bare place, he was minded to dismount and trample them with his boots, but this impulse he overcame. Ever and again he turned in his saddle, and looked back at the smoke.

"Spiders," he muttered over and over again. "Spiders! Well, well.... The next time I must spin a web."

GHOSTS IN THE TORNADO
BY ΠICKOLAUS ΑLBERΤ PΑCIONE

Looking to the skies I found myself looking into the documents of time when the storms touch landfall, often the case when I see myself asking the question of if ghosts make themselves present if they were the dead of a natural disaster. As some kind of offering to the skies above when either a tornado or a hurricane makes landfall, more so in Illinois where this is tornado country. When the supernatural combine their presence with the devastating winds, their way of saying the living will end up joining them soon.

Much as it was years ago in 1983, when a young child perished in a tornado just outside of the Lake County region. Such the idea that the supernatural come out of the dead of natural disasters is often unheard of but in the recent years when they found the rot in the streets after all the flash flooding it is often that observation that comes to mind, all the shadows left from the ghosts in the tornado when the dead are picked up in the eye. Crawling from the death green skies one can hear the screams of the dead within the nightmares. I sometimes seen a few knock upon my door asking for shelter then disappear without a trace.

Especially from the place I call a residence in and around Zion, Illinois, I found the ghosts from the storm wandering within the streets of the downtown area in the dead of winter. This is the case back in 1995, no one really knows the full details of the complete story or how it happened except for bits and pieces appearing in form of scraps of clothing that belonged to the dead just as they died. Such accounts of the dead were documented in the local papers and magazines by photo journalists.

I was looking into the old scrapbooks and looked at some of the photos my father took of the tornado that happened in 1983. There was very little I remember of the storm but to give some a time frame of how old I am now, I am about 24. Everything at the time was a damned blur to me about the actual funnel cloud, but I remember the photos of the debris captured on film. Everything about the area after the storm was almost something from the pages of Rod Serling's work. Just that I remember about the storm afterward was a dead silence, not the kind of silence one knows well enough unless they know that someone perished in the storm.

As I was looking at the photo scrapbook about the storm, I heard someone knocking on the door. Didn't know exactly who it was so I put on a pair of hiking boots and a hooded sweatshirt.

"Hello, can I help you?" I found myself asking.

No one was at the door, almost if someone disappeared without a trace.

Just a pair of ghostly footprints in the snow almost if no one was even there to begin with.

"What the fuck is going on?" I whispered to myself, the lady was upstairs and was new to the area after living in Des Moines, Iowa. I am starting to become rather creeped out knowing that someone that was already dead making themselves a guest to my residence. I felt all the cold spots within the house, and the girlfriend knew nothing about what was happening.

"Uh, Craig what the hell is going on around here?" I found her walking down the stairs dressed in a black denim skirt with skulls on her back pockets and throwing on a hooded sweatshirt over her Night of the Living Dead t-shirt.

She was running down the stairs in a bit of an alarm of knowing what was going on, not giving herself any time to put her make-up on wearing just her fishnet stockings – wondering why there were nothing but foot prints in the snow.

"I will tell you later, there is a story I want to tell you and it goes with all the scrapbooks that I was left and received in the mail the past few days. It was a strange morning, someone knocked on the door then vanished. A ghost from the tornado, remember the story I told you in the mail about a bunch of people dying during a tornado in Zion, Illinois, back in 1983 – the area is actually haunted by the dead produced by the funnel."

"I've seen things like this happen back in 1993, but I never heard of ghosts coming out of the remains of a flood or a tornado. This was the first time I've heard of stories like that, ghosts coming out of the wake of a natural disaster," she said with a little bit of an alarm, "Ghosts? I believe they exist but never heard of this happening – ghosts coming out of the wake of a tornado, and two this is in middle of winter."

I could just see everything in the back of my mind about what happened when looking back at those scrapbooks –- every horror, and every picture of tragedy. Every wind blowing against the sky and maelstrom, all the horrors within the last hours of those dead documented on still camera and news camera. What I imagined was coming true before my eyes – and it was in that March when the young and old died equally by the hands of Mother Nature. I pulled out the scrapbook that was left behind for me to show the girlfriend.

"I better make you some coffee before I tell you the story behind these photos, and the reason why this area is haunted by the ghosts left behind in the storm. Everything you're about to hear within this narrative I am going to relate would make you think that I am going to be giving the details of a horror film, but every detail is true. The person who left behind the scrapbook is a good friend of mine whose mother died in that tornado, she was a journalist for a magazine in the area. Some would try to explain the deaths involved being the act of a vengeful God, but no one can really explain why a storm like that would touch down when it wasn't quite spring – snow was still on the ground at the time. When the supernatural collides with the theories of science, not even the religious or science communities can explain away the unexplained," I said while sitting her down with the scrapbook. I got up to fix her some coffee because she would be there awhile because I have no real explanation why there were the dead coming back to visit the house.

"Damn, what the hell is really going on? I don't always understand the supernatural but this is freaking me out," she said when she was looking at the pages, "I do believe in ghosts and everything, just never heard that ghosts do return from the demises at the hand of nature. Did that many people really die in this?"

She was looking at the article about how many young and old passed on from the devastating winds. Apparently she was rather freaked out, and wondered why some of those ghosts come to the residence where I live now – turned out it used to be the house of one of the dead. I've known Riley for awhile now, and she's always been a bit spooked by the idea of tornadoes yet she lived in blizzard country in middle of the winter months. For her to hear about this story, it was entirely new -- and in some ways despite her dressing Goth, something like that freaked her out even more than many of the novels she has in the house.

I've seen her react in some ways to the supernatural that would make some others respond in a rather uncomfortable nature, but for her to squirm at the fact that this was a place were a few people died in a tornado -- it was sensory overload. This was one of those things where I didn't know what to say or how to explain exactly what happened in the pages of that scrapbook to her. That happened when I was really young, and my sister's best friend kept the book all this time.

So the coffee was done and poured her a cup because I knew that she was going to need it after seeing the scrapbook. I wanted her wide awake so I can give her more details about what happened. Deep down no one knows what kind of horrors that mother nature, everything with mother nature and the psyche playing off the belief of the supernatural and the afterlife becomes the beginning of her sensory overload.

"Are you fucking serious about this house being the location of a family who died in the tornado?" she asked while taking a sip of her coffee, almost gagging when she learned of the story.

"A family of four died in this house before I got it," I answered, "a young couple with two preteen children, the funnel ripped out their roof and the mother got pulled up into the vortex. They found the body broken in two almost two miles down the road while the rest of the family died in the house. Some could sometimes still hear the woman's scream in the bed room about 10:30 at night, because that was when the funnel cloud picked her up and later killed her by dropping her about 100 feet in the air. Her body snapped in half as well as from her neck."

I was reading about that too the moment I got the scrapbook in fact it was the first thing I opened to since that was actually photographed for the newspaper. They found her body actually bent in half, backwards. Folded like a piece of paper, her head was touching her heels as it was seen in the photo.

"The family is about our age exactly, the woman even looks like you but didn't dress like you. Sometimes you would hear footsteps in middle of the night and sometimes a door closing or two when no one is there, and this was something I didn't notice until I was five months into living here. It is kind of harrowing at times when I heard the footsteps when no one was there and sometimes I would hear something that sounds like a freight train but nothing is there either."

"It is a big unknown, combine the factor of ghosts with the unpredictability of natural disasters. I've seen floods happen and seen people die in the floods, but never heard of the thought that their ghost can return from something like this – it scares me to death to be honest," Rita said when she was taking a small drag of her cigarette while turning the page of the scrapbook.

As she was turning the page, the door started knocking again and I went to go answer it. It looks like someone came by with something but I can't say exactly what it was.

Opening the door, "Hello, I had a weird fucking day what do you want?"

The person said nothing but handed me a video cassette with the note saying, "play me on it."

I push play and it showed footage of the house, the sound of the tornado became louder at the same time the video plays. Weird shit, I swear to God – but nothing like this ever had happened. The house was shaking but nothing being ripped off the roof or anything going into the walls. Just that I started to hear the footsteps, this time frantic running up to the room and a scream here and there. I didn't know what the hell was going on but the notion was there – something was happening around the property that the person who sold us the house didn't tell us about, something that the person who gave me the video knew what happened here. Knowing that – it seemed to be a direct photograph to what exactly happened there, the horror of knowing and the actual footage of the funnel collecting who used to live here. This was their actual will and testament, for at the time – people could barely afford a video camera.

"What is the cassette?"

"Don't know, I am playing it to see what it is but I don't want to know – it must be some kind of last will and testament of the people who died in the house."

She knew that I was a bit frightened by what I've seen by playing the cassette, and I don't think anyone could take in if they've received the same thing I did. They must of felt that they were in middle of an apocalypse when they did that final will and testament. In their video they were praying to God and reading the Bible hoping that their God will deliver them from the grim fate that was handed them. End time prophecy to what they knew and the damnation that followed within the devastating winds. A half hour passed as the videocassette played, I felt the sound of the winds blaring much stronger as the cold spots within the room became even more intense.

Places such as Lake County, tornadoes are not very common but I've seen one rip apart a neighborhood without warning. Almost it was the sign of the coming Apocalypse, as they would preach in the churches -- all those hellfire and brimstone ministers while there are some out there who believe that only 144,001 are going to heaven but what happens when the storm touches down and rips away their beloved Kingdom Hall. All their fucking **Awake** magazines being caught up in the storm; God must really hate them. That was exactly in the video too -- a devastating wind ripping the roof off a Kingdom Hall of Jehovah's Witnesses. Knowing it was captured, what stood within the walls and screen will always be the reality wandering in the horrors that lived within the walls of this house. Devastating winds and horrors seen in the pages and all the documented memory as they were played on film.

All that was seen on the tape appeared unreal, like a horror movie but I felt every footstep run up the stairs and the house itself was a receiver for the supernatural. All my girlfriend was able to do but watch as the entities appeared and disappeared up and down the stairs, they were trying to tell us something or show us but I couldn't fully describe what was going on. Even to the backdrop of heavy metal music blasting in the background, the atmosphere just seemed even more frightening and alien to me -- the ghosts made themselves at home within our residence, without any sign of entry they made themselves existent.

In one observation of another, it becomes relative in the sense of everything that was going on. The spirits of the deceased had no place to go after they passed, or don't even know that they've died. Just the kind of thing becomes the question, does the living even know when they would end up becoming one with the dead? Always comes to mind when one looks at the footage, death for them does come in form of the devastating winds -- as they become the entity of their own, I've seen the ghosts that were produced by the tornado's dead. It was an entity in itself, as the storm on the screen ripped everything apart -- almost if it was God's way of saying, "everything must be destroyed."

It was at this moment when I heard the phone ring, and then stop -- then rang once more. I felt like I was wandering within another dimension when that phone hung up because I heard another set of footsteps go up the stairs and it wasn't my girlfriends. That was when the phone rang once again.

"Hello?" I picked up the phone.

"Is this Ryan Decker?" the person on the phone asked.

"Speaking, what's going on?" I asked with a little puzzlement.

"Did you get the video?" the person inquired.

"It is playing right now, and some weird shit is happening in the house.

Shutters slamming open and shut, but no winds around such as a tornado -- the kind of thing more common with tornadoes than anything."

"The house is haunted by the old residents who died in a tornado."

"My girlfriend sensed some weird things happening in the house too, sometimes she feels something sharp impaling her but nothing is there. She describes it as glass cutting her flesh, but there isn't any glass around -- as in nothing breaking from the windows but she felt it when she would get out of bed in the morning."

"That was how the original residents died in the tornado, shards of glass impaled different parts of their body and eventually they bled to death."

"How do you know this," I asked, there was an icy chill starting to go down my spine at this point.

"I used to be one of their neighbors, who did you buy the house from?" he asked.

"It was from a family friend at a low price, they didn't say the reason why they were selling it that low," I answered.

"Must have been my grandfather. He knew the family well, the family had a strong knowledge of storms and some of them used to be storm chasers. Also a few of them did believe in the supernatural, so you'll see a few bibles in the house," the person responded, "one of them actually felt the storm coming before it came."

"What is your name then, I remember that the last name of the person who sold us the house was a relator named Hollins, the person didn't look that old but he was older than he carried himself to be," I became more intrigued by the story he related.

"My name is Joseph Blake Hollins, you can call me J.B. I don't live in the area anymore but I knew that the haunting started just after they've died. The family before you are a rather young one, and the person who sold you the house is named Edward Hollins. He was sketchy because he didn't want to go into detail about what happened, all he told you is that the house was in a tornado," he introduced himself.

"So that explains why he wasn't going into detail about selling the house, people died in the house!" I listened while it all fell together, now I understand a little bit why the hauntings were starting to happen. They were the shades left behind by the tornado, spirits of the dead who were once alive but died in a violent death.

The case of ghosts are more common with either a suicide or homicide, but the event of ghosts appearing after the death in a natural disaster it is something that no one really began to think about. The ghosts formed from the death gray skies, looking on as they forgot that they've passed on. Becoming the detail that stands, one would want to be anywhere but there at the time when the family passed on.

The lady sat down on the couch and continued to watch the video that was sent in, and while looking at the clippings in the scrapbook they started to come together. Everything within the footage and the clippings, began to compliment each other. The storm induced entities being the ghosts from the family who died, down to the disappearing woman at the door.

"Ryan? Did you know what was going on?" Lia asked as she began to shiver after seen the clippings and the video cassette footage. The cold in the room was so intense that she reached for the blanket that was on the couch and covered herself up. She was able to see her own breath because it was so cold in the room, but she couldn't explain why it became that cold that fast. Her small frame couldn't take the death-like conditions that were happening in the room.

"Someone is whispering but I don't know from where," she also whimpered, "but no one is in the room but us! But is it possible for there to be ghosts existing from the result of a natural disaster? This is really scaring me the idea of ghosts in the house from a tornado, especially knowing this was their last will and testament."

In the backdrop of all this happening she decides to pull out her cassette player and play some Dead Can Dance to take her mind off all the strange happenings around her environment.

"As some of my friends say, I do like the dark but this is just becoming too eerie even for me," Lia whispered because her voice was starting to become strained from the cold, "It was almost if I was stepping into the pages of a really fucked up horror novel. In some ways I felt the winds that impaled and killed the family cut into my flesh but there are no cut marks on my body."

The air in the room felt quite similar to how it was walking into a cryogenics lab, with as much spectral activity going on within the house and the videotape playing -- it was if everything that happened on the video in 1983 was starting to happen once again. I felt everything happen including the windows blowing open (the house had the doorway windows that opened from either the inside or the outside.) Everything about this house, it feels like I've been being watched by the old owners from beyond the grave! It seems that the video and the scrapbook was their way of trying to communicate with the people who live in the house currently -- being which referring to us.

From the duration of the time that I've lived within that house in Zion, one had heard stories of the haunting that happened along the block before. From different web blogs as well as newsgroups, just that some of us here did witness that first hand and it started from a collection of newspaper clippings and a videotape. It wasn't necromancy per say, but them trying to communicate to us through some of their old neighbors - they way of saying that their story must be documented. Science trying to show us how the dead tried to speak to us, no matter how we can explain what happened.

Within the realms of death and hell, the devil and God move human souls as pawns in chess -- often the case when they describe spiritual warfare. As they said and documented in the Bible they've used natural disasters to destroy mankind; and this was the case that religion couldn't explain why the spirits of the dead still remain in the house.   It crawls within the silent air of the walls, but in that silence becomes the whispers that ask for the living to help the deceased.   Another mass questioning as it stands within the eyes of the Watchtower Society when another miracle rips apart their beloved temple. As what I am -- just a mere observer of everything that could not be explained, and the horrors that should not be.   Your everyday guy who falls into circumstances no one can even explain, not even myself or my girlfriend.

Even if it was a little more than a decade or so passed, it was if they were watching to see if the new people were taking care of the old home years after the devastating winds.   The neighbors who were long moved away, were behind the actual leaving behind of the scrapbook and the video. As Lia fell asleep, the phone rang once again -- she answered the phone this time.

"Hello?" she answered, "Do you even know what time it is?"

"Hey Lia, it's Vicky. I heard about the rough day you and the boyfriend where having," the familiar voice responded, "I guess no one told you that the house you lived in was haunted. I visited the house long before you moved in there and felt all the sharp objects -- or seemed as they were that sticking into my arms but couldn't explain what they were. I wasn't bleeding but felt a lot of red spots appear on my arms. I described as glass cutting into my veins."

"I felt the temperature drop nearly twenty degrees, I actually fell asleep in my sweatshirt and what I had on today," Lia responded, "Ryan got a package in the mail today that triggered a lot of what was going on, no one understood why until he got a call from a former neighbor who've seen the demise happen as it was videotaped."

"Damn, are you serious about that?"   Vicky questioned with an absolute shock, "I heard about the cold spot thing happening but never like that, wait a second --I have heard of something like that happening. Somewhere in the south where a young couple felt a ghost scratching their flesh while in bed."

Lia sat up further on the couch to speak more into detail, "I had to bundle up every time I lay on the couch and I don't always know why it is so cold in the house especially in the living room.   Sometimes Ryan has to keep a comforter on the couch for me at times when I come over, I don't know why but I am ultra -sensitive to activity of things beyond the grave."

The wanderers from the storm and the eyes are seen from the vortex of the gray funnel cloud as it appeared on the television screen.   It draws from the horrors seen, and the entities in the house as the footsteps scramble up and down the stairwells yet there isn't a trace of anyone around except for herself and I.   With all the stories of the devastating winds, it stood in the back of our minds knowing what happened -- and from the results become the ghosts in our house. The ghosts in the tornado are what remained after the tragedy.

AПCIEПT LIGHTS

BY ALGERПOП BLACKWOOD

From Southwater, where he left the train, the road led due west. That he knew; for the rest he trusted to luck, being one of those born walkers who dislike asking the way. He had that instinct, and as a rule it served him well. "A mile or so due west along the sandy road till you come to a stile on the right; then across the fields. You'll see the red house straight before you." He glanced at the post-card's instructions once again, and once again he tried to decipher the scratched-out sentence — without success. It had been so elaborately inked over that no word was legible. Inked-out sentences in a letter were always enticing. He wondered what it was that had to be so very carefully obliterated.

The afternoon was boisterous, with a tearing, shouting wind that blew from the sea, across the Sussex weald. Massive clouds with rounded, piled-up edges, cannoned across gaping spaces of blue sky. Far away the line of Downs swept the horizon, like an arriving wave. Chanctonbury Ring rode their crest — a scudding ship, hull down before the wind. He took his hat off and walked rapidly, breathing great draughts of air with delight and exhilaration. The road was deserted; no horsemen, bicycles, or motors; not even a tradesman's cart; no single walker. But anyhow he would never have asked the way. Keeping a sharp eye for the stile, he pounded along, while the wind tossed the cloak against his face, and made waves across the blue puddles in the yellow road. The trees showed their under leaves of white. The bracken and the high new grass bent all one way. Great life was in the day, high spirits and dancing everywhere. And for a Croydon surveyor's clerk just out of an office this was like a holiday at the sea.

It was a day for high adventure, and his heart rose up to meet the mood of Nature. His umbrella with the silver ring ought to have been a sword, and his brown shoes should have been top-boots with spurs upon the heels. Where hid the enchanted Castle and the princess with the hair of sunny gold? His horse...

The stile came suddenly into view and nipped adventure in the bud. Everyday clothes took him prisoner again. He was a surveyor's clerk, middle-aged, earning three pounds a week, coming from Croydon to see about a client's proposed alterations in a wood — something to ensure a better view from the dining-room window. Across the fields, perhaps a mile away, he saw the red house gleaming in the sunshine; and resting on the stile a moment to get his breath he noticed a copse of oak and hornbeam on the right. "Aha," he told himself "so that must be the wood he wants to cut down to improve the view? I'll 'ave a look at it." There were boards up, of course, but there was an inviting little path as well. "I'm not a trespasser," he said; "it's part of my business, this is." He scrambled awkwardly over the gate and entered the copse. A little round would bring him to the field again.

But the moment he passed among the trees the wind ceased shouting and a stillness dropped upon the world. So dense was the growth that the sunshine only came through in isolated patches. The air was close. He mopped his forehead and put his green felt hat on, but a low branch knocked it off again at once, and as he stooped an elastic twig swung back and stung his face. There were flowers along both edges of the little path; glades opened on either side; ferns curved about in damper corners, and the smell of earth and foliage was rich and sweet. It was cooler here. What an enchanting little wood, he thought, turning down a small green glade where the sunshine flickered like silver wings. How it danced and fluttered and moved about! He put a dark blue flower in his buttonhole. Again his hat, caught by an oak branch as he rose, was knocked from his head, falling across his eyes. And this time he did not put it on again. Swinging his umbrella, he walked on with uncovered head, whistling rather loudly as he went. But the thickness of the trees hardly encouraged whistling, and something of his gaiety and high spirits seemed to leave him. He suddenly found himself treading circumspectly and with caution. The stillness in the wood was so peculiar.

There was a rustle among the ferns and leaves and something shot across the path ten yards ahead, stopped abruptly an instant with head cocked sideways to stare, then dived again beneath the underbrush with the speed of a shadow. He started like a frightened child, laughing the next second that a mere pheasant could have made him jump. In the distance he heard wheels upon the road, and wondered why the sound was pleasant. "Good old butcher's cart," he said to himself—then realised that he was going in the wrong direction and had somehow got turned round. For the road should be behind him, not in front.

And he hurriedly took another narrow glade that lost itself in greenness to the right.

"That's my direction, of course," he said; "the trees has mixed me up a bit, it seems"—then found himself abruptly by the gate he had first climbed over. He had merely made a circle.

Surprise became almost discomfiture then. And a man, dressed like a gamekeeper in browny green, leaned against the gate, hitting his legs with a switch. "I'm making for Mr. Lumley's farm," explained the walker. "This is his wood, I believe—" then stopped dead, because it was no man a reconstruct the singular illusion, but the wind shook the branches roughly here on the edge of the wood and the foliage refused to reconstruct the figure. The leaves all rustled strangely. And just then the sun went behind a cloud, making the whole wood look otherwise. Yet h almost seemed to him the man had answered, spoken—or was this the shuffling noise the branches made ?—and had pointed with his switch to the notice-board upon the nearest tree.

The words rang on in his head, but of course he had imagined them: "No, it's not his wood.

It's ours." And some village wit, moreover, had changed the lettering on the weather-beaten board, for it read quite plainly, "Trespassers will be persecuted."

And while the astonished clerk read the words and chuckled, he said to himself, thinking what a tale he'd have to tell his wife and children later – "The blooming wood has tried to chuck me out. But I'll go in again. Why, it's only a matter of a square acre at most. I'm bound to reach the fields on the other side if I keep straight on." He remembered his position in the office. He had a certain dignity to maintain.

The cloud passed from below the sun, and light splashed suddenly in all manner of unlikely places. The man went straight on. He felt a touch of puzzling confusion somewhere; this way the copse had of shifting from sunshine into shadow doubtless troubled sight a little. To his relief at last, a new glade opened through the trees and disclosed the fields with a glimpse of the red house in the distance at the far end. But a little wicket gate that stood across the path had first to be climbed, and as he scrambled heavily over – for it would not open – he got the astonishing feeling that it slid off sideways beneath his weight, and towards the wood. Like the moving staircases at Harrod's and Earl's Court, it began to glide off with him. It was quite horrible. He made a violent effort to get down before it carried him into the trees, but his feet became entangled with the bars and umbrella, so that he fell heavily upon the farther side, arms spread across the grass and nettles, boots clutched between the first and second bars. He lay there a moment like a man crucified upside down, and while he struggled to get disentangled – feet, bars, and umbrella formed a regular net – he saw the little man in browny green go past him with extreme rapidity through the wood.

The man was laughing. He passed across the glade some fifty yards away, and he was not alone this time. A companion like himself went with him. The clerk, now upon his feet again, watched them disappear into the gloom of green beyond. "They're tramps, not gamekeepers," he said to himself, half mortified, half angry. But his heart was thumping dreadfully, and he dared not utter all his thought.

He examined the wicket gate, convinced it was a trick gate somehow – then went hurriedly on again, disturbed beyond belief to see that the glade no longer opened into fields, but curved away to the right. What in the world had happened to him? His sight was so utterly at fault. Again the sun flamed out abruptly and lit the floor of the wood with pools of silver, and at the same moment a violent gust of wind passed shouting overhead. Drops fell clattering everywhere upon the leaves, making a sharp pattering as of many footsteps.

The whole copse shuddered and went moving.

"Rain, by George," thought the clerk, and feeling for his umbrella, discovered he had lost it. He turned back to the gate and found it lying on the farther side. To his amazement he saw the fields at the far end of the glade, the red house, too, ashine in the sunset. He laughed then, for, of course, in his struggle with the gate, he had somehow got turned round — had fallen back instead of forwards. Climbing over, this time quite easily, he retraced his steps.

The silver band, he saw, had been torn from the umbrella. No doubt his foot, a nail, or something had caught in it and ripped it off. The clerk began to run; he felt extraordinarily dismayed.

But, while he ran, the entire wood ran with him, round him, to and fro, trees shifting like living things, leaves folding and unfolding, trunks darting backwards and forwards, and branches disclosing enormous empty spaces, then closing up again before he could look into them. There were footsteps everywhere, and laughing, crying voices, and crowds of figures gathering just behind his back till the glade, he knew, was thick with moving life. The wind in his ears, of course, produced the voices and the laughter, while sun and clouds, plunging the copse alternately in shadow and bright dazzling light, created the figures. But he did not like it, and went as fast as ever his sturdy legs could take him. He was frightened now. This was no story for his wife and children. He ran like the wind. But his feet made no sound upon the soft mossy turf.

Then, to his horror, he saw that the glade grew narrow, nettles and weeds stood thick across it, it dwindled down into a tiny path, and twenty yards ahead it stopped finally and melted off among the trees. What the trick gate had failed to achieve, this twisting glade accomplished easily — carried him in bodily among the dense and crowding trees.

There was only one thing to do — turn sharply and dash back again, run headlong into the life that followed at his back, followed so closely too that now it almost touched him, pushing him in. And with reckless courage this was what he did. It seemed a fearful thing to do. He turned with a sort of violent spring, head down and shoulders forward, hands stretched before his face. He made the plunge; like a hunted creature he charged full tilt the other way, meeting the wind now in his face.

Good Lord! The glade behind him had closed up as well; there was no longer any path at all. Turning round and round, like an animal at bay, he searched for an opening, a way of escape, searched frantically, breathlessly, terrified now in his bones. But foliage surrounded him, branches blocked the way; the trees stood close and still, unshaken by a breath of wind; and the sun dipped that moment behind a great black cloud. The entire wood turned dark and silent. It watched him.

Perhaps it was this final touch of sudden blackness that made him act so foolishly, as though he had really lost his head. At any rate, without pausing to think, he dashed headlong in among the trees again. There was a sensation of being stiflingly surrounded and entangled, and that he must break out at all costs — out and away into the open of the blessed fields and air. He did this ill-considered thing, and apparently charged straight into an oak that deliberately moved into his path to stop him. He saw it shift across a good full yard, and being a measuring man, accustomed to theodolite and chain, he ought to know. He fell, saw stars, and felt a thousand tiny fingers tugging and pulling at his hands and neck and ankles. The stinging nettles, no doubt, were responsible for this. He thought of it later. At the moment it felt diabolically calculated.

But another remarkable illusion was not so easily explained. For all in a moment, it seemed, the entire wood went sliding past him with a thick deep rustling of leaves and laughter, myriad footsteps, and tiny little active, energetic shapes; two men in browny green gave him a mighty hoist — and he opened his eyes to find himself lying in the meadow beside the stile where first his incredible adventure had begun. The wood stood in its usual place and stared down upon him in the sunlight. There was the red house in the distance as before.

Above him grinned the weather-beaten notice-board: "Trespassers will be prosecuted."

Dishevelled in mind and body, and a good deal shaken in his official soul, the clerk walked slowly across the fields. But on the way he glanced once more at the postcard of instructions, and saw with dull amazement that the inked-out sentence was quite legible after all beneath the scratches made across it: "There is a short cut through the wood — the wood I want cut down — if you care to take it." Only "care" was so badly written, it looked more like another word; the "c" was uncommonly like "d."

"That's the copse that spoils my view of the Downs, you see," his client explained to him later, pointing across the fields, and referring to the ordnance map beside him. "I want it cut down and a path made so and so." His finger indicated direction on the map. "The Fairy Wood — it's still called, and it's far older than this house. Come now, if you're ready, Mr. Thomas, we might go out and have a look at it. . ."

SCARLET FROST
BY JAMES WATTS

I.

John McPearson was swiveling around so fast that the Styrofoam cup of hot coffee in his hand nearly slipped away from him, and would have landed on his crotch if it had.

"What the hell was that?" his query fell on deaf ears as he was the only one in the small aluminum Gaurdco building on this dreary, snow driven night. Ed Patterson, the other guard on duty, was out on site patrol and wouldn't be back for another two hours or more. This left John to figure this one out on his own.

Yea, that was a comforting thought.

He glared passed Ed's cluttered desk, passed the old metal lockers to the back wall where the noise had come from. It sounded like someone had fired buckshot into the aluminum siding and was almost loud enough to drown out the whistling wind outside, but not quite.

Another gust of wind roared and the small stack of tin on the buildings northeast corner shuddered violently.

"You're just being paranoid," he told himself but there was no confidence in his voice, only a slow welling fear that he could not justify.

He sat in silence, for how long he didn't know, praying that what he had heard had been nothing more than the wind blowing something against the building or that maybe he had dozed off and dreamed what he had heard. But he knew, just as he knew that the lazy winter flurries outside were growing into a small blizzard, that he had not dozed off; nor had he imagined what he'd heard. And it damn sure hadn't been the wind. If you walked in, now, and asked him how he knew that as fact...he couldn't explain it...couldn't even begin to speculate. He just knew.

Then it hit again, louder, the sound like a cannon ball punching through sheet metal, and he saw the wall shake and tremble, the pictures on the wall doing a little jig on the nails from which they hung. John snapped his head towards the two-way radios, they were resting in a line of chargers between two Panasonic security monitors and he grabbed the first one in the line. Beads of sweat had formed on his brow, his uniform shirt was sticking to his chest, and back and his hands started to shake.

It took more effort than he thought himself capable of, but he managed and slowly calmed himself and pushed in the talk button. "Hey, Ed." He nearly screamed--wanted to scream--the transmission. "I mean...shit, unit one to rover." He hated radio communication and loathed Guardco's radio protocol.

There was an uncomfortable silence, well except for the roar in the wind outside, then a cackle of static followed by a deep baritone voice. "I hear ya, kid but the signal's kind of weak. And knock off all the damn radio talk. We are the only two people on duty."

"Yea, sure," John replied in as steady a voice as he could manage. "You seen or heard anything funny on your end?"

"Nothing on my end, Johnny Boy." Ed's voice slightly distorted through the static. "Got a spot of trouble on your end, do ya?"

"Maybe, maybe n..." the words died in his throat and he jumped, nearly dropping the radio in the process. The noise repeated, even louder this time and the wall did more than shake from the unknown force slamming into it. The paneling cracked into big splintered

shards and the few pictures that hung on the wall fell and shattered against the uncarpeted plywood floor, lying in crazy little clusters of broken wood and glass at the base of the wall.

Followed by this was an unnatural high-pitched metallic screech, or more like a wail, which not only reverberated in his ears, but also seemed as if it were digging--no, more like clawing-- its way into his mind. Then in few seconds, seconds that past by like an eternity, the wail died away and nothing but the winter wind remained.

"What the hell?" Ed shot over the two-way. "What the hell was that, Johnny?" Just what the hell was that?"

"I...do...don...don't know, Ed." John stuttered, his heart doing its best "Thumper the

Rabbit" imitation in his chest, and his eyes gridlocked on the spot on the back wall where the broken paneling jutted out the way diseased teeth would jut from bloody, infected gums.

His complexion, usually salon style tanned, had now went as white as the snow capped frozen earth just beyond the shack's front door. "I just might aught to grab a rifle and check it out."

Which he knew, knew deep down, that he was afraid to go anywhere near that spot on the wall.

"Damn that, boy!" Ed shouted, the fizz and hum of the static growing worse and John knew that before too long all radio communication would be lost. "You just stay put and wait on old Ed, ya hear. Keep your eyes and ears open, now, and make sure that head popper of yours has some rounds in 'er."

"No shit." John responded sourly, then, as if maybe, somehow, the bullets had magically disappeared from his gun, he removed the .38 revolver from the holster on his right hip and popped open the cylinder. A small sigh escaped his lips once he verified it was loaded then he popped the cylinder back in place and holstered the .38.

"10-4 on that. Just hold tight and I'll be headin' back directly. Now keep your head, boy and don't go shootin' at no ghosts."

"Sure thing, old man," trying to sound confident and failing miserably. The waver in his voice was sure to give him up. "I ain't green you know."

The two-way cackled its static laughter, then, "Don't matter in sheep shit if'n ya green or ain'tcha. Grown men can get a fright ever' now and again, too, ya know. Just don't go poppin' old Ed, ya hear."

"Don't go worrying any more grey hairs over that, old man. See you when you get here."

With the short communication over John set the two-way back into its charger and took a few breaths. Maybe this all in my head...just the product of my mind working overtime, John thought and that's when the banging started and John Mcpearson became a living corpse; his complexion cotton ball white, his heart sized by terror.

AIIa Dull grey snow clouds loomed across the sky somewhere beyond the dark abyss of the night while an onslaught of snow, mixed with just a hint of ice, pelted the Earth. Ed Patterson stepped from beneath the eve of one of the yellow-tan storage buildings that lined up along the far end of the Fisher and Stevens construction site and snugged the two-way on his belt.

The overhead security lights cast his stocky shadow over the virgin snow in a way that looked more like a bulging dark blot than the shadow of a man. Ed looked around and a frown put a crease in his already wrinkled, cragged face. Only twenty-four hours into the year's first winter snowfall and two hours into the winter's first snowstorm, there were fine sheets of snow covering everything in sight, and probably a good foot or two of the white fluff was covering the ground. He thrust his hands into the navy blue Guardco bomber jacket and trudged forward. There was a slight crunch underfoot as he moved and his feet sunk about four inches into the snow, maybe more and Ed realized that the snow was still soft and not yet hard packed. Won't be long, though, he thought, Way she's comin' down it'll be hard travelin' come mornin'.

A chill coursed an icy path throughout his body and he shivered and mentally chastised himself for not putting on his thermals before he left out for work, he had been in too big a rush to get to work--wanting to hit the clock at exactly 11:00 and not after. One more time punching in late and he might as well go down to the nearest unemployment office and stand in line. Can't ice that cake now...it's gobbled and gone. And right now he had to check in with base--or so he liked to think of it as such(which in reality it was no more than an aluminum storage shed with a few windows, running water, electricity and a half-ass working central heat and air unit)--and see what in God's name was happening up there. Young Mr.

"I'm not green, you know" had probably shit his pants by now. Of course, Ed figured he'd be pretty damned scared too if he were in John's shoes. That ghastly wail curdled his blood and in all of Ed Patterson's forty-eight years living and breathing, he had never heard such a horrendous sound.

Like the majority of the people settled in Cradle Caverns, Edward Milton

Patterson had been born and raised in town. He used to play in the woods just north of town as a boy and in all those years of scraping knees and telling tales too tall for the tallest of tales…he had never heard anything like what had squealed over the two-way tonight. It was the sound worn brake pads make when it's metal against metal, the sound of fingernails scratching across a chalkboard, a pinch of crunching Styrofoam to seal the deal. What ever made that racket didn't sound human, nor did it sound like any animal he'd ever heard for that matter. In his early twenties Ed had been in the ownership of the U.S. Navy, well that's how he looked at it anyway, he never really thought anyone in the military actually belonged to themselves anymore, but more or less became property of the U.S. like planes, tanks, and guns.

In the ten years he was traveling around the world he'd seen hell on Earth and thought he'd heard every evil, terrifying noise that this old world had to offer--now he wasn't so sure.

As Ed neared the point where the land sloped down toward the service roads he could see the Guardco Ford Explorer parked, with its amber lights flashing faintly, by a small cropping of pines; snow dusted needles giving them an odd similarity to frosted Christmas

Tree cookies, just where he'd left it. A cold gust whipped around him as he moved, hugged him in an icy embrace, and he hunched his shoulders and lowered his head, as if he could actually sink lower into the bomber for protection like some kind of burly turtle. The wind howled its dismal cries and slapped at him with undaunted fury as he moved between two front-end loaders parked at the crest of the hill, avoiding the concrete walkway; its surface glazed by sheets of ice, and lumbered downward. There was something in the air, more than the chill that was spewing from grandfather winters frozen maw, something that chilled him the way a deserted funeral parlor on Halloween night would. It seemed as if there was a presence in the air, the trees--hell in every damn inch of this wasteland of a construction site.

Like the equipment itself would come to life at any moment, mechanical beasts thirsting for human blood, or the ground might rupture and send jagged spikes reaching for the sky, and he would be no more; impaled and lifeless.

Don't let yourself get to thinking' crazy thoughts, Edward. Drive ya to the loony bin or put ya in the ground before ya time.

He turned his head back towards the front-end loaders, their imposing bulks seemed monstrous from their perch atop the snow packed crest of the hill and Ed half expected to hear them roar to life, growling like big metal demons, and rush down the hill to plow him under. But they jut set there, cold, dark and layered in white. He shook his head to wave off those childish fantasies of fears, fears of ghosts and goblins living under beds and inhabiting every dark corner of God's green Earth.

Those aught'n be the thoughts runnin' in the minds o' men. Unlessen you want'n t'be a pissy pants baby all ya life.

Ed shuddered, but not from the twenty below temperature or the knife-like wind-chill, but from that voice that had just blared in his head, the voice that sounded so much like his dead father. From somewhere deep, possibly some dark corner of God's green Earth, his father had come back to take a stab at him…a stab at his mind. And it felt as cold as the wind around him, as if someone had stuck their frost-bitten hands through the back of his skull and caressed his brain with their blackened, frozen fingers. But maybe "caress" was too soft a word to describe what he was experiencing. Squeezed, clamped, or even constricted would suite that horrendous feel better.

Impossible.

There were no such things as ghosts, of that he was sure since his father had beat that belief into his fragile child's mind some forty-two years before. On the same note people didn't rise from the dead or turn into wolf men by the light of a full moon. It was that simple. Or was it? His father's voice, or the voice he had imagined belonged to his father, had sounded so clear in his head; couldn't have sounded any clearer if his old man had been standing right next to him on this bank of snow and ice. That, for the lack of a better comparison, was as ridiculous as Gary Coleman running for president of the good old U.S. of A or Barry Manilow becoming the next great rap artist. His father, after all, was twenty years dead and buried, died of a massive heart stroke back in the summer of '83, the summer before Ed had become an enlisted man. But Ed remembered that night forty-two years ago, when he was six, back in 1961, it was.

It was the night that he lay in is room and screamed into the darkness, screamed that something was trying to claw its way into his room via the window. His father had come in on the run and flicked on the light, his face haggard, a tangle of concern and anger flashed from his eyes. There wasn't much for the light to fall on: a dresser, a bed (with one scared as hell six-year old boy occupying it) and a small wooden chest nestled underneath his window.

His father was still dressed in the stained coveralls from his days work and smelling of sweat and Earth (his father rarely bathed) and his agitation radiated off him in waves. Which, Ed guessed, that being woke up at two in the morning after working the land all day long, under the blaze of the sun, would be enough to piss off just about anyone.

Laurence Pattereson was a tall, lanky man with a thin face and thinning grey hair, his skin was tan and his hands heavy with calluses from working the family farm all his life, from childhood to adulthood. He was also a man that didn't take to the frivolous ranting of a child, especially when said child should have been good and asleep, as said child had to be up in three hours to start his chores.

"What'n the world's ailing you, boy?" His father had asked as he sat on the edge of Ed's bed, the bed that Laurence Patterson had built with his callused hands.

"There's a monster a tryin' to come in my window, Pa," Ed remembered replying as he cuddled even further under the patchwork quilt his mother had sewn with her fragile woman's hands. "It's gonna eat me up."

The memory of his father's face just then, a horrid memory that had the same effect as a walk in freezer, somehow erie and hollow, contorted to a mask of anger and said. "Those aught'n be the thoughts runnin' in the minds o'men. Unlessin you want'n t'be a pissy pants baby all your life."

At that moment, and to Ed's surprise his father had backhanded him hard across his right cheek and pain stung that side of his face like a thousand needles pricking him at once, his teeth rattled and a warm trickle of blood ran from the corner of his mouth. Ed had stared blankly at his father scared and confused by the fact that his father had struck him--a father that had never struck him outside of a leather belt or a hickory branch across his backside.

But what scared him most, and this memory was clearer then the snow at his feet, was what he had seen beneath his fathers eyes, beneath the anger. What he had saw was fear. Fear of what he had never been able to find out.

"I'm sorry as the dickens about doin' that, boy," his father had said, calm and reassuring.

"But'n you need to understand it was for yer own good, ya hear. Can't have no boy o' mine bein' scared o' the dark. Now shut yer eyes and go to sleep. We'll talk more on this subject come sunrise."

II.

Edward had shut his eyes just as his father had told him to do, but sleep did not claim him, not that night, and he pulled the quilt over his head; his force shield against the infamous boogeyman. He heard his father leave his room, gone back to the bed that he had shared with Ed's mother, back to whatever disillusioned fantasies that had served him as dreams until five o'clock chores came around. Ed received his first and only beating from his father that next day, behind the old red barn and away from his mother's loving eyes. A beating that was for more or less thinking of monsters in the dark rather than for waking the old man up in the middle of the night. That beating had been their talk on the "subject" and had closed it for Ed's father, although Ed continued to lay awake at night huddled underneath the old hand sewn quilt for another two years forced to hold back his cries of fear.

The gap between 1961 and 2003 closed in suddenly as Ed felt his feet slip out from under him, landing hard on his backside he barreled down the snow packed incline. He slid, at first, on his back until his feet struck something buried in the snow and then he was tumbling head over heels, arms flailing like a bird in the midst of an epileptic fit, trying to grab onto anything that would halt this crazy decent. Something hard, and thank God, smooth, poked him in the ribs on his downward spill and pain stabbed his left side. Then it was over, as abruptly as it started, with Ed on his back and looking up into the night sky, flakes of snow rushing to meet him. After a few moments, and with effort, he managed to sit up, the disorientation beginning to fade, looked around and discovered a new pain settled in his neck and shoulders. Well I made it to the bottom, he thought with a humorless grin spread across his face. He was in the shallow irrigation ditch at the base of the hill and even though the snow was denser here than up on the slope of the hill, the gravel lining the bottom of the ditch was hard and unyielding in its presence underneath its winters tomb.

"Damn, me!" Ed cursed himself, rubbed a hand across his forehead, and pulled it away moist with blood. "I don't remember see'n this shit on the application." His hand went to his forehead one more time and felt along the small gash there. And it was a small gash, or more of a small cut, and sighed relief.

It took even more effort to stand up then it had to sit up, but Ed managed to get to his feet and did his best to ignore the pain that shot fire up his legs and dusted the snow from his shoulders that lay there like frozen dandruff. After a brief examination to make sure nothing was broken, other than his pride, that is, he clambered from the irrigation ditch and headed towards the Explorer on unsure feet. A bout of dizziness stifled his vision, his head throbbed painfully at his temples, and for a second he thought he would end up face down in the snow, but it passed and his vision cleared, his head only throbbing slightly. He just hoped that if there was any such thing as a God in the Heavens that would shine the tiniest thread of hope on his fabled bad luck; he hadn't suffered a concussion. All he needed was to pass out and lay out here until he froze to death, perfect ending to an imperfect life, he supposed. Which, of course, Lady Luck had a way of pushing you down rather tahn helping you up and then kicking you in the face until she pulled her foot away from your pulverized face and laughing, maybe getting a few of your teeth stuck in her dainty little blood stained shoe.

And Edward Patterson had worse luck than a one-legged blind leper.

With a few heavy limped strides Ed staggered up to the Explorer, unlocked the door (thank God for keyless entry) and climbed in. Icy fingers crept from the black leather seat, pinched his pasty white bottom through the thin fabric of his navy blue slacks, and caused a shiver and a grimace. The Explorer's engine would not be able to warm up soon enough to please the grouch inside this confused forty-eight-year old man.

"Damn God forsaken snow," he mumbled in the tone of a man who was angry at the world and in essence he was--sight, sound, taste, touch--a cool temperament had never been apart of Edward Patterson's persona and never would be. "Goin' to be the death of these old bones, yet, by God."

He gave the engine another few minutes to idle then shifted the Explorer into drive and eased forward, snow and ice losing their battle against the snow chains on the Ford's tires. Ed silently thanked whoever it was that had enough brains in their head to be prepared for the changing of the season, fall over to winter, then mentally slapped him(or her it could have

very have been a woman, can't go getting politically incorrect eh Ed) on the back , as if to say, "Good job! Way to go!" Still, even with reassurance of the chains, he piloted the

Explorer over the frozen terrain slow and careful. Can't afford to be mangled up in a ditch or wrapped around a tree, now can I? Taking risks may have been a part of his long since departed youth, but now he was damn near fifty; an old man half a century old. Moreover, old men didn't go around acting like ballsy teenage boys, now did they? Nope. They fished, they drank, and they ate (not necessarily in that order) and bitched to the younger generations about how it was when they were growing up. That's what old men did. None of that rip-roaring and vandalizing that the kids of today were into, none of that rap and heavy metal. Satanic music they seemed to worship.

He drove along the deserted service roads for another ten minutes and past the big sign that read: Future Home of Chemtech Industries Megaplex #34, before mild and comforting warmth poured from the vents and circulated through the Explorer. A red-bricked building with a shingled roof loomed into view through the drifting snow on the other side of the windshield, as did the fork in the road that veered off to either side of the building. The building, he knew, was one of the twenty or more maintenance sheds scattered along all the service and delivery roads that circumferanced the 120 acre complex. 120 acres, he thought dismally. And those bastards at Guardco actually thought that two guards were enough for such a big stretch of land. Cheap sons'-of-bitches.

Ed focused his attention on the fork in the road ahead and…and really had no words to describe what he felt at that moment, an incongruous tingling all over his body combined with a state of utopia that no drug that he was aware of could produce. Drawing him. Yes, that was it, drawn towards something. Something beyond that scraggly V in the road, a macabre "Pied Piper" calling his children with a knotted old wooden ocarina, corralling his children together…corralling them for what? He had no answer for that question and had no idea why such a nightmarish thought had crossed his mind. A sickly vision of a skinny old man in rags, with long, scraggly white hair, thin around the edges and a scrawny and pale face; eyes like fire and a nose as sharp as broken glass. Surrounding him, in a tightly woven circle, were the blank, expressionless faces of children, hundreds of children, lost and confused. And the whole time he sat on the stump of an old poplar playing his enchanted melodies that kept the children under his spell. Disturbing an image as it was, Ed couldn't shake it, at least not right away and he felt the pangs of fear well up inside him.

Crazy thoughts for a crazy scared old man, his father's voice booming from the bleak corners of the world beyond the grave. Ed dismissed it, reassuring himself again that his father was dead and the only voice he heard was his own; somehow twisted and maliciously recreated in his mind to sound like that of his dead father.

As he neared closer to the split in the road, he veered the Ford to the left, the right path lead to the unfinished, skeletal frames of the complex's office buildings, and accelerated slightly. He had to get to Johnny and see if the boy was ok and that nothing terrible had happened to him. Had to make sure ol' Johnny wasn't dead. Now why would Johnny be dead? Of course, Ed concluded, that Mr. "I'm not green, ya know" would not be surviving the night. This was a fact, not his imagination, and he believed strongly that he knew that John McPearson was either already dead or would be soon.

"Johnny, Johnny, Johnny," he said. "You just do as old Ed said and stay put. I'll be there as soon's I can."

Although Ed knew, no matter how soon he got there, no matter how fast he risked driving on the ice-slicked service roads--it would not be soon enough. The instigator of the fear that rampaged through his mind was that God-awful wail he'd heard over John's end of the two-way. Earlier he would have sworn on his mother's grave, his father's grave, hell, on everyone hanging on his family tree, that he had never in his life heard such a disturbing sound, but now he wasn't so sure. However strange it seemed in his mind, the wispy tendrils of recognition were picking at him like that nosey neighbor that could never drill you enough for anything that would feed their gossip and was never truly happy, or so it seemed, unless they were prying into your business. Why hadn't he remembered when he'd first heard it? Why couldn't he remember where in the past he had heard it? These questions were scary because he couldn't form an answer with which he could dispense of them entirely. They continuely nagged at him. Nag. Nag. Nag. Demanding an answer to quench his thirst... was demanding satisfaction for his limited human concept of rationality.

There was a large thud then and the Explorer shook and slid. Ed brought the Ford under control, eased into a stop, and shifted into park. For a moment, there was only the almost silent hum of the engine then the wind, whipping and wailing in the night. Ed sat there listening to the wind and watching the flurries of snow, headlights shooting for a short way before they tapered off into the dark--a silent foreboding dark that seemed as eternal as time itself. Ed pushed open the door, cold air creeping in to greet him and playing tug-of-war with the Explorer's heater and he shivered. The chill was immediate as he left the warmth of the Ford behind and moved towards the back of the Explorer, realizing for the first time that night that the small blizzard that had plagued him all night had dropped off into a small flurry. Thank God for small favors, he thought with no real relief. It could start up again at any minute, and given how unpredictable the weather could be, it was bound to be worse than the first time around. He reached the rear fender of the Explorer and frowned. The security lights on the corners of the maintainance building were too dim and he had parked too far away for him to see anything clearly. A string of curses fled from his mouth as he trudged back towards the open drivers' side door of the Explorer and reached in under the seat. He pulled out an old Eveready flashlight and flicked it on, then turned and headed back to the fender, followed the small beam of the flashlight stopping suddenly as his light landed on the culprit.

III.

Ed felt like kicking his own ass, just reaching his foot back in an angle beyond human capability and planting his foot right into the seat of his pants. Apparently, he had scraped up against one of the yellow concrete safety poles. Bastards'll probably deduct this from my pay. Who was he kiddin'...they'd probably flat out ax 'em. Well hell, like the ol' man used to say, "Luck is one quarter good luck and three quarters a barrel of shit." A halfhearted snicker escaped his lips. The old man had many made-up sayings that he had spouted to Ed about a million times up until his death--and ninety percent of them to do with something being full of shit. Ed used to wonder, and still did from time-to-time, just how full of shit his father had been and if the old man ever realized what other people had thought of him.

Probably if he did, he didn't give a damn one way or another. A turn the other cheek kinda guy was the ol' man.

Depressing. Thinking of his father was always so damn depressing. He pushed those memories as far back into his mind as possible and climbed into the Explorer. He hadn't thought of his father this much in twelve years or more. Why now? Did it have anything to do with what was happening with John? No! That's bull and you know it! The ol' man's been holdin' a spot in the ground since '83! You're just getting' sentimental in your old age, is all.

The dead stay dead and they don't talk to crazy old sons that are still livin' and breathin' so get hold of yourself and get a move on. Johnny needs ya. Don't go letting' that boy down, ya hear.

"Yea. Got to get a move on, old man," Ed said as he climbed back in the Explorer and slammed the door. "Got to keep right on a movin'."

The snow had done more than slack off as the twin beams of the Explorer's headlamps bobbed unsteadily up the small hill leading to the guard shack, it had completely stopped, replaced now by an eerie calm and a partially clouded sky. The moon was peeking from beneath a small group of clouds and casting a dull glow over the land as the wind screamed through the night and all around the site the temperature rapidly dropped to a degree that no one on this Earth would have believed possible; ice as hard as steel; snow as hard as rock. At the exact same moment the Ford's heater stopped, cold air flowing from the vents. Ed, cursing like a drunken sailor, attacked the heating controls in every combination possible before giving up on it and slamming his hand against the dash. The heater was beyond his control.

"Damned piece of Junk!" Ed mumbled as he crested the hill and the Ford's headlights washed over the guard shack.

He pulled up next to the little aluminum building, threw the Ford into park and killed the engine. Shuddering a cold breath, and then taking another deep breath and letting it out he flicked off the headlights. It was cold, too cold, and all Ed wanted to do at this point was to be in the comfort of his old house, with its old gas furnace blowing its warmth throughout the house. He wanted nothing more to do with this job or with John McPearson.

His toes and fingers were numb and probably in the early stages of frost bite. The wise thing would be to drive up to old doc Clandenburg's after hours' clinic and get medical attention, but he wasn't going to do that. Ed didn't feel there were a great many options open for his immediate future--any options save for death, that is.

Besides…there is only one other thing old men do well, eh, Ed old boy.

They die.

Reaching for the door handle Ed froze, his eyes filling up with the pale, silvery glow of the moon. It was free of all cloud cover and served as the only illumination in this cold January night, like a lackluster low wattage bulb, dangling on an unseen cord from the Heavens--and Ed Patterson felt utter horror blanket his senses. That uneasy feeling was back and all of sudden Ed wanted desperately to get away from Cradle Caverns, but he didn't think somewhe his throat and seizing his heart. He couldn't ever remember being as scared as he was at this moment, except for that time, cuddled underneath the old patchwork quilt back in 1961; the night he thought something was trying to get into his room, some beast from the nightmares of his childish mind.

A new feeling was creeping into his old bones now, a feeling of being watched; observed like some sort of speciman in some scientists lab. A thousand sets of yellowed eyes staring at him from the abysmal edges of the dark. The wind rustled the few trees around the guard shack and a high-pitched wailing echoed all around him. Ed felt his skin rippling in gooseflesh and his trembling hand uncontrolled over the door handle. I can't go out there!

His mind screamed. I'll stay in here and lock the doors and…I…I will be safe. Safe from that damned wailin' monster. If'n I open the door it'll gobble me up. Eat me alive.

Despite the cold, Ed broke out into an involuntary sweat. Get a hold of yourself, damnit.

It's just the wind, is all. Nothin' creepin' out there but snow…and…and Scarlet Frost. No!

No such thing as Scarlet Frost. A myth! She's a damed myth created by some old fogies with a gut full 'o whiskey. Just a child's horror tale is what is or ever will be. NOW GET OUT THERE AND CHECK ON JOHNNY!

Ed, reaching for the door handle, took another deep breath, let it out in a breath of steam and climbed out of the Explorer. The numbness in his fingers and toes, having spread to his ears and his nose, was no longer a concern, or in fact was no longer noticed by Ed Patterson and whatever inkling of thought he had had earlier about seeking medical attention was forgotten. None of this mattered to Edward Milton Patterson as he trekked away from the open door of the Ford in a hazy fashion; eyes glazed and dreamy and completely unaware of the virgin white snow under his feet changing into a bright bloody red, a scarlet frost one might call it and it was snowing again; flakes floating down like frozen, bloody tears. As he rounded the guard shack, his jaw dropped and his eyes wanted to bulge from their sockets.

John McPearson was standing in front the guard shack in a small swash of light that was pouring dimly from the small building. The right side of his face looking as if it were ripped off--no--more like something had clawed it off and was dangling from a thin strip of skin just below his jaw along with his right eye. The entire front of his uniform was soaked in blood and spatters of bone and brain matter clung to it like obscene Christmas decorations from hell. He cocked his head a little, grinning widely through his ruined mouth and that last little strip of skin gave up its fight to remain apart of John McPearson's mutilated features and hit the ground with a greasy thud, that dead right eye boring a hole into Ed's soul.

"What took you so long, old man?" John's voice grated through the air. "Thought you'd never get your ass up here."

"Wh-wha-wha-wha," Ed stutterd, trying to find the words but all abilty to speak was lost.

When John McPearson began moving towards him Ed's face became a pale mask of horror, the .38 revolver at his side blinked from existence in his tormented mind and he was suddenly reminded of that old movie about the zombies; the living dead. This, however, was no movie. This was real. And Ed felt his heart beating rapidly in his chest and his breaths, quick and shallow, sent steam into the night.

"You ain't sceered are ya, old man?" John said, his voice as dead as he was. "Not tryin' to be a pissy pants little baby, are ya?"

Ed wanted to scream for him to be gone...that he wasn't real...just some hallucination.

But his words remained behind some imaginary locked door in his minds eye and the key had been lost around the same time his sense of rationality had been so heinously murdered by the apparition that now stood only an arm's length in front of him.

"I need you to come with me, now, Edward. I need you to come with me to meet Lady Scarlet...she's been waitin' on you for a very long time."

A smell like soured milk rolled from John's grated gums and Ed felt nausea churning in his stomach. "No," he croaked through craked lips. "NO!"

John was grinning like a demented elf, the skin on his hands and face becoming a liquid ooze, falling to the bloody snow in clumps. "Ed. You know better than that! What the lady wants, the lady gets. And she wants you, old man."

"IT'S A MTYH!" Ed cried out at the creature before him that no longer bore any resemblance to John McPearson. "AND YOU'RE...YOU'RE CRAZY!"

"No, old man," John said as he was placing one meaty hand on Ed's shoulder, and placing the other over Ed's face. "I am sane. I am eternal. I am her's"

The last thought to fleet through Edward Patterson's mind before it was crushed beneath John McPearson's bloody hand was an image of his father's laughing face...a face that was all of a sudden a pale young girl with hair the color of autum fire. Then there was nothing more.

IV.

As the sun rose over the small town of Cradle Caverns, Sheriff Cole Bukins pulled his old

Chevy Tahoe to a stop next to the the Guardco Ford Explorer parked with its driver side door standing open. Deputy Jenkins waved him over to the front of the guard shack once he'd got out of the Tahoe and shut the door. Cole didn't like this...hated it, in fact. Him and

Ed Patterson had went to school together, had been good friends the better part of thirty years or so. And now his good friend lay dead no more then ten feet away from him, along with Rickey McPearson's oldest boy, John. He had been a good boy as far as Cole was concerned, which is what made this case so strange.

"Damnedest, thing Cole," Jenkins was saying as Cole knelt beside the bodies.

"Damnedest thing I ever saw."

"It's a fuckin' shame," Cole said, shaking his head. "Ed had no relatives, that I know of.

But the McPearson boy...good God how am I going to tell Rickey that his boy's dead. Jesus."

"What you make of it, Cole?"

Cole Bukins looked down at the two corpses, frozen, pale husks in the snow, arms locked around one another's throats in death grips. "Well, Deputy, looks like they choked each other, doesn't it. Get on the horn, get the boy's on up here and bag 'em."

"Yes, sir," Jenkins said and turned towards his cruiser, then turned and asked. "Cole... what you think would make 'em go at each other like that?"

"Cabin fever...bad mojo...who knows. You just get a hold of dispatch and let's get this mess cleaned up."

"Yes, sir."

Cole listened to Jenkins feet crunching in the snow as the Deputy headed to his cruiser and thought come.

The bitch is back. And she's pissed.

Bathtime

By Alistair Canlin

There was so much to be arranged, so much that had to be put in place, tidied and prepared.

This moment had been a long time coming, something that I had dreamed of for a long time.

A fantasy that was about to become true.

She was everything I had dreamed she could ever be. Funny, intelligent, beautiful. I shook when I first saw her, that instant, that very second I knew it had to be her.

But I digress, there was much work to be done. The dinner was on, pasta, her favourite, nice and simple for my culinary level. Next the cleaning, must be prepared, cannot afford to be caught out by a simple mistake. I had the tools to hand. It's strange, but why do they not do rubber gloves in black or white? It seems almost inappropriate to choose between yellow or pink. I plumped for yellow, the lesser of two evils. They snap and squeak as I pulled them on, a feeling of security came over me. Emboldened, I climb the stairs to the bathroom, knowing which one creaks I sidestep gently.

The bathroom door was slightly ajar, my rubber clad hand pushed the door open. The white tiled walls and floor greeted me with their customary coldness. My bare feet almost recoil from their touch. With gentle persuasion they relent and I entered the bathroom.

The small plastic container of cleaning products I had left earlier is in the corner. I leaned over and started the cold tap running, then I carefully selected the cleaning products, no trade names, I don't want to give away all my secrets. The thin, but belligerent, grey line slowly disappeared as I worked on it. A steady rhythm and the job is done before I know it.

Another step closer.

My heart accelerated in anticipation. I could almost smell her, the prospect of her touch.

Snap out of it!

Jobs to be done.

I won't bore you with every detail of the cleaning, that would just be too boring, unless of course you're into that kind of thing?

No?

Well we'll jump to the juicy part.

The doorbell rang, against my natural instinct I don't run to it instantly. Don't want to appear too eager. I wait until my body is nearly bursting at every sinew and the doorbell rang again. Then I sauntered casually forward and opened the door, putting on my best winning smile.

And there she is.

The vision.

"I was worried you were out." Her voice was like a nightingale.

She leaned forward and her ruby lips gently caressed my cheek, I could feel her silken hair brush against me and I breathed in her smell, an intoxicating mix of exotic flowers.

"Come in." Not much for an opening gambit, but it was all I could manage.

"This is such a lovely place."

"It's been in the family for years, I was left it by my grandfather." That was a lie, my grandfather was in an old folks home spending his days staring into space and pissing into a bag.

Her movement was graceful, the way she held herself, almost an air of superiority.

"Can I take your coat?" Oh I'm a consummate charmer.

Why can't I say what I feel?

Because that would get me into trouble.

The form of her back revealed itself to me as I removed her coat.

I wanted to reach out, to trace the line of her spine. But no, there would be time enough for that later.

"Please, go through to the living room."

Her left eyebrow arched slightly.

"Second on the left."

She smiled and turned.

I watched her walk, the rhythmic sway that seemed to beckon.

The spell broke as she entered the living room.

I could feel my heart beating loudly as I put her coat away. I would have to control myself if I wanted things to have a successful outcome.

When I entered the living room she was seated on the sofa, gently flicking through a magazine, her legs crossed and it seemed the material of her knee length black skirt was stretched to almost breaking point.

My eyes followed the line of her thigh over her knee, down her gently shimmering shin to a thin and slender ankle. Her foot, encased in an elaborate black shoe, gently rocked up and down.

"I was surprised you called." She smiled as she looked up from the magazine.

"A pleasant surprise I hope?"

She let out a surprisingly girly giggle.

At that moment I think I loved her more than ever.

"What are you thinking?" Her left eyebrow arched again.

I couldn't tell her the truth, that would be ungentle manly.

"About us."

She smiled, revealing a glint in her eye, her tongue gliding against the tip of her teeth.

A slight shiver travelled down my back, I don't think it was guilt.

"So what're you cooking?"

"Your favourite."

Her face lit up.

It was almost too easy.

"I'd better check on it." I left and headed to the kitchen. If I'd planned everything correctly she'd use this as an opportunity to nose around. And of course, she'd only find what

I'd want her to find.

It was all a game, all heading towards the same conclusion, all I had to do was keep a clear head. It was then that I added the special ingredients and carried the two plates through.

She seemed to be straightening her skirt, or at least that's what she wanted me to think.

I placed both plates on the perfectly set table.

"Dinner is served madam."

There was that girly giggle again.

She rose elegantly and seemed to glide towards the table. Her walk was captivating, like an entrancing dance, a mixture of allure and power.

"Why thank you." She smiled as I held her seat for her, my finger momentarily brushed against her arm. My own body feeling as if it was being charged by her power.

"This looks good."

"It's just something simple I threw together." The compliment made me blush and almost threw me off my stride.

"Have I made you blush?"

"No." I was mortified I'd let it show.

"I have, haven't I?"

"I'm just not used to compliments." I tried to get control of my emotions.

"You surprise me." Her hand reached across, one of her fingers stroked between my index finger and thumb.

I felt so alive.

As if I would explode there and then.

Her power engorging mine.

"This tastes amazing." Her hand moved away, her fingers now dabbed at imaginary stains at the corner of her mouth.

"I don't think I can cope with all these compliments."

There was the girly giggle again.

I could watch her eat for hours, the parting of those lips, the way she savoured every morsel, the look of satisfaction.

"You really should give me the recipe." her eyes burned bright.

"Oh I couldn't possibly do that."

"Aaw." A look of sheer devastated disappointment spread across her face.

"An old family secret I'm afraid."

Her eyes did a wonderful job of pleading.

"Now you wouldn't want me to betray my ancestors, would you?"

The puppy dog eyes relented.

At that very moment I could have done anything I wanted, anything at all. But no. I decided to wait, to wait until the moment was right.

To be honest, deep down, I knew that moment wasn't far away. All I had to do was bide my time.

"I can't work you out?" She looked at me with mild confusion.

"There's nothing to work out." I wondered if she'd somehow worked out my plan.

"You're not....?" She couldn't finish the sentence.

"Not what?"

"Like other men."

Inside I was laughing like a drain. If only she knew.

"How so?"

"Most guys would've been all over me by now, y'know, any excuse for a quick grope."

I hoped I was using a sympathetic smile.

"Don't get me wrong, I'm enjoying it. The wining and dining, it makes a change to be treated like a human being rather than just a piece of meat." Her eyes looked sad, like a person resigned to their lot in life.

"Believe me I see you as far more." Part of me wanted to reach across and hold her, tell her she was special, and make everything alright. But I knew that would be the wrong thing, that would be a weakness. If I wanted everything I couldn't be weak.

I noticed her plate was almost empty.

"Do you wish some more?"

"Oh no I couldn't."

"I won't tell anyone."

"No I need to be good."

"Go on. We all need to be bad sometime."

"You're just trying to get me into trouble."

She must've noticed something in my face, her expression changed, she seemed wary.

Maybe things had changed.

Maybe things were working.

"Are you okay?" I thought I'd test the waters.

"Feel a bit funny." She held her hand up to her head.

"It's not my cooking?"

"I'll be fine." She dismissed me with a wave.

"The bathroom's first on the left as you go up the stairs."

She moved quickly, her arms outstretched for balance. I sat, quite contentedly, and finished the last of my meal. The stairs creaked, I knew exactly where she was.

The pasta tasted quite bland, not enough spice.

I gathered up the plates and took them through to the kitchen. On with the rubber gloves again I scrubbed all trace of the meal from the dishes. It felt almost therapeutic, the feeling of the water pounding against the gloves, the clammy rubber against my skin.

Maybe I'm just strange.

There was a noise from upstairs, it could be time, but I waited. After all they do say that the best things come to those who wait.

My heart was pounding with excitement, I could hear my blood roaring past my ears, my skin tingled and seemed to be turning pink.

I could wait no longer and headed for the stairs, my hands felt warm and sticky inside their rubber casing, I instinctively avoided the creaky step. I could see the bathroom door was slightly ajar, she hadn't had time to lock it. Nice of her to be so considerate.

I was sure the whole world could hear my heart pounding as I pushed open the bathroom door.

She seemed quite still, almost peaceful, until I noticed the slight rise and fall of her chest. She looked almost perfect, apart from a small puddle of vomit by her head, little bits of pasta and tomato sauce. A little bit dribbled down her cheek.

The urge to clean it was strong, but like I said, I can wait.

The rise and falls of her chest became few and far between, there was also a low rasping hiss escaping her mouth.

I sat on the toilet seat and watched and waited. As I watched her I felt almost envious, I don't know why I can't explain it, but I did. From where I sat her face was slightly hidden, I didn't want to see the vomit, but I reached across and gently pulled her hair away from her face. Her cheeks looked ashen, the sparkle had faded from her eyes, as they now just stared blankly ahead.

I almost wanted her to cry out for help, not that it would've made any difference, I wasn't willing to let anything spoil this moment. I counted as her final seconds slipped by, I made it to thirty two and then there was a long slow sigh. Her chest deflated for a final time.

People say you look peaceful in death, as I rolled her onto her back all I could see was a look of confusion staring back at me.

Some people talk a lot of shit.

For things to be right I had to tackle the vomit, if it was left then sure as eggs is eggs I'd end up standing in it, and that would just spoil the fun.

I reached over to the container of cleaning products, which I was pleased to see were undisturbed, I removed some anti-septic cloths and wiped away the vomit, making sure to move the cloth away from her so as not to get any in her hair or let any find its way under the body and annoy me later. I flushed the detritus down the toilet.

I took greater care over removing the slight trail from her face. Cradling her head on my lap I gently wiped her face clean. I was delighted when her makeup remained intact.

When I'd finished I laid her back down and took a step back to admire her.

She was perfect, almost serene.

My heart accelerated, my breathing shallow, my skin tingled.

I started with her shoes, the elaborate buckles and straps that wound their way round her slender ankles were tricky at first. My fingers shaking slightly. They soon got the hang of it.

Her toes looked slightly squashed as they were revealed. I have to admit I was disappointed, and hoped there wouldn't be any other imperfections hidden away.

I was relieved when I found she was wearing hold up stocking, not only was my life made a lot easier, but also I hated tights, nothing worse than tights. I decided to leave them on her for the moment as my hands removed her skirt. With a little bit of subtle persuasion it slid

off easily. I was impressed as I caught sight of the label, I folded it delicately and neatly, placing it carefully on top of the laundry basket.

She wore very attractive, and delicately embroidered, black lace hipsters.

I felt another tingle, as my fingers gently moved across her flat stomach, reaching and unfastening the buttons on her blouse, revealing a matching bra. An impressive work of art was being revealed, I could feel my skin begin to tingle. I had to lift her weight to ease off the blouse, her body still felt warm. The blouse felt expensive, but I didn't recognise the name on the label. Again I neatly folded it and placed it carefully on top of the laundry basket.

I took a moment and admired her, her silken dark hair lay around her, not like a halo, but more like a cloud of foreboding. Her makeup was still perfect and I was pleased to see that her toes, still slightly squashed at the bottom of her stockings, were the only imperfection.

All in all things had worked out well.

I reached across and opened the cupboard under the sink, and there they were, my little beauties, shining and glistening as the light fell upon them. With care and more than a little reverence I removed them one by one, placing them on a black felt cloth beside her body.

First the saw, which I had polished and sharpened only last week, then a smaller hacksaw, for the fiddly bits, a selection of different sized scalpels, which I had acquired for a bargain at a house clearance sale.

All looked beautiful.

All seemed to cry out, begging to be used.

All my body was surging with energy.

I couldn't resist running my fingers over her body, half expecting her to flinch or giggle, in fact I surprised myself when I had to stifle my own laughter. The excitement was becoming almost unbearable, I had to start.

I slowly rolled down each stocking, freeing her squashed feet. Her legs were silky smooth, she'd shaved them recently, probably in preparation for our date.

I peeled off her underwear, failing to stop myself from having a peek, a shiver ran down my back. Cradling her in my arms I lifted her, her head fell back, her hair cascading down my arm, she was beautiful, truly beautiful. I then placed her carefully into the bath.

The bath felt cold against my skin, the complete opposite to the pleasant warmth that came from her. I instinctively brushed her hair away from her face, she looked quite peaceful.

With the smallest scalpel I reached across her and cut her throat, the blood flowed freely out of her, my waiting had cut down on the mess. The blood was dark, staining everything it touched, but at first because the scalpel had gone through so easily I feared I had done nothing at all. The sight of the blood was reassuring.

Her expressionless eyes were slightly unnerving, but I watched them, half hoping for a reaction as I drew the scalpel across her wrists. I tried to tell myself I something, but deep

down I knew I was kidding myself.

Most of the bath had turned a deep crimson, large and small droplets clinging to the sides as if unsure of what to do next. I on the other hand knew exactly what was next. Taking hold of the saw I started to remove her feet, the ugliest part of her, cutting midway up her shin.

This proved tougher that I had imagined, bone was a resilient substance and the noise was none too pleasant. With a bit of elbow grease, perspiration, and grim determination her feet were finally removed.

I have to say it was an improvement, a vast improvement.

I decided my next move would have to be an easier one, cutting bone was hard work. With one of the larger scalpels I cut across her flat, slightly tanned, stomach. A gash opened like a deep dark cavern, I pulled it wider and dived in up to my elbows. It felt warm, just like

I'd imagined, I could feel soft and hard things rubbing against my skin, my fingers caressing and stroking her insides. As I worked her head lolled about, almost as if she was watching me, it was the closest I'd get to a reaction and it kind of thrilled me.

A putrid smell started to fill my nostrils, a smell unlike any other. At first it made me nauseous, but then I let it envelop me, caress my senses, until it felt homely and just, well, right.

Her body sagged, her face looked drawn, her breasts lopsided. Not as beautiful, but still I loved her. Loved her with all my being, so much it almost hurt.

I pulled my arms out and stared at the blood soaked on them, it made me feel alive, closer to her. Yes closer to her, I had to get closer to her. I fully undressed and stood naked above her, part of me expected her to have moved, to have got up and run away, but after what I had done it was impossible, so I took it as a sign that she wanted to be there, she wanted this to happen.

Why else had she come after all?

Why?

Because she loved me.

I climbed into the bath and lay down next to her, cradling her in my arms. She was cold. I stroked her hair, whispered into her ear. Told her I loved her.

I felt tired.

I could feel the light hairs on her arm, they felt soft, my fingers traced little patterns until her skin felt rough and ragged. I looked down, my fingers were playing with the edge of her wound. Instinctively I recoiled, which made me laugh, loud and echoing. But then I became fascinated by the gaping wound, it felt unreal almost sensual without the barrier of the rubber gloves. Slowly my fingers crept deeper and deeper inside, the warmth was leaving her, but my fingers wanted more. I could feel her ribcage, the muscle wall. I couldn't resist, I lifted her face to mine and kissed her.

Time stood still.

My heart stopped.

It felt right.

I was in love.

My head filled with images, strolls along beaches, holding hands, laughing, stolen moments and knowing glances.

All I had to do was hold her and all those things were real, those things that someone like me could never have.

I must've at some stage fallen asleep, I could see it was dark outside and I could hear voices. Late night revellers, so called normal people enjoying normal lives.

How depressing.

She was cold now, her skin pale grey, her lips almost blue and she felt stiff. Her wounds were dark black and her eyes looked hollow, almost sad.

I heard the creaky stair first, but my brain was too slow, maybe I was loved up?

Whatever it was I didn't even react when the door came crashing in. A large jackboot and a masked face, garbled words shouted. I had to smile as one pulled off his mask and staggered from the room, the sound of vomiting almost made me laugh.

These men were incapable of love, they didn't understand.

I held her close, but I was manhandled out of the bath, and my grip was lost. I tried to shout, but hands were all over me, pinning me down.

The bathroom door was cold.

The cell floor is cold.

I have to wear a repulsive paper suit, which rustles loudly when I move. Every so often eyes peer in at me, cold unfeeling eyes.

My skin yearns for her touch.

They won't tell me where she is.

Every so often they take me to another room, ask me questions, endless questions.

I'm told I'm a monster.

I'm told I'm inhuman.

They look smug.

They think they've won.

In my cell I close my eyes.

She smiles at me and holds my hand. The soft sand feels warm on my bare feet. She laughs as the birds fly overhead. My whole body is singing out as I hold her close. Her skin

feels warm and welcoming. I soak her up.

They think they've won.

THE SHADOW ON THE PLAIN

BY JAMES HOWLETT

The car sped along the highway like a bullet gliding down a gun barrel, wing mirrors glinting in the sun. The smooth purr of the cars engine was the only sound that could be heard for miles.

Alex adjusted his sunglasses, and rested one arm on the door of his convertible. The wind breezed through his hair like a lover's breath, and the sun beat him like an abusive parent. He was sweating profusely. Earlier, he had driven with the hood up and the air conditioning on full blast, and it had felt like he was sitting in a freezer. Problem was, on the first toilet break he had taken, he had damn nearly fainted when stepping out of the car, the heat hitting him like the proverbial ton of bricks. After that, he decided to drive with the top down and use the air conditioning at a premium. It would conserve more petrol that way too, and therefore save money which was something near to Alex's heart. Money that was, not saving money.

He was driving through Arizona, on his way to see his Grandfather, in Phoenix. It had been three years since he had seen him, and the old fart was due to croak at any moment, and had asked to see his only remaining living relative, Alex. So the distressed phone call from his nurse had said, anyway. The only thing she was probably so upset about was the likely end to her easy little job (although cleaning his pecker wasn't a pleasant job) and nice little money maker. Maybe she was after something out of the will, too.

Alex did not care much for his Grandfather. He had hardly seen him as a child, and the only memory he had of him was someone who used to shout at his Grandmother a lot and reeked of gin or whiskey. The last time they had met had been at his Grandmother's funeral, who had 'fallen' down the stairs at home. They had both been drunk and things had definitely gotten out of hand, although nothing was ever proven of course.

This was probably not the best time to reappear, especially after everything that had been said between them, but he smelt wills and inheritance and the desperate repentance of an asshole who knows they have little time left, so this baking trek should be worth it. He was, after all, the only Grandchild. He had rights, didn't he? Maybe he should have read some books on the subject before jumping into his car and roaring toward the desert and the pot of gold at the end of the rainbow. Surely the old bastard would relinquish the stubborn hold of his bitterness before he went to the grave.

Doing a steady sixty-five, the road yawned out in front of him like the bulbous tongue of some unknown beast, rolling him greedily towards its mouth. He looked either side, hoping to see something of interest. All that was on offer were large rocks, small rocks and a huge expanse of desert. It stretched forever, it seemed. God, you could believe you were the only person left in the world out here.

The so-called state of the art expensive car stereo (fitted as standard you know) had packed up ten minutes previously, to his great annoyance. The eclectic mix of trashy pop and mindless babble was not to his taste, but had been mildly entertaining, for a short while. The only other station the stereo could apparently receive out here was some kind of religious drivel, spouting forth from the mouth of some agitated southerner, preaching about the sins and evil of man and how we were all damned to Hell.

The clock on the dashboard said eleven thirty. By his estimation, he had another four hours of this. Christ. He couldn't remember the last car he had seen. About sixty miles back, possibly. He really didn't know. This had better be worth it. It would be, a voice inside his head told him in a placating tone.

Alex had prepared in a hurry for this journey, eager to play the role of forgiving and deeply upset Grandson. It would be a galling experience in the sickest of pantomimes, but he was confident he could pull it off. That particular thought made Alex smile and he put his foot down a bit more, wanting to get this over with, and not wanting to miss the old man's last moments on this earth, if the truth be known.

Holding a packet of cigarettes up to his lips, Alex pulled one out with his teeth, and depressed the lighter button on his dash. A small gust of wind rustled the map on the passenger seat, and he stamped on it with his hand. Mustn't lose that for Christ sakes.

He weighed it down with his bottle of mineral water just in case. The button clicked out, and he lighted the cigarette. At least that thing still worked. Taking a long drag, he removed it and stretched out in the seat. The luxury leather interior was spot welding itself to him, along with his sweat soaked shirt. He tried the stereo again, out of hope, really. Nothing but static, which further enhanced his growing feeling of solitude.

Driving out here was like being swallowed by a vast feeling of alone, nothing like he had felt before. It made him uncomfortable, so he left the radio on, just blaring static. At least it was something. Who knows, it might blurt into life at any time, like a reliable old car does, just when you think its had it.

Speaking of cars, he would replace this piece of shit with its crap stereo when he got his money. Alex was not a technical man when it came to cars, but he knew what he wanted. This thought distracted him for a while, and made him forget about the present reality. This was good, as the present reality sucked. It was bad in other ways, as it caused the flashing oil light on the dashboard to go unnoticed.

* * * * *

The shit hit the fan, so to speak, around forty-five minutes later. Alex had been looking blankly at more goddamn rocks when the engine simply spluttered once and then stalled. The car then rolled slowly to a halt, and Alex guided it carefully off the road. The car resisted all

Alex's attempts to restart it, like a stubborn child who has not got its own way. A reasonable amount of steam had accompanied the stalling of the engine, adding its own sense of drama to what could end up being a very serious situation indeed.

"Fuck!!!" screamed Alex, and thrust the palms of his hands against the steering wheel in frustration. Loosening the seat belt, he got out of the immobilised vehicle.

He removed his sunglasses, and popped the bonnet up. Quite why he did this he did not know, as he had no real idea of what the hell he was looking at. It was more out of hope; maybe he would see something loose or a similar obvious looking problem causer. Steam bellowed out straight into his face, and he jerked up, catching his head on the raised bonnet.

"Fuck!!!" he yelled once more, struggling to get a grip as a sense of panic rose up in his body like a sick tidal wave. He stomped around the side of the car yelling the same expletive over and over. 'Fuck! Shit! Fuck! Shit! Fuck! Shit!!' He interspersed this with the occasional kick into the side of the car for good measure. Slowly, as he continued pacing, he began calming down a little, and decided to re-investigate the engine. Aiming for the only component he was aware of in a car engine, he slid the oil dipstick from its greasy metal cylinder. He thought he had prepared for this journey, but in his haste, he had not checked the oil level. The dipstick was bone dry and very, very hot to the touch. Disheartened and defeated, he feebly plunged the dipstick back into its holder.

What the hell was he to do now? The tide of panic that had temporarily begun to ebb began lapping at the periphery of his mind once more. Stuck in the middle of the desert and no oil. No cars had been past for hours, maybe there wouldn't be one for days!

Alex slumped forward, placing his ends on either side of the car, staring into the engine, which now seemed like a black abyss, swallowing his dreams of inheritance.

Before Alex could gather his thoughts properly, he was struck a solid blow to his nose.

Bright sparks shot before his eyes and he sank to his knees from the unexpected blow. He could taste blood. His blood, warm and coppery, like sucking on a piece of electrical cable.

Slowly opening his eyes, he wiped his nose with his sleeve, and looked around. What the hell had done that? There was no-one here, who could have punched him? He stood up, and swayed back against the car, the unexpected blow had rattled his senses. Throwing his hand

over his forehead, he surveyed the scene around him. Lots of sand, dotted rocks and nothing else. Was that a cactus in the distance?

Then, it came to him; under the car! They were hiding under the car! Shaking, and more than a little scared, Alex sniffed blood back up his nostrils, slowly knelt down and started to look under the car. Swallowing furiously, his chin touching the hot tarmac, he peered all the way under.

A small bead mingling with a drop of blood that had followed the same vigil, forming an unholy alliance with the tarmac. There was nothing under the car. He half expected to see a pair of shoes on the other side, but there was nothing. His hands were getting really hot off the tarmac, so he got back up. You could probably do a mixed grill on this godforsaken road, he thought.

Straightening up, he looked around once more for his assailant. There was nothing to be seen, but there was something to be heard. A dripping noise, slow but steady.

It was coming from the front of the car. Frowning, and now even more annoyed, Alex strode like a general to the front of the car. The steam had stopped, and so he was able to get a good look at what he surmised to be a ruptured fuel line (because he could smell petrol so strongly) that was dangling limply like the arms of a punch drunk boxer. There was definitely someone here! That fuel line was fine moments ago, he was sure of it. Holding the broken end to his face, he made closer inspection. It would be fairer to say the tube had been chewed in half, not broken, judging by the ragged strips. Someone or something had chewed through the damn thing. An animal? He angrily slapped the cable back into the engine compartment and placed his hands on his hips. What the fuck was going on here? Someone was fucking about with him and now he was stranded. The tide of panic was fast becoming a flood.

Just then, he was struck a reasonably hard blow to his lower back, which caused him to arc backwards, wincing, squeezing his eyes shut and gritting his teeth with the pain. He tossed his head to the right, just in time to glimpse a thin stalk-like shadow dart behind the wing of the car.

"You fucker!!! I'm coming for you, you fucker!!" Alex screamed, but his bold language belied the fact he was actually very frightened. Physical violence was a way of life for him, but it was he who often dealt it, and wasn't used to being on the receiving end.

Rubbing his back slightly, he began to edge around the side of the car, heading for the boot. His back hurt, but not that much. It was like they wanted his attention or something.

Well, they had damn well got it, and they would be sorry they had. It was bad enough running out of oil, but now with the fuel line broken, he was stuck here for the time it would take to get a mechanic, and out here that could be hours. Yes, they would pay all right. Keeping low to the side, he edged past the passenger door. The metal of the car was hot. His hair lay plastered to his forehead in long greasy strips. Perspiration mottled his face and run onto his lips, tasting salty.

Just past the edge of the boot, he saw a long, thin shadow of a man. From the position of the shadow, his attacker was standing at the rear of the car.

Alex frowned. Hold on; standing?

Why could he not see him? He halted his advance, and to his horror, the shadow raised its arms in a hostile gesture like a karate posture and turned in his direction. It was waiting for him. It crouched slightly, ready to pounce. If shadows could do that. Clearly this one could.

Alex was thinking fast, he had to do something. Just what the fuck was that thing at the back of his car? The invisible man? The heat playing tricks on him? A small drop of blood plopped onto his thigh to remind him this was no mind game, that punch and that thing were real.

The shadow made his mind up for him. It came haring round the side of his car, looking like a streak of black paint and before a startled Alex could react, firmly kicked him in the ribs. Winded, Alex instinctively rolled under the car, gasping for air. He turned his head slowly fro slowly through his clothes. The shadow was to his right, just standing there again, the fighting posture dropped for the time being. It seemed content just to wait apparently. Alex needed to think what to do. Laying there under the car for what seemed like ages, he pondered his dilemma. What was it waiting for? He couldn't stay here forever, but he needed to recover from the assault he had endured. He slowly closed his eyes and tried to clear his mind, let logic reassert itself, and figure out what on earth he was going to do to get out of this nightmarish situation.

Without knowing, he slipped into a fitful sleep. His sub-conscious made the connection with his posture, and he dreamt of his childhood, and the time he was chased by an angry, boisterous dog.

His mother had let him play soccer with his friends in the park, unsupervised for the first time. Normally, she would insist on his Dad accompanying him, but in an unprecedented act of kindness, had allowed Alex the independence that all ten year old boys like to think they have. Alex knew he mustn't screw up, or she'd never let him out on his own again for some time.

Things started to go bad when he saw Mr Daniels looming on the horizon with Stevie.

Mr Daniels was a grumpy old man who lived three houses up from him, and Stevie was his dog. Alex was not an expert on dogs, all he knew was this one chased you and barked a lot. It was a damn scary dog. To a ten year old, anyway.

As fate would have it, Mr Daniels let Stevie off the lead, and he galloped straight for the boys, and before they knew what had happened, Stevie had sank his fangs into the ball and burst it. The ball slowly deflated, covered in slimy strings of dog drool. Stevie looked around, baring his teeth and obviously pleased with his labours, deciding who to terrorise next. The boys had already begun to scatter, but you guessed it, ol' Stevie saw the appealing, rapidly retreating rear end of Alex, and promptly gave chase. He could remember the familiar cry from Mr Daniels of 'he's only being friendly', but ask anyone who's ever been chased by a dog, they don't seem friendly at the time. The fleeing boys looked like panicked ants, and Stevie was the aardvark. Alex began running for the house, as fast as he could, but three quarters of the way there, it was clear as fast as he could was not going to cut it.

Sensing the snapping salivating jaws of Stevie behind him, he quickly glanced from side to side, looking for another escape. He found one. There was a parked car on the opposite side of the road outside his house. Maybe he could get under it before Stevie got him.

Alex got a lucky break when his sudden veer to the right took Stevie unawares. Stevie had thought this was a no-contest, and that Alex was going to foolishly attempt to head for the sanctuary of home, but now the boy was headed for underneath that car. The fraction of a second it took the dog to adjust its body weight and momentum was enough for the poor, hysterical Alex to drop to his knees and roll under the car. He cried as he did so, because he had scuffed his knees on the hard gravel road surface. The dog stood by the car growling and bearing his teeth, in that 'only being friendly' way that dog owners' patent. Occasionally the dog's head appeared and snapped its jaws at him. Alex lay under the car, dirty, oily, bleeding and crying, literally not knowing what to do next. He hoped to hell Stevie would go away.

He prayed his mother would hear the noise and come outside to investigate. His Mother did not like coming outside, however. Too many bad people around, she would say. It was a miracle she had let him out, but she would never do that again after this episode. As if things couldn't get any worse, the dog lowered itself and poked its head under the car enough for it to be able to grab Alex's leg. It had hold of his jeans, and was slowly but surely pulling him out, growling as it did so. Alex screamed and grabbed hold of the exhaust pipe, yelling for his Mother.

Woken from his slumber, Alex fought his way through the dregs of the nightmare.

Banging his head on the underside of the engine brought him to his senses, but he still half expected to see a decomposed Stevie tugging at his leg. Instead, he saw nothing. Unless he looked down at the road surface. Just as before, he could see the shadow of a man, but now the shadow of a man who had hold of his leg, and was slowly pulling him out. Similar to his nightmare, he grabbed the exhaust pipe. Unlike his nightmare, the exhaust pipe was still very hot, and his instant reaction was to let go. At the same time, with one mighty tug, he was wrenched from under the car, scraping the palms of his hands on the tarmac as he desperately scrabbled for purchase.

Driven by pure fright, Alex leapt to his feet and simply ran for it. His brain did not plot a logical path, he just simply ran for it. Out into the desert, out into nowhere, but somewhere, he didn't care, just away from the shadow. Being the only nearest object to him, he made for a large rock, sitting lonely on the plain.

Alex waited until he reached the rock, panting, gasping, before he afforded the luxury of looking behind him. About sixty metres away he could see his car, glinting like a big jewel in the sun. His car appeared to be deserted. Looking nervously and quickly at the ground around him, he searched for the shadow.

He needn't have looked far. The shadow was roughly five metres and closing fast. Alex could not take anymore. There was no escaping his mystery assailant. He was lazy and out of condition, and no match for anyone or anything in a fight, his attitude had always carried him through. This time though, his bluff had been well and truly called by this dark invader.

He backed up to the rock, felt its hot stony surface against his back and slowly slumped down, resigned to whatever grisly fate the shadow had in store. It was three metres away, still closing, and Alex watched as it raised its right arm high above its head, preparing to bring it crashing down. Alex closed his eyes, and in a lame show of defiance, offered his middle finger as a last gesture of hatred for his mysterious assailant.

Nothing.

Peeking out between the splayed fingers of his left hand, his right still showing the bird and the sun obscuring his view like an interrogator's spotlight, Alex looked around. His heart backed down his throat, and took up its rightful place in his rib cage, although it still wasn't happy.

The shadow stood there, arms by its side, about two feet away. Why hadn't it struck him? Confused, Alex looked around him, his head whipping from side to side, looking for the answer. Then, it came to him; the rock he was slumped against cast a shadow of its own, and Alex was currently in it. It was a small shadow, roughly five feet across and three feet deep. Alex's own shadow was consumed in that of the rock's. Was this the reason? Eager to test out his theory, he shuffled backward and sideways, nearing the edge of his black safety zone.

The shadow stiffened, and he could make out its head tilting slightly, like a dog's when you speak to them.

Tentatively, he poked the edge of his foot into the light, never taking his eyes off his persecutor.

The shadow lunged forward, cat like, arms outstretched in the direction of the exposed body part.

Alex shot his toes back into the shadow, and the second he did, the shadow stopped its advance, and resumed its waiting posture.

So, he was safe for the time being, but how long would it be before this thing, this creature gave up on him? Maybe never, but that was a depressing thought, and one Alex was not prepared to consider at this juncture, now he had a means of defence.

Instead, he turned his mind to thoughts of escape. He now had time to think, without being chased. Obviously, when he had been stupid enough to doze off, his leg had trailed out from underneath the car enough for the shadow to grab hold of it. He must have been reenacting his madcap dash from Stevie under the car. If he had known then what he had known now, he would never have bolted from his four wheeled sanctuary. All he had achieved was to put a good sixty metres between him and the car. Given the speed of the shadow and his state of exhaustion, he would never make it back there.

At some point though, another car would pass, and it would be bound to stop and investigate. Then, he could call for help. Yes, that was it, he would play the thing at its own game and wait the bastard out.

He looked at his watch. It was one o'clock. The sun was at the zenith of its powers and the heat was already becoming stifling. Although the rock offered some protection, it was clear it would not be enough. Alex took up a foetal position at the base of the rock, and tried to hide himself as much as possible. From this vantage point, he could see his car and the road, for about three miles, he guessed. Alex looked longingly at the car, for on the passenger's seat was his bottle of water. It was probably tepid to warm, but water was water right now.

He wasn't totally alone though; Alex needed not to look far for his attacker, because, as if sensing his thoughts, the shadow took up a position right in front of him. Standing

between him and his car, daring him to make a break for it.

Another hour passed. No saviours, but still the shadow persisted.

Alex dozed off again, the baking sun sapping his strength slowly, like the tide eroding the shoreline. The two dark circles under his arms met the dark patch in the middle of his back on his shirt while he slept, encasing him in a tomb of his own perspiration.

Still, the shadow persisted.

Something woke him up, but this time it wasn't a dog or a shadow tugging at his leg, but something else, a low humming to be exact. He put his hand across his forehead looking around, then broke into a grin.

A car was approaching.

Alex jumped up, and started waving his arms around, completely forgetting about the shadow for the time being.

The car shimmered in the heat as it drew closer. Alex could tell that it was slowing down, obviously to see if the driver of the stricken car needed help. Well, he did, but he was over here and his car was over there. Now, he could make out its brake lights.

The car stopped next to his and the driver got out.

Alex shouted 'Hey! Hey!' and took a step forward.

Whoa, wait, the shadow, he reminded himself.

And of course, it was still there, and was still blocking his path. Alex remained in the protective shadow of the rock and gritted his teeth in frustration at his predicament. He clenched and unclenched his fists repeatedly, pacing in his little bar less cage like an expectant father, and began yelling again.

If the driver heard him, he didn't acknowledge him. Instead, he was perusing Alex's car, like a curious feline.

'Over here! Help!' cried Alex. He needed water. The thought had occurred to him that the driver of the other vehicle would probably fall foul to his shadowy tormentor, but he didn't care as at least he would be able to make a break a for it. He could steal the other guy's car and get the hell out of here.

Alex impatiently watched the guy snoop round his car. He thumped his fists against his legs in anger as he saw the guy pull out his water bottle and drain its contents, throwing his head back with the bottle to his lips, and then tossed the container carelessly onto the sand.

Impossible as it was, Alex was sure he could have seen the water chugging from the bottle into the bastard's throat. I hope you fucking choke on it, he thought. He stared at the shadow in fury, his eyes boring a hole through it, and it just stood there, like it had been doing all the time he was hiding in the safety of the rock. He yelled his frustration.

To add to it, the guy at his car turned and looked in his direction. Clearly, he had not heard him yelling before. This seemed to spook him, as he now dived into Alex's car and disappeared from view. He must have thought Alex had gone for a piss and was on his way back. After a few minutes, the man reappeared with something in his hand. His car stereo.

Obviously, Alex had hurried the guy into revealing his true intention and it certainly wasn't to aid Alex in any way.

'Hey! You bastard, that's my stereo!' Alex howled in vain, knowing it was no use.

The guy flipped him off, jumped in his car and pulled away, with a screech of tyres as he did so.

Slumping back down against the rock, defeated, Alex pondered his predicament once more.

What should he do now? He could wait for another car he supposed, but what was the point?

One might not come along for ages and anyway, people were bastards he decided. Alex of course, was not.

No, it was time to prioritise. Not get carried away with self pity. There had to be a way out. Where there's a will, there's a way. Literally.

First up, he had to drink.

Now he knew there was no water back in the car so that limited his options. The shadow was waiting for him to make a break for it, so he was stuck where he was right now, his only option was to drink his own urine, however ghastly a proposition it seemed. Alex had no choice.

Trouble was, he had no container to put it in.

With one eye on the shadow, he stood up once more for a look around. There was bound to be something in the car he could use, the empty bottle was still in on the ground outside it, because he had seen the guy throw it there. But he would never make it; the shadow was too fast for him. The longer he stayed here though, the weaker he would get, and the slower he would get as the sun gradually sapped his strength. His time to do something was rapidly dwindling.

Looking to his right, he saw another rock, one that he had not noticed before. It was about the same size as the one he was currently hiding against from what he could tell. But that wasn't all. Just above the highest point of the rock, Alex was sure he could make out something blowing in the wind. It looked like strands of a spider's web, but was in fact wispy hair. Was there someone else, caught in a similar manner, hiding behind that rock? They must be dead, as they didn't respond to his earlier shouting. But maybe, they had something he could use.

Alex decided he had to get over there whatever, and at least it gave his mind something to grab hold of. Alex felt a renewed burst of energy as his brain processed the necessary information.

The distance was about half the trek to his car he figured. The car was out of the question, but maybe this wasn't. Was there something he could do to trick the thing? After all, had had deceived it before, when he made his first wild dash out into the desert.

Alex stood up, and went to the edge of his gloomy cell. The shadow stood directly in front of him, and Alex was sure it was looking straight at him, although it was impossible to tell.

Alex caught sight of movement in the distance, behind the shadow, so to speak.

Something gleamed on the horizon. Was that a car, driving through the desert? Surely not.

He narrowed his eyes and cupped his hands around the sides of his head.

'Over here! Hey!' he began screaming, flapping his arms around like he was trying to land a jet. His voice was really lacking penetration now, his throat was becoming quite sore with the lack of hydration it had received. He kept on screaming anyway.

The shadow turned around.

Alex ran.

Alex really had underestimated what the sun had done to his stamina. Only half way there, and his legs were beginning to betray him. He began to take staggering steps, nearly falling over. It felt as if his legs could barely support his weight. But he would not stop now.

Alex dared not look behind him as he ran, so he did not get a chance to enjoy his first instance of good fortune for the day. The shadow had also made an underestimation, that of the courage of its beleaguered prey. Momentarily distracted, it had spent a vital five seconds or so scanning the horizon, to no avail.

Knowing it had been tricked, it began in Alex's direction without even turning around to see if Alex had indeed made a break for it. It glided forward like a fast moving oil slick, veering from its straight line only to swerve past the shadow of Alex's former hiding place.

Only when he was within five metres did Alex afford himself a look over his shoulder.

The shadow was gaining fast, but he could tell it wouldn't be fast enough.

Gratefully, he slowed down. It was just as well, as his lungs were on fire, and felt as if they would leap out of his mouth at any time. Furthermore, he had a terrible stitch as a result of all that lactic acid sloshing around in his gut. Placing his hand onto the rock, Alex gasped at the heat that flooded through his hand as he vaulted over and plopped into the shade.

The shadow had reached the point where Alex first looked behind him, so he still had a few seconds to jubilantly flick it off before crouching back into the shade. He didn't know if the shadow got it or not and also didn't care.

Now, to his new neighbour.

Having not seen a dead man before, nothing could have prepared Alex for the shock.

Indeed, had he have known what was lurking behind the rock, he may not have so eagerly jumped over it and made his acquaintance with this thing.

For a thing was truly what this was, no longer a human being. Lord knows how long it had been here. Suppressing a choking gag, Alex pulled his shirt up over his nose and took a look at his new neighbour.

The face was all but skeletal; flesh, grey and decomposing, hung in strips from the skull, particularly around the eyes, where Alex was sure he could see scratch marks on the bone.

Ouch. It looked as if this poor sod had been mauled by an animal, or worse. Alex shuddered and was reminded of the shadow. The mouth was open and starting to show signs of that bony grin of the truly dead. The eyes were missing from their sockets, and the mouth was open and starting to show signs of that bony grin of the truly dead. Worst of all, he stunk.

He didn't want to think what state the rest of the body was in under those clothes. Alex could not stay here long, before he choked to death.

Steeling himself, he undertook a search of the corpse hoping to find something of use.

He could barely force himself to grope around the body, and it was only the sight of the shadow that compelled him to do it.

There was nothing of course. Deep inside, he knew there wouldn't be. It just wasn't his day, he joked. Or was his luck about to change?

The corpse, a man (Alex could tell by the clothes, there was no way of telling from the face) was resting on a backpack, that he had not noticed earlier. Alex shoved the body forward, momentarily forgetting his disgust in favour of haste. Or desperation, take your pick. The bag certainly felt as if it had something in it. Alex eagerly ripped open the straps and looked inside.

There was a snake.

Alex screamed and instinctively threw the bag into the air. It landed about four feet in front of him.

In the sun.

With the Shadow.

He thought he could almost see it laugh at him, revelling in his misfortune. There had been plenty of that today. The snake, for its part, slithered out of the bag, no doubt wondering what on earth it was doing there, and how it got there so damn quickly.

Drawing his legs up to his chest, Alex folded his arms across his knees and lowered his head, contemplating this latest setback. A dehydration headache had begun pounding at his temples. Maybe it had been there earlier, but he was now only aware of it. His eyes cleared his thoughts for him.

There was a bottle, between his legs. Alex held it in his hands in awe, as if he were holding the holy grail itself.

A bottle! Nothing in it, but a receptacle nonetheless. Alex didn't know much about the human anatomy, but he was sure he had read somewhere that you could get away with drinking some urine, for a period, as a last ditch resort for liquid. Preferably someone else's urine, but someone else wasn't here to piss in the bottle for him. Well, there was this shrivelled up grotesquery next to him, but the piss had dried up in that thing along time ago.

As he unbuckled, he laughed at his predicament. After all, he was about to piss into a bottle and drink it. It was the kind of thing kids dared each other to do. As he relieved himself, he wondered if it was the sunstroke that was making the proposition more acceptable. For someone partially de-hydrated, he had an awful lot of piss in him.

Holding back his disgust, putting a lock on his stomach, Alex drained the bottle in one.

For five agonising seconds he fought his gag reflex and kept the salty, acrid fluid down.

'Ha!' he spat at the shadow, urine droplets peppering the sand in front of him like raindrops. 'Tastes good!' Suddenly he retched, but brought up nothing but stringy saliva, which he quickly pushed back into his mouth. The performance was finished off nicely with a belch which tasted foul, worse than the piss.

It was then he remembered he had a mobile phone. How could he forget? Damn sun.

Plopping back down he plucked it from his jeans pocket. The screen was blank. The battery cover was missing along with the battery. No! He must have knocked it loose scrabbling over the rock to safety. It could be anywhere.

A sharp glint caught his attention. Alex looked round and at the shadow, which held his potential Grail in its hand, tilting it so that it caught the sun enough to grab Alex's attention.

Alex groaned and slumped back against the rock.

Mockingly, the shadow placed the battery on the verge of Alex's safety shadow and crouched down in front of it, daring Alex to break his cover for the one second it would take to grab the battery.

For that one second it would take the shadow to grab him, he knew that.

'You bastard,' Alex sighed. He looked at his watch. Four o'clock. He was out of time and options.

What the hell would happen when it got dark? Alex didn't want to think about that, actually.

Would another car come past? Maybe. Then again, maybe not.

He was hungry, he was thirsty and now he had a stomach ache.

The shadow had won, he was out of options, but Alex decided he would make it wait the longest time possible, until it was dark.

Alex stared defiantly at the shadow, which was now raising and spreading its arms to the sky. What was it doing?

The shadow began very slowly bringing its arms together above its head, and at the same time, the corners of Alex's vision darkened slightly. Alex wearily looked up at the sky.

Squadrons of tiny black clouds had appeared from somewhere, and somehow, the shadow was dragging them towards the sun.

It meant to create its own artificial night time. Alex figured he had maybe an hour.

'You bastard. You dirty bastard,' Alex groaned.

What had started out as a laborious journey to collect his inheritance had ended up as a fight for his very life. It was a fight he had lost. Alex would have gladly traded the money to get out of this situation, but the shadow cared not for wealth, it seemed. If only he could have his time again. But isn't that always the way? The sudden remorse of the person who has never displayed any? Wanting to be granted the mercy that he never really afforded to anyone else?

The thing in front of him was not born of mercy and certainly knew no mercy. It would show Alex none, he was sure. So he did the only thing he could do, the only thing there was left for him to do.

At the rate the clouds were closing, he figured he had maybe twenty minutes. Their progress was slow, like a troop of snails across a garden, but their progress was assured.

'What do you say Joe? Thought so!' Alex grinned at the corpse. 'You can't beat me!' he yelped, choking back the tears.

Alex reached for the battery.

THE SEER

BY BRAM STOKER

I had just arrived at Cruden Bay on my annual visit, and after a late breakfast was sitting on the low wall which was a continuation of the escarpment of the bridge over the Water of Cruden. Opposite to me, across the road and standing under the only little clump of trees in the place was a tall, gaunt old woman, who kept looking at me intently. As I sat, a little group, consisting of a man and two women, went by. I found my eyes follow them, for it seemed to me after they had passed me that the two women walked together and the man alone in front carrying on his shoulder a little black box-a coffin. I shuddered as I thought, but a moment later I saw all three abreast as they had been. The old woman was now looking at me with eyes that blazed. She came across the road and said to me without preface:

"What saw ye then, that yer e'en looked so awed?" I did not like to tell her so I did not answer. Her great eyes were fixed keenly upon me, seeming to look me through and through.

I felt that I grew quite red, whereupon she said, apparently to herself: "I thocht so! Even I did not see that which he saw."

"How do you mean?" I queried. She answered ambiguously:

"Wait! Ye shall perhaps know before this hour to-morrow!"

Her answer interested me and I tried to get her to say more; but she would not. She moved away with a grand stately movement that seemed to become her great gaunt form.

After dinner whilst I was sitting in front of the hotel, there was a great commotion in the village; much running to and fro of men and women with sad mien. On questioning them I found that a child had been drowned in the little harbour below. Just then a woman and a man, the same that had passed the bridge earlier in the day, ran by with wild looks. One of the bystanders looked after them pityingly as he said:

"Puir souls. It's a sad home-comin' for them the nicht."

"Who are they?" I asked. The man took off his cap reverently as he answered:

"The father and mother of the child that was drowned!" As he spoke I looked round as though someone had called me.

There stood the gaunt woman with a look of triumph on her face.

The curved shore of Cruden Bay, Aberdeenshire, is backed by a waste of sandhills in whose hollows seagrass and moss and wild violets, together with the pretty "grass of Parnassus" form a green carpet. The surface of the hills is held together by bent-grass and is eternally shifting as the wind takes the fine sand and drifts it to and fro. All behind is green, from the meadows that mark the southern edge of the bay to the swelling uplands that stretch away and away far in the distance, till the blue mist of the mountains at Braemar sets a kind of barrier. In the centre of the bay the highest point of the land that runs downward to the sea looks like a miniature hill known as the Hawklaw; from this point onward to the extreme south the land runs high with a gentle trend downwards.

Cruden sands are wide and firm and the sea runs out a considerable distance. When there is a storm with the wind on shore the whole bay is a mass of leaping waves and broken water that threatens every instant to annihilate the stake-nets which stretch out here and there along the shore. More than a few vessels have been lost on these wide stretching sands, and it was perhaps the roaring of the shallow seas and the terror which they inspired which sent the crews to the spirit room and the bodies of those of them which came to shore later on, to the churchyard on the hill.

If Cruden Bay is to be taken figuratively as a mouth, with the sand hills for soft palate, and the green Hawklaw as the tongue, the rocks which mark the extremities are its teeth. To the north the rocks of red granite rise jagged and broken. To the south, a mile and a half away as the crow flies, Nature seems to have manifested its wildest forces. It is here, where the little promontory called Whinnyfold juts out, that the two great geological features of the Aberdeen coast meet. The red sienite of the north joins the black gneiss of the south.

That union must have been originally a wild one; there are evidences of an upheaval which must have shaken the earth to its centre. Here and there are great masses of either species of rock hurled upwards in every conceivable variety of form, sometimes fused or pressed together so that it is impossible to say exactly where gneiss ends or sienite begins; but broadly speaking here is an irregular line of separation. This line runs seawards to the east and its strength is shown in its outcrop. For half a mile or more the rocks rise through the sea singly or in broken masses ending in a dangerous cluster known as "The Skares" and which has had for centuries its full toll of wreck and disaster. Did the sea hold its dead where they fell, its floor around the Skares would be whitened with their bones, and new islands could build themselves with the piling wreckage. At times one may see here the ocean in her fiercest mood; for it is when the tempest drives from the south-east that the sea is fretted amongst the rugged rocks and sends its spume landwards.

The rocks that at calmer times rise dark from the briny deep are lost to sight for moments in the grand onrush of the waves. The seagulls which usually whiten them, now flutter around screaming, and the sound of their shrieks comes in on the gale almost in a continuous note, for the single cries are merged in the multitudinous roar of sea and air.

The village, squatted beside the emboucher of the Water of Cruden at the northern side of the bay is simple enough; a few rows of fishermen's cottages, two or three great red-tiled drying-sheds nestled in the sand-heap behind the fishers' houses. For the rest of the place as it was when first I saw it, a little lockout beside a tall flagstaff on the northern cliff, a few scattered farms over the inland prospect, one little hotel down on the western bank of the

Water of Cruden with a fringe of willows protecting its sunk garden which was always full of fruits and flowers.

From the most southern part of the beach of Cruden Bay to Whinnyfold village the distance is but a few hundred yards; first a steep pull up the face of the rock; and then an even way, beside part of which runs a tiny stream. To the left of this path, going towards Whinnyfold, the ground rises in a bold slope and then falls again all round, forming a sort of wide miniature hill of some eighteen or twenty acres. Of this the southern side is sheer, the black rock dipping into the waters of the little bay of Whinnyfold, in the centre of which is a picturesque island of rock shelving steeply from the water on the northern side, as is the tendency of all the gneiss and granite in this part. But to east and north there are irregular bays or openings, so that the furthest points of the promotory stretch out like fingers. At the tips of these are reefs of sunken rock falling down to deep water and whose existence can only be suspected in bad weather when the rush of the current beneath sends up swirling eddies or curling masses of foam. These little bays are mostly curved and are green where falling earth or drifting sand have hidden the outmost side of the rocks and given a foothold to the seagrass and clover. Here have been at some time or other great caves, now either fallen in or silted up with sand, or obliterated with the earth brought down in the rush of surface-water in times of long rain. In one of these bays, Broad Haven, facing right out to the

Skares, stands an isolated pillar of rock called locally the "Puir mon" through whose base, time and weather have worn a hole through which one may walk dryshod.

Through the masses of rocks that run down to the sea from the sides and shores of all these bays are here and there natural channels with straight edges as though cut on purpose for the taking in of the cobbles belonging to the fisher folk of Whinnyfold.

When first I saw the place I fell in love with it. Had it been possible I should have spent my summer there, in a house of my own, but the want of any place in which to live forbade such an opportunity. So I stayed in the little hotel, the Kilmarnock Arms.

The next year I came again, and the next, and the next. And then I arranged to take a feu at Whinnyfold and to build a house overlooking the Skares for myself. The details of this kept me constantly going to Whinnyfold, and my house to be was always in my thoughts.

Hitherto my life had been an uneventful one. At school I was, though secretly ambitious, dull as to results. At College I was better off, for my big body and athletic powers gave me a certain position in which I had to overcome my natural shyness. When I was about eight and twenty I found myself nominally a barrister, with no knowledge whatever of the practice of law and but little less of the theory, and with a commission in the Devil's Own-the irrelevant name given to the Inns of Court Volunteers. I had few relatives, but a comfortable, though not great, fortune; and I had been round the world, dilettante fashion.

All that night I thought of the dead child and of the peculiar vision which had come to me. Sleeping or waking it was all the same; my mind could not leave the parents in procession as seen in imagination, or their distracted mien in reality. Mingled with them was the great-eyed, aquiline-featured, gaunt old woman who had taken such an interest in the affair; and in my part of it. I asked the landlord if he knew her, since from his position as postmaster he knew almost everyone for miles around. He told me that she was a stranger to the place. Then he added:

"I can't imagine what brings her here. She has come over from Peterhead two or three times lately; but she doesn't seem to have anything at all to do. She has nothing to sell and she buys nothing. She's not a tripper, and she's not a beggar, and she's not a thief, and she's not a worker of any sort. She's a queer-looking lot anyhow. I fancy from her speech that she's from the west; probably from some of the far-out islands. I can tell that she has the Gaelic from the way she speaks."

Later on in the day, when I was walking on the shore near the Hawklaw, she came up to speak to me.

The shore was quite lonely, for in those days it was rare to see anyone on the beach except when the salmon fishers drew their nets at the ebbing tide. I was walking towards Whinnyfold when she came upon me silently from behind. She must have been hidden among the bent-grass of the sandhills for had she been anywhere in view I must have seen her on that desolate shore. She was evidently a most imperious person; she at once addressed me in a tone and manner which made me feel as though I were in some way an inferior, and in somehow to blame:

"What for did ye no tell me what ye saw yesterday?" Instinctively I answered:

"I don't know why. Perhaps because it seemed so ridiculous." Her stern features hardened into scorn as she replied:

"Are Death and the Doom then so redeekulous that they pleasure ye intil silence?" I somehow felt that this was a little too much and was about to make a sharp answer, when suddenly it struck me as a remarkable thing that she knew already. Filled with surprise I straightway asked her:

"Why, how on earth do you know? I told no one." I stopped for I felt all at sea; there was some mystery here which I could not fathom. She seemed to read my mind like an open book, for she went on looking at me as she spoke, searchingly and with an odd smile.

"Eh! laddie, do ye no ken that ye hae een that can see? Do ye no understand that ye hae een that can speak? Is it that one with the Gift o' Second Sight has no an understandin' o' it.

Why, yer face when ye saw the mark o' the Doom, was like a printed book to een like mine."

"Do you mean to tell me," I asked, "that you could tell what I saw, simply by looking at my face?"

"Na! na! laddie. Not all that, though a Seer am I; but I knew that you had seen the Doom!

It's no that varied that there need be any mistake. After all Death is only one, in whatever way we may speak!" After a pause of thought I asked her:

If you have the power of Second Sight why did you not see the vision, or whatever it was, yourself?"

"Eh! laddie," she answered, shaking her head, "'Tis little ye ken o' the wark o' the Fates!

Learn ye then that the Voice speaks only as it listeth into chosen ears, and the Vision comes to chosen een. None can will to hear or to see, to pleasure theirsels."

"Then," I said, and I felt that there was a measure of triumph in my tone, "if to none but the chosen is given to know, how comes it that you, who seem not to have been chosen on this occasion at all events, know all the same?" She answered with a touch of impatience:

"Do ye ken, young sir, that even mortal een have power to see much, if there be behind them the thocht, an' the knowledge and the experience to guide them aright. How, think ye, is it that some can see much, and learn much as they gang; while others go blind as the mowdiwart, at the end o' the journey as before it?"

"Then perhaps you will tell me how much you saw, and how you saw it?"

"Ah! to them that have seen the Doom there needs but sma' guidance to their thochts.

Too lang, an' too often hae I mysen seen the death-sark an' the watch-candle an' the dead-hole, not to know when they are seen tae ither een. Na, na! laddie, what I kent o' yer seein' was no by the Gift but only by the use o' my proper een. I kent not the muckle o' what ye saw. Not whether it was ane or ither o' the garnishins o' the dead; but weel I kent that it was o' death."

"Then," I said interrogatively, "Second Sight is altogether a matter of chance?"

"Chance! chance!" she repeated with scorn. "Na! young sir; when the Voice has spoken there is no more chance than that the nicht will follow the day."

"You mistake me," I said, feeling somewhat superior now that I had caught her in an error,

"I did not for a moment mean that the Doom-whatever it is-is not a true forerunner. What I meant was that it seems to be a matter of chance in whose ear the Voice-whatever it isspeaks; when once it has been ordained that it is to sound in the ear of some one." Again she answered with scorn:

"Na, na! there is no chance o' ocht about the Doom. Them that send forth the Voice and the Seein' know well to whom it is sent and why. Can ye no comprehend that it is for no bairn-play that such goes forth. When the Voice speaks, it is mainly followed by tears an' woe an' lamentation! Nae! nor is it only one bit manifestation that stands by its lanes, remote and isolate from all ither. Truly 'tis but a pairt o' the great scheme o' things; an' be sure that who so is chosen to see or to hear is chosen weel, an' must hae their pairt in what is to be, on to the verra end."

"Am I to take it," I asked, "that Second Sight is but a little bit of some great purpose which has to be wrought out by means of many kinds; and that who so sees the Vision or hears the Voice is but the blind unconscious instrument of Fate?"

"Aye! laddie. Weel eneuch the Fates know their wishes an' their wark, no to need the help or the thocht of any human-blind or seein', sane or silly, conscious or unconscious."

All through her speaking I had been struck by the old woman's use of the word "Fate," and more especially when she used it in the plural.

It was evident that, Christian though she might be-and in the West they are generally devout observants of the duties of their creed-her belief in this respect came from some of the old pagan mythologies. I should have liked to question her on this point; but I feared to shut her lips against me. Instead I asked her:

"Tell me, will you, if you don't mind, of some case you have known yourself of Second

Sight?"

"'Tis no for them to brag or boast to whom has been given to see the wark o' the hand o' Fate. But sine ye are yerself a Seer an' would learn, then I may speak. I hae seen the sea ruffle wi'oot cause in the verra spot where later a boat was to gang doon, I hae heard on a lone moor the hammerin' o' the coffin-wright when one passed me who was soon to dee. I hae seen the death-sarli fold round the speerit o' a drowned one, in baith ma sleepin' an' ma wakin' dreams.

I hae heard the settin' doom o' the spaiks, an' I hae seen the weepers on a' the crood that walked. Aye, an' in money anither way hae I seen an' heard the Coming o' the Doom."

"But did all the seeings and hearings come true?" I asked. "Did it ever happen that you heard queer sounds or saw strange sights and that yet nothing came of them? I gather that you do not always know to whom something is going to happen; but only that death is coming to some one!" She was not displeased at my questioning but replied at once: "Na doot! but there are times when what is seen or heard has no manifest following. But think ye, young sir, how money a corp, still waited for, lies in the depths o' the sea; how money lie oot on the hillsides, or are fallen in deep places where their bones whiten unkent.

Nay! more, to how many has Death come in a way that men think the wark o' nature when his hastening has come frae the hand of man, untold." This was a difficult matter to answer so I changed or rather varied the subject.

"How long must elapse before the warning comes true?"

"Ye know yersel', for but yestreen ye hae seen, how the Death can follow hard upon the Doom; but there be times, nay mostly are they so, when days or weeks pass away ere the Doom is fulfilled."

"Is this so?" I asked, "when you know the person regarding whom the Doom is spoken."

She answered with an air of certainty which somehow carried conviction, secretly, with it.

"Even so! I know one who walks the airth now in all the pride o' his strength. But the Doom has been spoken of him. I saw him with these verra een lie prone on rocks, wi' the water runnin' down from his hair. An' again I heard the minute bells as he went by me on a road where is no bell for a score o' miles. Aye, an' yet again I saw him in the kirk itsel' wi' corbies flyin' round him, an' mair gatherin' from afar!"

Here was indeed a case where Second Sight might be tested; so I asked her at once, though to do so I had to overcome a strange sort of repugnance:

"Could this be proved? Would it not be a splendid case to make known; so that if the death happened it would prove beyond all doubt the existence of such a thing as Second Sight. "My suggestion was not well received. She answered with slow scorn:

"Beyon' all doot! Doot! Wha is there that doots the bein' o' the Doom? Learn ye too, young sir, that the Doom an' all thereby is no for traffickin' wi' them that only cares for curiosity and publeecity. The Voice and the Vision o' the Seer is no for fine madams and idle gentles to while away their time in play-toy make-believe!" I climbed down at once.

"Pardon me!" I said, "I spoke without thinking. I should not have said so-to you at any rate." She accepted my apology with a sort of regal inclination; but the moment after she showed by her words she was after all but a woman!

"I will tell ye; that so in the full time ye may hae no doot yersel'. For ye are a Seer and as Them that has the power hae gien ye the Gift it is no for the like o' me to cumber the road o' their doin'. Know ye then, and remember weel, how it was told ye by Gormala MacNiel that Lauchlane Macleod o' the Outer Isles hae been Called; tho' as yet the Voice has no sounded in his ears but only in mine. But ye will see the time-"

She stopped suddenly as though some thought had struck her, and then went on impressively:

"When I saw him lie prone on the rocks there was ane that bent ower him that I kent not in the nicht wha it was, though the licht o' the moon was around him. We shall see! We shall see!"

Without a word more she turned and left me. She would not listen to my calling after her; but with long strides passed up the beach and was lost among the sandhills.

The Derelict

By William Hope Hodgson

"IT'S the material," said the old ship's doctor — "the material plus the conditions — and, maybe," he added slowly, "a third factor — yes, a third factor; but there, there — —" He broke off his half-meditative sentence and began to charge his pipe.

"Go on, doctor," we said encouragingly, and with more than a little expectancy. We were in the smoke-room of the Sand-a-lea, running across the North Atlantic; and the doctor was a character. He concluded the charging of his pipe, and lit it; then settled himself, and began to express himself more fully.

"The material," he said with conviction, "is inevitably the medium of expression of the life-force — the fulcrum, as it were; lacking which it is unable to exert itself, or, indeed, to express itself in any form or fashion that would be intelligible or evident to us. So potent is the share of the material in the production of that thing which we name life, and so eager the life-force to express itself, that I am convinced it would, if given the right conditions, make itself manifest even through so hopeless seeming a medium as a simple block of sawn wood; for I tell you, gentlemen, the life-force is both as fiercely urgent and as indiscriminate as fire — the destructor; yet which some are now growing to consider the very essence of life rampant. There is a quaint seeming paradox there," he concluded, nodding his old grey head.

"Yes, doctor," I said. "In brief, your argument is that life is a thing, state, fact, or element, call it what you like, which requires the material through which to manifest itself, and that given the material, plus the conditions, the result is life. In other words, that life is an evolved product, manifested through matter and bred of conditions — eh?"

"As we understand the word," said the old doctor. "Though, mind you, there may be a third factor. But, in my heart, I believe that it is a matter of chemistry — conditions and a suitable medium; but given the conditions, the brute is so almighty that it will seize upon anything through which to manifest itself. It is a force generated by conditions; but, nevertheless, this does not bring us one iota nearer to its explanation, any more than to the explanation of electricity or fire. They are, all three, of the outer forces — monsters of the void. Nothing we can do will create any one of them, our power is merely to be able, by providing the conditions, to make each one of them manifest to our physical senses. Am I clear?"

"Yes, doctor, in a way, you are," I said. "But I don't agree with you, though I think I understand you. Electricity and fire are both what I might call natural things, but life is an abstract something — a kind of all-permeating wakefulness. Oh, I can't explain it! Who could? But it s spiritual, not just a thing bred out of a condition, like fire, as you say, or electricity. It's a horrible thought of yours. Life's a kind of spiritual mystery − −"

"Easy, my boy!" said the old doctor, laughing gently to himself. "Or else I may be asking you to demonstrate the spiritual mystery of life of the limpet, or the crab, shall we say." He grinned at me with ineffable perverseness. "Anyway," he continued, "as I suppose you've all guessed, I've a yarn to tell you in support of my impression that life is no more a mystery or a miracle than fire or electricity. But, please to remember, gentlemen, that because we've succeeded in naming and making good use of these two forces, they're just as much mysteries, fundamentally as ever. And, anyway, the thing I'm going to tell you won't explain the mystery of life, but only give you one of my pegs on which I hang my feeling that life is as I have said, a force made manifest through conditions − that is to say, natural chemistry − and that it can take for its purpose and need, the most incredible and unlikely matter; for without matter it cannot come into existence − it cannot become manifest − −"

"I don't agree with you, doctor," I interrupted. "Your theory would destroy all belief in life after death. It would − −"

"Hush, sonny," said the old man, with a quiet little smile of comprehension. "Hark to what I've to say first; and, anyway, what objection have you to material life after death? And if you object to a material framework, I would still have you remember that I am speaking of life, as we understand the word in this our life. Now do be a quiet lad, or I'll never be done:

"It was when I was a young man, and that is a good many years ago, gentlemen. I had passed my examinations, but was so run down with overwork that it was decided that I had better take a trip to sea. I was by no means well off, and very glad in the end to secure a nominal post as doctor in the sailing passenger clipper running out to China.

"The name of the ship was the Bheospse, and soon after I had got all my gear aboard she cast off, and we dropped down the Thames, and next day were well away out in the Channel.

"The captain's name was Gannington, a very decent man, though quite illiterate. The first mate, Mr. Berlies, was a quiet, sternish, reserved man, very well-read. The second mate, Mr. Selvern, was, perhaps, by birth and upbringing, the most socially cultured of the three, but he lacked the stamina and indomitable pluck of the two others. He was more of a sensitive, and emotionally and even mentally, the most alert man of the three.

"On our way out, we called at Madagascar, where we landed some of our passengers; then we ran eastward, meaning to call at North-West Cape; but about a hundred degrees east we encountered very dreadful weather, which carried away all our sails, and sprung the jibboom and foret'gallantmast.

"The storm carried us northward for several hundred miles, and when it dropped us finally, we found ourselves in a very bad state. The ship had been strained, and had taken some three feet of water through her seams; the maintopmast had been sprung, in addition to the jibboom and foret'gallantmast, two of our boats had gone, as also one of the pigstys, with three fine pigs, these latter having been washed overboard but some half-hour before the wind began to ease, which it did very quickly, though a very ugly sea ran for some hours after.

"The wind left us just before dark, and when morning came it brought splendid weather — a calm, mildly undulating sea, and a brilliant sun, with no wind. It showed us also that we were not alone, for about two miles away to the westward was another vessel, which Mr.

Selvern, the second mate, pointed out to me.

"'That's a pretty rum-looking, packet, doctor,' he said, and handed me his glass.

"I looked through it at the other vessel, and saw what he meant; at least, I thought I did.

"'Yes, Mr. Selvern,' I said. 'She's got a pretty old-fashioned look about her.'

"He laughed at me in his pleasant way.

"'It's easy to see you're not a sailor, doctor,' he remarked. 'There's a dozen rum things about her. She's a derelict, and has been floating round, by the look of her, for many a score of years. Look at the shape of her counter, and the bows and cutwater. She's as old as the hills, as you might say, and ought to have gone down to Davy Jones a good while ago. Look at the growths on her, and the thickness of her standing rigging; that's all salt encrustations, I fancy, if you notice the white colour. She's been a small barque; but, don't you see, she's not a yard left aloft. They've all dropped out of the slings; everything rotted away; wonder the standing rigging hasn't gone, too. I wish the old man would let us take the boat and have a look at her. She'd be well worth it.'

"'There seemed little chance, however, of this, for all hands were turned to and kept hard at it all day long repairing the damage to the masts and gear; and this took a long while, as you may think. Part of the time I gave a hand heaving on one of the deck capstans, for the exercise was good for my liver. Old Captain Gannington approved, and I persuaded him to come along and try some of the same medicine, which he did; and we got very chummy over the job.

"We got talking about the derelict, and he remarked how lucky we were not to have run full tilt on to her in the darkness, for she lay right away to leeward of us, according, to the way that we had been drifting in the storm. He also was of the opinion that she had a strange look about her, and that she was pretty old; but on this latter point he plainly had far less knowledge than the second mate, for he was, as I have said, an illiterate man, and knew nothing of seacraft beyond what experience had taught him. He lacked the book knowledge which the second mate had of vessels previous to his day, which it appeared the derelict was.

"'She's an old 'un, doctor,' was the extent of observations in this direction.

"Yet, when I mentioned to him that it would be interesting to go aboard and give her a bit of an overhaul, he nodded his head as if the idea had been already in his mind and accorded with his own inclinations.

"'When the work's over, doctor,' he said. 'Can't spare the men now, ye know. Got to get all shipshape an' ready as smart as we can. But, we'll take my gig, an' go off in the second dogwatch.

The glass is steady, an' it'll be a bit of gam for us.'

"That evening, after tea, the captain gave orders to clear the gig and get her overboard.

The second mate was to come with us, and the skipper gave him word to see that two or three lamps were put into the boat, as it would soon fall dark. A little later we were pulling across the calmness of the sea with a crew of six at the oars, and making very good speed of it.

"Now, gentlemen, I have detailed to you with great exactness all the facts, both big and little, so that you can follow step by step each incident in this extraordinary affair, and I want you now to pay the closest attention. I was sitting in the stern-sheets with the second mate and the captain, who was steering, and as we drew nearer and nearer to the stranger I studied her with an ever-growing attention, as, indeed, did Captain Gannington and the second mate. She was, as you know, to the west-ward of us, and the sunset was making a great flame of red light to the back of her, so that she showed a little blurred and indistinct by reason of the halation of the light, which almost defeated the eye in any attempt to see her rotting spars and standing rigging, submerged, as they were, in the fiery glory of the sunset.

"It was because of this effect of the sunset that we had come quite close, comparatively, to the derelict before we saw that she was all surrounded by a sort of curious scum, the colour of which was difficult to decide upon by reason of the red light that was in the atmosphere, but which afterwards we discovered to be brown. This scum spread all about the old vessel for many hundreds of yards in a huge, irregular patch, a great stretch of which reached out to the eastward, upon the starboard side of the boat some score or so fathoms away.

"'Queer stuff,' said Captain Gannington, leaning to the side and looking over. 'Something in the cargo as 'as gone rotten, and worked out through 'er seams.'

"'Look at her bows and stern,' said the second mate. 'Just look at the growth on her!'

"There were, as he said, great clumpings of strange-looking sea-fungi under the bows and the short counter astern. From the stump of her jibboom and her cutwater great beards of rime and marine growths hung downward into the scum that held her in. Her blank starboard side was presented to us — all a dead, dirtyish white, streaked and mottled vaguely with dull masses of heavier colour.

"'There's a steam or haze rising off her,' said the second mate, speaking again. 'You can see it against the light. It keeps coming and going. Look!'

"I saw then what he meant — a faint haze or steam, either suspended above the old vessel or rising from her. And Captain Gannington saw it also.

"'Spontaneous combustion!' he exclaimed. 'We'll 'ave to watch when we lift the 'atches, 'nless it's some poor devil that's got aboard of 'er. But that ain't likely.'

"We were now within a couple of hundred yards of the old derelict, and had entered into the brown scum. As it poured off the lifted oars I heard one of the men mutter to himself, 'Dam' treacle!' And, indeed, it was not something unlike it. As the boat continued to forge nearer and nearer to the old ship the scum grew thicker and thicker, so that, at last, it perceptibly slowed us.

"'Give way, lads! Put some beef to it!' sang out Captain Gannington. And thereafter there was no sound except the panting of the men and the faint, reiterated suck, suck of the sullen brown scum upon the oars as the boat was forced ahead. As we went, I was conscious of a peculiar smell in the evening air, and whilst I had no doubt that the puddling of the scum by the oars made it rise, I could give no name to it; yet, in a way, it was vaguely familiar.

"We were now very close to the old vessel, and presently she was high about us against the dying light. The captain called out then to 'in with the bow oars and stand by with the boat-hook,' which was done.

"'Aboard there! Ahoy! Aboard there! Ahoy!' shouted Captain Gannington; but there came no answer, only the dull sound his voice going lost into the open sea, each time he sung out.

"'Ahoy! Aboard there! Ahoy!' he shouted time after time, but there was only the weary silence of the old hulk that answered us; and, somehow as he shouted, the while that I stared up half expectantly at her, a queer little sense of oppression, that amounted almost to nervousness, came upon me. It passed, but I remember how I was suddenly aware that it was growing dark. Darkness comes fairly rapidly in the tropics, though not so quickly as many fiction writers seem to think; but it was not that the coming dusk had perceptibly deepened in that brief time of only a few moments, but rather that my nerves had made me suddenly a little hypersensitive. I mention my state particularly, for I am not a nervy man normally, and my abrupt touch of nerves is significant, in the light of what happened.

"'There's no one on board there!' said Captain Gannington. 'Give way, men!' For the boat's crew had instinctively rested on their oars, as the captain hailed the old craft. The men gave way again; and then the second mate called out excitedly, 'Why, look there, there's our pigsty! See, it's got Bheospse painted on the end. It's drifted down here and the scum's caught it. What a blessed wonder!'

"It was, as he had said, our pigsty that had been washed overboard in the storm; and most extraordinary to come across it there.

"'We'll tow it off with us, when we go,' said the captain, and shouted to the crew to get down to their oars; for they were hardly moving the boat, because the scum was so thick, close in around the old ship, that it literally clogged the boat from moving. I remember that it struck me, in a half-conscious sort of way, as curious that the pigsty, containing our three dead pigs, had managed to drift in so far unaided, whilst we could scarcely manage to force the boat in, now that we had come right into the scum. But the thought passed from my mind, for so many things happened within the next few minutes.

"The men managed to bring the boat in alongside, within a couple of feet of the derelict, and the man with the boat-hook hooked on.

"''Ave ye got 'old there, forrard?' asked Captain Gannington.

"'Yessir!' said the bowman; and as he spoke there came a queer noise of tearing.

"'What's that?' asked the Captain.

"'It's tore, sir. Tore clean away!' said the man, and his tone showed that he had received something of a shock.

"'Get a hold again, then!' said Captain Gannington irritably. 'You don't s'pose this packet was built yesterday! Shove the hook into the main chains' The man did so gingerly, as you might say, for it seemed to me, in the growing dusk, that he put no strain on to the hook, though, of course there was no need — you see the boat could not go very far of herself, in the stuff in which she was imbedded. I remember thinking this, also as I looked up at the bulging side of the old vessel. Then I heard Captain Gannington's voice:

"'Lord, but she s old! An' what a colour, doctor! She don't half want paint, do she? Now then, somebody, one of them oars.' An oar was passed to him, and he leant it up against the ancient, bulging side; then he paused, and called to the second mate to light a couple of the lamps, and stand by to pass them up, for darkness had settled down now upon the sea.

"The second mate lit two of the lamps, and told one of the men to light a third, and keep it handy in the boat; then he stepped across, with a lamp in each hand, to where Captain Gannington stood by the oar against the side of the ship.

"'Now, my lad,' said the captain to the man who had pulled stroke, 'up with you, an' we'll pass ye up the lamps.'

"The man jumped to obey, caught the oar, and put his weight upon it; and as he did so, something seemed to give way a little.

"'Look!' cried out the second mate, and pointed, lamp in hand. 'It's sunk in!'

"This was true. The oar had made quite an indentation into the bulging, somewhat slimy side of the old vessel.

"'Mould, I reckon,' said Captain Gannington, bending towards the derelict to look. Then to the man:

"'Up you go, my lad, and be smart! Don't stand there waitin'!'

"At that the man, who had paused a moment as he felt the oar give beneath his weight began to shin' up, and in a few seconds he was aboard, and leant out over the rail for the lamps. These were passed up to him, and the captain called to him to steady the oar. Then

Captain Gannington went, calling to me to follow, and after me the second mate.

"As the captain put his face over the rail, he gave a cry of astonishment.

"'Mould, by gum! Mould — tons of it. Good lord!'

"As I heard him shout that I scrambled the more eagerly after him, and in a moment or two I was able to see what he meant — everywhere that the light from the two lamps struck there was nothing but smooth great masses and surfaces of a dirty white coloured mould. I climbed over the rail, with the second mate close behind, and stood upon the mould covered decks. There might have been no planking beneath the mould, for all that our feet could feel.

It gave under our tread with a spongy, puddingy feel. It covered the deck furniture of the old ship, so that the shape of each article and fitment was often no more than suggested through it.

"Captain Gannington snatched a lamp from the man and the second mate reached for the other. They held the lamps high, and we all stared. It was most extraordinary, and somehow most abominable. I can think of no other word, gentlemen, that so much describes the predominant feeling that affected me at the moment.

"'Good lord!' said Captain Gannington several times. 'Good lord!' But neither the second mate nor the man said anything, and, for my part I just stared, and at the same time began to smell a little at the air, for there was a vague odour of something half familiar, that somehow brought to me a sense of half-known fright.

"I turned this way and that, staring, as I have said. Here and there the mould was so heavy as to entirely disguise what lay beneath, converting the deck-fittings into indistinguishable mounds of mould all dirty-white and blotched and veined with irregular, dull, purplish markings.

"There was a strange thing about the mould which Captain Gannington drew attention to — it was that our feet did not crush into it and break the surface, as might have been expected, but merely indented it.

"'Never seen nothin' like it before! Never!' said the captain after having stooped with his lamp to examine the mould under our feet. He stamped with his heel, and the mould gave out a dull, puddingy sound. He stooped again, with a quick movement, and stared, holding the lamp close to the deck. 'Blest if it ain't a reg'lar skin to it!'

"The second mate and the man and I all stooped and looked at it. The second mate progged it with his forefinger, and I remember I rapped it several times with my knuckles, listening to the dead sound it gave out, and noticing the close, firm texture of the mould.

"'Dough!' the second mate. 'It's just like blessed dough! Pouf!' He stood up with a quick movement. 'I could fancy it stinks a bit,' he said.

"As he said this I knew, suddenly, what the familiar thing was in the vague odour that hung about us — it was that the smell had something animal-like in it; something of the same smell, only heavier, that you would smell in any place that is infested with mice. I began to look about with a sudden very real uneasiness. There might be vast numbers of hungry rats aboard. They might prove exceedingly dangerous, if in a starving condition; yet, as you will understand, somehow I hesitated to put forward my idea as a reason for caution, it was too fanciful.

"Captain Gannington had begun to go aft along the mould-covered main-deck with the second mate, each of them holding their lamps high up, so as to cast a good light about the vessel. I turned quickly and followed them, the man with me keeping close to my heels, and plainly uneasy. As we went, I became aware that there was a feeling of moisture in the air, and I remembered the slight mist, or smoke, above the hulk, which had made Captain Gannington suggest spontaneous combustion in explanation.

"And always, as we went, there was that vague, animal smell; suddenly I found myself wishing we were well away from the old vessel.

"Abruptly, after a few paces, the captain stopped and pointed at a row of mould-hidden shapes on each side of the maindeck. 'Guns,' he said. 'Been a privateer in the old days, I guess — maybe worse! We'll 'ave a look below, doctor; there may be something worth touchin'.

She's older than I thought. Mr. Selvern thinks she's about two hundred years old; but I scarce think it.'

"We continued our way aft, and I remember that I found myself walking as lightly and gingerly as possible, as if I were subconsciously afraid of treading through the rotten, mouldhid decks. I think the others had a touch of the same feeling, from the way that they walked.

Occasionally the soft stuff would grip our heels, releasing them with a little sullen suck.

"The captain forged somewhat ahead of the second mate; and I know that the suggestion he had made himself, that perhaps there might be something below worth carrying away, had stimulated his imagination. The second mate was, however, beginning to feel somewhat the same way that I did; at least I have that impression. I think, if it had not been for what I might truly describe as Captain Gannington's sturdy courage, we should all of us have just gone back over the side very soon, for there was most certainly an unwholesome feeling abroad that made one feel queerly lacking in pluck; and you will soon see that this feeling was justified.

"Just as the captain reached the few mould-covered steps leading up on to the short halfpoop, I was suddenly aware that the feeling of moisture in the air had grown very much more definite. It was perceptible now, intermittently, as a sort of thin, moist, fog-like vapour, that came and went oddly, and seemed to make the decks a little indistinct to the view, this time and that. Once an odd puff of it beat up suddenly from somewhere, and caught me in the face, carrying a queer, sickly, heavy odour with it that somehow frightened me strangely with a suggestion of a waiting and half-comprehended danger.

"We had followed Captain Gannington up the three mould covered steps, and now went slowly along the raised after-deck. By the mizzenmast Captain Gannington paused, and held his lantern near to it. 'My word, mister,' he said to the second mate, 'it's fair thickened up with mould! Why, I'll g'antee it's close on four foot thick.' He shone the light down to where it met the deck. 'Good lord!' he said. 'Look at the sea-lice on it!' I stepped up, and it was as he had said; the sea-lice were thick upon it, some of them huge, not less than the size of large beetles, and all a clear, colourless shade, like water, except where there were little spots of grey on them.

"'I've never seen the like of them, 'cept on a live cod,' said Captain Gannington, in an extremely puzzled voice. 'My word! But they're whoppers!' Then he passed on; but a few paces farther aft he stopped again, and held his lamp near to the mould-hidden deck.

"'Lord bless me, doctor,' he called out, in a low voice, 'did ye ever see the like of that?

Why, it's a foot long, if it's a hinch!'

"I stooped over his shoulder, and saw what he meant; it was a clear, colourless creature about a foot long, and about eight inches high, with a curved back that was extraordinarily narrow. As we stared, all in a group, it gave a queer little flick, and was gone.

"'Jumped!' said the captain. 'Well, if that ain't a giant of all the sea-lice that ever I've seen.

I guess it's jumped twenty foot clear.' He straightened his back, and scratched his head a moment, swinging the lantern this way and that with the other hand, and staring about us.

'Wot are they doin' aboard 'ere?' he said. 'You'll see 'em — little things — on fat cod an' such-like. I'm blowed, doctor, if I understand.'

"He held his lamp towards a big mound of the mould that occupied part of the after portion of the low poop-deck, a little foreside of where there came a two-foot high 'break' to a kind of second and loftier poop, that ran away aft to the taffrail. The mound was pretty big, several feet across, and more than a yard high. Captain Gannington walked up to it.

"'I reck'n this's the scuttle,' he remarked, and gave it a heavy kick. The only result was a deep indentation into the huge, whiteish hump of mould, as if he had driven his foot into a mass of some doughy substance. Yet I am not altogether correct in saying that this was the only result, for a certain other thing happened. From the place made by the captain's foot there came a sudden gush of a purplish fluid, accompanied by a peculiar smell, that was, and was not, half familiar. Some of the mould-like substance had stuck to the toe of the captain's boot, and from this likewise there issued a sweat, as it were, of the same colour.

"'Well?' said Captain Gannington, in surprise, and drew back his foot to make another kick at the hump of mould. But he paused at an exclamation from the second mate:

"'Don't sir,' said the second mate.

"I glanced at him, and the light from Captain Gannington's lamp showed me that his face had a bewildered, half-frightened look, as if he were suddenly and unexpectedly half afraid of something, and as if his tongue had given away his sudden fright, without any intention on his part to speak. The captain also turned and stared at him.

"'Why, mister?' he asked, in a somewhat puzzled voice, through which there sounded just the vaguest hint of annoyance. 'We've got to shift this muck, if we're to get below.'

"I looked at the second mate, and it seemed to me that, curiously enough he was listening less to the captain than to some other sound. Suddenly he said, in a queer voice, 'Listen, everybody!'

"Yet we heard nothing, beyond the faint murmur of the men talking together in the boat alongside.

"'I don't, hear nothing,' said Captain Gannington, after a short pause. 'Do you, doctor?'

"'No,' I said.

"'Wot was it you thought you heard?' the captain, turning again to the second mate. But the second mate shook his head in a curious, almost irritable way, as if the captain's question interrupted his listening. Captain Gannington stared a moment at him, then held his lantern up and glanced about him almost uneasily. I know I felt a queer sense of strain. But the light showed nothing beyond the greyish dirty-white of the mould in all directions.

"'Mister Selvern,' said the captain, at last, looking at him, 'don't get fancying, things. Get hold of your bloomin' self. Ye know ye heard nothin'?'

"'I'm quite broke off sharply, and appeared to listen with an almost painful intensity.

"'What did it sound like?' I asked.

"'It's all right, doctor,' said Captain Gannington, laughing gently. 'Ye can give him a tonic when we get back. I'm goin' to shift this stuff.' He drew back, and kicked for the second time at the ugly mass which he took to hide the companionway. The result of his kick was startling, for the whole thing wobbled sloppily, like a mound of unhealthy-looking jelly.

"He drew his foot out of it quickly, and took a step backward, staring, and holding his lamp towards it. 'By gum,' he said, and it was plain that he was generally startled, 'the blessed thing's gone soft!'

"The man had run back several steps from the suddenly flaccid mound, and looking horribly frightened. Though of what, I am sure he had not the least idea. The second mate stood where he was, and stared. For my part, I know I had a most hideous uneasiness upon me. The captain continued to hold his light towards the wobbling mound and stare.

"'It's gone squashy all through,' he said. 'There's no scuttle there. There's no bally woodwork inside that lot! Phoo! What a rum smell!'

"He walked round to the after side of the strange mound, to see whether there might be some signs of an opening, into the hull at the back of the great heap of mould-stuff. And then:

"'Listen!' said the second mate again, in the strangest sort of voice.

"Captain Gannington straightened himself upright, and there succeeded a pause of the most intense quietness, in which there was not even the hum of talk from the men alongside in the boat. We all heard it — a kind of dull, soft thud, thud, thud, thud, somewhere in the hull under us, yet so vague as to make me half doubtful I heard it, only that the others did so, too.

"Captain Gannington turned suddenly to where the man stood.

"'Tell them — —' he began. But the fellow cried out something, and pointed. There had come a strange intensity into his somewhat unemotional face, so that the captain's glance followed his action instantly. I stared also as you may think. It was the great mound at which the man was pointing. I saw what he meant. From the two gapes made in the mould-like stuff by Captain Gannington's boot, the purple fluid was jetting out in a queerly regular fashion, almost as if it were being forced out by a pump. My word! But I stared! And even as I stared a larger jet squirted out, and splashed as far as the man, spattering his boots and trouser legs.

"The fellow had been pretty nervous before, in a stolid, ignorant sort of way, and his funk had been growing steadily; but at this he simply let out a yell, and turned about to run. He paused an instant,as if a sudden fear of the darkness that held the decks, between him and the boat, had taken him. He snatched at the second mate's lantern, tore it out of his hand, and plunged heavily away over the vile stretch of mould.

"Mr. Selvern, the second mate, said not a word; he was just staring, staring at the strangesmelling twin-streams of dull purple that were jetting out from the wobbling mound.

Captain Gannington, however, roared an order to the man to come back, but the man plunged on and on across the mould, his feet seeming to be clogged by the stuff, as if it had grown suddenly soft. He zigzagged as he ran, the lantern swaying, in wild circles as he wrenched his feet free with a constant plop, plop; and I could hear his frightened gasps even from where I stood.

"'Come back with that lamp!' roared the captain again; but still the man took no notice.

"And Captain Gannington was silent an instant, his lips working in a queer, inarticulate fashion, as if he were stunned momentarily by the very violence of his anger at the man's insubordination. And in the silence I heard the sounds again — thud, thud, thud, thud! Quite distinctly now, beating, it seemed suddenly to me, right down under my feet, but deep.

"I stared down at the mould on which I was standing, with a quick, disgusting sense of the terrible all about me; then I looked at the captain, and tried to say something, without appearing frightened. I saw that he had turned again to the mound, and all the anger had gone out of his face. He had his lamp out towards the mound, and was listening. There was another moment of absolute silence, at least, I knew that I was not conscious of any sound at all in all the world, except that extraordinary thud, thud, thud, thud, down somewhere in the huge bulk under us.

"The captain shifted his feet with a sudden, nervous movement, and as he lifted them the mould went plop, plop! He looked quickly at me, trying to smile, as if he were not thinking anything very much about it.

"'What do you make of it, doctor?' he said.

"'I think − −' I began. But the second mate interrupted with a single word, his voice pitched a little high, in a tone that made us both stare instantly at him.

"'Look!' he said, and pointed at the mound. The thing was all of a slow quiver. A strange ripple ran outward from it, along the deck, like you will see a ripple run inshore out of a calm sea. It reached a mound a little foreside of us, which I had supposed to be the cabin skylight, and in a moment the second mound sank nearly level with the surrounding decks, quivering floppily in a most extraordinary fashion. A sudden quick tremor took the mould right under the second mate, and he gave out a hoarse little cry, and held his arms out on each side of him, to keep his balance. The tremor in the mould spread, and Captain Gannington swayed, and spread out his feet with a sudden curse of fright. The second mate jumped across to him, and caught him by the wrist.

"'The boat, sir!' he said, saying the very thing that I had lacked the pluck to say. 'For

God's sake − −'

"But he never finished, for a tremendous hoarse scream cut off his words. They hove themselves round and looked. I could see without turning. The man who had run from us was standing in the waist of the ship, about a fathom from the starboard bulwarks. He was swaying from side to side, and screaming, in a dreadful fashion. He appeared to be trying to lift his feet, and the light from his swaying lantern showed an almost incredible sight. All about him the mould was in active movement. His feet had sunk out of sight. The stuff appeared to be lapping at his legs and abruptly his bare flesh showed. The hideous stuff had rent his trouser-leg away as if it were paper. He gave out a simply sickening scream, and, with a vast effort, wrenched one leg free. It was partly destroyed. The next instant he pitched face downward, and the stuff heaped itself upon him, as if it were actually alive, with a dreadful, severe life. It was simply infernal. The man had gone from sight. Where he had fallen was now a writhing, elongated mound, in constant and horrible increase, as the mould appeared to move towards it in strange ripples from all sides.

"Captain Gannington and the second mate were stone silent, in amazed and incredulous horror, but I had begun to reach towards a grotesque and terrific conclusion, both helped and hindered by my professional training.

"From the men in the boat alongside there was a loud shouting. and I saw two of their faces appear suddenly above the rail. They showed clearly a moment in the light from the lamp which the man had snatched from Mr. Selvern; for, strangely enough, this lamp was standing upright and unharmed on the deck, a little way foreside of that dreadful, elongated, growing mound, that still swayed and writhed with an incredible horror. The lamp rose and fell on the passing ripples of the mould, just — for all the world — as you will see a boat rise and fall on little swells. It is of some interest to me now, psychologically, to remember how that rising and falling lantern brought home to me more than anything the incomprehensible dreadful strangeness of it all.

"The men's faces disappeared with sudden yells, as if they had slipped, or been suddenly hurt; and there was a fresh uproar of shouting from the boat. The men were calling to us to come away — to come away. In the same instant I felt my left boot drawn suddenly and forcibly downward, with a horrible, painful grip. I wrenched it free, with a yell of angry fear.

Forrard of us, I saw that the vile surface was all amove, and abruptly I found myself shouting in a queer, frightened voice, 'The boat, captain! The boat, captain!'

"Captain Gannington stared round at me, over his right shoulder, in a peculiar, dull way, that told me he was utterly dazed with bewilderment and the incomprehensibleness of it all. I took a quick, clogged, nervous step towards him, and gripped his arm, and shook it fiercely.

'The boat!' I shouted at him. 'The boat! For God's sake, tell the men to bring the boat aft!'

"Then the mound must have drawn his feet down, for abruptly he bellowed fiercely with terror, his momentary apathy giving place to furious energy. His thickset, vastly muscular body doubled and writhed with his enormous effort, and he struck out madly dropping the lantern. He tore his feet free, something ripping as he did so. The reality and necessity of the situation had come upon him brutishly real, and he was roaring to the men in the boat, 'Bring the boat aft! Bring 'er aft! Bring 'er aft!' The second mate and I were shouting the same thing madly.

"'For God's sake, be smart, lads!' roared the captain, and stooped quickly for his lamp, which still burned. His feet were gripped again, and he hove them out, blaspheming breathlessly, aud leaping a yard high with his effort. Then he made a run for the side, wrenching his feet free at each step. In the same instant the second mate cried out something, and grabbed at the captain.

"'It's got hold of my feet! It's got hold of my feet!' he screamed. His feet, had disappeared up to his boot-tops, and Captain Gannington caught him round the waist with his powerful left arm, gave a mighty heave, and the next instant had him free; but both his boot-soles had gone. For my part, I jumped madly from foot to foot, to avoid the plucking of the mould; and suddenly I made a run for the ship's side. But before I could get there, a queer gape came in the mould between us and the side, at least a couple of feet wide, and how deep I don't know. It closed up in an instant, and all the mould where the cape had been vent into a sort of flurry of horrible ripplings, so that I ran back from it; for I did not dare to put my foot upon it. Then the captain was shouting to me:

"'Aft, doctor! Aft, doctor! This way, doctor! Run!' I saw then that he had passed me, and was up on the after raised portion of the poop. He had the second mate, thrown like a sack, all loose and quiet, over his left shoulder; for Mr. Selvern had fainted, and his long legs flogged limp and helpless against the captain's massive knees as he ran. I saw, with a queer, unconscious noting of minor details, how the torn soles of the second mate's boots flapped and jigged as the captain staggered aft.

"'Boat ahoy! Boat ahoy! Boat ahoy!' shouted the captain; and then I was beside him, shouting also. The men were answering with loud yells of encouragement, and it was plain they were working desperately to force the boat aft through the thick scum about the ship.

"We reached the ancient, mould-hid taffrail, and slewed about breathlessly in the halfdarkness to see what was happening. Captain Gannington had left his lantern by the big mound when he picked up the second mate; and as we stood, gasping we discovered suddenly that all the mould between us and the light was full of movement. Yet, the part on which we stood, for about six or eight feet forrard of us, was still firm.

"Every couple of seconds we shouted to the men to hasten, and they kept on calling to us that they would be with us in an instant. And all the time we watched the deck of that dreadful hulk, feeling, for my part, literally sick with mad suspense, and ready to jump overboard into that filthy scum all about us.

"Down somewhere in the huge bulk of the ship there was all the time that extraordinary dull, ponderous thud, thud, thud, thud growing ever louder. I seemed to feel the whole hull of the derelict, beginning to quiver and thrill with each dull beat. And to me, with the grotesque and hideous suspicion of what made that noise, it was at once the most dreadful and incredible sound I have ever heard.

"As we waited desperately for the boat, I scanned incessantly so much of the grey white bulk as the lamp showed. The whole of the decks seemed to be in strange movement. Forrard of the lamp, I could see indistinctly the moundings of the mould swaying and nodding hideously beyond the circle of the brightest rays. Nearer, and full in the glow of the lamp, the mound which should have indicated the skylight, was swelling steadily. There were ugly, purple veinings on it, and as it swelled, it seemed to me that the veinings and mottlings on it were becoming plainer, rising as though embossed upon it, like you will see the veins stand out on the body of a powerful, full-blooded horse. It was most extraordinary. The mound that we had supposed to cover the companionway had sunk flat with the surrounding mould, and I could not see that it jetted out any more of the purplish fluid.

"A quaking movement of the mound began away forrard of the lamp, and came flurrying away aft towards us, and at the sight of that I climbed up on to the spongy-feeling taffrail, and yelled afresh for the boat. The men answered with a shout, which told me they were nearer, but the beastly scum was so thick that it was evidently a fight to move the boat at all.

Beside me, Captain Gannington was shaking the second mate furiously, and the man stirred and began to moan. The captain shook him again, 'Wake up! Wake up, mister!' he shouted.

"The second mate staggered out of the captain's arms, and collapsed suddenly, shrieking: 'My feet! Oh, God! My feet!' The captain and I lugged him off the mound, and got him into a sitting position upon the taffrail, where he kept up a continual moaning.

"'Hold 'im, doctor,' said the captain. And whilst I did so, he ran forrard a few yards, and peered down over the starboard quarter rail. 'For God's sake, be smart, lads! Be smart! Be smart!' he shouted down to the men, and they answered him, breathless, from close at hand, yet still too far away for the boat to be any use to us on the instant.

"I was holding the moaning, half-unconscious officer, and staring forrard along the poop decks. The flurrying of the mould was coming aft, slowly and noiselessly. And then, suddenly, I saw something closer:

"'Look out, captain!' I shouted. And even as I shouted, the mould near to him gave a sudden, peculiar slobber. I had seen a ripple stealing towards him through the mould. He gave an enormous, clumsy leap, and landed near to us on the sound part of the mould, but the movement followed him. He turned and faced it, swearing fiercely. All about his feet there came abruptly little gapings, which made horrid sucking noises. 'Come back, captain!' I yelled. 'Come back, quick!' As I shouted, a ripple came at his feet — lipping at them; and he stamped insanely at it, and leaped back, his boot torn half off his foot. He swore madly with pain and anger, and jumped swiftly for the taffrail.

"'Come on, doctor! Over we go!' he called. Then he remembered the filthy scum, and hesitated, and roared out desperately to the men to hurry. I stared down, also.

"'The second mate?' I said.

"'I'll take charge doctor,' said Captain Gannington, and caught hold of Mr. Selvern. As he spoke, I thought I saw something beneath us, outlined against the scum. I leaned out over the stern, and peered. There was something under the port-quarter.

"'There's something down there, captain!' I called, and pointed in the darkness. He stooped far over, and stared.

"'A boat, by gum! A boat!' he yelled, and began to wriggle swiftly along the taffrail, dragging the second mate after him. I followed. 'A boat it is, sure!' he exclaimed a few moments later, and, picking up the second mate clear of the rail, he hove him down into the boat, where he fell with a crash into the bottom.

"'Over ye go, doctor!' he yelled at me, and pulled me bodily off the rail and dropped me after the officer. As he did so, I felt the whole of the ancient, spongy rail give a peculiar, sickening quiver, and begin to wobble. I fell on to the second mate, and the captain came after, almost in the same instant, but, fortunately, he landed clear of us, on to the fore thwart, which broke under his weight, with a loud crack and splintering of wood.

"'Thank God!' I heard him mutter. 'Thank God! I guess that was a mighty near thing to going to Hades.'

"He struck a match, just as I got to my feet, and between us we got the second mate straightened out on one of the after fore-and-aft thwarts. We shouted to the men in the boat, telling them where we were, and saw the light of their lantern shining round the starboard counter of the derelict. They called back to us to tell us they were doing their best, and then, whilst we waited, Captain Gannington struck another match, and began to overhaul the boat we had dropped into. She was a modern, two-bowed boat, and on the stern there was painted

'Cyclone, Glasgow.' She was in pretty fair condition, and had evidently drifted into the scum and been held by it.

"Captain Gannington struck several matches, and went forrard towards the derelict. Suddenly he called to me, and I jumped over the thwarts to him. 'Look, doctor,' he said, and I saw what he meant — a mass of bones up in the bows of the boat. I stooped over them, and looked; there were the bones of at least three people, all mixed together in an extraordinary fashion, and quite clean and dry. I had a sudden thought concerning the bones, but I said nothing, for my thought was vague in some ways, and concerned the grotesque and incredible suggestion that had come to me as to the cause of that ponderous, dull thud, thud, thud thud, that beat on so infernally within the hull, and was plain to hear even now that we had got off the vessel herself. And all the while, you know, I had a sick, horrible mental picture of that frightful, wriggling mound aboard the hulk.

"As Captain Gannington struck a final match, I saw something that sickened me and the captain saw it in the same instant. The match went out, and he fumbled clumsily for another, and struck it. We saw the thing again. We had not been mistaken. A great lip of grey-white was protruding in over the edge of the boat — a great lappet of the mould was coming stealthily towards us — a live mass of the very hull itself! And suddenly Captain Gannington yelled out in so many words the grotesque and incredible thing I was thinking: '*She's alive!*'

"I never heard such a sound of comprehension and terror in a man's voice.

The very horrified assurance of it made actual to me the thing that before had only lurked in my subconscious mind. I knew he was right; I knew that the explanation my reason and my training both repelled and reached towards was the true one. Oh, I wonder whether anyone can possibly understand our feelings in that moment? The unmitigated horror of it and the incredibleness!

"As the light of the match burned up fully, I saw that the mass of living matter coming towards us was streaked and veined with purple, the veins standing out, enormously distended. The whole thing quivered continuously to each ponderous thud, thud, thud, thud, of that gargantuan organ that pulsed within the huge grey-white bulk. The flame of the match reached the captain's fingers, and there came to me a little sickly whiff of burned flesh, but he seemed unconscious of any pain. Then the flame went out in a brief sizzle, yet at the last moment I had seen an extraordinary raw look become visible upon the end of that monstrous, protruding lappet. It had become dewed with a hideous, purplish sweat. And with the darkness there came a sudden charnel-like stench.

"I heard the matchbox split in Captain Gannington's hands as he wrenched it open. Then he swore, in a queer frightened voice, for he had come to the end of his matches. He turned clumsily in the darkness, and tumbled over the nearest thwart, in his eagerness to get to the stern of the boat; and I after him. For we knew that thing was coming towards us through the darkness, reaching over that piteous mingled heap of human bones all jumbled together in the bows. We shouted madly to the men, and for answer saw the bows of the boat emerge dimly into view round the starboard counter of the derelict.

"'Thank God!' I gasped out. But Captain Gannington roared to them to show a light. Yet this they could not do, for the lamp had just been stepped on in their desperate efforts to force the boat round to us.

"'Quick! Quick!' I shouted.

"'For God's sake, be smart, men!' roared the captain.

"And both of us faced the darkness under the port-counter, out of which we knew — but could not see — the thing was coming to us.

"'An oar! Smart, now — pass me an oar!' shouted the captain; and reached out his hands through the gloom towards the on-coming boat. I saw a figure stand up in the bows, and hold something out to us across the intervening yards of scum. Captain Gannington swept his hands through the darkness, and encountered it.

"'I've got it! Let go there!' he said, in a quick, tense voice.

"In the same instant the boat we were in was pressed over suddenly to starboard by some tremendous weight. Then I heard the captain shout, 'Duck y'r head, doctor!' And directly afterwards he swung the heavy, fourteen-foot oar round his head, and struck into the darkness. There came a sudden squelch, and he struck again, with a savage grunt of fierce energy. At the second blow the boat righted with a slow movement, and directly afterwards the other boat bumped gently into ours.

"Captain Gannington dropped the oar, and, springing across to the second mate, hove him up off the thwa then he shouted to me to follow, which I did, and he came after me, bringing the oar with him. We carried the second mate aft, and the captain shouted to the men to back the boat a little; then they got her bows clear of the boat we had just left, and so headed out through the scum for the open sea.

"'Where's Tom 'Arrison?" gasped one of the men, in the midst of his exertions. He happened to be Tom Harrison's particular chum, and Captain Gannington answered him briefly enough:

"'Dead! Pull! Don't talk!'

"Now, difficult as it had been to force the boat through the scum to our rescue, the difficulty to get clear seemed tenfold. After some five minutes pulling, the boat seemed hardly to have moved a fathom, if so much, and a quite dreadful fear took me afresh, which one of the panting men put suddenly into words, 'It's got us!' he gasped out. 'Same as poor Tom!' It was the man who had inquired where Harrison was.

"'Shut y'r mouth an' pull!' roared the captain. And so another few minutes passed.

Abruptly, it seemed to me that the dull, ponderous thud, thud, thud, thud came more plainly through the dark, and I stared intently over the stern. I sickened a little, for I could almost swear that the dark mass of the monster was actually nearer — that it was coming nearer to us through the darkness. Captain Gannington must have had the same thought, for, after a brief look into the darkness, he jumped forrard, and began to double-bank the stroke-oar.

"'Get forrid under the oars, doctor,' he said to me rather breathlessly. 'Get in the bows, an' see if you can't free the stuff a bit round the bows.'

"I did as he told me, and a minute later I was in the bows of the boat, puddling the scum from side to side, and trying to break up the viscid, clinging muck. A heavy almost animallike smell rose off it, and all the air seemed full of the deadening, heavy smell. I shall never find words to tell anyone on earth the whole horror of it all — the threat that seemed to hang in the very air around us, and but a little astern that incredible thing, coming, as I firmly believed, nearer, and scum holding us, like half-melted glue.

"The minutes passed in a deadly, eternal fashion, and I kept staring back astern into the darkness but never ceasing to puddle that filthy scum, striking at it and switching it from side to side until I sweated.

"Abruptly Captain Gannington sang out: 'We're gaining, lads. Pull!' And I felt the boat forge ahead perceptibly, as they gave way with renewed hope and energy. There was soon no doubt of it, for presently that hideous thud, thud, thud, thud had grown quite dim and vague somewhere astern and I could no longer see the derelict, for the night had come down tremendously dark and all the sky was thick, overset with heavy clouds. As we drew nearer and nearer to the edge of the scum, the boat moved more and more perceptibly, until suddenly we emerged with a clean, sweet, fresh sound into the open sea.

"'Thank God!' I said aloud, and drew in the boathook, and made my way aft again to where Captain Gannington now sat once more at the tiller. I saw him looking anxiously up at the sky and across to where the lights of our vessel burned, and again he would seem to listen intently, so that I found myself listening also.

"'What's that, Captain?' I said sharply; for it seemed to me that I heard a sound far astern, something, between a queer whine and a low whistling. 'What's that?'

"'It's wind, doctor.' he said in a low voice. 'I wish to God we were aboard.' Then to the men: 'Pull! Put y'r backs into it, or ye'll never put y'r teeth through good bread again!' The men obeyed nobly, and we reached the vessel safely, and had the boat safely stowed before the storm came, which it did in a furious white smother out of the west. I could see it for some minutes beforehand, tearing the sea in the gloom into a wall of phosphorescent foam; and as it came nearer, that peculiar whining, piping sound grew louder and louder, until it was like a vast steam whistle rushing towards us. And when it did come, we got it very heavy indeed, so that the morning showed us nothing but a welter of white seas, with that grim derelict many a score of miles away in the smother, lost as utterly as our hearts could wish to lose her.

"When I came to examine the second mate's feet, I found them in a very extraordinary condition. The soles of them had the appearance of having been partly digested. I know of no other word that so exactly describes their condition, and the agony the man suffered must have been dreadful.

"Now," concluded the doctor, "that is what I call a case in point. If we could know exactly what the old vessel had originally been loaded with, and the juxtaposition of the various articles of her cargo, plus the heat and time she had endured, plus one or two other only guessable quantities, we should have solved the chemistry of the life-force, gentlemen. Not necessarily the origin, mind you; but, at least, we should have taken a big step on the way.

I've often regretted that gale, you know — in a way, that is, in a way. It was a most amazing discovery, but at the same time I had nothing but thankfulness to be rid of it. A most amazing chance. I often think of the way the monster woke out of its torpor. And that scum!

The dead pigs caught in i! I fancy that was a grim kind of a net, gentlemen. It caught many things. It − −"

The old doctor sighed and nodded.

"If I could have had her bill of lading," he said, his eyes full of regret. "If − − It might have told me something to help. But, anyway − −" He began to fill his pipe again. "I suppose," he ended, looking round at us gravely, "I s'pose we humans are an ungrateful lot of beggars at the best! But − but, what a chance? What a, chance, eh?"

A Thousand Deaths

BY JACK LONDON

I had been in the water about an hour, and cold, exhausted, with a terrible cramp in my right calf, it seemed as though my hour had come. Fruitlessly struggling against the strong ebb tide, I had beheld the maddening procession of the water-front lights slip by, but now a gave up attempting to breast the stream and contended myself with the bitter thoughts of a wasted career, now drawing to a close.

It had been my luck to come of good, English stock, but of parents whose account with the bankers far exceeded their knowledge of child-nature and the rearing of children. While born with a silver spoon in my mouth, the blessed atmosphere of the home circle was to me unknown. My father, a very learned man and a celebrated antiquarian, gave no thought to his family, being constantly lost in the abstractions of his study; while my mother, noted far more for her good looks than her good sense, sated herself with the adulation of the society in which she was perpetually plunged. I went through the regular school and college routine of a boy of the English bourgeoisie, and as the years brought me increasing strength and passions, my parents suddenly became aware that I was possessed of an immortal soul, and endeavoured to draw the curb. But it was too late; I perpetrated the wildest and most audacious folly, and was disowned by my people, ostracised by the society I had so long outraged, and with the thousand pounds my father gave me, with the declaration that he would neither see me again nor give me more, I took a first-class passage to Australia.

Since then my life had been one long peregrination--from the Orient to the Occident, from the Arctic to the Antarctic--to find myself at last, an able seaman at thirty, in the full vigour of my manhood, drowning in San Francisco bay because of a disastrously successful attempt to desert my ship.

My right leg was drawn up by the cramp, and I was suffering the keenest agony. A slight breeze stirred up a choppy sea, which washed into my mouth and down my throat, nor could

I prevent it. Though I still contrived to keep afloat, it was merely mechanical, for I was rapidly becoming unconscious. I have a dim recollection of drifting past the sea-wall, and of catching a glimpse of an upriver steamer's starboard light; then everything became a blank.

* * *

I heard the low hum of insect life, and felt the balmy air of a spring morning fanning my cheek. Gradually it assumed a rhythmic flow, to whose soft pulsations my body seemed to respond. I floated on the gentle bosom of a summer's sea, rising and falling with dreamy pleasure on each crooning wave. But the pulsations grew stronger; the humming, louder; the waves, larger, fiercer--I was dashed about on a stormy sea. A great agony fastened upon me.

Brilliant, intermittent sparks of light flashed athwart my inner consciousness; in my ears there was the sound of many waters; then a sudden snapping of an intangible something, and I awoke.

The scene, of which I was protagonist, was a curious one. A glance sufficed to inform me that I lay on the cabin floor of some gentleman's yacht, in a most uncomfortable posture. On either side, grasping my arms and working them up and down like pump handles, were two peculiarly clad, dark-skinned creatures. Though conversant with most aboriginal types, I could not conjecture their nationality. Some attachment had been fastened about my head, which connected my respiratory organs with the machine I shall next describe. My nostrils, however, had been closed, forcing me to breathe through my mouth. Foreshortened by the obliquity of my line of vision, I beheld two tubes, similar to small hosing but of different composition, which emerged from my mouth and went off at an acute angle from each other.

The first came to an abrupt termination and lay on the floor beside me; the second traversed the floor in numerous coils, connecting with the apparatus I have promised to describe.

In the days before my life had become tangential, I had dabbled not a little in science, and, conversant with the appurtenances and general paraphernalia of the laboratory, I appreciated the machine crude sort which is employed for experimentative purposes. A vessel of water was surrounded by an air chamber, to which was fixed a vertical tube, surmounted by a globe. In the centre of this was a vacuum gauge. The water in the tube moved upwards and downwards, creating alternate inhalations and exhalations, which were in turn communicated to me through the hose. With this, and the aid of the men who pumped my arms, so vigorously, had the process of breathing been artificially carried on, my chest rising and falling and my lungs expanding and contracting, till nature could be persuaded to again take up her wonted labour.

As I opened my eyes the appliance about my head, nostrils and mouth was removed.

Draining a stiff three fingers of brandy, I staggered to my feet to thank my preserver, and confronted--my father. But long years of fellowship with danger had taught me self-control, and I waited to see if he would recognise me. Not so; he saw in me no more than a runaway sailor and treated me accordingly.

Leaving me to the care of the blackies, he fell to revising the notes he had made on my resuscitation. As I ate of the handsome fare served up to me, confusion began on deck, and from the chanteys of the sailors and the rattling of blocks and tackles I surmised that we were getting under way. What a lark! Off on a cruise with my recluse father into the wide Pacific! Little did I realise, as I laughed to myself, which side the joke was to be on. Aye, had I known, I would have plunged overboard and welcomed the dirty fo'c'sle from which I had just escaped.

I was not allowed on deck till we had sunk the Farallones and the last pilot boat. I appreciated this forethought on the part of my father and made it a point to thank him heartily, in my bluff seaman's manner. I could not suspect that he had his own ends in view, in thus keeping my presence secret to all save the crew. He told me briefly of my rescue by his sailors, assuring me that the obligation was on his side, as my appearance had been most opportune. He had constructed the apparatus for the vindication of a theory concerning certain biological phenomena, and had been waiting for an opportunity to use it.

"You have proved it beyond all doubt," he said; then added with a sigh, "But only in the small matter of drowning." But, to take a reef in my yarn--he offered me an advance of two pounds on my previous wages to sail with him, and this I considered handsome, for he really did not need me. Contrary to my expectations, I did not join the sailor' mess, for'ard, being assigned to a comfortable stateroom and eating at the captain's table. He had perceived that I was no common sailor, and I resolved to take this chance for reinstating myself in his good graces. I wove a fictitious past to account for my education and present position, and did my best to come in touch with him. I was not long in disclosing a predilection for scientific pursuits, nor he in appreciating my aptitude. I became his assistant, with a corresponding increase in wages, and before long, as he grew confidential and expounded his theories, I was as enthusiastic as himself.

The days flew quickly by, for I was deeply interested in my new studies, passing my waking hours in his well-stocked library, or listening to his plans and aiding him in his laboratory work. But we were forced to forego many enticing experiments, a rolling ship not being exactly the proper place for delicate or intricate work. He promised me, however, many delightful hours in the magnificent laboratory for which we were bound. He had taken possession of an uncharted South Sea island, as he said, and turned it into a scientific paradise.

We had not been on the island long, before I discovered to horrible mare's nest I had fallen into. But before I describe the strange things which came to pass, I must briefly outline the causes which culminated in as startling an experience as ever fell to the lot of man.

Late in life, my father had abandoned the musty charms of antiquity and succumbed to the more fascinating ones embraced under the general head of biology. Having been thoroughly grounded during his youth in the fundamentals, he rapidly explored all the higher branches as far as the scientific world had gone, and found himself on the no man's land of the unknowable. It was his intention to pre-empt some of this unclaimed territory, and it was at this stage of his investigations that we had been thrown together. Having a good brain, though I say it myself, I had mastered his speculations and methods of reasoning, becoming almost as mad as himself. But I should not say this. The marvellous results we afterwards obtained can only go to prove his sanity. I can but say that he was the most abnormal specimen of cold-blooded cruelty I have ever seen.

After having penetrated the dual mysteries of physiology and psychology, his thought had led him to the verge of a great field, for which, the better to explore, he began studies in higher organic chemistry, pathology, toxicology and other sciences and sub-sciences rendered kindred as accessories to his speculative hypotheses. Starting from the proposition that the direct cause of the temporary and permanent arrest of vitality was due to the coagulation of certain elements and compounds in the protoplasm, he had isolated and subjected these various substances to innumerable experiments. Since the temporary arrest of vitality in an organism brought coma, and a permanent arrest death, he held that by artificial means this coagulation of the protoplasm could be retarded, prevented, and even overcome in the extreme states of solidification. Or, to do away with the technical nomenclature, he argued that death, when not violent and in which none of the organs had suffered injury, was merely suspended vitality; and that, in such instances, life could be induced to resume its functions by the use of proper methods. This, then, was his idea: To discover the method--and by practical experimentation prove the possibility--of renewing vitality in a structure from which life had seemingly fled. Of course, he recognised the futility of such endeavour after decomposition had set in; he must have organisms which but the moment, the hour, or the day before, had been quick with life. With me, in a crude way, he had proved this theory. I was really drowned, really dead, when picked from the water of San Francisco bay--but the vital spark had been renewed by means of his aerotherapeutical apparatus, as he called it.

Now to his dark purpose concerning me. He first showed me how completely I was in his power. He had sent the yacht away for a year, retaining only his two blackies, who were utterly devoted to him. He then made an exhaustive review of his theory and outlined the method of proof he had adopted, concluding with the startling announcement that I was to be his subject.

I had faced death and weighed my chances in many a desperate venture, but never in one of this nature. I can swear I am no coward, yet this proposition of journeying back and forth across the borderland of death put the yellow fear upon me. I asked for time, which he granted, at the same time assuring me that but the one course was open--I must submit. Escape from the Island was out of the question; escape by suicide was not to be entertained, though really preferable to what it seemed I must undergo; my only hope was to destroy my captors.

But this latter was frustrated through the precautions taken by my father. I was subjected to a constant surveillance, even in my sleep being guarded by one or the other of the blacks.

Having pleaded in vain, I announced and proved that I was his son. It was my last card, and I had played all my hopes upon it. But he was inexorable; he was not a father but a scientific machine. I wonder yet have it ever came to pass that he married my mother or begat me, for there was not the slightest grain of emotion in his make-up. Reason was all in all to him, nor could he understand such things as love or sympathy in others, except as petty weaknesses which should be overcome. So he informed me that in the beginning he had given me life, and who had better right to take it away than he? Such, he said, was not his desire, however; he merely wished to borrow it occasionally, promising to return it punctually at the appointed time. Of course, there was a liability of mishaps, but I could do no more than take the chances, since the affairs of men were full of such.

The better to insure success, he wished me to be in the best possible condition, so I was dieted and trained like a great athlete before a decisive contest. What could I do? If I had to undergo the peril, it were best to be in good shape. In my intervals of relaxation he allowed me to assist in the arranging of the apparatus and in the various subsidiary experiments. The interest I took in all such operations can be imagined. I mastered the work as thoroughly as he, and often had the pleasure of seeing some of my suggestions or alterations put into effect.

After such events I would smile grimly, conscious of officiating at my own funeral. He began by inaugurating a series of experiments in toxicology. When all was ready, I was killed by a stiff dose of strychnine and allowed to lie dead for some twenty hours. During that period my body was dead, absolutely dead. All respiration and circulation ceased; but the frightful part of it was, that while the protoplasmic coagulation proceeded, I retained consciousness and was enabled to study it in all its ghastly details.

The apparatus to bring me back to life was an air-tight chamber, fitted to receive my body. The mechanism was simple--a few valves, a rotary shaft and crank, and an electric motor. When in operation, the interior atmosphere was alternately condenses and rarefied, thus communicating to my lungs an artificial respiration without the agency of the hosing previously used. Though my body was inert, and, for all I knew, in the first stages of decomposition, I was cognisant of everything that transpired. I knew when they placed me in the chamber, and though all my senses were quiescent, I was aware of hypodermic injections of a compound to react upon the coagulatory process. Then the chamber was closed and the machinery started. My anxiety was terrible; but the circulation became gradually restored, the different organs began to carry on their respective functions, and in an hour's time I was eating a hearty dinner.

It cannot be said that I participated in this series, nor in the subsequent ones, with much verve; but after two ineffectual attempts of escape, I began to take quite an interest. Besides, I was becoming accustomed. My father was beside himself at his success, and as the months rolled by his speculations took wilder and yet wilder flights. We ranged through the three great classes of poisons, the neurotics, the gaseous and the irritants, but carefully avoided some of the mineral irritants and passed the whole group of corrosives. During the poison regime I became quite accustomed to dying, and had but one mishap to shake my growing confidence. Scarifying a number of lesser blood vessels in my arm, he introduced a minute quantity of that most frightful of poisons, the arrow poison, or curare. I lost consciousness at the start, quickly followed by the cessation of respiration and circulation, and so far had the solidification of the protoplasm advanced, that he gave up all hope. But at the last moment he applied a discovery he had been working upon, receiving such encouragement as to redouble his efforts.

In a glass vacuum, similar but not exactly like a Crookes' tube, was placed a magnetic field. When penetrated by polarised light, it gave no phenomena of phosphorescence nor the rectilinear projection of atoms, but emitted non-luminous rays, similar to the X ray. While the X ray could reveal opaque objects hidden in dense mediums, this was possessed of far subtler penetration. By this he photographed my body, and found on the negative an infinite number of blurred shadows, due to the chemical and electric motions still going on. This was an infallible proof that the rigor mortis in which I lay was not genuine; that is, those mysterious forces, those delicate bonds which held my soul to my body, were still in action.

The resultants of all other poisons were unapparent, save those of mercurial compounds, which usually left me languid for several days.

Another series of delightful experiments was with electricity. We verified Tesla's assertion that high currents were utterly harmless by passing 100,000 volts through my body.

As this didnot affect me, the current was reduced to 2,500, and I was quickly electrocuted.

This time he ventured so far as to allow me to remain dead, or in a state of suspended vitality, for three days. It took four hours to bring me back.

Once, he superinduced lockjaw; but the agony of dying was so great that I positively refused to undergo similar experiments. The easiest deaths were by asphyxiation, such as drowning, strangling, and suffocation by gas; while those by morphine, opium, cocaine and chloroform, were not at all hard.

Another time, after being suffocated, he kept me in cold storage for three months, not permitting me to freeze or decay. This was without my knowledge, and I was in a great fright on discovering the lapse of time. I became afraid of what he might do with me when I lay dead, my alarm being increased by the predilection he was beginning to betray towards vivisection. The last time I was resurrected, I discovered that he had been tampering with my breast. Though he had carefully dressed and sewed the incisions up, they were so severe that I had to take to my bed for some time. It was during this convalescence that I evolved the plan by which I ultimately escaped.

While feigning unbounded enthusiasm in the work, I asked and received a vacation from my moribund occupation. During this period I devoted myself to laboratory work, while he was too deep in the vivisection of the many animals captured by the blacks to take notice of my work.

It was on these two propositions that I constructed my theory: First, electrolysis, or the decomposition of water into its constituent gases by means of electricity; and, second, by the hypothetical existence of a force, the converse of gravitation, which Astor has named "apergy". Terrestrial attraction, for instance, merely draws objects together but does not combine them; hence, apergy is merely repulsion. Now, atomic or molecular attraction not only draws objects together but integrates them; and it was the converse of this, or a disintegrative force, which I wished to not only discover and produce, but to direct at will.

Thus, the molecules of hydrogen and oxygen reacting on each other, separate and create new molecules, containing both elements and forming water. Electrolysis causes these molecules to split up and resume their original condition, producing the two gases separately. The force I wished to find must not only do this with two, but with all elements, no matter in what compounds they exist. If I could then entice my father within its radius, he would be instantly disintegrated and sent flying to the four quarters, a mass of isolated elements.

It must not be understood that this force, which I finally came to control, annihilated matter; it merely annihilated form. Nor, as I soon discovered, had it any effect on inorganic structure; but to all organic form it was absolutely fatal. This partiality puzzled me at first, though had I stopped to think deeper I would have seen through it. Since the number of atoms in organic molecules is far greater than in the most complex mineral molecules, organic compounds are characterised by their instability and the ease with which they are split up by physical forces and chemical reagents.

By two powerful batteries, connected with magnets constructed specially for this purpose, two tremendous forces were projected. Considered apart from each other, they were perfectly harmless; but they accomplished their purpose by focusing at an invisible point in mid-air. After practically demonstrating its success, besides narrowly escaping being blown into nothingness, I laid my trap. Concealing the magnets, so that their force made the whole space of my chamber doorway a field of death, and placing by my couch a button by which I could throw on the current from the storage batteries, I climbed into bed.

The blackies still guarded my sleeping quarters, one relieving the other at midnight. I turned on the current as soon as the first man arrived. Hardly had I begun to doze, when I was aroused by a sharp, metallic tinkle. There, on the mid-threshold, lay the collar of Dan, my father's St. Bernard. My keeper ran to pick it up. He disappeared like a gust of wind, his clothes falling to the floor in a heap. There was a slight wiff of ozone in the air, but since the principal gaseous components of his body were hydrogen, oxygen and nitrogen, which are equally colourless and odourless, there was no other manifestation of his departure. Yet when I shut off the current and removed the garments, I found a deposit of carbon in the form of animal charcoal; also other powders, the isolated, solid elements of his organism, such as sul got up and removed the remains of the second black, and then slept peacefully till morning.

I was awakened by the strident voice of my father, who was calling to me from across the laboratory. I laughed to myself. There had been no one to call him and he had overslept. I could hear him as he approached my room with the intention of rousing me, and so I sat up in bed, the better to observe his translation--perhaps apotheosis were a better term. He paused a moment at the threshold, then took the fatal step. Puff! It was like the wind sighing among the pines. He was gone. His clothes fell in a fantastic heap on the floor. Besides ozone, I noticed the faint, garlic-like odour of phosphorus. A little pile of elementary solids lay among his garments. That was all. The wide world lay before me. My captors were no more.

18 MILES FROM PITTSBURGH
BY TIFFANY L. PROCTOR

I'm driving down the highway. I don't know where I'm going. And I don't care. Anywhere but where I am.

The song is playing on the radio. Our song. My song. Shane's song.

I'm running. Again. I was running when I came here. I'm still running.

And I pray that the demons won't find me.

But let me tell it from the beginning.

I don't know what drew me to L.A. in the first place. Maybe it was the lights, the glam. Or maybe it was the promise of a better life, with fame and riches and supermodel girlfriends. Whatever the reason, it was the first place I fled when I was old enough to leave home.

I grew up just outside of San Francisco. My father was an amazing guitar player. My fondest memories of him were the nights when he would invite the members of his band over and they would practice in the basement of our house. He taught me how to play when I was really young and sometimes if I was lucky he would let me jam with him. He used to say to me "You sure have talent, Grant," and you'd think I had just won the lottery. A compliment from my dad or one of his bandmates was enough to keep my head in the clouds for a week. That's all I ever remember wanting to do. To play in a band. To be like my dad.

But then there were the nights when he would come home drunk and forget that I was there. He would take my mother into the bedroom and they would scream at each other for hours. I don't know what went on behind the closed bedroom door. I hope that I never do. I was afraid of my father when he was like that.

The guy had real talent. He could have been someone. He could have made it. But he threw all of it away with his drinking. Eventually his band broke up and he spent more and more nights alone, drinking to ease the pain of what he had lost. When I got older I made a vow that I would never let anything get in the way of my future. In that respect, I didn't want to be anything like my dad. I vowed that I would never touch a drop of alcohol. Alcohol was my enemy. It had destroyed my family.

When I came of age, I took the money that I had saved for college and moved to Los Angeles, the city of my dreams. I never saw either of my parents again.

I guess that I expected life to be easy once I got out there. But what I found was a cold, empty city. For the first time in my life I was completely alone and I didn't know what I was supposed to do. I couldn't do anything except play the guitar. Those first few weeks were the hardest of my life.

I was able to make some money as a waiter at a restaurant on the east side of the city. It wasn't how I had always pictured my life in L.A., but I was able to save enough money to rent a small apartment and buy a car. I didn't get to play my guitar much (apartments and late night rock sessions don't exactly go well together), and as the weeks went by I began to lose track of my dream of becoming a rock star. I wasn't happy, but the routine I was living in became my life. And not much else existed for me.

I finally talked myself into going out one Saturday night. There was a night club on the other side of town that I had heard boasted some of the best local music around. It was a bit of a drive, but I figured I could use a break from the monotony of my life.

When I got there the place was packed. There was a band on the stage getting ready to play. I found a spot in the back of the club where I had a pretty good view.

And then the music started. Within seconds it had completely washed over me, and all of my dreams came rushing back. It was almost as if I could picture myself up on the stage with those guys, playing with them. The song they were playing was the most beautiful song I had ever heard. That song had power. It stirred something inside of me. A spark that kept building and building until it threatened to explode... then the song ended and the spell broke.

Right away the band launched into another song. The lyrics intrigued me, and I listened, fascinated. "...And I pray that the demons won't find me./ Now I'm 18 miles from Pittsburgh, maybe/ One day you'll forget you hate me..."

When the second song ended, the band introduced themselves as Verbatim. There were four of them, a drummer, a bass player, a guitarist, and a singer who sometimes played the guitar. The singer intrigued me immensely. He had to be one of the most gorgeous people I had ever seen in my life. He was of average height, and slight of build. He had dark hair, and gray eyes that seemed as if they could look straight through my soul. I was completely awed by him. I wanted to be him.

Something made me stick around that night after the band had finished their set. I lingered at the back of the club as the other people filed out around me. I don't know what prompted me to stay. But I was just about to forget about it and leave when the I heard a commotion on the stage. The singer was arguing with his guitar player. I didn't mean to eavesdrop, but they were yelling pretty loud...

The singer was clearly angry. "Something's got to change, Joel. You can't even show up on time anymore. You stumble in an hour late and can barely make it through a half hour set.

This has gone too far. You have to make a choice. If you don't, I'll find someone to replace you. See if I won't."

The guitar player, Joel, looked like he was ready to spit daggers at the singer. "What about you? You put yourself way up a pedestal away from the rest of us down here on earth.

Maybe it's time you came back to the real world and stopped living in the clouds. I'm not changing my lifestyle for you, or anyone else. Replace me if you want. Why the hell do I stay with you guys anyway? You'll never go anywhere. You'll still be playing in this little hole-in-the-wall ten years from now."

I thought the argument was about to come to blows when the guitar player took a flying leap off the stage and shoved past me out the door. I realized that I had subconsciously stepped closer to the stage to listen to the argument. The singer spotted me and called out.

"Hey. Who the hell are you and what do you want?"

I didn't know what to say. I just stood there staring. I didn't know whether to run or to answer his question. My mind went blank. What did I want? Why was I standing there?

The singer seemed to sense my unease because he smiled, jumped down off the stage and offered me his hand. "I'm Shane."

I still couldn't move. I must have looked like an idiot, standing there like I was.

Shane shrugged, took his hand back, and turned away from me.

My voice found its way back.

"Um... my name is Grant."

Shane didn't turn around. "Nice to meet you."

"Yeah, you too... um, that first song you played... it's amazing. I've never heard anything like it before"

That comment seemed to interest Shane because he finally turned back around to face me. "It's something I've been working on. It's not completely finished yet. It's called 'Alone.'

It's kind of about my life, I guess you could say."

Now I was on a roll. "The song you sang after that reminded me of myself. I ran away to L.A. a few months ago. I came out here to find my dream. I play the guitar and I've always wanted to play in a band. I--" I might have rambled on all night long, had Shane not interrupted me.

"You play the guitar? No kidding? You any good?"

"I ah, well... I... I haven't done much practicing lately."

"You want to play in a band, huh? How about this one?"

"I ah..." There I went, losing my voice again. What were we talking about? A band? This band? Me?

Shane, aware of my unease, said "Tell you what. Why don't you come over to my house Monday evening? The guys will be there. Bring your guitar and we'll jam. We'll see if you

can play or not. Sound like a deal?"

"Sure, I... ah... I would love to." What else could I say?

"Great. Let me give you directions."

Later my sense of reality kicked back in and it all seemed like a dream. I went from having no friends and no life to being invited to play with this great band, all in one night.

Was it a simple twist of fate or just a matter of being in the right place at the right time? Or something else entirely? I had no idea.

I spent a couple of sleepless night wondering what would happen Monday evening. What if they didn't like me? Or what if they did? Which would be worse? Oh God, what had I gotten myself into?

My nerves were on edge the entire weekend. I couldn't think properly. I spent Monday morning on pins and needles. I didn't belong with these people. Surely they would pick up on that.

Shane lived across town and the drive to his house took the better part of an hour. On the way over it occurred to me that this might all have been a crazy dream and that when I arrived I would find out that there was no Verbatim, and that Shane and his bandmates didn't really exist. I almost turned around and went home. Somehow, I kept driving.

Finally I arrived at the address Shane had given me. The house was fairly large and set apart from its neighbors. There was a long driveway leading up the front porch and a garage to the side of the house. There were several cars already parked at the end of the driveway, so I figured I must be at the right place.

With shaking steps I managed to get out of the car and walk up the steps to the front door. I rang the bell and waited. "I'm not ready for this," I muttered under my breath.

"Grant. I'm glad you decided to come."

I hadn't realize that I had been staring at the ground until I looked up to see Shane standing in the doorway. I hesitated for a moment, but he gestured for me to come inside, so I did.

I must say that for a struggling musician, Shane didn't live too badly. He had expensive taste and the house was exquisitely furnished. As Shane led me past the living room I caught a glimpse of a fancy coffee table made entirely of glass that was sitting in the middle of the floor. The legs were frosted and there was some kind of design etched on the top of it. It wasn't something I would buy, but I supposed that it had probably cost a fortune, and it was nice... if you were into that sort of thing. Shane led me down into the basement where the other members of the band were busy setting up equipment. I was introduced to the drummer, Chad, and the bass player, Steven.

But I hardly glanced at them. My eyes were drawn to a woman standing in the corner. She was, by far, the most beautiful woman I had ever laid eyes on. She was the perfect Hollywood icon come to life. She had long blonde hair, a body to die for, a face like a supermodel... I could go on. Shane introduced her to me as his girlfriend, Serena. I was in love.

I don't remember what happened next. I was too absorbed with being nervous and staring at Serena to notice anything else. But then the band started to play and as I joined them I became totally absorbed in the music and forgot all about being nervous. I even, for a minute or two, forgot about Serena. Well, maybe not completely...

We rocked for about an hour. It was the first time I had really enjoyed myself in a long time. I never wanted it to end.

When we were finished playing, Shane got together with his bandmates. I took a seat near Serena and we struck up a conversation. I don't remember what it was about.

A few minutes later, Shane came over and sat down beside me.

"So what do you think of the band?"

"Honestly? I think you guys are awesome. I would love to be able to do this everyday. I could do it all day long."

Shane didn't say anything for a minute. He seemed to be thinking something over. He continued. "The band came together four or five years ago. We were fresh out of high school. I've known all the guys since my freshmen year."

I did the math and figured Shane to be about three or four years older than me.

"In high school, Joel and I were really close. We would jam at each other's houses every night after school until our parents threatened to call the cops. He got into drugs our senior year. He said it wasn't a big deal. He said he only was selling them to make money, and that he wasn't taking them. It was for the band, he said. I could have given him money if that's want he wanted, but I didn't complain. Once out of school, we got together with the other guys and Verbatim was born. We wrote some songs, played some gigs, and figured ourselves to be the greatest rock band that ever graced the planet. For a while we were doing really well. And then last year things took a turn for the worst. Joel was into some pretty heavy drugs by then and it was too late for me to do anything about it. He started showing up late for gigs. Sometimes he wouldn't show up at all and we'd have to cancel at the last minute.

That really pissed off the club owners and we found it harder and harder to find a place to play. I knew Joel had a problem and I tried to help him. But every time I confronted him about it he blew up at me. And then the other night I finally lost it. He was almost an hour late. I practically had to beg to get us that gig. I was afraid that he wasn't going to show, and I knew that if that happened we wouldn't have any choice but to try and play without him. I could tell he was on something the moment walked through the door, but there was nothing I could do about it. It was a wonder that he made it through the set. But I had it. I told him what I thought, and he got angry and left. The band needs someone to replace him, Grant.

How about you?"

I had been dre that this question might one day be asked of me. I knew the truth. It wasn't that my unbelievable skill with the guitar had awed Shane and his bandmates to tears. They were in a spot and I was the closest thing around that could help get them out of it. And part of it was Shane's ego. Shane had boasted to Joel that he could find a replacement for him. To fire Joel one night and find someone else to take his place two days later was a major ego boost for Shane. I knew all that and I didn't care. My opportunity had finally been handed to me. I took it and ran.

"Yes," was all that I said. It was all that I needed to say. Shane went upstairs to fix drinks while the other members of the band (my band), and Serena, congratulated me. I was the happiest that I had ever been in my entire life.

Shane came back in and offered me a drink. I remembered the vow that I had made when I left home. I had promised myself that I wouldn't so much as touch a drop of alcohol as long as I lived. So far I had stuck to it. I didn't want to end up like my father. But I stared into Shane's eyes, the eyes of the man I worshiped, and I knew that I would do anything he asked me to. I smiled, and took a drink. I had broken my vow. And it felt good.

As I was leaving that night (or maybe it was early the next morning... after a few drinks it became hard to tell), Serena slipped me her phone number on a piece of paper. I couldn't have been more excited if she had handed me a million dollars. And so ended the night that my life began to come together for the first time. And the night that it began to completely come apart.

I devoted my entire life to Verbatim. I quit my job at the restaurant and concentrated on writing songs with Shane. Shane and I became inseparable. We did everything together. I never really got that close with the other guys in Verbatim. They both had families and lives outside of the band. Shane and I only had each other.

Shane was a difficult person to understand. I was often reminded of the comment that Joel had made on the night that he left the band. About Shane putting himself up on a pedestal and refusing to come down and mingle with the rest of the world. Joel was right about that, somewhat. Shane was a very introspective person and he had a hard time letting his feelings show on the outside. He was a very caring person once you got to know him, but to strangers he could appear almost callous. Not cold really, but indifferent. It's like he had his own private concerns to deal with and he was above the problems of the everyday world.

He was a loner. As close as we were, I never really felt like I could totally reach him. He could be so warm one minute and then say something totally off-the-wall cold the next. I don't think he ever meant to hurt anyone with what he said. He simply didn't realize what he was saying, or how it sounded to someone else.

Shane didn't talk about his past much. I knew that he had grown up in Los Angeles and that his parents had left him a lot of money. That was about it. He never offered to talk about his childhood, and I never pushed him about it.

The band really began to take off. Shane and I finished the song, "Alone," that Shane had been working on for years. We were so proud of that song.

"I see fragments of my life in every line." Shane told me one day. "That's why I had such a hard time finishing it. I still have a hard time sharing it with other people. It's like I give a piece of myself to the audience every time I sing it, and I'm scared to death that they'll reject it."

It was a beautiful song. The audience didn't reject it. They loved it.

The months flew by and we found a manager, signed a record deal, and started recording our album. "Alone" was to be our first single. We were on our way to becoming huge stars.

Or so we thought.

I was seeing my best friend's girlfriend behind his back. Sometimes I felt like a jerk for doing it, but I was in love. It seemed like love, anyway.

Serena aside, my relationship with Shane couldn't have been any better. We would have died for each other. At least we liked to believe that we would have. We never dreamed that one day we might actually have to.

I'll never forget that fateful night. I was sleeping soundly in my apartment. Serena was sleeping naked beside me. The phone downstairs rang and woke me up. It was around 2 in the morning. There was no way I was getting up to answer it.

Serena stirred beside me. "Grant..."

"Go back to sleep," I muttered.

The phone downstairs had just stopped ringing when my cell phone went off. The thing was stuffed somewhere in the pocket of the pants that I had tossed off before getting into bed. The ringing was coming from somewhere down the hall. I ignored it. It stopped. It started again. It was a terribly annoying ring-tone.

I cursed myself for choosing that particular tone as I got up and started digging around for my pants. I was vaguely aware of Serena watching me with an amused look on her face.

The phone kept ringing. I finally found my pants, lying half under the couch in the living room. In a sleepy haze I grabbed a hold of the phone and was about to turn it off when I saw and recognized the number on the caller ID. It was Shane. "Oh shit," I said to myself. "He can't know about me and Serena!" I answered the phone.

Now like I said, Shane had never been the kind of person to wear his emotions on his sleeve. But when I picked up the phone that night, he was hysterical. It kind of freaked me out and I knew immediately that something was very, very wrong.

"Grant?" I could hardly make out what Shane was trying to say.

"I'm here. Calm down for a sec. What's the matter?"

"Oh God, Grant. I... I need you to come over... now. Please. I... I can't... handle this by myself. Please."

Shivers went up my spine. What in the world could have happened that would shake. Shane up like that? I was terrified. By then I was wide awake and nothing could have kept me from going over to see Shane.

"I'll be right over."

The line went dead.

"What the hell was that about?" Serena had found her clothes (some of them) and was standing behind me.

"I don't know. Something happened to Shane. I've got to go over to his place. Get the

heck out of here and if anyone asks, you didn't see me at all last night, okay?" Serena looked annoyed, but she agreed. She certainly didn't seem too concerned about Shane. She found the rest of her clothing and walked out the door. Grabbing my keys off of the floor, I was right behind her.

There was very little traffic at that hour. I made it to Shane's house in record time. My

hands were shaking and I don't know how I managed to stay on the road.

As I pulled into the familiar driveway and got out of my car, Shane bolted out the front door and stood on the front porch steps. It was hard to make him out in the darkness, but at first glance it looked like he was soaking wet. I ran up to the porch and he grabbed my arm.

He was sobbing, and he held onto me for a long time. When I pulled away I realized that my friend wasn't soaking wet at all. He was covered in blood. It had soaked through his clothing, his hair was plastered in it, and it was all over his face and hands.

"What the hell?" I didn't know what to say. I was in total shock, taking it all in.

"I didn't mean to. It was an accident, I swear." Shane was hysterical again, and I had to keep him from falling down.

"Calm down. What was an accident?" I tried to stay calm even though I was about to lost the contents of my stomach. The sight and smell of the blood was getting to me.

"Come inside." Shane slowly staggered back into the house, and I followed.

I was completely unprepared for what I saw when I stepped into the living room.

The expensive solid glass table was shattered into broken pieces. The whole room was covered in blood. It stained the carpet, the walls, the furniture. And in the middle of the mess was Joel's body, it too covered in blood and bits of glass.

"Oh my God..." My knees buckled and I had to swallow back the bile that was rising in my throat. Shane grabbed me and pulled me into the dinning room.

I was trembling all over. "We've got to call an ambulance. What the hell happened in there?"

I had my cell phone in my hand but Shane grabbed it from me as I fumbled with the buttons. "It won't do any good. He's dead, Grant."

"Then we have to call the cops."

"No. Please no, Grant. I'll go to jail. Listen to me. Please."

"You fucking killed him, didn't you?" Now I was on the verge of hysterics. "Tell me what the hell happened!"

"I'm trying to, Grant. Give me a second."

I shoved a stack of dirty dishes off of the dinning room table and shoved Shane down onto a chair. "Tell me what happened."

For a while he just sat there with his head on the table, sobbing. Soothingly, I took one of his hands and he seemed to calm down a bit. He started to talk.

"Joel came over. It was the first time I had seen him since he stormed out of the club that night. He was wired.He... he wanted money. He had this crazy look in his eyes. I wouldn't give him any. I told him to leave. And then he got angry. He ridiculed me. God, Grant, he told me about the song... and he knew about Serena."

"What song? What about Serena? You're not making any sense. Tell me Shane, or I'll call the cops."

Shane took a deep breath and continued. "Every word that Joel spoke to me tonight tore a piece of my heart out and threw it against the wall. But every word he spoke to me is true.

The song. My song. 'Alone.' Joel was sleeping with the producer's wife. So he heard things.

He told me that the record company is giving our song to some other group. Some other group that's more 'marketable' than we are. They're planning on dropping us the first chance they get. Our songs are going to be recorded by someone else."

"C'mon, Shane. Get real. They can't do that," I said. "We signed a contract."

Shane's eyes took on a faraway look and he seemed to stare straight through the wall and into the next room. "Oh? Can't they, Grant? Tell me something. Did you ever actually read that contract we signed? Or were you like me? Too damn excited and immature to care about what it said. It was a record contract, after all. It had to be legit"

"I..." I didn't know how to answer that question. "So you murdered Joel?"

"I didn't murder anybody! But I couldn't just stand there and listen to Joel put down everything that meant something in my life. I was so angry. But I didn't mean to hurt anyone.

I... I shoved Joel. Hard. He wasn't expecting it and he stumbled backward and fell onto the glass table. It broke, and he stood back up covered in blood. He was mad. He took out a knife. He was going to kill me, Grant! I didn't have a choice. I had to do something. So I... grabbed the biggest piece of glass that I could find. I was only going to use it to get him to back off. But he lunged at me. And then... I... I hit him with the jagged end of the glass. I hit him in the neck. And blood spurted everywhere. And he fell... and he didn't get up again. Oh

God, Grant, help me."

I held him as he collapsed into another bout of hysterics. "You believe me, don't you? I didn't mean to kill him."

"Yeah," I whispered, not sure whether I meant it or not. "I believe you." I honestly didn't know what to think. But something else was bothering me.

"Shane, what did you mean when you said that Joel 'knew about Serena'?"

In a flash, Shane became angry. "You slept with her too, didn't you, Grant? Oh don't pretend you don't know what I'm talking about. Serena slept with every one of us at some point. And you never even guessed, did you? Well everyone else knew about it!" He pulled away from me.

"Death was something that I meant to give myself tonight, not Joel. I was going to kill myself tonight, Grant. But look who's lying on the floor!"

"Why, Shane? Why? Who cares if the record company stole our songs? We can write more songs. We'll get another record deal. Why would you want to kill yourself?"

Shane shook his head slowly. "Oh you poor, ignorant bastard. You really have no idea, do you, Grant?. Serena has AIDS."

There was a pause.

"And I have it too."

I felt like a bomb had exploded inside my head. The room was spinning and blurring around me.

And from somewhere far away, Shane spoke to me, softly.

"Did you use a condom, Grant?"

I don't remember when I regained my senses. I do remember that before the sun came up

Shane and I dumped Joel's body in an abandoned lot. There wasn't much in the way of an investigation after the body was found. I suppose the police figured it was just another drug deal gone bad and thumbs up to whoever chose to rid the world of another useless druggie.

It's not like Joel had any family or anyone to miss him. Isn't it a wonderful world we live in?

I also remember driving home the next morning. The sun was just beginning to rise. The city was at my back, the wind was running through my hair, and just two nights prior, I would have marveled at the possibilities. But it wasn't two nights two prior.

"So this is how it all goes down," I thought to myself. "Joel's dead. Serena is going to die.

Shane is going to die. I'm probably going to die." It hit me. Hard. I almost drove into the guardrail. For the first time ever, I began to understand Shane. I began to understand the despair that made him want to take his own life. And I began to understand the desperation that drove him to kill someone else. And I hated myself for it. I had lived my entire life afraid that I would turn into a monster like my father. And looking back I hadn't. No. The monster I had become was much, much worse.

There wasn't much left of our lives after that. All of our cards where laid out on the table, and each and every one was tainted.

Serena got really sick. Shane went to visit her in the hospital once, and I went with him.

She seemed happy to see me, but I could finally see the truth. Her outer beauty had begun to melt away and I could see for the first time the ugliness that lay underneath it. I just wanted to get out of that hospital. It reeked of death. I never saw Serena again and I don't know what became of her. I don't really care.

Shane replaced the carpet in his living room and repainted the walls. We tried to cover up what had happened that horrible night, but we couldn't hide it up from ourselves.

The record company dumped us for a more marketable band. It was too much stress for us to handle, and Verbatim broke up. But Shane and I stayed together. We still jammed in his basement every night, and for a while life was tolerable. But then Shane started to get sick too, and I was forced to face reality. And it terrified me. Shane was all that I had in the world, and once he was gone I would be all alone again. I wondered what a cruel world I lived in that could harbor such a fate.

The last evening that Shane I had together we spent in the basement of his house. He was so weak by that point that I practically had to carry him down the stairs. He sat holding his guitar, trying to play a song. The notes came out thick and staccato, but I recognized them.

And suddenly I was swept away to another time and place. I was at the club where I had first heard that song. Shane was on the stage with his band. Joel was still alive. I had just walked in. And the song had captured me. The lyrics ran through my mind and I started to sing along with Shane.

"...But you don't have to be alone/Just let me in and show me home/'Cuz you've lost yourself in your own mind/And these lies you live in lead you blind."

I broke down then. I couldn't stand the thought of being alone. But Shane had been alone all his life. He chose to be that way. I tried to reach him. But he wouldn't let me.

That night as he lay dying in bed, Shane spoke to me. He talked of how he came to write the song "18 Miles from Pittsburgh."

"I was running away, Grant," he said. My band was falling apart, the girl I was engaged to was seeing someone else. I had lived here all my life and the city had finally gotten to me. I needed to get away from it. So I left. I drove clean across the country before I realized that it wasn't going to do me any good. I looked out my window and I saw one of those signs along the highway that tells you how many miles away you are from someplace. It said 'Pittsburgh, 18.' And that was when it hit me that it wasn't L.A. I was running away from. I was running away from myself. The only problem was that I would still be with me wherever I went. Pittsburgh, New York, Miami. I turned back around and came home. And I wrote that song.

I never lost my demons. They would have found me no matter where I went."

He paused for a second to glance at me.

"But what about you, Grant? Did you ever lose the demons you were running from?"

I looked into his eyes. He was frail, just a shadow of the man he had once been. I couldn't stand to see him like that. I looked away. "I thought I did. But they're still here."

Shane smiled. "You never lose them. They're a part of you. It takes a strong person to accept those demons and come to terms with them. That's the only way to be rid of them. I could never do it.

"You know, It's easy to blame other people for your misfortunes. But the key to letting go of the past is to stop feeling sorry for yourself and to take responsibility for your own decisions. Serena isn't responsible for the way that I am right now. It's no one's fault but my own. I made my own choices in life. You still have a chance to embrace your demons, Grant.

It's too late for me. But not for you."

I was stunned. Was that what I had been doing? Had I blamed alcohol for my father's problems? No one made him pick that bottle up. Had I run away from one demon only to come face to face with another? Had I blamed Serena for everything that had happened to

Shane and myself? No one had made me sleep with her. Just like no one made any of us sign our music over to that record company. We chose to do it. It was quite a revelation for me.

When I looked back at the bed, Shane was gone. But his dying words would stick with me for the rest of my life. I used to wish he had killed me instead of Joel that night. The emotional scars I suffered seemed much too heavy to bear. But on the night that Shane died, something changed inside of me. I was no longer quite as afraid of being alone as I had been.

That night I was on the verge of taking the first step toward embracing my demons.

Shane willed all of his belongings to me. But I didn't want them. I just wanted to get out of that city. I packed some clothes, got in my car, and drove off, leaving the City of Angels behind me forever. There was nothing there for me anymore. I didn't look back once.

So here I am, driving east. Shane is gone, Serena is gone, Verbatim is gone. Yet I'm still here. I wonder why. I wonder what greater purpose has kept me on earth for just a little bit longer.

But what about me, you ask. Do I have AIDS too?

No.

So far I don't. But the disease has been known to lie dormant for several years before surfacing. Perhaps I'll just keel over and die on the street one day. But somehow I don't think it will be that easy.

"Alone" is playing on the radio. My song. Shane's song. No. The words and the music are the same, but it sounds nothing like the song that Shane wrote. It's a good song, none the less.

I am still running. Except that this time I'm running in the right direction. Now I've shared my secrets, and the demons that follow me don't seem quite as scary anymore. I don't know where I'm going or what I'll do with myself once I get there. But as long as I have a future I have hope. I will make my own decisions and take responsibility for my own actions.

I might even have a drink or two every now and then. I won't let anything get in the way of my dreams. And dreams can always change.

I look out my window. The sun is just beginning to rise. The city is at my back, the wind is running through my hair, and I marvel at the possibilities. I turn the radio up and sing along. And I do a strange thing. I laugh.

THE GREAT MORGAN FAMILY REUNION AND SNIPE HUNT

BY ERIC R. LOWTHER

Tom was sure if there was a God he was laughing his ass off. They'd given him a huge burlap sack with marshmallows inside and an old-fashioned lantern then led him deep into the hollow. The moon was full in the cloudless sky, lighting up the clearing at the head of the blackberry thicket. The lantern, so they told him, was more to attract the snipe out of the thicket. Once it came out, all Tom would have to do was hold the bag open. No snipe could resist marshmallows, so he'd been told, and it would just waltz right into the bag. All he had to do was sit, still and quiet, and wait for the snipe to appear.

It was all a moot point to Tom, especially considering snipe weren't real in the first place.

If it was so important to these hicks to have their laugh at his expense then so be it. At the very least his father couldn't deny him his trust fund after this. As degrading as it was to sit in the woods in the middle of the night, waiting for the hillbilly equivalent of Charlie Brown's Great Pumpkin, it was less so than having to work at McDonalds to help pay his way through college.

Tom's parents had divorced shortly after the last Morgan reunion, a grand event that pulled the family back to the hills and hollers' of central West Virginia every ten years. His mother had refused to attend the last one, when she was still married to Tom's father, Henry. They had met in college, he a struggling hick on a full ride, she a pampered suburban princess. He managed to become an attorney, and through some lucky breaks had made his way into a lucrative corporate position in Charleston. Her refusal to attend this very event ten years before had spelled the end of their marriage. That's why Tom was surprised when his mother had begged him to go this time around.

It was time to start thinking about his future, and his father had set up a trust for Tom's education. If the man would divorce his wife over attending this back-woods jamboree it was a given that Tom's failure to attend could only hurt his father's good graces, and though sh was practically guaranteed lifelong income from their divorce Tom wouldn't be so lucky.

With his future at stake, he had no other option but accept his father's invitation. Besides, he'd never see these people again, and if it guaranteed a life of collegiate leisure he'd let them have their laugh at "fooling" the city boy into their redneck ritual.

It had been more than an hour since his father and several of his uncles had left him, promising they wouldn't be too far away. They needed to stay concealed and upwind of the briar patch but they'd still be close enough to help if things got dangerous, as snipe hunts could sometimes become. Tom had laughed at that. He had nothing to fear from an imaginary creature, especially one that could be bested by a lantern, marshmallows and a burlap sack. He sighed and adjusted his back against the old oak and wondered how long he should stay before trudging back empty-handed. The longer he stayed, the drunker they would be and the more satisfying the joke. He only hoped he could fake being the good sport enough to get him back to Cleveland and put this nightmare behind him for good.

The only sounds around him were the wind and the odd call of a night bird here and there. Tom rolled down his sock and pulled out a marijuana cigarette, thinking a good buzz would entertain him for enough time before heading back. He lit and held his breath, letting the smoke escape slowly through tightened lips. Just as he took another puff, he heard a soft rustling at the edge of the blackberry thicket. He continued holding his breath and squinted at the tangle of briars, waiting to see small, dirty hands and hear the giggles of his hick younger cousins. What he saw was a large bird the likes of which he'd never seen before. It looked like one of the wild turkeys he'd seen in petting zoos and nature shows though twice the size in both width and height. Its coloration was all wrong, too. Even in the moon and lantern light he could see the feathers of this bird were a bright, shining red. It took a few slow, cautious steps out of the thicket on its hand-sized feet, its six-inch talons sinking into the soft earth.

"What the hell..." Tom whispered to himself. The creature locked its near-glowing yellow eyes on his and stopped. The two sat motionless, staring across the ten or so feet of open ground between them. Tom reached up and slowly removed the smoldering joint from his lips then dropped it to the ground beside him. Either the animal before him was real or there was something seriously wrong with the weed. After several breathless moments, the bird finally broke eye contact and turned its attention to the bag in Tom's lap. It raised its long, barbed beak in the air and made a sniffing sound as if scenting the air.

"You've gotta' be kidding me..." he mumbled as the bird took another halting step closer, looked back to Tom's face then let out an ear-piercing caw. Tom jumped at the sudden, raspy sound but held his position. It called again, this time much more softly, almost cooing. "No way..."

He let his hands go to his lap slowly and pulled open the bag. He held it off to his side and opened it towards the bird, the length of the sack trailing out flat behind him. It craned its' long neck toward the opening and sniffed noisily, issuing a softer, mewling call. "Yeah... yeah... they're for you..." Tom found himself saying softly to it. "Nice and fresh..." It took several steps closer, its head nearly at the bag's mouth then looked up at him and cooed again as if in a question. Tom's hands were shaking now though he tried to still them. He took a deep breath and concentrated, making the tremors subside so as not to scare it away.

"Go ahead, little guy... go on..." he said reassuringly. It paused only a moment more before walking slowly ahead, right into the depths of the large burlap sack.

As soon as it was completely inside, Tom brought his hands together and closed the bag.

He suddenly remembered the animal's thick talons and sharp beak and quickly put the bag out at arm's reach. What the hell were these hillbillies thinking? Burlap was as good as tissue paper to hold something like this. He desperately wanted to let go of the bag, to get as far away from those rending claws that he was sure any minute now would be slicing through first the sack and then him. Still, he held the bag closed in a white-knuckled grip and listened to the soft slurping sounds from within. The thing was oblivious to its predicament, its full attention on the sweet sticky morsels within.

Tom stood, still keeping the bag at arm's length. It was surprisingly heavy and would be difficult to carry and still keep it away from his body. He froze suddenly as he felt the weight of his bundle shift slightly. He fully expected its claws and beak to break free of the bag now that it had finished its treat. Instead, the thing started cooing again, though this time a low, mournful sound. Well, it was a bird, wasn't it? If you wanted to calm a bird, you threw a drape over its cage. Tom only hoped this was the case, and that the calming effect wouldn't be lost as he moved the bird from the hollow and back to the farm.

Still unwilling to hold the bag close, he cast about and found a long, fallen oak branch.

He set the bag on the ground and with trembling hands tied the top into a large knot. The thing's cries had become constant now, its' mewling growing louder and more shrill with each passing moment. Tom cringed at the sound of it as he slid an end of the branch through the knot, meaning to carry his bundle hobo-style over his shoulder and well away from his body. Suddenly, the snipe's caterwauling turned to an ear-piercing, constant shriek more akin to a woman than a bird. Tom winced as the sound cut through his temples and brought on an immediate, throbbing headache. He stumbled away from the bag, leaned against the tree and covered his ears with his hands.

After what felt like minutes, the snipe finally stopped its keening. Tom moved his hands away from his ears slowly, waiting to see if it had truly stopped or if it was only catching its breath. That's when he heard another call from somewhere in the deep woods surrounding the blackberry thicket. Unlike the snipe's frightened wail, this new call was a deep, throaty and very angry sound. Tom spun on his heel, heart trip-hammering in his chest. The call came again, closer this time and accompanied by the sounds of something very large and very pissed-off coming through the woods at high speed.

Tom made to run but his legs wouldn't respond. Rooted by fear he could only watch as a

wad of leaves and thick branches some ten feet off the ground blew out of the wood line. A huge, bright red mass followed the tangle of fauna to the ground, crushing it to splinters beneath its massive, talon-tipped claws. It spun towards Tom and puffed out its chest, the sound from its' enraged call slamming against him in a palpable wave as it started towards him, its' foot-long talons churning the soft ground beneath it.

Tom screamed as the monster drew closer, his mind reeling out the scant few feet left between them the cracks of rifles and the booming of shotgun blasts filled the air around him, adding their noise to the cacophony of shrieks from beast and boy alike. Tom opened his eyes in time to see the giant bird rear back mere feet ahead of him, the bullets and buckshot blowing chunks of red-feathered flesh into the air. It teetered for a moment on wobbly legs then, still screeching its awful caw, fell slowly forward. He screamed and dropped to his knees, hands crossed over his head, waiting for the dying thing to collapse on him. Instead, he felt the ground shudder as the monster's weight fell in a dead heap beside him.

Shaking, Tom opened his eyes. Its head lay mere inches from him, its frozen, saucersized yellow eyes spattered with blood. The smaller creature in the bag behind him had gone quiet and still now, perhaps from the gunfire and the collective whoops and shouts that rang out from the men coming out of the woods, perhaps from the thundering absence of its mother's call. Tom got to his feet and wiped at the errant splatters of crimson on his face, his hands trembling almost too violently to accomplish the task. Henry Morgan walked up to him with his long-barreled shotgun held at port arms and smiled.

"Ya' did good, boy. Real good." he said, clasping his son's shoulder.

"What the..." Tom wheezed. He took a deep breath and started again. "What the hell just happened here? What the hell is that thing? Why didn't you tell me..."

"Easy, boy." Earl, Tom's uncle, said as he and the rest of the men joined them.

"Easy hell!" Tom screamed. "What the fuck is that thing?" he asked, pointing at the dead monster.

"It's a snipe, son." his father returned, deadpan. "That's what we was out here huntin' ain't it?"

"Snipe don't exist! Christ!" Tom said. He was shaking uncontrollably now as the late adrenaline rush and subconscious joy of not being dead rushed through him.

"Calm down, boy." Henry said softly. "Now, we told ya' we were snipe huntin', and we told ya' sometimes it can get dangerous, didn't we? It ain't our fault you didn't believe us."

"I... you..." Tom stammered. "This..." He pointed down at the cooling carcass again and swallowed a bit of bile that was creeping up on him. "Snipe aren't fucking real!" he blurted out finally.

"Looks like you got a lackin' in your education." Uncle Earl said, his Appalachian accent giving his words a slow, pondering feel. "You should read a book or two."

Tom whipped his head around and set a vicious gaze on his uncle. "Is this you idiots' idea of a God-damn joke?" he practically screamed. "I could have been killed!"

"Boy..." Henry said softly, "...you best check your tone. I understand it was a bit frightenin' an' all for a little man from the big city, but you take the Lord's name in vain agin' and I'll have to knock you into next week. You understand me, Tommy?" Tom turned his steely gaze on his father, but at that moment the surge of fear and adrenaline finished its course. He started shaking again, though far less violently than before. The look his father gave him told him the man would have no qualms about doing exactly what he said he'd do.

"Yes..." Tom finally responded, his head dropping wearily onto his chest.

"Yes, what?" his father prompted.

"Yes... sir." Tom answered. Henry squeezed his shoulder again and stood beside him as the rest of the men hoisted the bird up and onto their shoulders.

"Yes, sirree!" Uncle Earl called out between grunts as he helped shoulder the load. "It ain't a Morgan reunion without snipe for Sunday supper!" The rest of the men grunted in laugher and agreement as they began the arduous task of packing the massive bird out of the hollow and back to the farm.

"We better get you on back, Tom." his father said. Tom looked at his father for a moment then wiped his bloody hands on his jeans.

"You've never called me Tom before." Tom said softly.

"Well... guess it's 'cause you ain't never been a man before." Henry said thoughtfully.

Tom smiled at him and started to follow the rest out of the hollow. "Hey!" Henry called to him. "You forgettin' somethin'?" Tom turned back. His father was shining a flashlight beam onto the tied-off sack. "Pick up that poke and get it on up to the house."

"Oh... right..." Tom said, actually a little embarrassed to have so quickly forgotten his burden. He went to the bag, picked it up and regarded his father. "We aren't going to... kill it, are we?" Tom asked, swallowing hard.

"Naw." Henry answered. "Snipe ain't good eatin' till they get to be around ten or so.

See, when they're young like that one their mammas put 'em in the brush, like the blackberries here. You can't never get an adult snipe to come out. They're way too careful for that kind of thing. The only sure way to get 'em to come out is if they think their young is in danger. That's when they stop bein' careful and come at ya' with everything they got."

Tom hoisted the bag over his shoulder, adjusting his stance to compensate for the weight.

"So why don't I let him go now?"

"That ain't a him, it's a her, Tom." Henry said matter-of-factly. "Your Uncle Earl found some sign down over in Brinkman's holler' last week, thinks there's a tom snipe at just about breedin' age. Tomorrow morning, we're all gonna' go down there and release the little lady you caught here tonight, give that randy little buck some company, if you catch my meanin'.

Then we'll come on back and have our usual snipe dinner 'fore everybody heads back home.

By next reunion-time, those two'll have mated and that tom'll be all fattened up and ready to carry on the Morgan reunion tradition. Now let's get on back to the house. That snipe ain't goin' to pluck itself." Tom made a distasteful face to his back, shouldered his burden and fell in step behind his father.

"Hey, Dad..." Tom said between breaths as they climbed the steep, wooded hill back to the farm. "What does snipe taste like?"

"Snipe? Tastes exactly like chicken." Henry said over his shoulder. The answer stopped Tom dead in his track, his feet threatening to slide down the rocky bank. He thought about the snipe bursting out of the forest, how he'd pissed himself and how he'd almost died. His face turned red and hot as he shifted his load again between his shoulders.

"Exactly like chicken?" Tom echoed, his voice quivering slightly.

"Exactly." his father said.

"Then why the hell don't you rednecks just eat chicken in the first place?" Tom screamed at his back.

Henry stopped and looked back at his son, his feet balancing easily on the rough hill.

"You probably wouldn't know it, son, but chickens... well, chickens just ain't fun to hunt.

No challenge in it." Henry chuckled low under his breath and turned back to continue on up the hill. "You just make sure you come on down next summer." he called back after him.

"Why?" Tom called up the hill.

"Shit, son... don't you know nuthin'? Every eleven years is gryphon season..."

Night of the Black Malkin

By Joline Lieck

The big cats of the African jungles are fierce kings; in the rain forests they are agile predators with an unmatched grace. In ancient Egypt, seemingly ordinary house cats were regarded as gods as they sat beside the thrones of pharaohs, and whether mere legend or possible truth, they have often been depicted as familiars, or servants to witches. In more modern times, a cat's role has been to fulfill the lives of pet owners and to provide companionship to the lonely. The ancestry and history of these fascinating creatures is as rich as that of humankind.

Annaliese, a fair skinned, raven haired beauty with eyes of the clearest blue, was angelic in her looks and her mannerisms. She had a classy air that is often associated with the elite, and such grace about her that her soul could have been that of a cat incarnate. It seemed rather appropriate that her pets be nothing, ever, than a cat. And since she was a child, that was all that she had ever had.

She had loved Malkin, a big, sleek black cat, although she was reluctant at first. Her last cat went missing and was found dead a few blocks from her home; she knew it was him by the collar. Lavender with a floral print that was now streaked with blood. She figured that some animal had probably chased after him, as he never ventured far from the garden which was set in front of the large window in front of the house, and during the chase he must have been hit by the car. At least, this was what she had surmised.

Annaliese was of the belief that no one, including animals, could be replaced, but when a friend went through the trouble of finding her a new kitten to help her through her grief, she had no choice but to provide it with a new home, although she wasn't thrilled at the time.

It was soon after the death of the last cat, and of the six cats she had owned, this was the first to meet an unnatural end. But she would prevent any such event from happening again;

Malkin was to strictly be a house cat.

One day, whether by coincidence or act of pure fate, he escaped when she walked in the door after coming home from work. The more she ran after the cat, the further he ran from her. And then she lost sight of him completely.

She was upset as she always used extra caution to keep him indoors, and that day she hadn't even thought twice about it. She had now had the cat for over a year, a year and three months to be precise, and he had never acted so unpredictably. Maybe something had startled him.

But she knew in her heart he would come back. And he did, that very night.

The night would change her future eternally.

At first she heard a scratching and horrible wailing at the front door. It was 3:00 A.M.

She was still awake, worried, and she knew it was him and hoped he wasn't hurt, as he sounded as if he may have been at Death's door. She picked him up, noting the blood on his coat. The only animal doctor that was open this late was two hours away, so she inspected the cat herself. There was blood on his coat but no open wounds. Perhaps it was from a fight with another cat? Either way, she needed to get him to the vet, so she opted to take him in to get checked out first thing in the morning and to do what she could for him now.

She wet a soft sponge with warm water and added a drop of mild shampoo. She squeezed the sponge to create a lather, took him into the bathroom, set him in the sink basin, and gently applied the sponge to the blood-matted parts of his coat.

Without warning, Malkin dug his claws into her arm, leaving deep, long gashes from her elbow all the way down to her knuckles. He jumped out of the sink and stood in the doorway, hissing threateningly, and took off out of sight down the hall. This was out of character, even though she knew he didn't like water. He'd never once acted aggressively in the time that she'd had him; his initial reaction to conflict was flight. Her arm was covered with rivulets of blood that dripped into the sink and onto the floor. She cleaned up the mess along with her wounds and wrapped her arm with a towel, the best thing she had at the moment to stop the flow of blood for such a long gash.

She searched the house for him, and there he was. Under the bed. She had to use a flashlight to see him as his form blended into the darkness, but his eyes didn't gleam, not even in the light. Instead, they shone eerily dark. She'd never seen a cat's eyes take on a dark appearance when the light hit.

"Come on, Malkin," coaxed Annaliese as she reached slowly under the bed. "It's okay, I'm not mad."

She spoke to him as if he could understand, and she truly believed that all of her cats did in fact understand. Maybe that was a compensatory response from having no children of her own.

He scratched her again, catching his claw in the towel around her arm and biting on the bare part of her hand, clawing her with his three free paws until he finally came detached from the bloody towel.

She wrapped a clean towel around her arm after applying a salve, and then she settled down for the rest of the night. It was hopeless to tend to the cat any further so she just ignored him, figuring she would take him to the vet first thing in the morning.

What could it be? There was a full moon tonight. Could that be the reason behind his behaviour?

The next day she decided to take a day off from work, which she rarely ever did. The vet said Malkin was fine, and he was up on all of his vaccinations, but if it appeased her mind he would keep the cat overnight. Just in case....

As soon as she got home she jumped in the shower and didn't hear the message that came on her machine. Malkin had injured the veteranarian and had somehow escaped. It was a fairly bad injury considering that it came from a cat, and since Malkin was just a cat, he was exonerated of all blame. The vet's injuries were so bad that they required stitches for a few of the scratches and for two deep bite marks. The "New Message" light blinked, but Annaliese didn't think to check her messages when she got out of the shower as she hadn't been expecting any calls. Certainly not a call like this one.

The scratching and hideous wailing at the door caught her attention and with a towel wrapped tightly around herself, she peeked out the side of the front window only to see Malkin there, all alone. It was still early in the day, not even yet noon, and the drive from the vet's office was about twenty minutes. She had seen the vet take Malkin and put him into a kennel, and it didn't make sense how he could have gotten home so fast.

"What are you doing here?" she asked warmly, but he ran past her as soon as she opened the door.

She went to call the vet using the number on the card they had given her, but noticing the new message, she played it. How could a cat do so much damage as to require stitches? Her

scratches were pretty bad, but she didn't think it required stitching, although that may have been her own obstinacy speaking. The scratches would leave some pretty nasty scars; of that she could be certain.

She followed up the message with a call of concern for the sake of the veteranarian, and also to notify them that Malkin had returned home.

And then the strangeness really began, as if things weren't strange enough. Annalies always set her alarm clock to go off at 6:45 A.M. All she had to do was switch a button to turn the alarm on since the time was already set, and as with many alarm clocks, the alarm was programmed to sound again in ten minutes after hitting the snooze button.

Her alarm went off and she hit the snooze button as she laid there for a moment, letting the ticking of the clock on the wall lull her into a meditation of nothingness as she stared, unblinki and attributed it to her ordeal with Malkin, she decided to force herself out of bed.

She washed her face in the sink and started at her reflection in the mirror that overhung the basin. Stopping to glance into the mirror, she noticed that her eyes, usually a clear blue, took on a very dark appearance; she'd have said black. She heard the alarm go off in the bedroom, which caused her to jump, breaking her from the trance as her eyes returned to their familiar blue again.

She went to shut the clock off and though it should have read 6:55 A.M., the time was 3:10 A.M. She checked the other clocks in her bedroom and the time was correct. That meant the alarm had gone off at three in the morning! Something must be wrong with the clock, she figured, and set it for her usual time, hoping that it would work. And just as she'd hoped, it went off at 6:45, so she assumed that there was some reason for the glitch and ignored the problem; she didn't want to burden herself with more worries than she already had.

Malkin hadn't touched his food and she took extra care to monitor his food dish. He'd gone a whole day without eating. She hadn't seen him since he ran into the house the day before, and he barely made a sound, if any at all. She wondered if he was really there or if she had imagined him running inside the house the day before. But she knew he was around. She could somehow sense his presence.

Something was wrong, but she didn't know what to do. She didn't know if she should chance taking him to the vet again and the pound would probably have him euthanized with the way he had been behaving. In fact, she wanted to just take him and drop him off somewhere, anywhere, as long as he wouldn't come back, but her kindness overcame the uneasy feeling she now had about him.

The next night, the same thing happened. The alarm clock went off at 3:00 A.M. What was going on? She felt a madness rising within her. Three A.M. That was the same time Malkin had come home. Three days ago.

Her mind played a torturous overture, of what she couldn't place. It sounded all but pleasant, like instruments playing out of tune and out of synch. The sounds gradually turned to screams and yells. Painful moans. Unintelligible voices, possibly crying out for some sort of relief.

What was happening? She couldn't explain it or even describe it. The sounds were so horrendous that she knew she couldn't be dreaming or imagining it. Either that, or she was in fact experiencing a bout of madness.

And there was Malkin. Laying relaxed upon a shelf, licking his paw and then turning to stare at her. Behind him was an antique clock that ticked away, loudly, through the screams of the tortured souls that penetrated her mind and causing her great pain that wracked her body. There was a sickness in the pit of her stomach. A helplessness. Sympathy. She could do nothing but listen to the sounds of torture, and sharp pains jabbed her body as if she was experiencing the same horrible fate of those pour souls.

And she felt it. It was what she felt all along. How she knew Malkin was there, even though she couldn't see him. It was a dark presence. The presence crept all around her and she could feel it prying her soul from her body as the darkness overcame her. She watched

Malkin as it happened; his mouth remained motionless but he emitted such a horrendous sound, a cat-like wailing, a horrible wailing, along with the tortured moans. And he appeared to be smiling…smiling! Could it be?

And at the last minute, Annaliese made a decision. She knew it was a sin. An irreparable sin. Perhaps, in this instance, there might be an exception? But all logic was lost in her desperation.

She knew she couldn't fight this Darkness that she now realised was an

Entity. Not a feeling or emotion as she first had thought, but something that could be touched. The

Darkness was actually pursuing her.

She grabbed a golden letter opener that her father had given her, the first thing her eyes had fallen upon. She muttered the words, "God forgive me," hoping that He was listening, as that was possibly her final chance at salvation. She turned her fear into a strength, and with both hands wrapped around the letter opener she plunged it deep into her heart. There was some suffering, but it was over quickly. And in ending her life, she had possibly marred her eternity with a torture that had only been left to her imagination by the screams she had heard. Either way, the Darkness would have won. She was too weak to fight it and had damned her own soul in trying to save herself from the possession of this Entity.

Her lifeless body lay there, the clocks ticking and flashing away. It was 3:03 A.M. It's amazing how much can happen in so little time.

Malkin jumped from his perch, and the television flipped on by itself. It flipped stations andlanded on a "Breaking News" story of a house, not far from his own, that had been the meeting place for those involved in Satanic rituals. He sat in front of the television, as if watching. There were a few animals in cages, their coats covered in blood, and some had even been sacrificed, killed in ways too horrible to be detailed.

His mistress was dead, and now it was time to serve someone new. He listened to the list of names on the news and one name and face stood out. Antonius Rossi. He remembered the name "Tony" from the night of the "meeting" he had been taken to. In fact, he recognized the house they had showed on the news. Tony must have been a nickname because it was undoubtedly him.

Antonius had released the Darkness into the world, and now by contract, Malkin was his servant. Only the death of Antonius could break the contract and truly set the Darkness free, something the cat had to bear in mind. Accidents happen.

THE LEGEND OF SLEEPY HOLLOW
BY WASHINGTON IRVING

Found among the papers of the Late Diedrich Knickerbocker.

> A pleasing land of drowsy head it was,
> Of dreams that wave before the half-shut eye;
> And of gay castles in the clouds that pass,
> Forever flushing round a summer sky. -- Castle of Indolence

In the bosom of one of those spacious coves which indent the eastern shore of the Hudson, at that broad expansion of the river denominated by the ancient Dutch navigators the Tappan

Zee, and where they always prudently shortened sail and implored the protection of St. Nicholas when they crossed, there lies a small market town or rural port, which by some is called Greensburgh, but which is more generally and properly known by the name of Tarry Town. This name was given, we are told, in former days, by the good housewives of the adjacent country, from the inveterate propensity of their husbands to linger about the village tavern on market days. Be that as it may, I do not vouch for the fact, but merely advert to it, for the sake of being precise and authentic. Not far from this village, perhaps about two miles, there is a little valley or rather lap of land among high hills, which is one of the quietest places in the whole world. A small brook glides through it, with just murmur enough to lull one to repose; and the occasional whistle of a quail or tapping of a woodpecker is almost the only sound that ever breaks in upon the uniform tranquillity.

I recollect that, when a stripling, my first exploit in squirrel-shooting was in a grove of tall walnut-trees that shades one side of the valley. I had wandered into it at noontime, when all nature is peculiarly quiet, and was startled by the roar of my own gun, as it broke the Sabbath stillness around and was prolonged and reverberated by the angry echoes. If ever I should wish for a retreat whither I might steal from the world and its distractions, and dream quietly away the remnant of a troubled life, I know of none more promising than this little valley.

From the listless repose of the place, and the peculiar character of its inhabitants, who are descendants from the original Dutch settlers, this sequestered glen has long been known by the name of Sleepy Hollow, and its rustic lads are called the Sleepy Hollow Boys throughout all the neighboring country. A drowsy, dreamy influence seems to hang over the land, and to pervade the very atmosphere. Some say that the place was bewitched by a High German doctor, during the early days of the settlement; others, that an old Indian chief, the prophet or wizard of his tribe, held his powwows there before the country was discovered by Master Hendrick Hudson. Certain it is, the place still continues under the sway of some witching power, that holds a spell over the minds of the good people, causing them to walk in a continual reverie. They are given to all kinds of marvellous beliefs, are subject to trances and visions, and frequently see strange sights, and hear music and voices in the air. The whole neighborhood abounds with local tales, haunted spots, and twilight superstitions; stars shoot and meteors glare oftener across the valley than in any other part of the country, and the nightmare, with her whole ninefold, seems to make it the favorite scene of her gambols.

The dominant spirit, however, that haunts this enchanted region, and seems to be commander-in-chief of all the powers of the air, is the apparition of a figure on horseback, without a head. It is said by some to be the ghost of a Hessian trooper, whose head had been carried away by a cannon-ball, in some nameless battle during the Revolutionary War, and who is ever and anon seen by the country folk hurrying along in the gloom of night, as if on the wings of the wind. His haunts are not confined to the valley, but extend at times to the adjacent roads, and especially to the vicinity of a church at no great distance. Indeed, certain of the most authentic historians of those parts, who have been careful in collecting and collating the floating facts concerning this spectre, allege that the body of the trooper having been buried in the churchyard, the ghost rides forth to the scene of battle in nightly quest of his head, and that the rushing speed with which he sometimes passes along the Hollow, like a midnight blast, is owing to his being belated, and in a hurry to get back to the churchyard before daybreak.

Such is the general purport of this legendary superstition, which has furnished materials for many a wild story in that region of shadows; and the spectre is known at all the country firesides, by the name of the Headless Horseman of Sleepy Hollow.

It is remarkable that the visionary propensity I have mentioned is not confined to the native inhabitants of the valley, but is unconsciously imbibed by every one who resides there for a time. However wide awake they may have been before they entered that sleepy region, they are sure, in a little time, to inhale the witching influence of the air, and begin to grow imaginative, to dream dreams, and see apparitions.

I mention this peaceful spot with all possible laud, for it is in such little retired Dutch valleys, found here and there embosomed in the great State of New York, that population, manners, and customs remain fixed, while the great torrent of migration and improvement, which is making such incessant changes in other parts of this restless country, sweeps by them unobserved. They are like those little nooks of still water, which border a rapid stream, where we may see the straw and bubble riding quietly at anchor, or slowly revolving in their mimic harbor, undisturbed by the rush of the passing current. Though many years have elapsed since I trod the drowsy shades of Sleepy Hollow, yet I question whether I should not still find the same trees and the same families vegetating in its sheltered bosom.

In this by-pl say, some thirty years since, a worthy wight of the name of Ichabod Crane, who sojourned, or, as he expressed it, "tarried," in Sleepy Hollow, for the purpose of instructing the children of the vicinity. He was a native of Connecticut, a State which supplies the Union with pioneers for the mind as well as for the forest, and sends forth yearly its legions of frontier woodmen and country schoolmasters. The cognomen of Crane was not inapplicable to his person. He was tall, but exceedingly lank, with narrow shoulders, long arms and legs, hands that dangled a mile out of his sleeves, feet that might have served for shovels, and his whole frame most loosely hung together. His head was small, and flat at top, with huge ears, large green glassy eyes, and a long snipe nose, so that it looked like a weather-cock perched upon his spindle neck to tell which way the wind blew. To see him striding along the profile of a hill on a windy day, with his clothes bagging and fluttering about him, one might have mistaken him for the genius of famine descending upon the earth, or some scarecrow eloped from a cornfield.

His schoolhouse was a low building of one large room, rudely constructed of logs; the windows partly glazed, and partly patched with leaves of old copybooks. It was most ingeniously secured at vacant hours, by a withe twisted in the handle of the door, and stakes set against the window shutters; so that though a thief might get in with perfect ease, he would find some embarrassment in getting out,--an idea most probably borrowed by the architect, Yost Van Houten, from the mystery of an eelpot. The schoolhouse stood in a rather lonely but pleasant situation, just at the foot of a woody hill, with a brook running close by, and a formidable birch-tree growing at one end of it. From hence the low murmur of his pupils' voices, conning over their lessons, might be heard in a drowsy summer's day, like the hum of a beehive; interrupted now and then by the authoritative voice of the master, in the tone of menace or command, or, peradventure, by the appalling sound of the birch, as he urged some tardy loiterer along the flowery path of knowledge. Truth to say, he was a conscientious man, and ever bore in mind the golden maxim, "Spare the rod and spoil the child." Ichabod Crane's scholars certainly were not spoiled.

I would not have it imagined, however, that he was one of those cruel potentates of the school who joy in the smart of their subjects; on the contrary, he administered justice with discrimination rather than severity; taking the burden off the backs of the weak, and laying it on those of the strong. Your mere puny stripling, that winced at the least flourish of the rod, was passed by with indulgence; but the claims of justice were satisfied by inflicting a double portion on some little tough wrong-headed, broad-skirted Dutch urchin, who sulked and swelled and grew dogged and sullen beneath the birch. All this he called "doing his duty by their parents;" and he never inflicted a chastisement without following it by the assurance, so consolatory to the smarting urchin, that "he would remember it and thank him for it the longest day he had to live."

When school hours were over, he was even the companion and playmate of the larger boys; and on holiday afternoons would convoy some of the smaller ones home, who happened to have pretty sisters, or good housewives for mothers, noted for the comforts of the cupboard. Indeed, it behooved him to keep on good terms with his pupils. The revenue arising from his school was small, and would have been scarcely sufficient to furnish him with daily bread, for he was a huge feeder, and, though lank, had the dilating powers of an anaconda; but to help out his maintenance, he was, according to country custom in those parts, boarded and lodged at the houses of the farmers whose children he instructed. With these he lived successively a week at a time, thus going the rounds of the neighborhood, with all his worldly effects tied up in a cotton handkerchief.

That all this might not be too onerous on the purses of his rustic patrons, who are apt to consider the various ways of rendering himself both useful and agreeable. He assisted the farmers occasionally in the lighter labors of their farms, helped to make hay, mended the fences, took the horses to water, drove the cows from pasture, and cut wood for the winter fire. He laid aside, too, all the dominant dignity and absolute sway with which he lorded it in his little empire, the school, and became wonderfully gentle and ingratiating. He found favor in the eyes of the mothers by petting the children, particularly the youngest; and like the lion bold, which whilom so magnanimously the lamb did hold, he would sit with a child on one knee, and rock a cradle with his foot for whole hours together.

In addition to his other vocations, he was the singing- master of the neighborhood, and picked up many bright shillings by instructing the young folks in psalmody. It was a matter of no little vanity to him on Sundays, to take his station in front of the church gallery, with a band of chosen singers; where, in his own mind, he completely carried away the palm from the parson. Certain it is, his voice resounded far above all the rest of the congregation; and there are peculiar quavers still to be heard in that church, and which may even be heard half a mile off, quite to the opposite side of the millpond, on a still Sunday morning, which are said to be legitimately descended from the nose of Ichabod Crane. Thus, by divers little makeshifts, in that ingenious way which is commonly denominated "by hook and by crook," the worthy pedagogue got on tolerably enough, and was thought, by all who understood nothing of the labor of headwork, to have a wonderfully easy life of it.

The schoolmaster is generally a man of some importance in the female circle of a rural neighborhood; being considered a kind of idle, gentlemanlike personage, of vastly superior taste and accomplishments to the rough country swains, and, indeed, inferior in learning only to the parson. His appearance, therefore, is apt to occasion some little stir at the tea-table of a farmhouse, and the addition of a supernumerary dish of cakes or sweetmeats, or, peradventure, the parade of a silver teapot. Our man of letters, therefore, was peculiarly happy in the smiles of all the country damsels. How he would figure among them in the churchyard, between services on Sundays; gathering grapes for them from the wild vines that overran the surrounding trees; reciting for their amusement all the epitaphs on the tombstones; or sauntering, with a whole bevy of them, along the banks of the adjacent millpond; while the more bashful country bumpkins hung sheepishly back, envying his superior elegance and address.

From his half-itinerant life, also, he was a kind of travelling gazette, carrying the whole budget of local gossip from house to house, so that his appearance was always greeted with satisfaction. He was, moreover, esteemed by the women as a man of great erudition, for he had read several books quite through, and was a perfect master of Cotton Mather's History of New England Witchcraft, in which, by the way, he most firmly and potently believed.

He was, in fact, an odd mixture of small shrewdness and simple credulity. His appetite for the marvellous, and his powers of digesting it, were equally extraordinary; and both had been increased by his residence in this spell-bound region. No tale was too gross or monstrous for his capacious swallow. It was often his delight, after his school was dismissed in the afternoon, to stretch himself on the rich bed of clover bordering the little brook that whimpered by his schoolhouse, and there con over old Mather's direful tales, until the gathering dusk of evening made the printed page a mere mist before his eyes. Then, as he wended his way by swamp and stream and awful woodland, to the farmhouse where he happened to be quartered, every sound of nature, at that witching hour, fluttered his excited imagination,--the moan of the whip-poor-will from the hillside, the boding cry of the tree toad, that harbinger of storm, the dreary hooting of the screech owl, or the sudden rustling in the thicket of birds frightened from their roost. The fireflies, too, which sparkled most vividly in the darkest places, now and then startled him, as one of uncommon brightness would stream across his path; and if, by chance, a huge blockhead of a beetle came winging his blundering flight against him, the poor varlet was ready to give up the ghost, with the idea that he was struck with a witch's token. His only resource on such occasions, either to drown thought or drive away evil spirits, was to sing psalm tunes and the good people of Sleepy Hollow, as they sat by their doors of an evening, were often filled with awe at hearing his nasal melody, in linked sweetness long drawn out, floating from the distant hill, or along the dusky road.

Another of his sources of fearful pleasure was to pass long winter evenings with the old Dutch wives, as they sat spinning by the fire, with a row of apples roasting and spluttering along the hearth, and listen to their marvellous tales of ghosts and goblins, and haunted fields, and haunted brooks, and haunted bridges, and haunted houses, and particularly of the headless horseman, or

Galloping Hessian of the Hollow, as they sometimes called him. He would delight them equally by his anecdotes of witchcraft, and of the direful omens and portentous sights and sounds in the air, which prevailed in the earlier times of Connecticut; and would frighten them woefully with speculations upon comets and shooting stars; and with the alarming fact that the world did absolutely turn round, and that they were half the time topsy-turvy!

But if there was a pleasure in all this, while snugly cuddling in the chimney corner of a chamber that was all of a ruddy glow from the crackling wood fire, and where, of course, no spectre dared to show its face, it was dearly purchased by the terrors of his subsequent walk homewards. What fearful shapes and shadows beset his path, amidst the dim and ghastly glare of a snowy night! With what wistful look did he eye every trembling ray of light streaming across the waste fields from some distant window! How often was he appalled by some shrub covered with snow, which, like a sheeted spectre, beset his very path! How often did he shrink with curdling awe at the sound of his own steps on the frosty crust beneath his feet; and dread to look over his shoulder, lest he should behold some uncouth being tramping close behind him! And how often was he thrown into complete dismay by some rushing blast, howling among the trees, in the idea that it was the Galloping Hessian on one of his nightly scourings!

All these, however, were mere terrors of the night, phantoms of the mind that walk in darkness; and though he had seen many spectres in his time, and been more than once beset by Satan in divers shapes, in his lonely perambulations, yet daylight put an end to all these evils; and he would have passed a pleasant life of it, in despite of the Devil and all his works, if his path had not been crossed by a being that causes more perplexity to mortal man than ghosts, goblins, and the whole race of witches put together, and that was--a woman.

Among the musical disciples who assembled, one evening in each week, to receive his instructions in psalmody, was Katrina Van Tassel, the daughter and only child of a substantial Dutch farmer. She was a blooming lass of fresh eighteen; plump as a partridge; ripe and melting and rosy-cheeked as one of her father's peaches, and universally famed, not merely for her beauty, but her vast expectations. She was withal a little of a coquette, as might be perceived even in her dress, which was a mixture of ancient and modern fashions, as most suited to set off her charms. She wore the ornaments of pure yellow gold, which her great-great-grandmother had brought over from Saardam; the tempting stomacher of the olden time, and withal a provokingly short petticoat, to display the prettiest foot and ankle in the country round.

Ichabod Crane had a soft and foolish heart towards the sex; and it is not to be wondered at that so tempting a morsel soon found favor in his eyes, more especially after he had visited her in her paternal mansion. Old Baltus Van Tassel was a perfect picture of a thriving, contented, liberal-hearted farmer. He seldom, it is true, sent either his eyes or his thoughts beyond the boundaries of his own farm; but within those everything was snug, happy and well-conditioned. He was satisfied with his wealth, but not proud of it; and piqued himself upon the hearty abundance, rather than the style in which he lived. His stronghold was situated on the banks of the Hudson, in one of those green, sheltered, fertile nooks in which the Dutch farmers are so fond of nestling. A great elm tree spread its broad branches over it, at the foot of which bubbled up a spring of the softest and sweetest water, in a little well formed of a barrel; and then stole sparkling away through the grass, to a neighboring brook, that babbled along among alders and dwarf willows. Hard by the farmhouse was a vast barn, that might have served for a church; every window and crevice of which seemed bursting forth with the treasures of the farm; the flail was busily resounding within it from morning to night; swallows and martins skimmed twittering about the eaves; and rows of pigeons, some with one eye turned up, as if watching the weather, some with their heads under their wings or buried in their bosoms, and others swelling, and cooing, and bowing about their dames, were enjoying the sunshine on the roof. Sleek unwieldy porkers were grunting in the repose and abundance of their pens, from whence sallied forth, now and then, troops of sucking pigs, as if to snuff the air. A stately squadron of snowy geese were riding in an adjoining pond, convoying whole fleets of ducks; regiments of turkeys were gobbling through the farmyard, and Guinea fowls fretting about it, like ill-tempered housewives, with their peevish, discontented cry. Before the barn door strutted the gallant cock, that pattern of a husband, a warrior and a fine gentleman, clapping his burnished wings and crowing in the pride and gladness of his heart,--sometimes tearing up the earth with his feet, and then generously calling his ever-hungry family of wives and children to enjoy the rich morsel which he had discovered.

The pedagogue's mouth watered as he looked upon this sumptuous promise of luxurious winter fare. In his devouring mind's eye, he pictured to himself every roasting-pig running about with a pudding in his belly, and an apple in his mouth; the pigeons were snugly put to bed in a comfortable pie, and tucked in with a coverlet of crust; the geese were swimming in their own gravy; and the ducks pairing cosily in dishes, like snug married couples, with a decent competency of onion sauce. In the porkers he saw carved out the future sleek side of bacon, and juicy relishing ham; not a turkey but he beheld daintily trussed up, with its gizzard under its wing, and, peradventure, a necklace of savory sausages; and even bright chanticleer himself lay sprawling on his back, in a side dish, with uplifted claws, as if craving that quarter which his chivalrous spirit disdained to ask while living.

As the enraptured Ichabod fancied all this, and as he rolled his great green eyes over the fat meadow lands, the rich fields of wheat, of rye, of buckwheat, and Indian corn, and the orchards burdened with ruddy fruit, which surrounded the warm tenement of Van Tassel, his heart yearned after the damsel who was to inherit these domains, and his imagination expanded with the idea, how they might be readily turned into cash, and the money invested in immense tracts of wild land, and shingle palaces in the wilderness. Nay, his busy fancy already realized his hopes, and presented to him the blooming Katrina, with a whole family of children, mounted on the top of a wagon loaded with household trumpery, with pots and kettles dangling beneath; and he beheld himself bestriding a pacing mare, with a colt at her heels, setting out for Kentucky, Tennessee,--or the Lord knows where!

When he entered the house, the conquest of his heart was complete. It was one of those spacious farmhouses, with high- ridged but lowly sloping roofs, built in the style handed down from the first Dutch settlers; the low projecting eaves forming a piazza along the front, capable of being closed up in bad weather. Under this were hung flails, harness, various utensils of husbandry, and nets for fishing in the neighboring river. Benches were built along the sides for summer use; and a great spinning-wheel at one end, and a churn at the other, showed the various uses to which this important porch might be devoted. From this piazza the wondering Ichabod entered the hall, which formed the centre of the mansion, and the place of usual residence. Here rows of resplendent pewter, ranged on a long dresser, dazzled his eyes. In one corner stood a huge bag of wool, ready to be spun; in another, a quantity of linsey-woolsey just from the loom; ears of Indian corn, and strings of dried apples and peaches, hung in gay festoons along the walls, mingled with the gaud of red peppers; and a door left ajar gave him a peep into the best parlor, where the claw-footed chairs and dark mahogany tables shone like mirrors; andirons, with their accompanying shovel and tongs, glistened from their covert of asparagus tops; mock- oranges and conch-shells decorated the mantelpiece; strings of various-colored birds eggs were suspended above it; a great ostrich egg was hung from the centre of the room, and a corner cupboard, knowingly left open, displayed immense treasures of old silver and well-mended china.

From the moment Ichabod laid his eyes upon these regions of delight, the peace of his mind was at an end, and his only study was how to gain the affections of the peerless daughter of Van Tassel. In this enterprise, however, he had more real difficulties than generally fell to the lot of a knight-errant of yore, who seldom had anything but giants, enchanters, fiery dragons, and such like easily conquered adversaries, to contend with and had to make his way merely through gates of iron and brass, and walls of adamant to the castle keep, where the lady of his heart was confined; all which he achieved as easily as a man would carve his way to the centre of a Christmas pie; and then the lady gave him her hand as a matter of course. Ichabod, on the contrary, had to win his way to the heart of a country coquette, beset with a labyrinth of whims and caprices, which were forever presenting new difficulties and impediments; and he had to encounter a host of fearful adversaries of real flesh and blood, the numerous rustic admirers, who beset every portal to her heart, keeping a watchful and angry eye upon each other, but ready to fly out in the common cause against any new competitor.

Among these, the most formidable was a burly, roaring, roystering blade, of the name of Abraham, or, according to the Dutch abbreviation, Brom Van Brunt, the hero of the country round, which rang with his feats of strength and hardihood. He was broad-shouldered and double-jointed, with short curly black hair, and a bluff but not unpleasant countenance, having a mingled air of fun and arrogance. From his Herculean frame and great powers of limb he had received the nickname of Brom Bones, by which he was universally known.

He was famed for great knowledge and skill in horsemanship, being as dexterous on horseback as a Tartar. He was foremost at all races and cock fights; and, with the ascendancy which bodily strength always acquires in rustic life, was the umpire in all disputes, setting his hat on one side, and giving his decisions with an air and tone that admitted of no gainsay or appeal. He was always ready for either a fight or a frolic; but had more mischief than ill-will in his composition; and with all his overbearing roughness, there was a strong dash of waggish good humor at bottom. He had three or four boon companions, who regarded him as their model, and at the head of whom he scoured the country, attending every scene of feud or merriment for miles round. In cold weather he was distinguished by a fur cap, surmounted with a flaunting fox's tail; and when the folks at a country gathering descried this wellknown crest at a distance, whisking about among a squad of hard riders, they always stood by for a squall. Sometimes his crew would be heard dashing along past the farmhouses at midnight, with whoop and halloo, like a troop of Don Cossacks; and the old dames, startled out of their sleep, would listen for a moment till the hurry-scurry had clattered by, and then exclaim, "Ay, there goes Brom Bones and his gang!" The neighbors looked upon him with a mixture of awe, admiration, and good-will; and, when any madcap prank or rustic brawl occurred in the vicinity, always shook their heads, and warranted Brom Bones was at the bottom of it.

This rantipole hero had for some time singled out the blooming Katrina for the object of his uncouth gallantries, and though his amorous toyings were something like the gentle caresses and endearments of a bear, yet it was whispered that she did not altogether discourage his hopes. Certain it is, his advances were signals for rival candidates to retire, who felt no inclination to cross a lion in his amours; insomuch, that when his horse was seen tied to Van Tassel's paling, on a Sunday night, a sure sign that his master was courting, or, as it is termed, "sparking," within, all other suitors passed by in despair, and carried the war into other quarters.

Such was the formidable rival with whom Ichabod Crane had to contend, and, considering all things, a stouter man than he would have shrunk from the competition, and a wiser man would have despaired. He had, however, a happy mixture of pliability and perseverance in his nature; he was in form and spirit like a supple-jack--yielding, but tough; though he bent, he never broke; and though he bowed beneath the slightest pressure, yet, the moment it was away--jerk!--he was as erect, and carried his head as high as ever.

To have taken the field openly against his rival would have been madness; for he was not a man to be thwarted in his amours, any more than that stormy lover, Achilles. Ichabod, therefore, made his advances in a quiet and gently insinuating manner. Under cover of his character of singing-master, he made frequent visits at the farmhouse; not that he had anything to apprehend from the meddlesome interference of parents, which is so often a stumbling-block in the path of lovers. Balt Van Tassel was an easy indulgent soul; he loved his daughter better even than his pipe, and, like a reasonable man and an excellent father, let her have her way in everything. His notable little wife, too, had enough to do to attend to her housekeeping and manage her poultry; for, as she sagely observed, ducks and geese are foolish things, and must be looked after, but girls can take care of themselves. Thus, while the busy dame bustled about the house, or plied her spinning-wheel at one end of the piazza, honest Balt would sit smoking his evening pipe at the other, watching the achievements of a little wooden warrior, who, armed with a sword in each hand, was most valiantly fighting the wind on the pinnacle of the barn. In the mean time, Ichabod would carry on his suit with the daughter by the side of the spring under the great elm, or sauntering along in the twilight, that hour so favorable to the lover's eloquence.

I profess not to know how women's hearts are wooed and won. To me they have always been matters of riddle and admiration. Some seem to have but one vulnerable point, or door of access; while others have a thousand avenues, and may be captured in a thousand different ways. It is a great triumph of skill to gain the former, but a still greater proof of generalship to maintain possession of the latter, for man must battle for his fortress at every door and window. He who wins a thousand common hearts is therefore entitled to some renown; but he who keeps undisputed sway over the heart of a coquette is indeed a hero. Certain it is, this was not the case with the redoubtable Brom Bones; and from the moment Ichabod Crane made his advances, the interests of the former evidently declined: his horse was no longer seen tied to the palings on Sunday nights, and a deadly feud gradually arose between him and the preceptor of Sleepy Hollow.

Brom, who had a degree of rough chivalry in his nature, would fain have carried matters to open warfare and have settled their pretensions to the lady, according to the mode of those most concise and simple reasoners, the knights-errant of yore,-- by single combat; but Ichabod was too conscious of the superior might of his adversary to enter the lists against him; he had overheard a boast of Bones, that he would "double the schoolmaster up, and lay him on a shelf of his own schoolhouse;" and he was too wary to give him an opportunity.

There was something extremely provoking in this obstinately pacific system; it left Brom no alternative but to draw upon the funds of rustic waggery in his disposition, and to play off boorish practical jokes upon his rival. Ichabod became the object of whimsical persecution to Bones and his gang of rough riders. They harried his hitherto peaceful domains; smoked out his singing school by stopping up the chimney; broke into the schoolhouse at night, in spite of its formidable fastenings of withe and window stakes, and turned everything topsy-turvy, so that the poor schoolmaster began to think all the witches in the country held their meetings there. But what was still more annoying, Brom took all opportunities of turning him into ridicule in presence of his mistress, and had a scoundrel dog whom he taught to whine in the mos psalmody.

In this way matters went on for some time, without producing any material effect on the relative situations of the contending powers. On a fine autumnal afternoon, Ichabod, in pensive mood, sat enthroned on the lofty stool from whence he usually watched all the concerns of his little literary realm. In his hand he swayed a ferule, that sceptre of despotic power; the birch of justice reposed on three nails behind the throne, a constant terror to evil doers, while on the desk before him might be seen sundry contraband articles and prohibited weapons, detected upon the persons of idle urchins, such as half-munched apples, popguns, whirligigs, fly-cages, and whole legions of rampant little paper gamecocks. Apparently there had been some appalling act of justice recently inflicted, for his scholars were all busily intent upon their books, or slyly whispering behind them with one eye kept upon the master; and a kind of buzzing stillness reigned throughout the schoolroom.

It was suddenly interrupted by the appearance of a negro in tow-cloth jacket and trowsers, a round-crowned fragment of a hat, like the cap of Mercury, and mounted on the back of a ragged, wild, halfbroken colt, which he managed with a rope by way of halter. He came clattering up to the school door with an invitation to Ichabod to attend a merry-making or "quilting frolic," to be held that evening at Mynheer Van Tassel's; and having delivered his message with that air of importance, and effort at fine language, which a negro is apt to display on petty embassies of the kind, he dashed over the brook, and was seen scampering away up the hollow, full of the importance and hurry of his mission.

All was now bustle and hubbub in the late quiet schoolroom. The scholars were hurried through their lessons without stopping at trifles; those who were nimble skipped over half with impunity, and those who were tardy had a smart application now and then in the rear, to quicken their speed or help them over a tall word. Books were flung aside without being put, away on the shelves, inkstands were overturned, benches thrown down, and the whole school was turned loose an hour before the usual time, bursting forth like a legion of young imps, yelping and racketing about the green in joy at their early emancipation.

The gallant Ichabod now spent at least an extra half hour at his toilet, brushing and furbishing up his best, and indeed only suit of rusty black, and arranging his locks by a bit of broken looking-glass that hung up in the schoolhouse. That he might make his appearance before his mistress in the true style of a cavalier, he borrowed a horse from the farmer with whom he was domiciliated, a choleric old Dutchman of the name of Hans Van Ripper, and, thus gallantly mounted, issued forth like a knight- errant in quest of adventures. But it is meet I should, in the true spirit of romantic story, give some account of the looks and equipments of my hero and his steed. The animal he bestrode was a broken-down plow-horse, that had outlived almost everything but its viciousness. He was gaunt and shagged, with a ewe neck, and burs; one eye had lost its pupil, and was glaring and spectral, but the other had the gleam of a genuine devil in it. Still he must have had fire and mettle in his day, if we may judge from the name he bore of Gunpowder. He had, in fact, been a favorite steed of his master's, the choleric Van Ripper, who was a furious rider, and had infused, very probably, some of his own spirit into the animal; for, old and broken-down as he looked, there was more of the lurking devil in him than in any young filly in the country.

Ichabod was a suitable figure for such a steed. He rode with short stirrups, which brought his knees nearly up to the pommel of the saddle; his sharp elbows stuck out like grasshoppers'; he carried his whip perpendicularly in his hand, like a sceptre, and as his horse jogged on, the motion of his arms was not unlike the flapping of a pair of wings. A small wool hat rested on the top of his nose, for so his scanty strip of forehead might be called, and the skirts of his black coat fluttered out almost to the horses tail. Such was the appearance of Ichabod and his steed as they shambled out of the gate of Hans Van Ripper, and it was altogether such an apparition as is seldom to be met with in broad daylight.

It was, as I have said, a fine autumnal day; the sky was clear and serene, and nature wore that rich and golden livery which we always associate with the idea of abundance. The forests had put on their sober brown and yellow, while some trees of the tenderer kind had been nipped by the frosts into brilliant dyes of orange, purple, and scarlet. Streaming files of wild ducks began to make their appearance high in the air; the bark of the squirrel might be heard from the groves of beech and hickory- nuts, and the pensive whistle of the quail at intervals from the neighboring stubble field.

The small birds were taking their farewell banquets. In the fullness of their revelry, they fluttered, chirping and frolicking from bush to bush, and tree to tree, capricious from the very profusion and variety around them. There was the honest cock robin, the favorite game of stripling sportsmen, with its loud querulous note; and the twittering blackbirds flying in sable clouds; and the golden-winged woodpecker with his crimson crest, his broad black gorget, and splendid plumage; and the cedar bird, with its red-tipt wings and yellow-tipt tail and its little monteiro cap of feathers; and the blue jay, that noisy coxcomb, in his gay light blue coat and white underclothes, screaming and chattering, nodding and bobbing and bowing, and pretending to be on good terms with every songster of the grove.

As Ichabod jogged slowly on his way, his eye, ever open to every symptom of culinary abundance, ranged with delight over the treasures of jolly autumn. On all sides he beheld vast store of baskets and barrels for the market; others heaped up in rich piles for the cider-press. Farther on he beheld great fields of Indian corn, with its golden ears peeping from their leafy coverts, and holding out the promise of cakes and hasty- pudding; and the yellow pumpkins lying beneath them, turning up their fair round bellies to the sun, and giving ample prospects of the most luxurious of pies; and anon he passed the fragrant buckwheat fields breathing the odor of the beehive, and as he beheld them, soft anticipations stole over his mind of dainty slapjacks, well buttered, and garnished with honey or treacle, by the delicate little dimpled hand of Katrina Van Tassel.

Thus feeding his mind with many sweet thoughts and "sugared suppositions," he journeyed along the sides of a range of hills which look out upon some of the goodliest scenes of the mighty Hudson. The sun gradually wheeled his broad disk down in the west.

The wide bosom of the Tappan Zee lay motionless and glassy, excepting that here and there a gentle undulation waved and prolonged the blue shadow of the distant mountain. A few amber clouds floated in the sky, without a breath of air to move them. The horizon was of a fine golden tint, changing gradually into a pure apple green, and from that into the deep blue of the mid-heaven. A slanting ray lingered on the woody crests of the precipices that overhung some parts of the river, giving greater depth to the dark gray and purple of their rocky sides. A sloop was loitering in the distance, dropping slowly down with the tide, her sail hanging uselessly against the mast; and as the reflection of the sky gleamed along the still water, it seemed as if the vessel was suspended in the air.

It was toward evening that Ichabod arrived at the castle of the Heer Van Tassel, which he found thronged with the pride and flower of the adjacent country. Old farmers, a spare leathern- faced race, in homespun coats and breeches, blue stockings, huge shoes, and magnificent pewter buckles. Their brisk, withered little dames, in close-crimped caps, longwaisted short gowns, homespun petticoats, with scissors and pincushions, and gay calico pockets hanging on the outside. Buxom lasses, almost as antiquated as their mothers, excepting where a straw hat, a fine ribbon, or perhaps a white frock, gave symptoms of city innovation. The sons, in short square-skirted coats, with rows of stupendous brass buttons, and their hair generally queued in the fashion of the times, especially if they could procure an eel-skin for the purpose, it being esteemed throughout the country as a potent nourisher and strengthener of the hair.

Brom Bones, however, was the hero of the scene, having come to the gathering on his favorite steed Daredevil, a creature, like himself, full of mettle and mischief, and which no one but himself could manage. He was, in fact, noted for preferring vicious animals, given to all kinds of t well-broken horse as unworthy of a lad of spirit.

Fain would I pause to dwell upon the world of charms that burst upon the enraptured gaze of my hero, as he entered the state parlor of Van Tassel's mansion. Not those of the bevy of buxom lasses, with their luxurious display of red and white; but the ample charms of a genuine Dutch country tea-table, in the sumptuous time of autumn. Such heaped up platters of cakes of various and almost indescribable kinds, known only to experienced Dutch housewives! There was the doughty doughnut, the tender oly koek, and the crisp and crumbling cruller; sweet cakes and short cakes, ginger cakes and honey cakes, and the whole family of cakes. And then there were apple pies, and peach pies, and pumpkin pies; besides slices of ham and smoked beef; and moreover delectable dishes of preserved plums, and peaches, and pears, and quinces; not to mention broiled shad and roasted chickens; together with bowls of milk and cream, all mingled higgledy- piggledy, pretty much as I have enumerated them, with the motherly teapot sending up its clouds of vapor from the midst--

Heaven bless the mark! I want breath and time to discuss this banquet as it deserves, and am too eager to get on with my story. Happily, Ichabod Crane was not in so great a hurry as his historian, but did ample justice to every dainty.

He was a kind and thankful creature, whose heart dilated in proportion as his skin was filled with good cheer, and whose spirits rose with eating, as some men's do with drink. He could not help, too, rolling his large eyes round him as he ate, and chuckling with the possibility that he might one day be lord of all this scene of almost unimaginable luxury and splendor. Then, he thought, how soon he'd turn his back upon the old schoolhouse; snap his fingers in the face of Hans Van Ripper, and every other niggardly patron, and kick any itinerant pedagogue out of doors that should dare to call him comrade!

Old Baltus Van Tassel moved about among his guests with a face dilated with content and good humor, round and jolly as the harvest moon. His hospitable attentions were brief, but expressive, being confined to a shake of the hand, a slap on the shoulder, a loud laugh, and a pressing invitation to "fall to, and help themselves."

And now the sound of the music from the common room, or hall, summoned to the dance. The musician was an old gray-headed negro, who had been the itinerant orchestra of the neighborhood for more than half a century. His instrument was as old and battered as himself. The greater part of the time he scraped on two or three strings, accompanying every movement of the bow with a motion of the head; bowing almost to the ground, and stamping with his foot whenever a fresh couple were to start.

Ichabod prided himself upon his dancing as much as upon his vocal powers. Not a limb, not a fibre about him was idle; and to have seen his loosely hung frame in full motion, and clattering about the room, you would have thought St. Vitus himself, that blessed patron of the dance, was figuring before you in person. He was the admiration of all the negroes; who, having gathered, of all ages and sizes, from the farm and the neighborhood, stood forming a pyramid of shining black faces at every door and window, gazing with delight at the scene, rolling their white eyeballs, and showing grinning rows of ivory from ear to ear. How could the flogger of urchins be otherwise than animated and joyous? The lady of his heart was his partner in the dance, and smiling graciously in reply to all his amorous oglings; while Brom Bones, sorely smitten with love and jealousy, sat brooding by himself in one corner.

When the dance was at an end, Ichabod was attracted to a knot of the sager folks, who, with Old Van Tassel, sat smoking at one end of the piazza, gossiping over former times, and drawing out long stories about the war.

This neighborhood, at the time of which I am speaking, was one of those highly favored places which abound with chronicle and great men. The British and American line had run near it during the war; it had, therefore, been the scene of marauding and infested with refugees, cowboys, and all kinds of border chivalry. Just sufficient time had elapsed to enable each storyteller to dress up his tale with a little becoming fiction, and, in the indistinctness of his recollection, to make himself the hero of every exploit.

There was the story of Doffue Martling, a large blue-bearded Dutchman, who had nearly taken a British frigate with an old iron nine-pounder from a mud breastwork, only that his gun burst a being too rich a mynheer to be lightly mentioned, who, in the battle of White Plains, being an excellent master of defence, parried a musket-ball with a small sword, insomuch that he absolutely felt it whiz round the blade, and glance off at the hilt; in proof of which he was ready at any time to show the sword, with the hilt a little bent. There were several more that had been equally great in the field, not one of whom but was persuaded that he had a considerable hand in bringing the war to a happy termination.

But all these were nothing to the tales of ghosts and apparitions that succeeded. The neighborhood is rich in legendary treasures of the kind. Local tales and superstitions thrive best in these sheltered, long-settled retreats; but are trampled under foot by the shifting throng that forms the population of most of our country places. Besides, there is no encouragement for ghosts in most of our villages, for they have scarcely had time to finish their first nap and turn themselves in their graves, before their surviving friends have travelled away from the neighborhood; so that when they turn out at night to walk their rounds, they have no acquaintance left to call upon. This is perhaps the reason why we so seldom hear of ghosts except in our long-established Dutch communities.

The immediate cause, however, of the prevalence of supernatural stories in these parts, was doubtless owing to the vicinity of Sleepy Hollow. There was a contagion in the very air that blew from that haunted region; it breathed forth an atmosphere of dreams and fancies infecting all the land. Several of the Sleepy Hollow people were present at Van Tassel's, and, as usual, were doling out their wild and wonderful legends. Many dismal tales were told about funeral trains, and mourning cries and wailings heard and seen about the great tree where the unfortunate Major André was taken, and which stood in the neighborhood. Some mention was made also of the woman in white, that haunted the dark glen at Raven Rock, and was often heard to shriek on winter nights before a storm, having perished there in the snow.

The chief part of the stories, however, turned upon the favorite spectre of Sleepy Hollow, the Headless Horseman, who had been heard several times of late, patrolling the country; and, it was said, tethered his horse nightly among the graves in the churchyard.

The sequestered situation of this church seems always to have made it a favorite haunt of troubled spirits. It stands on a knoll, surrounded by locust-trees and lofty elms, from among which its decent, whitewashed walls shine modestly forth, like Christian purity beaming through the shades of retirement. A gentle slope descends from it to a silver sheet of water, bordered by high trees, between which, peeps may be caught at the blue hills of the Hudson.

To look upon its grass-grown yard, where the sunbeams seem to sleep so quietly, one would think that there at least the dead might rest in peace. On one side of the church extends a wide woody dell, along which raves a large brook among broken rocks and trunks of fallen trees. Over a deep black part of the stream, not far from the church, was formerly thrown a wooden bridge; the road that led to it, and the bridge itself, were thickly shaded by overhanging trees, which cast a gloom about it, even in the daytime; but occasioned a fearful darkness at night. Such was one of the favorite haunts of the Headless Horseman, and the place where he was most frequently encountered. The tale was told of old Brouwer, a most heretical disbeliever in ghosts, how he met the Horseman returning from his foray into

Sleepy Hollow, and was obliged to get up behind him; how they galloped over bush and brake, over hill and swamp, until they reached the bridge; when the Horseman suddenly turned into a skeleton, threw old Brouwer into the brook, and sprang away over the tree-tops with a clap of thunder.

This story was immediately matched by a thrice marvellous adventure of Brom Bones, who made light of the Galloping Hessian as an arrant jockey. He affirmed that on returning one night from the neighboring village of Sing Sing, he had been overtaken by this midnight trooper; that he had offered to race with him for a bowl of punch, and should have won it too, for Daredevil beat the goblin horse all hollow, but just as they came to the church

bridge, the Hessian bolted, and vanished in a flash of fire.

All these tales, told in that drowsy undertone with which men talk in the dark, the countenances of the listeners only now and then receiving a casual gleam from the glare of a pipe, sank deep in the mind of Ichabod. He repaid them in kind with large extracts from his invaluable author, Cotton Mather, and added many marvellous events that had taken place in his native State of Connecticut, and fearful sights which he had seen in his nightly walks about Sleepy Hollow.

The revel now gradually broke up. The old farmers gathered together their families in their wagons, and were heard for some time rattling along the hollow roads, and over the distant hills. Some of the damsels mounted on pillions behind their favorite swains, and their light-hearted laughter, mingling with the clatter of hoofs, echoed along the silent woodlands, sounding fainter and fainter, until they gradually died away,--and the late scene of noise and frolic was all silent and deserted. Ichabod only lingered behind, according to the custom of country lovers, to have a tête-à-tête with the heiress; fully convinced that he was now on the high road to success. What passed at this interview I will not pretend to say, for in fact I do not know. Something, however, I fear me, must have gone wrong, for he certainly sallied forth, after no very great interval, with an air quite desolate and chapfallen.

Oh, these women! these women! Could that girl have been playing off any of her coquettish tricks? Was her encouragement of the poor pedagogue all a mere sham to secure her conquest of his rival? Heaven only knows, not I! Let it suffice to say, Ichabod stole forth with the air of one who had been sacking a henroost, rather than a fair lady's heart. Without looking to the right or left to notice the scene of rural wealth, on which he had so often gloated, he went straight to the stable, and with several hearty cuffs and kicks roused his steed most uncourteously from the comfortable quarters in which he was soundly sleeping, dreaming of mountains of corn and oats, and whole valleys of timothy and clover.

It was the very witching time of night that Ichabod, heavy-hearted and crestfallen, pursued his travels homewards, along the sides of the lofty hills which rise above Tarry Town, and which he had traversed so cheerily in the afternoon. The hour was as dismal as himself. Far below him the Tappan Zee spread its dusky and indistinct waste of waters, with here and there the tall mast of a sloop, riding quietly at anchor under the land. In the dead hush of midnight, he could even hear the barking of the watchdog from the opposite shore of the Hudson; but it was so vague and faint as only to give an idea of his distance from this faithful companion of man. Now and then, too, the long-drawn crowing of a cock, accidentally awakened, would sound far, far off, from some farmhouse away among the hills--but it was like a dreaming sound in his ear. No signs of life occurred near him, but occasionally the melancholy chirp of a cricket, or perhaps the guttural twang of a bullfrog from a neighboring marsh, as if sleeping uncomfortably and turning suddenly in his bed.

All the stories of ghosts and goblins that he had heard in the afternoon now came crowding upon his recollection. The night grew darker and darker; the stars seemed to sink deeper in the sky, and driving clouds occasionally hid them from his sight. He had never felt so lonely and dismal. He was, moreover, approaching the very place where many of the scenes of the ghost stories had been laid. In the centre of the road stood an enormous tuliptree, which towered like a giant above all the other trees of the neighborhood, and formed a kind of landmark. Its limbs were gnarled and fantastic, large enough to form trunks for ordinary trees, twisting down almost to the earth, and rising again into the air. It was connected with the tragical story of the unfortunate André, who had been taken prisoner hard by; and was universally known by the name of Major André's tree. The common people regarded it with a mixture of respect and superstition, partly out of sympathy for the fate of its ill- starred namesake, and partly from the tales of strange sights, and doleful lamentations, told concerning it.

As Ichabod approached this fearful tree, he began to whistle; he thought his whistle was answered; it was but a blast sweeping sharply through the dry branches. As he approached a little nearer, he thought he saw something white, hanging in the midst of the tree: he paused and ceased whistling but, on looking more narrowly, perceived that it was a place where the tree had been scathed by lightning, and the white wood laid bare. Suddenly he heard a groan-- his teeth chattered, and his knees smote against the saddle: it was but the rubbing of one huge bough upon an but new perils lay before him.

About two hundred yards from the tree, a small brook crossed the road, and ran into a marshy and thickly-wooded glen, known by the name of Wiley's Swamp. A few rough logs, laid side by side, served for a bridge over this stream. On that side of the road where the brook entered the wood, a group of oaks and chestnuts, matted thick with wild grape-vines, threw a cavernous gloom over it. To pass this bridge was the severest trial. It was at this identical spot that the unfortunate André was captured, and under the covert of those chestnuts and vines were the sturdy yeomen concealed who surprised him. This has ever since been considered a haunted stream, and fearful are the feelings of the schoolboy who has to pass it alone after dark.

As he approached the stream, his heart began to thump; he summoned up, however, all his resolution, gave his horse half a score of kicks in the ribs, and attempted to dash briskly across the bridge; but instead of starting forward, the perverse old animal made a lateral movement, and ran broadside against the fence. Ichabod, whose fears increased with the delay, jerked the reins on the other side, and kicked lustily with the contrary foot: it was all in vain; his steed started, it is true, but it was only to plunge to the opposite side of the road into a thicket of brambles and alder bushes. The schoolmaster now bestowed both whip and heel upon the starveling ribs of old Gunpowder, who dashed forward, snuffling and snorting, but came to a stand just by the bridge, with a suddenness that had nearly sent his rider sprawling over his head. Just at this moment a plashy tramp by the side of the bridge caught the sensitive ear of Ichabod. In the dark shadow of the grove, on the margin of the brook, he beheld something huge, misshapen and towering. It stirred not, but seemed gathered up in the gloom, like some gigantic monster ready to spring upon the traveller.

The hair of the affrighted pedagogue rose upon his head with terror. What was to be done? To turn and fly was now too late; and besides, what chance was there of escaping ghost or goblin, if such it was, which could ride upon the wings of the wind? Summoning up, therefore, a show of courage, he demanded in stammering accents, "Who are you?"

He received no reply. He repeated his demand in a still more agitated voice. Still there was no answer. Once more he cudgelled the sides of the inflexible Gunpowder, and, shutting his eyes, broke forth with involuntary fervor into a psalm tune. Just then the shadowy object of alarm put itself in motion, and with a scramble and a bound stood at once in the middle of the road. Though the night was dark and dismal, yet the form of the unknown might now in some degree be ascertained. He appeared to be a horseman of large dimensions, and mounted on a black horse of powerful frame. He made no offer of molestation or sociability, but kept aloof on one side of the road, jogging along on the blind side of old Gunpowder, who had now got over his fright and waywardness.

Ichabod, who had no relish for this strange midnight companion, and bethought himself of the adventure of Brom Bones with the Galloping Hessian, now quickened his steed in hopes of leaving him behind. The stranger, however, quickened his horse to an equal pace.

Ichabod pulled up, and fell into a walk, thinking to lag behind,--the other did the same. His heart began to sink within him; he endeavored to resume his psalm tune, but his parched tongue clove to the roof of his mouth, and he could not utter a stave. There was something in the moody and dogged silence of this pertinacious companion that was mysterious and appalling. It was soon fearfully accounted for. On mounting a rising ground, which brought the figure of his fellow-traveller in relief against the sky, gigantic in height, and muffled in a cloak, Ichabod was horror-struck on perceiving that he was headless!--but his horror was still more increased on observing that the head, which should have rested on his shoulders, was carried before him on the pommel of his saddle! His terror rose to desperation; he rained a shower of kicks and blows upon Gunpowder, hoping by a sudden movement to give his companion the slip; but the spectre started full jump with him. Away, then, they dashed

through thick and thin; stones flying and sparks flashing at every bound. Ichabod's flimsy garments fluttered in the air, as he stretched his long lank body away over his horse's head, in the eagerness of his flight.

They had now reached the road which turns off to Sleepy Hollow; but Gunpowder, who seemed possessed with a demon, instead of keeping up it, made an opposite turn, and plunged headlong downhill to the left. This road leads through a sandy hollow shaded by trees for about a quarter of a mile, where it crosses the bridge famous in goblin story; and just beyond swells the green knoll on which stands the whitewashed church.

As yet the panic of the steed had given his unskilful rider an apparent advantage in the chase, but just as he had got half way through the hollow, the girths of the saddle gave way, and he felt it slipping from under him. He seized it by the pommel, and endeavored to hold it firm, but in vain; and had just time to save himself by clasping old Gunpowder round the neck, when the saddle fell to the earth, and he heard it trampled under foot by his pursuer.

For a moment the terror of Hans Van Ripper's wrath passed across his mind,--for it was his Sunday saddle; but this was no time for petty fears; the goblin was hard on his haunches; and (unskilful rider that he was!) he had much ado to maintain his seat; sometimes slipping on one side, sometimes on another, and sometimes jolted on the high ridge of his horse's backbone, with a violence that he verily feared would cleave him asunder.

An opening in the trees now cheered him with the hopes that the church bridge was at hand. The wavering reflection of a silver star in the bosom of the brook told him that he was not mistaken. He saw the walls of the church dimly glaring under the trees beyond. He recollected the place where Brom Bones's ghostly competitor had disappeared. "If I can but reach that bridge," thought Ichabod, "I am safe." Just then he heard the black steed panting and blowing close behind him; he even fancied that he felt his hot breath. Another convulsive kick in the ribs, and old Gunpowder sprang upon the bridge; he thundered over the resounding planks; he gained the opposite side; and now Ichabod cast a look behind to see if his pursuer should vanish, according to rule, in a flash of fire and brimstone. Just then he saw the goblin rising in his stirrups, and in the very act of hurling his head at him. Ichabod endeavored to dodge the horrible missile, but too late. It encountered his cranium with a tremendous crash,--he was tumbled headlong into the dust, and Gunpowder, the black steed, and the goblin rider, passed by like a whirlwind.

The next morning the old horse was found without his saddle, and with the bridle under his feet, soberly cropping the grass at his master's gate. Ichabod did not make his appearance at breakfast; dinner-hour came, but no Ichabod. The boys assembled at the schoolhouse, and strolled idly about the banks of the brook; but no schoolmaster. Hans Van Ripper now began to feel some uneasiness about the fate of poor Ichabod, and his saddle. An inquiry was set on foot, and after diligent investigation they came upon his traces. In one part of the road leading to the church was found the saddle trampled in the dirt; the tracks of horses' hoofs deeply dented in the road, and evidently at furious speed, were traced to the bridge, beyond which, on the bank of a broad part of the brook, where the water ran deep and black, was found the hat of the unfortunate Ichabod, and close beside it a shattered pumpkin.

The brook was searched, but the body of the schoolmaster was not to be discovered.

Hans Van Ripper as executor of his estate, examined the bundle which contained all his worldly effects. They consisted of two shirts and a half; two stocks for the neck; a pair or two of worsted stockings; an old pair of corduroy small- clothes; a rusty razor; a book of psalm tunes full of dog's-ears; and a broken pitch-pipe. As to the books and furniture of the schoolhouse, they belonged to the community, excepting Cotton Mather's History of Witchcraft, a New England Almanac, and a book of dreams and fortune-telling; in which last was a sheet of foolscap much scribbled and blotted in several fruitless attempts to make a copy of verses in honor of the heiress of Van Tassel. These magic books and the poetic scrawl were forthwith consigned to the flames by Hans Van Ripper; who, from that time forward, determined to send his children no more to school, observing that he never knew any good come of this same reading and writing. Whatever money the schoolmaster possessed, and he had received his quarter's pay but a day or two before, he must have had about his person at the time of his disappearance.

The mysterious event caused much speculation at the church on the following Sunday.

Knots of gazers and gossips were collected in the churchyard, at the bridge, and at the spot where the hat and pumpkin had been found. The stories of Brouwer, of Bones, and a whole budget of others were called to mind; and when they had diligently considered them all, and compared them with the symptoms of the present case, they shook their heads, and came to the conclusion that Ichabod had been carried off by the Galloping Hessian. As he was a bachelor, and in nobody's debt, nobody troubled his head any more about him; the school was removed to a different quarter of the hollow, and another pedagogue reigned in his stead.

It is true, an old farmer, who had been down to New York on a visit several years after, and from whom this account of the ghostly adventure was received, brought home the intelligence that Ichabod Crane was still alive; that he had left the neighborhood partly through fear of the goblin and Hans Van Ripper, and partly in mortification at having been suddenly dismissed by the heiress; that he had changed his quarters to a distant part of the country; had kept school and studied law at the same time; had been admitted to the bar; turned politician; electioneered; written for the newspapers; and finally had been made a justice of the Ten Pound Court. Brom Bones, too, who, shortly after his rival's disappearance conducted the blooming Katrina in triumph to the altar, was observed to look exceedingly knowing whenever the story of Ichabod was related, and always burst into a hearty laugh at the mention of the pumpkin; which led some to suspect that he knew more about the matter than he chose to tell.

The old country wives, however, who are the best judges of these matters, maintain to this day that Ichabod was spirited away by supernatural means; and it is a favorite story often   told about the neighborhood round the winter evening fire. The bridge became more than ever an object of superstitious awe; and that may be the reason why the road has been altered of late years, so as to approach the church by the border of the millpond. The schoolhouse being deserted soon fell to decay, and was reported to be haunted by the ghost of the unfortunate pedagogue and the plowboy, loitering homeward of a still summer evening, has often fancied his voice at a distance, chanting a melancholy psalm tune among the tranquilsolitudes of Sleepy Hollow.

The End

THE MONKEY'S PAW
BY W. W. JACOBS

I.

WITHOUT, the night was cold and wet, but in the small parlour of Laburnam Villa the blinds were drawn and the fire burned brightly. Father and son were at chess, the former, who possessed ideas about the game involving radical changes, putting his king into suchsharp and unnecessary perils that it even provoked comment from the white-haired old lady knitting placidly by the fire.

"Hark at the wind," said Mr. White, who, having seen a fatal mistake after it was too late, was amiably desirous of preventing his son from seeing it.

"I'm listening," said the latter, grimly surveying the board as he stretched out his hand.

"Check."

"I should hardly think that he'd come to-night," said his father, with his hand poised over the board.

"Mate," replied the son.

"That's the worst of living so far out," bawled Mr. White, with sudden and unlooked-for violence; "of all the beastly, slushy, out-of-the-way places to live in, this is the worst.

Pathway's a bog, and the road's a torrent. I don't know what people are thinking about. I suppose because only two houses on the road are let, they think it doesn't matter."

"Never mind, dear," said his wife soothingly; "perhaps you'll win the next one."

Mr. White looked up sharply, just in time to intercept a knowing glance between mother and son. The words died away on his lips, and he hid a guilty grin in his thin grey beard.

"There he is," said Herbert White, as the gate banged to loudly and heavy footsteps came toward the door.

The old man rose with hospitable haste, and opening the door, was heard condoling with the new arrival. The new arrival also condoled with himself, so that Mrs. White said, "Tut, tut!" and coughed gently as her husband entered the room, followed by a tall burly man, beady of eye and rubicund of visage.

"Sergeant-Major Morris," he said, introducing him.

The sergeant-major shook hands, and taking the proffered seat by the fire, watched contentedly while his host got out whiskey and tumblers and stood a small copper kettle on the fire.

At the third glass his eyes got brighter, and he began to talk, the little family circle regarding with eager interest this visitor from distant parts, as he squared his broad shoulders in the chair and spoke of strange scenes and doughty deeds; of wars and plagues and strange peoples.

"Twenty-one years of it," said Mr. White, nodding at his wife and son. "When he went away he was a slip of a youth in the warehouse. Now look at him."

"He don't look to have taken much harm," said Mrs. White, politely.

"I'd like to go to India myself," said the old man, "just to look round a bit, you know."

"Better where you are," said the sergeant-major, shaking his head. He put down the empty glass, and sighing softly, shook it again.

"I should like to see those old temples and fakirs and jugglers," said the old man. "What was that you started telling me the other day about a monkey's paw or something, Morris?"

"Nothing," said the soldier hastily. "Leastways, nothing worth hearing."

"Monkey's paw?" said Mrs. White curiously.

"Well, it's just a bit of what you might call magic, perhaps," said the sergeant-major offhandedly.

His three listeners leaned forward eagerly. The visitor absentmindedly put his empty glass to his lips and then set it down again. His host filled it for him.

"To look at," said the sergeant-major, fumbling in his pocket, "it's just an ordinary little paw, dried to a mummy."

He took something out of his pocket and proffered it. Mrs. White drew back with a grimace, but her son, taking it, examined it curiously.

"And what is there special about it?" inquired Mr. White, as he took it from his son and, having examined it, placed it upon the table.

"It had a spell put on it by an old fakir," said the sergeant-major, "a very holy man. He wanted to show that fate ruled people's lives, and that those who interfered with it did so to their sorrow. He put a spell on it so that three separate men could each have three wishes from it."

His manner was so impressive that his hearers were conscious that their light laughter jarred somewhat.

"Well, why don't you have three, sir?" said Herbert White cleverly.

The soldier regarded him in the way that middle age is wont to regard presumptuous youth. "I have," he said quietly, and his blotchy face whitened.

"And did you really have the three wishes granted?" asked Mrs. White.

"I did," said the sergeant-major, and his glass tapped against his strong teeth.

"And has anybody else wished?" inquired the old lady.

"The first man had his three wishes, yes," was the reply. "I don't know what the first two were, but the third was for death. That's how I got the paw."

His tones were so grave that a hush fell upon the group.

"If you've had your three wishes, it's no good to you now, then, Morris," said the old man at last. "What do you keep it for?"

The soldier shook his head. "Fancy, I suppose," he said slowly.

"If you could have another three wishes," said the old man, eyeing him keenly, "would you have them?"

"I don't know," said the other. "I don't know."

He took the paw, and dangling it between his front finger and thumb, suddenly threw it upon the fire. White, with a slight cry, stooped down and snatched it off.

"Better let it burn," said the soldier solemnly.

"If you don't want it, Morris," said the old man, "give it to me."

"I won't," said his friend doggedly. "I threw it on the fire. If you keep it, don't blame me for what happens. Pitch it on the fire again, like a sensible man."

The other shook his head and examined his new possession closely. "How do you do it?" he inquired.

"Hold it up in your right hand and wish aloud,' said the sergeant-major, "but I warn you of the consequences."

"Sounds like the Arabian Nights," said Mrs White, as she rose and began to set the supper.

"Don't you think you might wish for four pairs of hands for me?"

Her husband drew the talisman from his pocket and then all three burst into laughter as the sergeant-major, with a look of alarm on his face, caught him by the arm.

"If you must wish," he said gruffly, "wish for something sensible."

Mr. White dropped it back into his pocket, and placing chairs, motioned his friend to the table. In the business of supper the talisman was partly forgotten, and afterward the three sat listening in an enthralled fashion to a second instalment of the soldier's adventures in India.

"If the tale about the monkey paw is not more truthful than those he has been telling us," said Herbert, as the door closed behind their guest, just in time for him to catch the last train, "we shan't make much out of it."

"Did you give him anything for it, father?" inquired Mrs. White, regarding her husbandclosely.

"A trifle," said he, colouring slightly. "He didn't want it, but I made him take it. And he pressed me again to throw it away."

"Likely," said Herbert, with pretended horror. "Why, we're going to be rich, and famous, and happy. Wish to be an emperor, father, to begin with; then you can't be henpecked."

He darted round the table, pursued by the maligned Mrs. White armed with an antimacassar.

Mr. White took the paw from his pocket and eyed it dubiously. "I don't know what to wish for, and that's a fact," he said slowly. "It seems to me I've got all I want."

"If you only cleared the house, you'd be quite happy, wouldn't you?" said Herbert, with

his hand on his shoulder. "Well, wish for two hundred pounds, then; that'll just do it."

His father, smiling shamefacedly at his own credulity, held up the talisman, as his son, with a solemn face somewhat marred by a wink at his mother, sat down at the piano and struck a few impressive chords.

"I wish for two hundred pounds," said the old man distinctly.

A fine crash from the piano greeted the words, interrupted by a shuddering cry from the old man. His wife and son ran toward him.

"It moved, he cried, with a glance of disgust at the object as it lay on the floor. "As I wished it twisted in my hands like a snake."

"Well, I don't see the money," said his son, as he picked it up and placed it on the table, "and I bet I never shall."

"It must have been your fancy, father," said his wife, regarding him anxiously.

He shook his head. "Never mind, though; there's no harm done, but it gave me a shock all the same."

They sat down by the fire again while the two men finished their pipes. Outside, the wind was higher than ever, and the old man started nervously at the sound of a door banging upstairs. A silence unusual and depressing settled upon all three, which lasted until the old couple rose to retire for the night.

"I expect you'll find the cash tied up in a big bag in the middle of your bed," said Herbert, as he bade them good-night, "and something horrible squatting up on top of the wardrobe watching you as you pocket your ill-gotten gains."

He sat alone in the darkness, gazing at the dying fire, and seeing faces in it. The last face was so horrible and so simian that he gazed at it in amazement. It got so vivid that, with a little uneasy laugh, he felt on the table for a glass containing a little water to throw over it.

His hand grasped the monkey's paw, and with a little shiver he wiped his hand on his coat and went up to bed.

II.

IN the brightness of the wintry sun next morning as it streamed over the breakfast table

Herbert laughed at his fears. There was an air of prosaic wholesomeness about the room which it had lacked on the previous night, and the dirty, shrivelled little paw was pitched on the sideboard with a carelessness which betokened no great belief in its virtues.

"I suppose all old soldiers are the same," said Mrs White. "The idea of our listening to such nonsense! How could wishes be granted in these days? And if they could, how could two hundred pounds hurt you, father?"

"Might drop on his head from the sky," said the frivolous Herbert.

"Morris said the things happened so naturally," said his father, "that you might if you so wished attribute it to coincidence."

"Well, don't break into the money before I come back," said Herbert, as he rose from the table. "I'm afraid it'll turn you into a mean, avaricious man, and we shall have to disown you."

His mother laughed, and following him to the door, watched him down the road, and returning to the breakfast table, was very happy at the expense of her husband's credulity. All of which did not prevent her from scurrying to the door at the postman's knock, nor prevent her from referring somewhat shortly to retired sergeant-majors of bibulous habits when she found that the post brought a tailor's bill.

"Herbert will have some more of his funny remarks, I expect, when he comes home," she said, as they sat at dinner.

"I dare say," said Mr. White, pouring himself out some beer; "but for all that, the thing moved in my hand; that I'll swear to."

"You thought it did," said the old lady soothingly.

"I say it did," replied the other. "There was no thought about it; I had just---- What's the matter?"

His wife made no reply. She was watching the mysterious movements of a man outside, who, peering in an undecided fashion at the house, appeared to be trying to make up his mind to enter. In mental connection with the two hundred pounds, she noticed that the stranger was well dressed and wore a silk hat of glossy newness. Three times he paused at the gate, and then walked on again. The fourth time he stood with his hand upon it, and then with sudden resolution flung it open and walked up the path. Mrs. White at the same moment placed her hands behind her, and hurriedly unfastening the strings of her apron, put that useful article of apparel beneath the cushion of her chair.

She brought the stranger, who seemed ill at ease, into the room. He gazed at her furtively, and listened in a preoccupied fashion as the old lady apologized for the appearance of the room, and her husband's coat, a garment which he usually reserved for the garden. She then waited as patiently as her sex would permit, for him to broach his business, but he was at first strangely silent.

"I--was asked to call," he said at last, and stooped and picked a piece of cotton from his trousers. "I come from Maw and Meggins."

The old lady started. "Is anything the matter?" she asked breathlessly. "Has anything happened to Herbert? What is it? What is it?"

Her husband interposed. "There, there, mother," he said hastily. "Sit down, and don't jump to conclusions. You've not brought bad news, I'm sure, sir" and he eyed the other wistfully.

"I'm sorry----" began the visitor.

"Is he hurt?" demanded the mother.

The visitor bowed in assent. "Badly hurt," he said quietly, "but he is not in any pain."

"Oh, thank God!" said the old woman, clasping her hands. "Thank God for that!

Thank----"

She broke off suddenly as the sinister meaning of the assurance dawned upon her and she saw the awful confirmation of her fears in the other's averted face. She caught her breath, and turning to her slower-witted husband, laid her trembling old hand upon his. There was a long silence.

"He was caught in the machinery," said the visitor at length, in a low voice.

"Caught in the machinery," repeated Mr. White, in a dazed fashion, "yes."

He sat staring blankly out at the window, and taking his wife's hand between his own, pressed it as he had been wont to do in their old courting days nearly forty years before.

"He was the only one left to us," he said, turning gently to the visitor. "It is hard."

The other coughed, and rising, walked slowly to the window. "The firm wished me to convey their sincere sympathy with you in your great loss," he said, without looking round.

"I beg that you will understand I am only their servant and merely obeying orders."

There was no reply; the old woman's face was white, her eyes staring, and her breath inaudible; on the husband's face was a look such as his friend the sergeant might have carried into his first action.

"I was to say that Maw and Meggins disclaim all responsibility," continued the other.

"They admit no liability at all, but in consideration of your son's services they wish to present you with a certain sum as compensation."

Mr. White dropped his wife's hand, and rising to his feet, gazed with a look of horror at his visitor. His dry lips shaped the words, "How much?"

"Two hundred pounds," was the answer.

Unconscious of his wife's shriek, the old man smiled faintly, put out his hands like a sightless man, and dropped, a senseless heap, to the floor.

III.

IN the huge new cemetery, some two miles distant, the old people buried their dead, and came back to a house steeped in shadow and silence. It was all over so quickly that at first they could hardly realize it, and remained in a state of expectation as though of something else to happen--something else which was to lighten this load, too heavy for old hearts to bear.

But the days passed, and expectation gave place to resignation--the hopeless resignation of the old, sometimes miscalled, apathy. Sometimes they hardly exchanged a word, for now they had nothing to talk about, and their days were long to weariness.

It was about a week after that that the old man, waking suddenly in the night, stretched out his hand and found himself alone. The room was in darkness, and the sound of subdued weeping came from the window. He raised himself in bed and listened.

"Come back," he said tenderly. "You will be cold."

"It is colder for my son," said the old woman, and wept afresh.

The sound of her sobs died away on his ears. The bed was warm, and his eyes heavy with sleep. He dozed fitfully, and then slept until a sudden wild cry from his wife awoke him with a start.

"The paw!" she cried wildly. "The monkey's paw!"

He started up in alarm. "Where? Where is it? What's the matter?"

She came stumbling across the room toward him. "I want it," she said quietly. "You've not destroyed it?"

"It's in the parlour, on the bracket," he replied, marvelling. "Why?"

She cried and laughed together, and bending over, kissed his cheek.

"I only just thought of it," she said hysterically. "Why didn't I think of it before? Why didn't you think of it?"

"Think of what?" he questioned.

"The other two wishes," she replied rapidly. "We've only had one."

"Was not that enough?" he demanded fiercely.

"No," she cried, triumphantly; "we'll have one more. Go down and get it quickly, and wish our boy alive again."

The man sat up in bed and flung the bedclothes from his quaking limbs. "Good God, you are mad!" he cried aghast.

"Get it," she panted; "get it quickly, and wish---- Oh, my boy, my boy!"

Her husband struck a match and lit the candle. "Get back to bed," he said, unsteadily.

"You don't know what you are saying."

"We had the first wish granted," said the old woman, feverishly; "why not the second."

"A coincidence," stammered the old man.

"Go and get it and wish," cried the old woman, quivering with excitement.

The old man turned and regarded her, and his voice shook. "He has been dead ten days, and besides he--I would not tell you else, but--I could only recognize him by his clothing. If he was too terrible for you to see then, how now?"

"Bring him back," cried the old woman, and dragged him toward the door. "Do you think I fear the child I have nursed?"

He went down in the darkness, and felt his way to the parlour, and then to the mantelpiece. The talisman was in its place, and a horrible fear that the unspoken wish might bring his mutilated son before him ere he could escape from the room seized upon him, and he caught his breath as he found that he had lost the direction of the door. His brow cold with sweat, he felt his way round the table, and groped along the wall until he found himself in the small passage with the unwholesome thing in his hand.

Even his wife's face seemed changed as he entered the room. It was white and expectant, and to his fears seemed to have an unnatural look upon it. He was afraid of her.

"Wish!" she cried, in a strong voice.

"It is foolish and wicked," he faltered.

"Wish!" repeated his wife.

He raised his hand. "I wish my son alive again."

The talisman fell to the floor, and he regarded it fearfully. Then he sank trembling into a chair as the old woman, with burning eyes, walked to the window and raised the blind.

He sat until he was chilled with the cold, glancing occasionally at the figure of the old woman peering through the window. The candle end, which had burnt below the rim of the china candlestick, was throwing pulsating shadows on the ceiling and walls, until, with a flicker larger than the rest, it expired. The old man, with an unspeakable sense of relief at the failure of the talisman, crept back to his bed, and a minute or two afterward the old woman came silently and apathetically beside him.

Neither spoke, but both lay silently listening to the ticking of the clock. A stair creaked, and a squeaky mouse scurried noisily through the wall. The darkness was oppressive, and after lying for some time screwing up his courage, the husband took the box of matches, and striking one, went downstairs for a candle.

At the foot of the stairs the match went out, and he paused to strike another, and at the same moment a knock, so quiet and stealthy as to be scarcely audible, sounded on the front door.

The matches fell from his hand. He stood motionless, his breath suspended until the knock was repeated. Then he turned and fled swiftly back to his room, and closed the door behind him. A third knock sounded through the house.

"What's that?" cried the old woman, starting up.

"A rat," said the old man, in shaking tones--"a rat. It passed me on the stairs."

His wife sat up in bed listening. A loud knock resounded through the house.

"It's Herbert!" she screamed. "It's Herbert!"

She ran to the door, but her husband was before her, and catching her by the arm, held her tightly.

"What are you going to do?" he whispered hoarsely.

"It's my boy; it's Herbert!" she cried, struggling mechanically. "I forgot it was two miles

away. What are you holding me for? Let go. I must open the door."

"For God's sake, don't let it in," cried the old man trembling.

"You're afraid of your own son," she cried, struggling. "Let me go. I'm coming, Herbert;   I'm coming."

There was another knock, and another. The old woman with a sudden wrench broke free and ran from the room. Her husband followed to the landing, and called after her appealingly as she hurried downstairs. He heard the chain rattle back and the bottom bolt drawn slowly and stiffly from the socket. Then the old woman's voice, strained and panting.

"The bolt," she cried loudly. "Come down. I can't reach it."

But her husband was on his hands and knees groping wildly on the floor in search of the paw. If he could only find it before the thing outside got in. A perfect fusillade of knocks reverberated through the house, and he heard the scraping of a chair as his wife put it down in the passage against the door. He heard the creaking of the bolt as it came slowly back, and at the same moment he found the monkey's paw, and frantically breathed his third and last wish.

The knocking ceased suddenly, although the echoes of it were still in the house. He heard the chair drawn back and the door opened. A cold wind rushed up the staircase, and a long loud wail of disappointment and misery from his wife gave him courage to run down to her side, and then to the gate beyond. The street lamp flickering opposite shone on a quiet and deserted road.

THE TEMPLE

BY H·P· LOVECRAFT

(Manuscript found on the coast of Yucatan.)

On August 20, 1917, I, Karl Heinrich, Graf von Altberg-Ehrenstein, Lieutenant-Commander in the Imperial German Navy and in charge of the submarine U-29, deposit this bottle and record in the Atlantic Ocean at a point to me unknown but probably about N. Latitude 20°, W. Longitude 35°, where my ship lies disabled on the ocean floor. I do so because of my desire to set certain unusual facts before the public; a thing I shall not in all probability survive to accomplish in person, since the circumstances surrounding me are as menacing as they are extraordinary, and involve not only the hopeless crippling of the U-29, but the impairment of my iron German will in a manner most disastrous.

On the afternoon of June 18, as reported by wireless to the U-61, bound for Kiel, we torpedoed the British freighter Victory, New York to Liverpool, in N. Latitude 45° 16', W. Longitude 28° 34'; permitting the crew to leave in boats in order to obtain a good cinema view for the admiralty records. The ship sank quite picturesquely, bow first, the stern rising high out of the water whilst the hull shot down perpendicularly to the bottom of the sea. Our camera missed nothing, and I regret that so fine a reel of film should never reach Berlin. After that we sank the lifeboats with our guns and submerged.

When we rose to the surface about sunset a seaman's body was found on the deck, hands gripping the railing in curious fashion. The poor fellow was young, rather dark, and very handsome; probably an Italian or Greek, and undoubtedly of the Victory's crew. He had evidently sought refuge on the very ship which had been forced to destroy his own—one more victim of the unjust war of aggression which the English pig-dogs are waging upon the Fatherland. Our men searched him for souvenirs, and found in his coat pocket a very odd bit of ivory carved to represent a youth's head crowned with laurel. My fellow-officer, Lieut. Klenze, believed that the thing was of great age and artistic value, so took it from the men for himself. How it had ever come into the possession of a common sailor, neither he nor I could imagine.

As the dead man was thrown overboard there occurred two incidents which created much disturbance amongst the crew. The fellow's eyes had been closed; but in the dragging of his body to the rail they were jarred open, and many seemed to entertain a queer delusion that they gazed steadily and mockingly at Schmidt and Zimmer, who were bent over the corpse. The Boatswain Müller, an elderly man who would have known better had he not been a superstitious Alsatian swine, became so excited by this impression that he watched the body in the water; and swore that after it sank a little it drew its limbs into a swimming position and sped away to the south under the waves. Klenze and I did not like these displays of peasant ignorance, and severely reprimanded the men, particularly Müller.

The next day a very troublesome situation was created by the indisposition of some of the crew. They were evidently suffering from the nervous strain of our long voyage, and had had bad dreams. Several seemed quite dazed and stupid; and after satisfying myself that they were not feigning their weakness, I excused them from their duties. The sea was rather rough, so we descended to a depth where the waves were less troublesome. Here we were comparatively calm, despite a somewhat puzzling southward current which we could not identify from our oceanographic charts. The moans of the sick men were decidedly annoying; but since they did not appear to demoralise the rest of the crew, we did not resort to extreme measures. It was our plan to remain where we were and intercept the liner Dacia, mentioned in information from agents in New York.

In the early evening we rose to the surface, and found the sea less heavy. The smoke of a battleship was on the northern horizon, but our distance and ability to submerge made us safe. What worried us more was the talk of Boatswain Müller, which grew wilder as night came on. He was in a detestably childish state, and babbled of some illusion of dead bodies drifting past the undersea portholes; bodies which looked at him intensely, and which he recognised in spite of bloating as having seen dying during some of our victorious German exploits. And he said that the young man we had found and tossed overboard was their leader. This was very gruesome and abnormal, so we confined Müller in irons and had him soundly whipped. The men were not pleased at his punishment, but discipline was necessary. We also denied the request of a delegation headed by Seaman Zimmer, that the curious carved ivory head be cast into the sea.

On June 20, Seamen Bohm and Schmidt, who had been ill the day before, became violently insane. I regretted that no physician was included in our complement of officers, since German lives are precious; but the constant ravings of the two concerning a terrible curse were most subversive of discipline, so drastic steps were taken. The crew accepted the event in a sullen fashion, but it seemed to quiet Müller; who thereafter gave us no trouble. In the evening we released him, and he went about his duties silently.

In the week that followed we were all very nervous, watching for the Dacia. The tension was aggravated by the disappearance of Müller and Zimmer, who undoubtedly committed suicide as a result of the fears which had seemed to harass them, though they were not observed in the act of jumping overboard. I was rather glad to be rid of Müller, for even his silence had unfavourably affected the crew. Everyone seemed inclined to be silent now, as though holding a secret fear. Many were ill, but none made a disturbance. Lieut. Klenze chafed under the strain, and was annoyed by the merest trifles—such as the school of dolphins which gathered about the U-29 in increasing numbers, and the growing intensity of that southward current which was not on our chart.

It at length became apparent that we had missed the Dacia altogether. Such failures are not uncommon, and we were more pleased than disappointed; since our return to Wilhelmshaven was now in order. At noon June 28 we turned northeastward, and despite some rather comical entanglements with the unusual masses of dolphins were soon under way.

The explosion in the engine room at 2 P.M. was wholly a surprise. No defect in the machinery or carelessness in the men had been noticed, yet without warning the ship was racked from end to end with a colossal shock. Lieut. Klenze hurried to the engine room, finding the fuel-tank and most of the mechanism shattered, and Engineers Raabe and Schneider instantly killed. Our situation had suddenly become grave indeed; for though the chemical air regenerators were intact, and though we could use the devices for raising and submerging the ship and opening the hatches as long as compressed air and storage batteries might hold out, we were powerless to propel or guide the submarine. To seek rescue in the lifeboats would be to deliver ourselves into the hands of enemies unreasonably embittered against our great German nation, and our wireless had failed ever since the Victory affair to put us in touch with a fellow U-boat of the Imperial Navy.

From the hour of the accident till July 2 we drifted constantly to the south, almost without plans and encountering no vessel. Dolphins still encircled the U-29, a somewhat remarkable circumstance considering the distance we had covered. On the morning of July 2 we sighted a warship flying American colours, and the men became very restless in their desire to surrender. Finally Lieut. Klenze had to shoot a seaman named Traube, who urged this un-German act with especial violence. This quieted the crew for the time, and we submerged unseen.

The next afternoon a dense flock of sea-birds appeared from the south, and the ocean began to heave ominously. Closing our hatches, we awaited developments until we realised that we must either submerge or be swamped in the mounting waves. Our air pressure and electricity were diminishing, and we wished to avoid all unnecessary use of our slender mechanical resources; but in this case there was no choice. We did not descend far, and when after several hours the sea was calmer, we decided to return to the surface. Here, however, a new trouble developed; for the ship failed to respond to our direction in spite of all that the mechanics could do. As the men grew more frightened at this undersea imprisonment, some of them began to mutter again about Lieut. Klenze's ivory image, but the sight of an automatic pistol calmed them. We kept the poor devils as busy as we could, tinkering at the machinery even when we knew it was useless.

Klenze and I usually slept at different times; and it was during my sleep, about 5 A.M., July 4, that the general mutiny broke loose. The six remaining pigs of seamen, suspecting that we were lost, had suddenly burst into a mad fury at our refusal to surrender to the Yankee battleship two days before; and were in a delirium of cursing and destruction. They roared like the animals they were, and broke instruments and furniture indiscriminately; screaming about such nonsense as the curse of the ivory image and the dark dead youth who looked at them and swam away. Lieut. Klenze seemed paralysed and inefficient, as one might expect of a soft, womanish Rhinelander. I shot all six men, for it was necessary, and made sure that none remained alive.

We expelled the bodies through the double hatches and were alone in the U-29. Klenze seemed very nervous, and drank heavily. It was decided that we remain alive as long as possible, using the large stock of provisions and chemical supply of oxygen, none of which had suffered from the crazy antics of those swine-hound seamen. Our compasses, depth gauges, and other delicate instruments were ruined; so that henceforth our only reckoning would be guesswork, based on our watches, the calendar, and our apparent drift as judged by any objects we might spy through the portholes or from the conning tower. Fortunately we had storage batteries still capable of long use, both for interior lighting and for the searchlight. We often cast a beam around the ship, but saw only dolphins, swimming parallel to our own drifting course. I was scientifically interested in those dolphins; for though the ordinary Delphinus delphis is a cetacean mammal, unable to subsist without air, I watched one of the swimmers closely for two hours, and did not see him alter his submerged condition.

With the passage of time Klenze and I decided that we were still drifting south, meanwhile sinking deeper and deeper. We noted the marine fauna and flora, and read much on the subject in the books I had carried with me for spare moments. I could not help observing, however, the inferior scientific knowledge of my companion. His mind was not Prussian, but given to imaginings and speculations which have no value. The fact of our coming death affected him curiously, and he would frequently pray in remorse over the men, women, and children we had sent to the bottom; forgetting that all things are noble which serve the German state. After a time he became noticeably unbalanced, gazing for hours at his ivory image and weaving fanciful stories of the lost and forgotten things under the sea. Sometimes, as a psychological experiment, I would lead him on in these wanderings, and listen to his endless poetical quotations and tales of sunken ships. I was very sorry for him, for I dislike to see a German suffer; but he was not a good man to die with. For myself I was proud, knowing how the Fatherland would revere my memory and how my sons would be taught to be men like me.

On August 9, we espied the ocean floor, and sent a powerful beam from the searchlight over it. It was a vast undulating plain, mostly covered with seaweed, and strown with the shells of small molluscs. Here and there were slimy objects of puzzling contour, draped with weeds and encrusted with barnacles, which Klenze declared must be ancient ships lying in their graves. He was puzzled by one thing, a peak of solid matter, protruding above the ocean bed nearly four feet at its apex; about two feet thick, with flat sides and smooth upper surfaces which met at a very obtuse angle.

I called the peak a bit of outcropping rock, but Klenze thought he saw carvings on it. After a while he began to shudder, and turned away from the scene as if frightened; yet could give no explanation save that he was overcome with the vastness, darkness, remoteness, antiquity, and mystery of the oceanic abysses. His mind was tired, but I am always a German, and was quick to notice two things; that the U-29 was standing the deep-sea pressure splendidly, and that the peculiar dolphins were still about us, even at a depth where the existence of high organisms is considered impossible by most naturalists. That I had previously overestimated our depth, I was sure; but none the less we must still be deep enough to make these phenomena remarkable. Our southward speed, as gauged by the ocean floor, was about as I had estimated from the organisms passed at higher levels.

It was at 3:15 P.M., August 12, that poor Klenze went wholly mad. He had been in the conning tower using the searchlight when I saw him bound into the library compartment where I sat reading, and his face at once betrayed him. I will repeat here what he said, underlining the words he emphasised: "He is calling! He is calling! I hear him! We must go!" As he spoke he took his ivory image from the table, pocketed it, and seized my arm in an effort to drag me up the companionway to the deck. In a moment I understood that he meant to open the hatch and plunge with me into the water outside, a vagary of suicidal and homicidal mania for which I was scarcely prepared. As I hung back and attempted to soothe him he grew more violent, saying: "Come now—do not wait until later; it is better to repent and be forgiven than to defy and be condemned." Then I tried the opposite of the soothing plan, and told him he was mad—pitifully demented. But he was unmoved, and cried: "If I am mad, it is mercy! May the gods pity the man who in his callousness can remain sane to the hideous end! Come and be mad whilst he still calls with mercy!"

This outburst seemed to relieve a pressure in his brain; for as he finished he grew much milder, asking me to let him depart alone if I would not accompany him. My course at once became clear. He was a German, but only a Rhinelander and a commoner; and he was now a potentially dangerous madman. By complying with his suicidal request I could immediately free myself from one who was no longer a companion but a menace. I asked him to give me the ivory image before he went, but this request brought from him such uncanny laughter that I did not repeat it. Then I asked him if he wished to leave any keepsake or lock of hair for his family in Germany in case I should be rescued, but again he gave me that strange laugh. So as he climbed the ladder I went to the levers, and allowing proper time-intervals operated the machinery which sent him to his death. After I saw that he was no longer in the boat I threw the searchlight around the water in an effort to obtain a last glimpse of him; since I wished to ascertain whether the water-pressure would flatten him as it theoretically should, or whether the body would be unaffected, like those extraordinary dolphins. I did not, however, succeed in finding my late companion, for the dolphins were massed thickly and obscuringly about the conning tower.

That evening I regretted that I had not taken the ivory image surreptitiously from poor Klenze's pocket as he left, for the memory of it fascinated me. I could not forget the youthful, beautiful head with its leafy crown, though I am not by nature an artist. I was also sorry that I had no one with whom to converse. Klenze, though not my mental equal, was much better than no one. I did not sleep well that night, and wondered exactly when the end would come. Surely, I had little enough chance of rescue.

The next day I ascended to the conning tower and commenced the customary searchlight explorations. Northward the view was much the same as it had been all the four days since we had sighted the bottom, but I perceived that the drifting of the U-29 was less rapid. As I swung the beam around to the south, I noticed that the ocean floor ahead fell away in a marked declivity, and bore curiously regular blocks of stone in certain places, disposed as if in accordance with definite patterns. The boat did not at once descend to match the greater ocean depth, so I was soon forced to adjust the searchlight to cast a sharply downward beam. Owing to the abruptness of the change a wire was disconnected, which necessitated a delay of many minutes for repairs; but at length the light streamed on again, flooding the marine valley below me.

I am not given to emotion of any kind, but my amazement was very great when I saw what lay revealed in that electrical glow. And yet as one reared in the best Kultur of Prussia I should not have been amazed, for geology and tradition alike tell us of great transpositions in oceanic and continental areas. What I saw was an extended and elaborate array of ruined edifices; all of magnificent though unclassified architecture, and in various stages of preservation. Most appeared to be of marble, gleaming whitely in the rays of the searchlight, and the general plan was of a large city at the bottom of a narrow valley, with numerous isolated temples and villas on the steep slopes above. Roofs were fallen and columns were broken, but there still remained an air of immemorially ancient splendour which nothing could efface.

Confronted at last with the Atlantis I had formerly deemed largely a myth, I was the most eager of explorers. At the bottom of that valley a river once had flowed; for as I examined the scene more closely I beheld the remains of stone and marble bridges and sea-walls, and terraces and embankments once verdant and beautiful. In my enthusiasm I became nearly as idiotic and sentimental as poor Klenze, and was very tardy in noticing that the southward current had ceased at last, allowing the U-29 to settle slowly down upon the sunken city as an aëroplane settles upon a town of the upper earth. I was slow, too, in realising that the school of unusual dolphins had vanished.

In about two hours the boat rested in a paved plaza close to the rocky wall of the valley. On one side I could view the entire city as it sloped from the plaza down to the old river-bank; on the other side, in startling proximity, I was confronted by the richly ornate and perfectly preserved facade of a great building, evidently a temple, hollowed from the solid rock. Of the original workmanship of this titanic thing I can only make conjectures. The facade, of immense magnitude, apparently covers a continuous hollow recess; for its windows are many and widely distributed. In the centre yawns a great open door, reached by an impressive flight of steps, and surrounded by exquisite carvings like the figures of Bacchanals in relief. Foremost of all are the great columns and frieze, both decorated with sculptures of inexpressible beauty; obviously portraying idealised pastoral scenes and processions of priests and priestesses bearing strange ceremonial devices in adoration of a radiant god. The art is of the most phenomenal perfection, largely Hellenic in idea, yet strangely individual. It imparts an impression of terrible antiquity, as though it were the remotest rather than the immediate ancestor of Greek art. Nor can I doubt that every detail of this massive product was fashioned from the virgin hillside rock of our planet. It is palpably a part of the valley wall, though how the vast interior was ever excavated I cannot imagine. Perhaps a cavern or series of caverns furnished the nucleus. Neither age nor submersion has corroded the pristine grandeur of this awful fane—for fane indeed it must be—and today after thousands of years it rests untarnished and inviolate in the endless night and silence of an ocean chasm.

I cannot reckon the number of hours I spent in gazing at the sunken city with its buildings, arches, statues, and bridges, and the colossal temple with its beauty and mystery. Though I knew that death was near, my curiosity was consuming; and I threw the searchlight's beam about in eager quest. The shaft of light permitted me to learn many details, but refused to shew anything within the gaping door of the rock-hewn temple; and after a time I turned off the current, conscious of the need of conserving power. The rays were now perceptibly dimmer than they had been during the weeks of drifting. And as if sharpened by the coming deprivation of light, my desire to explore the watery secrets grew. I, a German, should be the first to tread those aeon-forgotten ways!

I produced and examined a deep-sea diving suit of joined metal, and experimented with the portable light and air regenerator. Though I should have trouble in managing the double hatches alone, I believed I could overcome all obstacles with my scientific skill and actually walk about the dead city in person.

On August 16 I effected an exit from the U-29, and laboriously made my way through the ruined and mud-choked streets to the ancient river. I found no skeletons or other human remains, but gleaned a wealth of archaeological lore from sculptures and coins. Of this I cannot now speak save to utter my awe at a culture in the full noon of glory when cave-dwellers roamed Europe and the Nile flowed unwatched to the sea. Others, guided by this manuscript if it shall ever be found, must unfold the mysteries at which I can only hint. I returned to the boat as my electric batteries grew feeble, resolved to explore the rock temple on the following day.

On the 17th, as my impulse to search out the mystery of the temple waxed still more insistent, a great disappointment befell me; for I found that the materials needed to replenish the portable light had perished in the mutiny of those pigs in July. My rage was unbounded, yet my German sense forbade me to venture unprepared into an utterly black interior which might prove the lair of some indescribable marine monster or a labyrinth of passages from whose windings I could never extricate myself. All I could do was to turn on the waning searchlight of the U-29, and with its aid walk up the temple steps and study the exterior carvings. The shaft of light entered the door at an upward angle, and I peered in to see if I could glimpse anything, but all in vain. Not even the roof was visible; and though I took a step or two inside after testing the floor with a staff, I dared not go farther. Moreover, for the first time in my life I experienced the emotion of dread. I began to realise how some of poor Klenze's moods had arisen, for as the temple drew me more and more, I feared its aqueous abysses with a blind and mounting terror. Returning to the submarine, I turned off the lights and sat thinking in the dark. Electricity must now be saved for emergencies.

Saturday the 18th I spent in total darkness, tormented by thoughts and memories that threatened to overcome my German will. Klenze had gone mad and perished before reaching this sinister remnant of a past unwholesomely remote, and had advised me to go with him. Was, indeed, Fate preserving my reason only to draw me irresistibly to an end more horrible and unthinkable than any man has dreamed of? Clearly, my nerves were sorely taxed, and I must cast off these impressions of weaker men.

I could not sleep Saturday night, and turned on the lights regardless of the future. It was annoying that the electricity should not last out the air and provisions. I revived my thoughts of euthanasia, and examined my automatic pistol. Toward morning I must have dropped asleep with the lights on, for I awoke in darkness yesterday afternoon to find the batteries dead. I struck several matches in succession, and desperately regretted the improvidence which had caused us long ago to use up the few candles we carried.

After the fading of the last match I dared to waste, I sat very quietly without a light. As I considered the inevitable end my mind ran over preceding events, and developed a hitherto dormant impression which would have caused a weaker and more superstitious man to shudder. The head of the radiant god in the sculptures on the rock temple is the same as that carven bit of ivory which the dead sailor brought from the sea and which poor Klenze carried back into the sea.

I was a little dazed by this coincidence, but did not become terrified. It is only the inferior thinker who hastens to explain the singular and the complex by the primitive short cut of supernaturalism. The coincidence was strange, but I was too sound a reasoner to connect circumstances which admit of no logical connexion, or to associate in any uncanny fashion the disastrous events which had led from the Victory affair to my present plight. Feeling the need of more rest, I took a sedative and secured some more sleep. My nervous condition was reflected in my dreams, for I seemed to hear the cries of drowning persons, and to see dead faces pressing against the portholes of the boat. And among the dead faces was the living, mocking face of the youth with the ivory image.

I must be careful how I record my awaking today, for I am unstrung, and much hallucination is necessarily mixed with fact. Psychologically my case is most interesting, and I regret that it cannot be observed scientifically by a competent German authority. Upon opening my eyes my first sensation was an overmastering desire to visit the rock temple; a desire which grew every instant, yet which I automatically sought to resist through some emotion of fear which operated in the reverse direction. Next there came to me the impression of light amidst the darkness of dead batteries, and I seemed to see a sort of phosphorescent glow in the water through the porthole which opened toward the temple. This aroused my curiosity, for I knew of no deep-sea organism capable of emitting such luminosity. But before I could investigate there came a third impression which because of its irrationality caused me to doubt the objectivity of anything my senses might record. It was an aural delusion; a sensation of rhythmic, melodic sound as of some wild yet beautiful chant or choral hymn, coming from the outside through the absolutely sound-proof hull of the U-29. Convinced of my psychological and nervous abnormality, I lighted some matches and poured a stiff dose of sodium bromide solution, which seemed to calm me to the extent of dispelling the illusion of sound. But the phosphorescence remained, and I had difficulty in repressing a childish impulse to go to the porthole and seek its source. It was horribly realistic, and I could soon distinguish by its aid the familiar objects around me, as well as the empty sodium bromide glass of which I had had no former visual impression in its present location. The last circumstance made me ponder, and I crossed the room and touched the glass. It was indeed in the place where I had seemed to see it. Now I knew that the light was either real or part of an hallucination so fixed and consistent that I could not hope to dispel it, so abandoning all resistance I ascended to the conning tower to look for the luminous agency. Might it not actually be another U-boat, offering possibilities of rescue?

It is well that the reader accept nothing which follows as objective truth, for since the events transcend natural law, they are necessarily the subjective and unreal creations of my overtaxed mind. When I attained the conning tower I found the sea in general far less luminous than I had expected. There was no animal or vegetable phosphorescence about, and the city that sloped down to the river was invisible in blackness. What I did see was not spectacular, not grotesque or terrifying, yet it removed my last vestige of trust in my consciousness. For the door and windows of the undersea temple hewn from the rocky hill were vividly aglow with a flickering radiance, as from a mighty altar-flame far within.

Later incidents are chaotic. As I stared at the uncannily lighted door and windows, I became subject to the most extravagant visions—visions so extravagant that I cannot even relate them. I fancied that I discerned objects in the temple—objects both stationary and moving—and seemed to hear again the unreal chant that had floated to me when first I awaked. And over all rose thoughts and fears which centred in the youth from the sea and the ivory image whose carving was duplicated on the frieze and columns of the temple before me. I thought of poor Klenze, and wondered where his body rested with the image he had carried back into the sea. He had warned me of something, and I had not heeded—but he was a soft-headed Rhinelander who went mad at troubles a Prussian could bear with ease.

The rest is very simple. My impulse to visit and enter the temple has now become an inexplicable and imperious command which ultimately cannot be denied. My own German will no longer controls my acts, and volition is henceforward possible only in minor matters. Such madness it was which drove Klenze to his death, bareheaded and unprotected in the ocean; but I am a Prussian and a man of sense, and will use to the last what little will I have. When first I saw that I must go, I prepared my diving suit, helmet, and air regenerator for instant donning; and immediately commenced to write this hurried chronicle in the hope that it may some day reach the world. I shall seal the manuscript in a bottle and entrust it to the sea as I leave the U-29 forever.

I have no fear, not even from the prophecies of the madman Klenze. What I have seen cannot be true, and I know that this madness of my own will at most lead only to suffocation when my air is gone. The light in the temple is a sheer delusion, and I shall die calmly, like a German, in the black and forgotten depths. This daemoniac laughter which I hear as I write comes only from my own weakening brain. So I will carefully don my diving suit and walk boldly up the steps into that primal shrine; that silent secret of unfathomed waters and uncounted years.

Piece By Piece

By Ken Kupstis

Ever cut your hand off?

It can happen, especially around here. Better believe it. The saws have no conscience, no mercy. They don't care what color, age, religion or social class you are, and in the voracious consumption of human flesh, they are faster than you'll ever live to be.

The air is filled with the screams of metal: aluminum, steel and alloys battling with pneumatic hammers, bandsaws, table saws, massive punch presses and power drills. The machines win, the metals lose. More metals arrive and the battles begin again. In the midst of this metal thunder, a worker can "zone out." The sounds cut into your ears, into your brain, and you get numb to the monotonous work you're doing. Call it Work Hypnosis or the Zen of Metalshop. But enter that state and that's when the first piece of you will be taken away.

I was cutting sheet metal to the proper size for the cores of Patriot warheads, and this particular bandsaw was older than Ozzy Osbourne…Man, I wish they'd give us some new equipment once in a while! The bandsaw was resisting the aluminum, slowing it to a stop. I put more pressure on it to force it through the blade. Suddenly it did…taking my hand with it.

Against aluminum, this particular bandsaw was worth shit.

Against human flesh, it kicked ass and took names. The blade chewed a thick red slot three-quarters of the way through my wrist before I felt any pain, or even realized what had happ sacrificing precious flesh to this…this…thing, this traitorous schizo-demon of shrieking metal. I saw another part of my wrist surrender to the blade, then I ripped my arm back out.

Most of it. I was rewarded with a painless, spurting stump that I regarded with incredulous, bulging eyes. My hand flopped to the floor behind the saw. Strangely there was no pain, just a weird heat and a sickening feeling of wrongness. If you ever want something removed quickly and comfortably, a bandsaw's the way to do it.

Then the pain hit.

MOTHERRRRRRFUCKERRRRR!!!" I bellowed to the organized chaos of the metalshop. I clutched the stump in a death-grip and broke into moves that would make M.C. Hammer jump back and kill himself. I screamed, bled, cried, and bled some more.

Suddenly, everybody stopped what they were doing and rushed over. Even now, I wonder why. I mean, hell, it's a metalshop. Accidents will happen. The metals will still have to be hammered and sawed and cut and chopped into the shapes demanded. It would go on until the end of time, or until somebody thought up a replacement for mental. And if we didn't do the hammering and sawing and cutting and chopping, someone else would. Why the fuss over a hand?

"See if you can find it...fell behind the saw, I think..." Frank droned from somewhere far away.

"Poor sonofabitch. Bound to happen sooner or later, though..." Bill's voice trailed off into meaninglessness.

I didn't know whether it was the loss of blood, or the sight of it. I didn't normally faint at the sight of blood...until I started working at the metalshop.

The metalshop around me flickered from color to black and white, and finally just black.

I had a vague sensation of being picked up and carried. Then...

I remembered...

"Just wanted you to know there're no hard feelings. Beer?" I offered my replacement—Geoffrey something, I recalled, one of those high-class transplanted Florida Limeys. Just because he was British didn't mean he wasn't an immigrant. Good-looking bastard, though; elegantly coiffed blonde hair, sickeningly neat little goatee. And that accent! No wonder

Catherine had dropped me like a hot rock.

"Thanks! Cheers!" He said, swigging deeply off of the Rolling Rock I'd poured for him.

"You know, you're a weird bloke, Ryan. Most guys'd be thirsting for my blood right now—"

I am, "Geoffrey", I am—

"—And here you are, just dismissing the whole thing and taking it easy. Sure you're not British?" He guffawed, perhaps a bit too loudly.

I smiled calmly. "Quite sure. No, I just figured that Catherine's her own woman, not my possession or anything. Whatever she wants is okay with me. If I'd have been that serious, I would've married her." I watched his feet as I reeled off my nice-guy monologue. As he paced the metalshop I saw him stumble, ever so slightly. Ah, here we go...

"Well, I—bloody hell, you don't have enough saws here, mate! Y'ought to get s'more..."

He grinned around at my machines of loving grace. I snickered in compliance with his little joke. Little? Microscopic, just like his dick, his brain, his chance of escape.

"Oh, I've got all kinds of saws here. I can cut anything you want. Or anything I want, for that matter." I said, moving closer to him. He spilled beer in a circle around him without noticing.

"Hmmm? What? Mmmm—might I—have 'nother?" He looked at me stupidly, holding up his empty mug.

I smiled at him. "Sure with or without Seconal? One lump or two, asshole?

Better slow down, 'Geoffrey', you've got enough downers in you to knock out Mothra."

He made a choking noise, spun around, stumbled and fell. He lay on his back staring up at me, chest heaving, eyes bulging. My smile grew huge as I picked up a roll of electrician's tape. "And I'm not all that weird, Geoffrey. Just a little jealous, that's all. Now let me show you this really neat saw..."

The air is filled with the screams of metal. It woke me up, to stare at my fellow shopworkers.

"Zonin' out again, huh, Ryan? C'mon, we need two hundred and eighty more casings."

Frank said tonelessly. He wasn't ordering me around; he wasn't the boss. We all knew our jobs, and we did them.

I nodded, got busy, and stared down at the nothingness below my wrist. Just a tapering stub of flesh and bone. I'd lost the hand years ago, in an accident with a bandsaw, I think.

Funny how it only seems like yesterday.

Hire the handicapped, we're fun to watch. I can still work, though, even if I just have one hand. As I started punching out casings on the drill press, I remembered Catherine—

"Don't try to talk me out of it, Ryan." She warned me.

"I wouldn't dream of it." I said calmly, pouring myself a drink.

She was beautiful.

Pity.

"Just let it go. When Geoff comes to pick me up—"

"Geoff? Oh, he's not coming. I imagine he's halfway over the Atlantic by now. Wise choice." I sipped whiskey, sighing with pleasure and triumph.

"What are you talking about?" She demanded.

"We had a little chat today while I was at work. Told him I was more than happy for both of you, since I've got the AIDS virus and all." I giggled a little, and handed her a copy of my 'blood test'. It was startlingly realistic, the best that money can buy, and what would a British actor know about American medical documents anyway?

"What is this? Some kind of sick joke? It is, isn't it? Just the kind of thing your twisted little mind would dream up. Well, just 'cause you told him that you had it, doesn't mean that I---"

"Oh, don't worry. I 've got that covered. You've got it, too. Here's your copy." I handed it to her. She took it, glanced at it, and her beautiful brown eyes blazed with anger as she crumpled it and flung it to the floor. "He was beside himself with anger." I said, and how I managed to keep a straight face, I'll never know.

"So. You tricked him, sent him away..."

That's right, babe. Far, far away, piece by piece.

"...Did you think that would make me stay with you? You, a metalworker, when he's making more than you ever will? Now that I know what a petty schmuck you are, I think I'll be going." She turned away with a cascade of her pretty blonde hair, preparing her grandiose nose-in-the-air exit, and I took that as the opportune moment to smack her in the back of the head with my wrench. She dropped like a slughtered calf, and I began taping her up.

Wonderful stuff, that electrician's tape. Much better than handcuffs.

"Yes, my dear. You will be going. Far, far away, piece by piece." I said, finishing my whiskey.

She came to while I was putting her gag on. I was glad! "Actually, Cath, this has nothing to do with making you stay with me. This has everything to do with betrayal, and its consequences."

I put her in the trunk of my car and brought her to the Shop. It was late, and dark. I don't think I was spotted but I was curiously unconcerned. It was one of those crimes of passion where you don't care if you get away with it, as long as you accomplish it.

I unlocked the warehouse and dragged her inside, laying her down on the saw-table next to Geoffrey.

The left half of him, anyway.

Her eyes widened as she saw his cleanly-sliced cranium spilling forth pale jelly, his opened throat clotted with drying blood, his chest packed with wet and colorful organs. She freaked out, straining uselessly against her bonds and making pathetic bleats through her gag.

I found her devotion touching, but annoying. Because if she didn't hold still, it was going to be messy.

Well, messier.

I turned the saw on, and for a moment I felt strangely like Oilcan Harry in the old cartoons, tying a screaming heroine to the railroad tracks. A hideous power was rushing through me. I could see the legs of her jeans turning dark, and tears spilling out of her eyes as she fought even harder.

"What?! What are you crying about? You wanted to be with Geoff instead of me, right?

Well, you ought to thank me...'cause you're really going to be with him now. I'm going to bring the two of you closer together than you ever dreamed possible."

I hit her with the wrench again; I suppose I owed her the mercy of unconsciousness. She didn't black out, though. She wasn't going gentle into that bad night. I hit her again.

"You're going to be literally inseparable!"

I drove her head-first through the saw blade. The gag muted her death-scream, which only lasted a microsecond, and to feel her treacherous brains hitting my face was almost worth it.

Almost.

When it was done, I took one of the acetylene torches, lined up the halves of their bodies and cauterized them together.

The resulting creation smelled terrible, and didn't fit together as neatly as I'd hoped—Geoffrey was quite a few inches taller than Catherine—but I was impressed with the results nonetheless. Seeing them turned into dead jigsaw puzzles, joined at their black hearts, was a sight both horrifying and gratifying. If one is driven to murder, it shouldn't be a mere act of senseless violence, but a means of artistic expression!

I put one of the matched-set freaks into one of the shop's huge cardboard cartons, wrote EVIDENCE on it with a thick magic marker, and dropped them off a block from the police station. With a note:

Hi Guys!

Enclosed please find the partial remains of one Geoffrey Beamon and one Catherine

Reilly. Hope you don't mind if I keep one for myself. I've got a dozen doughnuts for the first one of you that catches me! Good luck!

I was able to spend a few lazy days on Daytona Beach before they caught me. They always catch you, always. I wasn't worried. I'd just had the ultimate revenge; what was there to worry about? To flee from justice would be cowardice.

And they always catch you. Always.

"RYAN! Watch what you're doi—" I heard Bill yell out in an angry warning, and then the power press closed on the stump of my arm, twenty-five tons of pressure per square inch.

In the second it took for the press to close, the bones were pulped into meal and the flesh was compressed to a quarter-inch thickness.

I pulled a grotesquely widened flipper of skin out of the press. Unlike my brief but torrid affair with the bandsaw, the pain didn't wait to show up. It was here at the door, smiling with suitcases in hand.

I raved and screamed as my blood tried to flow and couldn't. I knocked over a rack of Kalishnikov assault rifle barrels and smashed through some stacked boxes of unfinished grenades. "LET ME OUT! LET ME OUTTA HERE, I QUIT! I QUIT, DAMN IT! LET ME OUTTA HERE!!!"

Nobody tried to stop me.

How could they?

There was Frank, down to one finger and a thumb on his remaining arm. His left eye was a suppurating mess where one of the ancient stapleguns had misfired.

Then the the waist but he was still working, still working, good old Bill.

And the others, here, there, everywhere. Murderous metalshop Frankensteins, missing eyes, ears, arms, legs. Burned alive, flesh corroded into filthy pink pulp by acids or radiation.

Even worse, there were the 'oldtimers', like Ed Gein, John Wayne Gacy and Herman Mudgett, hired decades before I was. Their minds were quite gone, and they actually delighted in the 'accidents' now. One of their favorite things to do was their "Imitation of Christ": they'd stab power drills through their hands and feet, wrap razor wire around their heads into blasphemous crowns, and run around shrieking "I'm God! I'm GOD!"

They're trying to be macho, but I know it's just an act. We only have enough sanity left to keep cranking out weapon after weapon. You'd think they'd cut us some slack. But no; they just cut us, and send us back to the lake of fire, piece by piece.

The saws have no conscience, no mercy. Because none of us did, either.

Even so, I hear they're backlogged with 'applications'. New hires are coming in all the time...

"Yo! Ryan! Snap out of it, we need seventy more...LOOK OUT! SAW!" Frank screamed.

I snapped out of it, looking around wildly. A five foot long, inch-wide slot appeared in the concrete floor under my right foot. The slot was lit up from the eternal flames below, and a blackened radial saw blade popped up with a scream. It came for me with diabolical speed, but oddly I could still the five-pointed star etched into its side.

I pulled my foot back just in time, and both saw and slot vanished entirely. There was only firm concrete floor again...for the moment.

"Too fast for ya, Chief. But don't worry, I'll get back to work." I said to the shop, giggling. Man, that was close. I don't want to lose my feet and have to use a crawler like Bill.

Damn it, I'm down to ONE HAND!

But accidents happen.

Hell, it's a metalshop.

THE DAMNED THING

BY AMBROSE BIERCE

I.

By THE light of a tallow candle, which had been placed on one end of a rough table, a man was reading something written in a book. It was an old account book, greatly worn; and the writing was not, apparently, very legible, for the man sometimes held the page close to the flame of the candle to get a stronger light upon it. The shadow of the book would then throw into obscurity a half of the room, darkening a number of faces and figures; for besides the reader, eight other men were present. Seven of them sat against the rough log walls, silent and motionless, and, the room being small, not very far from the table. By extending an arm any one of them could have touched the eighth man, who lay on the table, face upward, partly covered by a sheet, his arms at his sides. He was dead.

The man with the book was not reading aloud, and no one spoke; all seemed to be waiting for something to occur; the dead man only was without expectation. From the blank darkness outside came in, through the aperture that served for a window, all the ever unfamiliar noises of night in the wilderness — the long, nameless note of a distant coyote; the stilly pulsing thrill of tireless insects in trees; strange cries of night birds, so different from those of the birds of day; the drone of great blundering beetles, and all that mysterious chorus of small sounds that seem always to have been but half heard when they have suddenly ceased, as if conscious of an indiscretion. But nothing of all this was noted in that company; its members were not overmuch addicted to idle interest in matters of no practical importance; that was obvious in every line of their rugged faces — obvious even in the dim light of the single candle. They were evidently men of the vicinity — farmers and woodmen.

The person reading was a trifle different; one would have said of him that he was of the world, worldly, albeit there was that in his attire which attested a certain fellowship with the organisms of his environment. His coat would hardly have passed muster in San Francisco: his footgear was not of urban origin, and the hat that lay by him on the floor (he was the only one uncovered) was such that if one had considered it as an article of mere personal adornment he would have missed its meaning. In countenance the man was rather prepossessing, with just a hint of sternness; though that he may have assumed or cultivated, as appropriate to one in authority. For he was a coroner. It was by virtue of his office that he had possession of the book in which he was reading; it had been found among the dead man's effects — in his cabin, where the inquest was now taking place.

When the coroner had finished reading he put the book into his breast pocket. At that moment the door was pushed open and a young man entered. He, clearly, was not of mountain birth and breeding: he was clad as those who dwell in cities. His clothing was dusty, however, as from travel. He had, in fact, been riding hard to attend the inquest.

The coroner nodded; no one else greeted him.

"We have waited for you," said the coroner. "It is necessary to have done with this business to-night."

The young man smiled. "I am sorry to have kept you," he said. "I went away, not to evade your summons, but to post to my newspaper an account of what I suppose I am called back to relate."

The coroner smiled.

"The account that you posted to your newspaper," he said, "differs probably from that which you will give here under oath."

"That," replied the other, rather hotly and with a visible flush, "is as you choose. I used manifold paper and have a copy of what I sent. It was not written as news, for it is incredible, but as fiction. It may go as a part of my testimony under oath."

"But you say it is incredible."

"That is nothing to you, sir, if I also swear that it is true."

The coroner was apparently not greatly affected by the young man's manifest resentment. He was silent for some moments, his eyes upon the floor. The men about the sides of the cabin talked in whispers, but seldom withdrew their gaze from the face of the corpse. Presently the coroner lifted his eyes and said: "We will resume the inquest."

The men removed their hats. The witness was sworn.

"What is your name?" the coroner asked.

"William Harker."

"Age?"

"Twenty-seven."

"You knew the deceased, Hugh Morgan?"

"Yes."

"You were with him when he died?"

"Near him."

"How did that happen—your presence, I mean?"

"I was visiting him at this place to shoot and fish. A part of my purpose, however, was to study him, and his odd, solitary way of life. He seemed a good model for a character in fiction. I sometimes write stories."

"I sometimes read them."

"Thank you."

"Stories in general—not yours."

Some of the jurors laughed. Against a sombre background humor shows high lights. Soldiers in the intervals of battle laugh easily, and a jest in the death chamber conquers by surprise.

"Relate the circumstances of this man's death," said the coroner. "You may use any notes or memoranda that you please."

The witness understood. Pulling a manuscript from his breast pocket he held it near the candle, and turning the leaves until he found the passage that he wanted, began to read.

II.

"...The sun had hardly risen when we left the house. We were looking for quail, each with a shotgun, but we had only one dog. Morgan said that our best ground was beyond a certain ridge that he pointed out, and we crossed it by a trail through the chaparral. On the other side was comparatively level ground, thickly covered with wild oats. As we emerged from the chaparral, Morgan was but a few yards in advance. Suddenly, we heard, at a little distance to our right, and partly in front, a noise as of some animal thrashing about in the bushes, which we could see were violently agitated.

"'We've started a deer,' said. 'I wish we had brought a rifle.'

"Morgan, who had stopped and was intently watching the agitated chaparral, said nothing, but had cocked both barrels of his gun, and was holding it in readiness to aim. I thought him a trifle excited, which surprised me, for he had a reputation for exceptional coolness, even in moments of sudden and imminent peril.

"'O, come!' I said. 'You are not going to fill up a deer with quail-shot, are you?'

"Still he did not reply; but, catching a sight of his face as he turned it slightly toward me, I was struck by the pallor of it. Then I understood that we had serious business on hand, and my first conjecture was that we had 'jumped' a grizzly. I advanced to Morgan's side, cocking my piece as I moved.

"The bushes were now quiet, and the sounds had ceased, but Morgan was as attentive to the place as before.

"'What is it? What the devil is it?' I asked.

"'That Damned Thing!' he replied, without turning his head. His voice was husky and unnatural. He trembled visibly.

"I was about to speak further, when I observed the wild oats near the place of the disturbance moving in the most inexplicable way. I can hardly describe it. It seemed as if stirred by a streak of wind, which not only bent it, but pressed it down—crushed it so that it did not rise, and this movement was slowly prolonging itself directly toward us.

"Nothing that I had ever seen had affected me so strangely as this unfamiliar and unaccountable phenomenon, yet I am unable to recall any sense of fear. I remember—and tell it here because, singularly enough, I recollected it then—that once, in looking carelessly out of an open window, I momentarily mistook a small tree close at hand for one of a group of larger trees at a little distance away. It looked the same size as the others, but, being more distinctly and sharply defined in mass and detail, seemed out of harmony with them. It was a mere falsification of the law of aerial perspective, but it startled, almost terrified me. We so rely upon the orderly operation of familiar natural laws that any seeming suspension of them is noted as a menace to our safety, a warning of unthinkable calamity. So now the apparently causeless movement of the herbage, and the slow, undeviating approach of the line of disturbance were distinctly disquieting. My companion appeared actually frightened, and I could hardly credit my senses when I saw him suddenly throw his gun to his shoulders and fire both barrels at the agitated grass! Before the smoke of the discharge had cleared away I heard a loud savage cry—a scream like that of a wild animal—and, flinging his gun upon the ground, Morgan sprang away and ran swiftly from the spot. At the same instant I was thrown violently to the ground by the impact of something unseen in the smoke—some soft, heavy substance that seemed thrown against me with great force.

"Before I could get upon my feet and recover my gun, which seemed to have been struck from my hands, I heard Morgan crying out as if in mortal agony, and mingling with his cries were such hoarse savage sounds as one hears from fighting dogs. Inexpressibly terrified, I struggled to my feet and looked in the direction of Morgan's retreat; and may heaven in mercy spare me from another sight like that! At a distance of less than thirty yards was my friend, down upon one knee, his head thrown back at a frightful angle, hatless, his long hair in disorder and his whole body in violent movement from side to side, backward and forward. His right arm was lifted and seemed to lack the hand—at least, I could see none. The other arm was invisible. At times, as my memory now reports this extraordinary scene, I could discern but a part of his body; it was as if he had been partly blotted out—I can not otherwise express it —then a shifting of his position would bring it all into view again.

"All this must have occurred within a few seconds, yet in that time Morgan assumed all the postures of a determined wrestler vanquished by superior weight and strength. I saw nothing but him, and him not always distinctly. During the entire incident his shouts and curses were heard, as if through an enveloping uproar of such sounds of rage and fury as I had never heard from the throat of man or brute!

"For a moment only I stood irresolute, then, throwing down my gun, I ran forward to my friend's assistance. I had a vague belief that he was suffering from a fit or some form of convulsion. Before I could reach his side he was down and quiet. All sounds had ceased, but, with a feeling of such terror as even these awful events had not inspired, I now saw the same mysterious movement of the wild oats prolonging itself from the trampled area about the prostrate man toward the edge of a wood. It was only when it had reached the wood that I was able to withdraw my eyes and look at my companion. He was dead."

III.

The coroner rose from his seat and stood beside the dead man. Lifting an edge of the sheet he pulled it away, exposing the entire body, altogether naked and showing in the candle light a clay-like yellow. It had, however, broad maculations of bluish-black, obviously caused by extravasated blood from contusions. The chest and sides looked as if they had been beaten with a bludgeon. There were dreadful lacerations; the skin was torn in strips and shreds.

The coroner moved round to the end of the table and undid a silk handkerchief, which had been passed under the chin and knotted on the top of the head. When the handkerchief was drawn away it exposed what had been the throat. Some of the jurors who had risen to get a better view repented their curiosity, and turned away their faces. Witness Harker went to the open window and leaned out across the sill, faint and sick. Dropping the handkerchief upon the dead man's neck, the coroner stepped to an angle of the room, and from a pile of clothing produced one garment after another, each of which he held up a moment for inspection. All were torn, and stiff with blood. The jurors did not make a closer inspection. They seemed rather uninterested. They had, in truth, seen all this before; the only thing that was new to them being Harker's testimony.

"Gentlemen," the coroner said, "we have no more evidence, I think. Your duty has been already explained to you; if there is nothing you wish to ask you may go outside and consider your verdict."

The foreman rose—a tall, bearded man of sixty, coarsely clad.

"I should like to ask one question, Mr. Coroner," he said. "What asylum did this yer last witness escape from?"

"Mr. Harker," said the coroner, gravely and tranquilly, "from what asylum did you last escape?"

Harker flushed crimson again, but said nothing, and the seven jurors rose and solemnly filed out of the cabin.

"If you have done insulting me, sir," said Harker, as soon as he and the officer were left alone with the dead man, "I suppose I am at liberty to go?"

"Yes."

Harker started to leave, but paused, with his hand on the door latch. The habit of his profession was strong in him—stronger than his sense of personal dignity. He turned about and said:

"The book that you have there—I recognize it as Morgan's diary. You seemed greatly interested in it; you read in it while I was testifying. May I see it? The public would like—"

"The book will cut no figure in this matter," replied the official, slipping it into his coat pocket; "all the entries in it were made before the writer's death."

As Harker passed out of the house the jury reentered and stood about the table on which the now covered corpse showed under the sheet with sharp definition. The foreman seated himself near the candle, produced from his breast pocket a pencil and scrap of paper, and wrote rather laboriously the following verdict, which with various degrees of effort all signed:

"We, the jury, do find that the remains come to their death at the hands of a mountain lion, but some of us thinks, all the same, they had fits."

IV.

In the diary of the late Hugh Morgan are certain interesting entries having, possibly, a scientific value as suggestions. At the inquest upon his body the book was not put in evidence; possibly the coroner thought it not worth while to confuse the jury. The date of the first of the entries mentioned can not be ascertained; the upper part of the leaf is torn away; the part of the entry remaining is as follows:

"... would run in a half circle, keeping his head turned always toward the centre and again he would stand still, barking furiously. At last he ran away into the brush as fast as he could go. I thought at first that he had gone mad, but on returning to the house found no other alteration in his manner than what was obviously due to fear of punishment.

"Can a dog see with his nose? Do odors impress some olfactory centre with images of the thing emitting them? . . .

"Sept. 2. — Looking at the stars last night as they rose above the crest of the ridge east of the house, I observed them successively disappear — from left to right. Each was eclipsed but an instant, and only a few at the same time, but along the entire length of the ridge all that were within a degree or two of the crest were blotted out. It was as if something had passed along between me and them; but I could not see it, and the stars were not thick enough to define its outline. Ugh! I don't like this. . . ."

Several weeks' entries are missing, three leaves being torn from the book.

"Sept. 27. — It has been about here again — I find evidences of its presence every day. I watched again all of last night in the same cover, gun in hand, double-charged with buckshot. In the morning the fresh footprints were there, as before. Yet I would have sworn that I did not sleep — indeed, I hardly sleep at all. It is terrible, insupportable! If these amazing experiences are real I shall go mad; if they are fanciful I am mad already.

"Oct. 3. — I shall not go — it shall not drive me away. No, this is my house, my land. God hates a coward....

"Oct. 5. — I can stand it no longer; I have invited Harker to pass a few weeks with me — he has a level head. I can judge from his manner if he thinks me mad.

"Oct. 7. — I have the solution of the problem; it came to me last night —

suddenly, as by revelation. How simple—how terribly simple!

"There are sounds that we can not hear. At either end of the scale are notes that stir no chord of that imperfect instrument, the human ear. They are too high or too grave. I have observed a flock of blackbirds occupying an entire treetop—the tops of several trees—and all in full song. Suddenly—in a moment—at absolutely the same instant—all spring into the air and fly away. How? They could not all see one another—whole treetops intervened. At no point could a leader have been visible to all. There must have been a signal of warning or command, high and shrill above the din, but by me unheard. I have observed, too, the same simultaneous flight when all were silent, among not only blackbirds, but other birds—quail, for example, widely separated by bushes—even on opposite sides of a hill.

"It is known to seamen that a school of whales basking or sporting on the surface of the ocean, miles apart, with the convexity of the earth between them, will sometimes dive at the same instant—all gone out of sight in a moment. The signal has been sounded—too grave for the ear of the sailor at the masthead and his comrades on the deck—who nevertheless feel its vibrations in the ship as the stones of a cathedral are stirred by the bass of the organ.

"As with sounds, so with colors. At each end of the solar spectrum the chemist can detect the presence of what are known as 'actinic' rays. They represent colors—integral colors in the composition of light—which we are unable to discern. The human eye is an imperfect instrument; its range is but a few octaves of the real 'chromatic scale' I am not mad; there are colors that we can not see.

"And, God help me! the Damned Thing is of such a color!"

THE MORTAL IMMORTAL

BY MARY SHELLEY

JULY 16, 1833. --This is a memorable anniversary for me; on it I complete my three hundred and twenty-third year!

The Wandering Jew?--certainly not. More than eighteen centuries have passed over his head. In comparison with him, I am a very young Immortal.

Am I, then, immortal? This is a question which I have asked myself, by day and night, for now three hundred and three years, and yet cannot answer it. I detected a gray hair amidst my brown locks this very day-- that surely signifies decay. Yet it may have remained concealed there for three hundred years--for some persons have become entirely white headed before twenty years of age.

I will tell my story, and my reader shall judge for me. I will tell my story, and so contrive to pass some few hours of a long eternity, become so wearisome to me. For ever! Can it be? to live for ever! I have heard of enchantments, in which the victims were plunged into a deep sleep, to wake, after a hundred years, as fresh as ever: I have heard of the Seven Sleepers--thus to be immortal would not be so burthensome: but, oh! the weight of never-ending time--the tedious passage of the still-succeeding hours! How happy was the fabled Nourjahad!----But to my task.

All the world has heard of Cornelius Agrippa. His memory is as immortal as his arts have made me. All the world has also heard of his scholar, who, unawares, raised the foul fiend during his master's absence, and was destroyed by him. The report, true or false, of this accident, was attended with many inconveniences to the renowned philosopher. All his scholars at once deserted him--his servants disappeared. He had no one near him to put coals on his ever-burning fires while he slept, or to attend to the changeful colours of his medicines while he studied. Experiment after experiment failed, because one pair of hands was insufficient to complete them: the dark spirits laughed at him for not being able to retain a single mortal in his service.

I was then very young--very poor--and very much. in love. I had been for about a year the pupil of Cornelius, though I was absent when this accident took place. On my return, my friends implored me not to return to the alchymist's abode. I trembled as I listened to the dire tale they told; I required no second warning; and when Cornelius came and offered me a purse of gold if I would remain under his roof, I felt as if Satan himself tempted me. My teeth chattered--my hair stood on end:--I ran off as fast as my trembling knees would permit.

My failing steps were directed whither for two years they had every evening been attracted,--a gently bubbling spring of pure living waters, beside which lingered a dark-haired girl, whose beaming eyes were fixed on the path I was accustomed each night to tread. I cannot remember the hour when I did not love Bertha; we had been neighbours and playmates from infancy--her parents, like mine, were of humble life, yet respectable--our attachment had been a source of pleasure to them. In an evil hour, a malignant fever carried off both her father and mother, and Bertha became an orphan. She would have found a home beneath my paternal roof, but, unfortunately, the old lady of the near castle, rich, childless, and solitary, declared her intention to adopt her. Henceforth Bertha was clad in silk--inhabited a marble palace--and was looked on as being highly favoured by fortune. But in her new situation among her new associates, Bertha remained true to the friend of her humbler days; she often visited the cottage of my father, and when forbidden to go thither, she would stray towards the neighbouring wood, and meet me beside its shady fountain.

She often declared that she owed no duty to her new protectress equal in sanctity to that which bound us. Yet still I was too poor to marry, and she grew weary of being tormented on my account. She had a haughty but an impatient spirit, and grew angry at the obstacles that prevented our union. We met now after an absence, and she had been sorely beset while I was away; she complained bitterly, and almost reproached me for being poor. I replied hastily,--

"I am honest, if I am poor!--were I not, I might soon become rich!"

This exclamation produced a thousand questions. I feared to shock her by owning the truth, but she drew it from me; and then, casting a look of disdain on me, she said--

"You pretend to love, and you fear to face the Devil for my sake!"

I protested that I had only dreaded to offend her;--while she dwelt on the magnitude of the reward that I should receive. Thus encouraged-- shamed by her--led on by love and hope, laughing at my late fears, with quick steps and a light heart, I returned to accept the offers of the alchymist, and was instantly installed in my office.

A year passed away. I became possessed of no insignificant sum of money. Custom had banished my fears. In spite of the most painful vigilance, I had never detected the trace of a cloven foot; nor was the studious silence of our abode ever disturbed by demoniac howls. I still continued my stolen interviews with Bertha, and Hope dawned on me-- Hope--but not perfect joy; for Bertha fancied that love and security were enemies, and her pleasure was to divide them in my bosom. Though true of heart, she was somewhat of a coquette in manner; and I was jealous as a Turk. She slighted me in a thousand ways, yet would never acknowledge herself to be in the wrong. She would drive me mad with anger, and then force me to beg her pardon. Sometimes she fancied that I was not sufficiently submissive, and then she had some story of a rival, favoured by her protectress. She was surrounded by silk-clad youths--the rich and gay--What chance had the sad-robed scholar of Cornelius compared with these?

On one occasion, the philosopher made such large demands upon my time, that I was unable to meet her as I was wont. He was engaged in some mighty work, and I was forced to remain, day and night, feeding his furnaces and watching his chemical preparations. Bertha waited for me in vain at the fountain. Her haughty spirit fired at this neglect; and when at last I stole out during the few short minutes allotted to me for slumber, and hoped to be consoled by her, she received me with disdain, dismissed me in scorn, and vowed that any man should possess her hand rather than he who could not be in two places at once for her sake. She would be revenged!--And truly she was. In my dingy retreat I heard that she had been hunting, attended by Albert Hoffer. Albert Hoffer was favoured by her protectress, and the three passed in cavalcade before my smoky window. Methought that they mentioned my name--it was followed by a laugh of derision, as her dark eyes glanced contemptuously towards my abode.

Jealousy, with all its venom, and all its misery, entered my breast. Now I shed a torrent of tears, to think that I should never call her mine; and, anon, I imprecated a thousand curses on her inconstancy. Yet, still I must stir the fires of the alchymist, still attend on the changes of his unintelligible medicines.

Cornelius had watched for three days and nights, nor closed his eyes. The progress of his alembics was slower than he expected: in spite of his anxiety, sleep weighed upon his eyelids. Again and again he threw off drowsiness with more than human energy; again and again it stole away his senses. He eyed his crucibles wistfully. "Not ready yet," he murmured; "will another night pass before the work is accomplished? Winzy, you are vigilant--you are faithful--you have slept, my boy--you slept last night. Look at that glass vessel. The liquid it contains is of a soft rose-colour: the moment it begins to change its hue, awaken me--till then I may close my eyes. First, it will turn white, and then emit golden flashes; but wait not till then; when the rose-colour fades, rouse me." I scarcely heard the last words, muttered, as they were, in sleep. Even then he did not quite yield to nature. "Winzy, my boy," he again said, "do not touch the vessel-- do not put it to your lips; it is a philter--a philter to cure love; you would not cease to love your Bertha--beware to drink!"

And he slept. His venerable head sunk on his breast, and I scarce heard his regular breathing. For a few minutes I watched the vessel--the rosy hue of the liquid remained unchanged. Then my thoughts wandered --they visited the fountain, and dwelt on a thousand charming scenes never to be renewed-- never! Serpents and adders were in my heart as the word "Never!" half formed itself on my lips. False girl!--false and cruel! Never more would she smile on me as that evening she smiled on Albert. Worthless, detested woman! I would not remain unrevenged--she should see Albert expire at her feet--she should die beneath my vengeance. She had smiled in disdain and triumph--she knew my wretchedness and her power. Yet what power had she?--the power of exciting my hate--my utter scorn--my--oh, all but indifference! Could I attain that--could I regard her with careless eyes, transferring my rejected love to one fairer and more true, that were indeed a victory!

A bright flash darted before my eyes. I had forgotten the medicine of the adept; I gazed on it with wonder: flashes of admirable beauty, more bright than those which the diamond emits when the sun's rays are on it, glanced from the surface of the liquid; an odour the most fragrant and grateful stole over my sense; the vessel seemed one globe of living radiance, lovely to the eye, and most inviting to the taste. The first thought, instinctively inspired by the grosser sense, was, I will--I must drink. I raised the vessel to my lips. "It will cure me of love--of torture!" Already I had quaffed half of the most delicious liquor ever tasted by the palate of man, when the philosopher stirred. I started--I dropped the glass--the fluid flamed and glanced along the floor, while I felt Cornelius's gripe at my throat, as he shrieked aloud, "Wretch! you have destroyed the labour of my life!"

The philosopher was totally unaware that I had drunk any portion of his drug. His idea was, and I gave a tacit assent to it, that I had raised the vessel from curiosity, and that, frighted at its brightness, and the flashes of intense light it gave forth, I had let it fall. I never undeceived him. The fire of the medicine was quenched--the fragrance died away--he grew calm, as a philosopher should under the heaviest trials, and dismissed me to rest.

I will not attempt to describe the sleep of glory and bliss which bathed my soul in paradise during the remaining hours of that memorable night. Words would be faint and shallow types of my enjoyment, or of the gladness that possessed my bosom when I woke. I trod air--my thoughts were in heaven. Earth appeared heaven, and my inheritance upon it was to be one trance of delight. "This it is to be cured of love," I thought; "I will see Bertha this day, and she will find her lover cold and regardless: too happy to be disdainful, yet how utterly indifferent to her!"

The hours danced away. The philosopher, secure that he had once succeeded, and believing that he might again, began to concoct the same medicine once more. He was shut up with his books and drugs, and I had a holiday. I dressed myself with care; I looked in an old but polished shield, which served me for a mirror; methought my good looks had wonderfully improved. I hurried beyond the precincts of the town, joy in my soul, the beauty of heaven and earth around me. I turned my steps towards the castle--I could look on its lofty turrets with lightness of heart, for I was cured of love. My Bertha saw me afar off, as I came up the avenue. I know not what sudden impulse animated her bosom, but at the sight, she sprung with a light fawn-like bound down the marble steps, and was hastening towards me. But I had been perceived by another person. The old high-born hag, who called herself her protectress, and was her tyrant, had seen me, also; she hobbled, panting, up the terrace; a page, as ugly as herself, held up her train, and fanned her as she hurried along, and stopped my fair girl with a "How, now, my bold mistress? whither so fast? Back to your cage--hawks are abroad!"

Bertha clasped her hands--her eyes were still bent on my approaching figure. I saw the contest. How I abhorred the old crone who checked the kind impulses of my Bertha's softening heart. Hitherto, respect for her rank had caused me to avoid the lady of the castle; now I disdained such trivial considerations. I was cured of love, and lifted above all human fears; I hastened forwards, and soon reached the terrace. How lovely Bertha looked! her eyes flashing fire, her cheeks glowing with impatience and anger, she was a thousand times more graceful and charming than ever--I no longer loved--Oh! no, I adored--worshipped--idolized her!

She had that morning been persecuted, with more than usual vehemence, to consent to an immediate marriage with my rival. She was reproached with the encouragement that she had shown him--she was threatened with being turned out of doors with disgrace and shame. Her proud spirit rose in arms at the threat; but when she remembered the scorn that she had heaped upon me, and how, perhaps, she had thus lost one whom she now regarded as her only friend, she wept with remorse and rage. At that moment I appeared. "O, Winzy!" she exclaimed, "take me to your mother's cot; swiftly let me leave the detested luxuries and wretchedness of this noble dwelling--take me to poverty and happiness."

I clasped her in my arms with transport. The old lady was speechless with fury, and broke forth into invective only when we were far on our road to my natal cottage. My mother received the fair fugitive, escaped from a gilt cage to nature and liberty, with tenderness and joy; my father, who loved her, welcomed her heartily; it was a day of rejoicing, which did not need the addition of the celestial potion of the alchymist to steep me in delight.

Soon after this eventful day, I became the husband of Bertha. I ceased to be the scholar of Cornelius, but I continued his friend. I always felt grateful to him for having, unawares, procured me that delicious draught of a divine elixir, which, instead of curing me of love (sad cure! solitary and joyless remedy for evils which seem blessings to the memory), had inspired me with courage and resolution, thus winning for me an inestimable treasure in my Bertha.

I often called to mind that period of trance-like inebriation with wonder. The drink of Cornelius had not fulfilled the task for which he affirmed that it had been prepared, but its effects were more potent and blissful than words can express. Nestors grey the apparent disparity of our ages by a thousand feminine arts bought star place mortal immortal the wonder and benefactor of the human species. leave no name behind.my name shall be recorded as one of the most famous among the sons of men.

EXPLOITED

BY CHRISTOPHER FROST

Colburn Tucker stood in the modest kitchen of his apartment on the third floor. He wore faded, ripped jeans and a black t-shirt. His face was a shadow of dark stubble from a week of neglected shaving. Colburn's head ached and he rubbed at his temples while pushing his shoulder length black hair out of his face, tucking a few strands behind his ear. In front of him a cabinet door was open and he was staring into it, hands shaking. It was what he called a medicine cabinet, where he kept all his prescriptions. There were at least twelve bottles on the bottom shelf of the cabinet, the labels turned away from him. His hand shook so badly that he kept clenching and unclenching his fists to try and get rid of the tremors that plagued him when he hadn't taken his meds. Lined like soldiers across the countertop were bottles of beer, liquor, and wine, all empty, except for the one that was in front of him. That one was half full. The fridge also was full of liquor, empty of food.

There was one bottle that he was looking for. The one that would take the edge off for just enough time so that he could get some sleep. He needed to sleep so badly. His eyes, bloodshot and swollen, an indication of the lack of rest. His shaking fingers reached out for the bottles and he moved them aside one by one until he found what he was looking for. The one. The one that would make the world fade away. More than anything he wished that he had stopped at the liquor store on his way home from work for something stronger than the beers that were left in the fridge. But the beer would have to do.

He withdrew the bottle from the other companions in his medicine cabinet. Colburn put the bottle down on the counter, let it go reaching for his drink, and finished the bottle. There was another full bottle of beer next to the newly empty one. He popped off the cap and took another long swig. Slamming the bottle down so that its contents began to foam inside. He reached for the medication and flipped off the top with his thumb and dumped four pills into his hand.

What the fuck am I doing? He asked himself. *Do I really need this shit?* He glanced down at his scarred arms where he had dragged knife blades, razors, even broken glass across his pale skin just to feel something other than the perpetual torment that raged in his soul and the resounded in his mind. He glanced over at the knives hung up by the stove and thought about grabbing one and dismissing the pills. As he reached for one of the knives his hand began to shake so badly that he retracted it and clenched it against his chest, trying to stop the tremors.

Four pills.

He popped them into his mouth and tipped back his head swallowing the rest of the beer. Colburn began rubbing his hands back and forth over his eyes as his mind began to take control of him. He started to wonder. That's what he called it when his mind couldn't stay focused on the moment and went to the shadow world of his soul.

Stop it, he thought.

You're never going to be sane. You'll never fit in anywhere. This world does not belong to you; you do not exist in it. These thoughts came from his deep subconscious, the ones that drove him to reach for knives and take them to his arms, chest, stomach, legs, any part of his body that would bleed, because that was really the only thing that gave him instant satisfaction and momentary peace. As his fingertips touched the knife and an electric current of arousal ran through his body, there was a knock at the door.

His fingers fell away from the blade as he walked from the kitchen to the front door. He never checked the peep hole to see who it was. In his mind, with any luck, it would be some home invader that would put a bullet in his chest and end the misery. That wasn't the case tonight. When he opened the door there was a woman standing at the threshold with tears streaking her face, black mascara running down her cheeks like some Gothic mask.

"What happened?" he asked.

"Can I come in?" she replied.

Colburn stepped to the side as she walked past him. She sat on the small love seat in the living room. The sofa was hidden out of the way behind his punching bag which was marked with dry blood stains. His torn and beaten knuckles evidence of what he would do to himself in any attempt for self mutilation. He felt neither pain nor emotion. Colburn floated through life, never part of it, always on the outside.

The crying woman had planted her face against her hands. She was shaking as bad as he had been but when he looked down at his hands they were no longer trembling at all. Colburn returned to the kitchen and grabbed a handful of paper towels for tissues. It wasn't regular practice for him to have weeping women at his doorstep. Opening the refrigerator he also took out two beers and popped the caps from both, returning to the living room, he sat down next to the woman.

"Here," he said handing her the beer. Ashley, a girl that he worked on the docks with, he more or less worked the shipping lines while she was up in the office doing the book work. They had grown close over the years of working together, heading out with the other dock workers to the local pub a block up from the docks after work. From his observations she was a tough chick. Took no shit from anyone, and brushed off the sexual remarks from the dock workers or threw some insulting line back in their face with a smile and a swig of a beer. In the three years that he had known her he had never seen a single tear roll from those green eyes. Sure she had her mood swings, who didn't? The guys on the dock would say that when she got those moods, that she was on the rag. Colburn just assumed she was like everyone else, had good days and bad, it didn't have anything to do with her menstrual cycle. Yet here she was, in the living room, on his love seat, dark mascara-laced-tears streaming freely from her eyes.

"What is it?"

There was a long hesitation. Dipping into her purse she withdrew a packet of pocket tissues and blew into one wiping the snot that was streaming over her upper lip. Her blood shot eyes, avoiding Colburn's, instead looking dead ahead at the vacant white wall. "Sean," she said gingerly as her voice cracked and was as shallow as a mouse squeak.

Sean Drake, a dock worker, who worked the shipping lines with Colburn. Ashley and Sean had been dating for roughly two years. As far as he knew they had never had so much as a fight, let alone one so bad that would bring her to his doorstep in the middle of the night. Colburn liked Sean, he was a good guy, hard worker, but when she said his name emphasized with the tears his fingers turned and clenched into fists.

Colburn reached out pulling her hands away from her face. She looked over at him, somewhat reluctantly. Beneath one of her eyes he could see the smallest round outline of red, maybe a mark that threatened to become a bruise. It was hard to tell with the tears.

"I'm sorry," she said standing up, "I shouldn't have come." Ashley started for the door but Colburn grabbed her loosely by the elbow pulling her back towards him. If what he thought had happened to her the last thing he wanted to do was scare her by being overly aggressive.

"Wait."

=Ashley collapsed into his arms pressing her breast against the lower part of his chest. He reluctantly wrapped his arms around her and as he did the world began to go out of focus. The drugs were kicking in.

"It's okay," he said in his most reassuring voice. "Everything's going to be okay." His hands stroked her chestnut hair.

"Why are you so good to me?" Ashley pulled slightly away from him but not out of his embrace and peered up into his dark eyes. Her trembling fingers stroked his cheek, the tears seeming to dry up while she was in his arms. "You're the most loyal person I have ever met. You have no expectations of people, but you are always there for anyone who needs you and you never ask for something in return. Why is that?"

Colburn didn't answer. Not because he didn't want to, but because he didn't honestly have an answer for her. She lifted up on tiptoe so that their mouths were only inches apart and when she closed her eyes Colburn stepped away from her.

"Don't," he said.

"Why?"

"Because I don't betray people," he looked away. More tears began to well at the corners of her eyes, staining her blush cheeks.

"Why do I always pick the worst guys to be with and ignore the ones that are standing right in front of me?"

Colburn looked at her bloodshot eyes and then broke away, looking down at the floor.

"Why are you here?" he asked.

"I can't," she sobbed and went for the door again. Colburn let her get to the door to test her, to see if she was just playing some woman-mind-game, but when she turned the door knob and opened the door to step out of the apartment he quickly crossed the room and pushed the door closed.

"What happened?" he asked again.

"It was just a fight. No big deal."

"If it wasn't a big deal than you wouldn't be here."

"It's nothing. I can handle it."

"Ash," Colburn said taking her hand, "Did he hit you?"

She turned away from him and buried her face once again in her hands. She was sobbing so heavily that she was on the verge of hyperventilating. Colburn came up behind her and placed a warm hand on her shoulder. But there was nothing warm in his soul anymore, if there ever was to begin with.

"Did he...hit...you?"

"It was just a fight. We had too much to drink and I said some things that I shouldn't have. Stupid things. How could I've been so stupid? I just should have kept my mouth shut. So stupid, so stupid." She began whacking her forehead with the palm of her hand, each blow harder than the last. "Dammit, I can be such an idiot. The things

I said…mean things, comments to intentionally hurt him. I shouldn't have, you know? I should have known that it would hurt him. Should've known better. It's not his fault, I provoked him. I know better than to…to push his buttons. It's not his fault, Colburn, it isn't. He just gets…you know, crazy when he's been drinking. I was just in such a bad mood because he had come home so late. He told me he was with the guys, that they'd gone out for a few, but when he wasn't home when he said he was…I just, I just overreacted. Started accusing him of things. It was childish," she wept.

Colburn approached her. "Ash, you didn't answer my question." Still her eyes averted him. "Did Sean hit you?"

"Can't you see it was my fault?"

"No."

An overwhelming sense of tunnel vision swept over him like a tornado. He was dizzy on his feet for a second as the oxygen escaped his lungs. He tried to take a deep breath but could not. The rational world dissipated. Arrangements of color that washed over the dingy apartment melted to red, literally, he saw his apartment as if looking through red-lensed goggles, or as if someone had splattered his visual world in blood. He felt the arousal of the drug. An electric current ran up his spine and through his neck which cracked with the flick of his head. He cracked each knuckle as the rage began to build inside of him.

That sonofabitch, he thought, *that **motherfucker!***

"Listen to me," he said to Ashley. She turned to face him, her crimson image looking up through tired and beaten eyes, her tears no longer dark from the mascara but appeared to be tears of blood dripping down her cheeks and falling off her chin. "This isn't your fault."

"Yes it is. I provoked him. I shouldn't have come to you, Colburn, I'm sorry. I just needed someone to talk to. Someone I felt safe with."

He knew where Sean Drake lived. Had even partied at his house on a few occasions. It was at least a thirty minute drive. Enough time for the drugs to get out of his system and have a clear mind when he got to his house.

"Stay here," he told her.

"What?"

"I'll be back in an hour, hour and a half at tops."

"What are you going to do?" she pleaded.

"I'm going to take care of it."

Colburn walked away from Ashley and went into his bedroom. He opened up the closet door and pulled his leather jacket off the coat hanger and put it on. Over to the night-stand he grabbed the keys to his car and tucked them into the pocket of his jeans. There was a gun in the drawer of the night-stand, a .45, but this was personal. He didn't want to make it quick and easy. Anyone who hits a woman should have to suffer as much as they make their victim suffer and a gun would be too quick.

When he emerged from the bedroom Ashley was standing in the kitchen leaning against the counter, beer in hand. She sipped generously from it, a cigarette between her fingers that she was flicking into the sink.

"I'll be back," he said as he opened the door and stepped out.

Ashley finished her beer. She reached into the refrigerator and took out another. Her cigarette was smoked down to a roach and she tossed it into the sink. Lighting another smoke, she pulled out her cell phone and dialed a preset number. The phone only rang twice before a voice answered on the other end.

"It's taken care of," she told the person on the other end of the line. "Your brother will be dead within the hour and you and I can be together."

"What about Tucker?" the voice on the other end asked.

"An anonymous phone call to the police should take care of him. Just be at the phone booth in an hour and make that call."

"I love the way you think," the voice laughed.

"It was the easiest thing I've ever done."

Colburn swung his car into the driveway of Sean Drake's house. If he had been thinking, if he had premeditated what was to come, he would have parked down the street where no one could have seen his car. Instead, he came headlights blazing into the driveway and hit the brakes, making the car slide down the driveway, leaving a trail of rubber in its wake. He flung the door open and leapt out of the car his soul filled with red rage as he peered up at the lights glowing in the open windows.

"Sean!" he screamed. Colburn made his way up the lawn to the front door and with one violent kick smashed the door from its hinges. The door flung open and crashed into the wall behind it. He stepped into the house and quickly memorized the layout and tried to figure where Sean would be at this hour at night. He had worked earlier this evening, the late shift like most of them did for the overtime. Sean was also a huge Bruin's fan and recorded all the games that he missed while at work. He would be in the living room Colburn guessed. He didn't have to wait long before Sean came rushing into the foyer with the phone in his hand.

"Tucker?" Sean said surprised. "What the fuck are you doing? You drunk, man?"

Colburn rushed him grabbing the phone out of his hand and throwing it against the wall hearing it smash behind him. He wouldn't let Sean call 911. No cop was going to save his woman-beating-ass.

"What the fuck?" Sean screamed. Colburn punched him in the face sending him careening across the wood floor into a lamp that toppled over and smashed in a spark of light. Before Sean could react Colburn had rushed him and kicked him in the gut sending a stream of puke out of Sean's mouth. Then he was on him, straddling his body as he laid down punch after punch to Sean's face. He could see Sean's mouth open, probably screaming, but he couldn't hear anything but the thundering echo of his heart in his ear drums. He landed punch after punch as Sean tried to defend himself, his hand up over his face but Colburn just punched through Sean's blocking forearms, desperate to save himself. Sean's bloody hand was reaching out, leaving marks and handprints of blood. Then his fingers touched cold metal, the sparking lamppost. He grasped it, pulled it up, and pushed it into Colburn's fact, burning him.

Colburn did not scream, but was caught off guard and fell off of Sean. The man quickly scurried away from his attacker and disappeared around the corner of the living room.

Splinters of glass and the fused electric edge of the lamp had burned and sliced into his left cheek. Colburn grasped the rod of the lamp and with one violent pull ripped it from his face. A volcano of blood shot from his cheek and splattered on the waxed wood floors.

"I was just going to rough you up, Seanny," Colburn spoke into the empty living room, knowing that Sean could hear every word he muttered, "But now I'm going to kill you. You hear me, Seanny?""

"I'm calling the police, Tucker. Do you hear me? I'm calling the police you fucking psycho!" The voice was distant and came from above. Sean Drake was upstairs, probably in the bedroom. But he wasn't calling the police. Colburn had been in this house before, had been in Sean's bedroom when he had showed him his collection of Boston Bruins memorabilia. There was no phone in the bedroom or any of the rooms upstairs. Sean Drake also didn't have a cell phone, he didn't believe in them the same way that Colburn didn't, it was one subject the two had discussed on Sean's porch one late night after work.

The last thing I want is someone to be able to get a hold of me no matter where I am, Sean said.

I hear that, man, Colburn laughed clanking his beer bottle against Sean's. *I have an answering machine for a reason. Sure as hell don't need a cell phone so everyone and anyone can reach me whenever the fuck they want.*

He could hear the patter of feet running around above him up on the second floor of the house. Through the living room to the right was the kitchen and in that room was an assortment of knives. He smiled through the pain.

Colburn had never killed a person in his life. He had come close once in the past. The love of his life, one Ginger Rose after she had been raped by a friend of hers in her dorm room in college. Colburn had attacked the man with viscous finality, even broken the son-of-a-bitch's neck but he hadn't done it properly, and only fractured a few vertebrae, didn't even paralyze the bastard. It had been his intent, to kill, not maim. It Women had always been his weakness, especially when one was the so called damsel-in-distress.

His ex-wife had never needed a hero. In fact it was one of the reasons that the two had gotten a divorce, she was an independent woman who didn't need a man to fight her battles. Colburn needed someone to save. Especially since he couldn't save himself. Iit was always easier to take out his own issues on someone else, even if it came down to murder.

Colburn was wobbling as he made his way towards the kitchen. The drugs that he had taken earlier were now fully affecting his judgment. The world had gone numb and distant, his vision wavering, a full erection threatening to pierce his jeans.

Once in the kitchen he reached into one of the drawers and pulled out a long, French knife. He pressed the blade to the side of his face like a man takes a woman's hand to feel her warm skin against his own. With the blade in hand he took the sharp edge and dragged it down the side of his face that wasn't wounded, cutting from his forehead over his eyebrow and down his cheek. The blood oozing from the open wound and tracing down his cheek bone and maneuvering over his neck. It made him shiver with excitement. The warm thick texture of the blood on his skin. The coppery taste in his mouth. There was an arousal from the wound, the feel of his flesh spliced and separating away from the edge of the blade.

"Oh God," he whispered as his erection threatened to explode in his pants. Colburn's eye lids were threatening to fall over his eyes, plunge him into sleep, the drugs coursing through his system. If he were to permit to the enveloping darkness, the battle would be lost. Sean would find him on the floor of his home, call 911, and Colburn would spend the rest of his life in jail, probably get two life sentences. No, he had to end this tonight.

Crawling towards the lit fireplace with the world growing blacker with each inch he pulled his failing body. From the fireplace he could feel the warm heat on his face. The sight of the burning logs reminded him of Christmas, one that he had never experienced himself. One he could imagine, standing in the Macy's furniture section where trees were decorated and boxes were wrapped with silver bows under a Christmas tree giving the illusion of Christmas cheer. He would see the families standing around the trees their hearts filled with the spirit of Christmas, children pondering whether or not Santa Claus had already come to the department store to lay out the vast amount of presents and the parents not wanting to explain that beneath the holiday paper were only empty boxes. It was nothing like his home, not the way that he had grown up – *home* -- in fact it had been years since he had thought about that hell his parents had put him through, it had even gotten worse around the holidays. No matter how many times he had been escorted off to a mental institution or exiled from his family, the hope of Christmas would always be a part of his soul.

Colburn thrust his hand into the fire. He bit down on his other hand silently screaming as the fire seared his skin, his teeth penetrating the flesh until warm spurts of blood splashed over his tongue. No longer was he about to pass out. In fact he felt more alive than he had in ages. The pain and rage coursing through is body was like an adrenaline rush – most likely that was exactly what was happening to his body – and suddenly he was more aware, more awake. The doctors had given him so many drugs to suppress not only his anxiety and whatever diagnosis of mental illness they were writing him up with in their neat little files. There was one, however, that they had forgotten. His uncontrollable rage that had lain dormant inside his psyche for the past ten years.

That had all changed.

Colburn withdrew his hand from the fire, his skin dark and burned from the flames. He felt a wash of euphoria as once again and old friend was invited home.

Pain.

Rage had kept him alive through the most tumultuous parts of his adolescence and once again he was free

One thing was for certain, he would not die tonight, not in this house. Perhaps later, but not now. He still had a mission to accomplish, a woman to save. This was going to be fun. When was the last time that he had saved a damsel-in-distress?

His head fell back on his shoulders and he felt the rush of the drugs working their magic to make him as high as a kite. It felt good. Invigorating. Freedom from the suppression of the drugs, which were supposed to keep him stable. From above him he could hear Sean scurrying from room to room, probably looking for a weapon that could take Colburn out, end his life. After all the police reports would read self defense if Sean had the balls to do what needed to be done. They both knew that he didn't. Sean didn't have that killer instinct.

Colburn danced into the kitchen, the wave of euphoria washing over him as he moved. He took out the knife. Walked back to the living room and knelt in front of the fireplace. He dipped the blade into the fire until its stainless steel blade turned dark from the fire. As the blade was removed he placed the hot metal against his skin, pushing down with all his might until he could smell the aroma of burning flesh. His teeth were pressed together and his head thrown back as the intoxication of the burn and the pain melded. Holding the blade in one hand he slowly drew deep slices through the burned flesh until his blood leaked out. With two fingers he dipped them into the wounds until each fingertip was lubricated with blood. Taking the blood drenched fingers he pulled them down his face making a macabre mask around his eyes and across his face.

"Seanny?" he whispered, sure that his once good friend could hear him.

Somewhere hidden on the upper floor was a terrified person who could not call 911. He was trapped like a Christian in the lion's pit of a coliseum.

At the footsteps leading up to the second floor, Colburn knelt on the first step peering up into the darkness. Only silence breathed through the house but he was sure that Sean hadn't escaped. The only exit would be for Sean to drop three stories to the rock ground below and then most likely slide into the Merrimack River where he would be swallowed by the current and dragged for miles down steam eventually drowning.

He had him.

"Seanny?" There was almost a gleeful laugh in his voice, beneath the contempt he felt for a woman abusing bitch.

He took a step up the stairs.

"This is cliché but I'll ask anyhow. Do you know why I am here, Seanny?"

No response.

"I understand. If the situations were reversed I wouldn't be speaking, not giving away my position. Good for you to have some kind of brain function," Colburn sneered. "So let me elaborate for you. This is how the situation went and how it is going to go. You hit Ashley. You abused her not only physically but emotionally. I promised you, when you got together with her, that if you ever harmed her I would kill you. Back then, that night we sat in your apartment smoking weed, I had to listen to your incessant crying, the whining, God how sickening it was to have to listen to a man spill his pathetic Dr. Phil emotions to me. To tell you the truth, you bored me. You made me sick and just sitting next to you made me feel less than a man. I should have snapped your neck then, or at least pulled out your tongue and sliced it off so I didn't have to listen to you pathetic whiny voice over and over again about how you valued our friendship and would do anything to save it.

"The funny thing is, she wasn't quite over her ex boyfriend at the time and after I left you she called me, and I went to her apartment. Are you listening?"

Silence.

"We fucked for three hours. Did you know that? Did she divulge that information to you? Hahahaha, god how we fucked for so long and she told me how you were too quick on the draw and never really satisfied her."

"You lie," Sean said.

There it was. Colburn had gotten under his skin and potentially revealed Sean's whereabouts.

"What the hell is this about, Colburn? I thought we were friends?" Sean yelled from somewhere on the second level.

"We were friends, good friends. That all changed the moment you put your hands on her. I warned you, Sean! You made the literal mistake of not believing me when I said I would kill you if you ever hurt her. Too late for that now, pal. I have come to collect on that promise." Colburn climbed three more steps. "Knock, knock," he laughed in hysterics, "Death has come and stands at your front door and he's come for you." There was a patter of feet from above and then nothing. Silence lingered throughout the house, Sean was silent, not even a whimper of fright. Colburn was growing agitated, frustrated that Sean wouldn't come out and face him, it almost made him want to laugh how pathetic the man was. "Hello? Is anyone home? Are you cowering under your bed, Seanny, I mean really. Where did you get that idea, some horror flick. Of course, the killer never looks under the bed, I don't get that. I mean seriously how silly is that. Why wouldn't you look under the bed?" He sniffed at the air though all his senses had suddenly become acute. "What's that stench? Jesus, Sean, is that what I think it is," he laughed to himself. "God, man, did you piss yourself? Is that what I smell? No, answer. Okay, no worries, I'll still find you, you must understand that." Silence. "Don't you know it's rude not to answer your buddy, now you're just being rude."

Once on the top step Colburn peered into the darkness allowing his eyes to adjust as he held his breath so that Sean couldn't pinpoint his direction. He looked down the hall to his left and then the right. No sign of Sean. He wasn't paying attention to the door in front of him, the one that led to the bathroom, but who would be so stupid to hide in such a small space? Where could he hide in a bathroom, behind a shower curtain? Too obvious, besides the mask of the shower curtain would have hidden Sean and given Colburn an easy assault, driving his knife through the shower curtain until Sean's dead body went limp in the bathtub basil where his crimson blood would circle the drain. He turned to head down the left corridor of the hallway when the bathroom door swung open and Sean charged him.

Caught off guard by the unexpected attack, Colburn just had time to look into the rage filled eyes of his one time friend as Sean slammed the shower rod into and through Colburn's stomach. There was an instant of pain at the realization he had just been impaled by a fucking shower rod. A bubble of blood exploded from his mouth and drooled down his chin. As Colburn collapsed to his knees still gripping the shower rod protruding from his abdomen and exiting out his back, he could feel the warm blood seeping around the foreign object, expanding around his T-shirt in a dark misshapen circle. From the exit wound blood spurted out in a stream, gushing down his back and into the crack of his ass soiling his boxers.

"Statistically, spousal abusers don't have the balls to pick fights with men, they enjoy the power of hitting women, makes 'em feel like men."

"Like I told you, Colburn, I never hit Ashley."

There was something different in his eyes, a truth that he hadn't seen. Not until a shower rod had been driven through his lower body.

"Fuck me," Colburn said realizing that Sean was telling the truth. "Shit."

As Colburn tried to back up his foot slipped on his blood and he went tumbling down the staircase, rolling over and over again down each wooden step until his back crashed into the wall at the bottom of the stairs. Sean now stood above him like a conquering Roman warrior. Slowly he began to descend toward Colburn, who was coughing up blood in giant chunks of red that splattered over his face and down his neck. His hands were on the shower curtain, plastic, he wasn't trying to pull it out, watching episodes of *ER* and other medical dramas he knew that was a death sentence. That didn't mean he couldn't snap the curtain outside his body. Straining with excruciating effort he gripped the shower curtain and snapped off the end that wasn't impaled in his abdomen, his hands soaked in blood, losing pints as it squirted out around the wound. The piece of shower curtain that was snapped off fell loosely from his hand and rolled across the floor in a wide roll much like that of a painters roller. He screamed in agony as it twisted inside the gaping wound.

Sean stood above Colburn now, looking down at the monster that had once been a man. His eyes were filled with sympathy, and disgust. This was no longer the man that Sean had known so well over the years. Colburn had become something different, more sinister, darker than anyone could have ever imagined a human being to become.

"I know you, Colburn, better than you think. You live by a code, a code of what is right and wrong, black and white, no matter how twisted your ethics have become. I knew a man that believed betrayal was the ultimate sin, and here you come into my home and attack me because you heard one side of a story from a scorned lover. Ashley and I haven't been together in quite some time. Granted we have this relationship, but it's mutual, just friends with benefits."

"Friends...with...benefits?" Colburn asked confused.

"Fuck buddies, buddy," Sean explained, "Simple as that. Just two people looking to hook up."

Colburn began to laugh.

"Help me?" he asked Sean.

A hesitation washed over Sean's face and he looked side to side as though expecting someone else to have magically appeared in the room that could offer him advice. Coming to a conclusion as he stepped down the stairs and knelt in front of Colburn he placed his hands on the protruding shower rod ready to pull it from Colburn. Unaware of the shard that was hidden behind Colburn.

"Thank you," Colburn said.

"You don't deserve this."

"No, I don't." A smile crossed his face as Sean began to pull on the shower rod.

Colburn pulled the shard of plastic from behind his back and shoved it up into Sean's throat. A loud gurgling sound emitted from his throat as blood spat over Colburn's face. He pushed the shower rod deeper into Sean until he was sure it struck his brain and Sean collapsed to one side...dead.

Ashley sat in her car outside of a 7 Eleven. She had her cell phone in hand, a cigarette in the other. Dialing the number to her lover, she listened to the ringing. There were no overhead lights where she had parked her car in the rear of the 7 Eleven, she had the night to herself. As she waited for the phone to pick up, she applied crimson lipstick to her full and pouty lips.

A shard of something sharp pressed into the side of her temple so hard that it drew a droplet of blood. She immediately looked into her rearview mirror and was just able to make out a figure behind her through the mirror. She saw Colburn, the left side of his face half melted off, dried blood clinging to his lips and chin, his eyes were dark and unfriendly, the eyes of someone who had only one intention on his mind.

"I thought I had friends," he said. "People that I could trust, people that understood what I was going through. It's laughable that I thought you were one of those people but you only wanted to expose my illness, my rage, you knew exactly what I would do if you told me that Sean had been beating you and shame on me for not paying more attention to the fact that there isn't a single bruise on you."

"Colburn, you don't understand. He never hit my face, he made sure that all the bruises he left could be covered by clothes," she exclaimed with a trace of fear.

"Save it," he demanded. "You got what you wanted. Sean is dead. But something tells me that he never laid a hand on you. Poor, poor, Ashley, thought she had the whole situation under control. Shame on you darling. You should've known better."

"What are you going to do? Turn me into the police?"

"No, darling, I have plans of my own for you. I have only minutes left before I bleed to death in the back of your car."

"We need to get you to a hospital, get our story straight, we can all walk away from this. There doesn't have to be any more death tonight."

"You are right, what was I thinking? I'm so confused, Ashley, what's happening to me?" Colburn said lowering his eyes to the number on the cell phone.

"It's okay." Ashley looked at his eyes in the mirror and tried to give him her most sympathetic smile. "I don't know what is happening to you but we can get through this together."

"You're right. We are going to get through this together."

"I'm glad you see it my way, now please lower your weapon."

"I will, just as soon as you tell me who you are talking to."

"It's my friend Becca."

"Really?"

"Yeah."

"Too bad the number you are calling is Sean's brother."

"Colburn listen...."

There was an eruption of blood that splattered across the windshield as Colburn drove the splinter of the shower rod through the back of her head and out her eye socket. Her body lolled to one side, her head hanging just above the passenger seat as blood spilled like an open faucet onto the seat.

Colburn reached down for the phone and picked it up as he heard the voice on the other end call Ashley's name for the third time.

"I'm sorry, Fadon, Ashley is unavailable at the moment, can I take a message?"

THE LIGHTHOUSE

BY EVERETTE BELL

David stopped in the gravel driveway, adjusting his grip on the cardboard box filled with paperbacks. An old memory of a faded photograph with curled edges came back to him. The lighthouse didn't look a bit different from the picture his grandfather had given his mother while on his deathbed back in 1972, but today was the first time he'd ever actually stepped foot on the ancestral homestead.

The scene was breathtaking; Cressmoor Point was a rocky outcropping that pierced about twenty yards into the dark waters of the Atlantic. On either side, coastline littered with rocks and driftwood snaked toward the horizon, and waves broke against the shore exploding foamy geysers into the chilly gray morning.

About a hundred yards back from the junction of ocean and wet stone, the hard earth succumbed to a blanket of tall grass. The fall-kissed, ankle high blades rustled in the gentle sea breeze. Further back the grassy expanse collided with a wall of trees separating Cressmoor Point from the rest of Maine, and a single gravel road dared to wind from the point into the dark wood.

In the center of the grassy shelf stood a lighthouse, majestic and strong. The weathered white tower looked out over the ocean like an ancient king surveying his realm. And like a kneeling peasant, a quaint Cape Cod style home sat at the feet of the lighthouse.

Inhaling deeply, David smiled at the beauty around him. The freshness of the breeze coming off the ocean was unlike anything he had every experienced in the city. He was glad to finally be home.

A look of satisfaction beamed from his face as he sat at the kitchen table with his wife and daughter. For the last sixteen years, Sharon had been patient while David put every dollar above expenses into the stock market. When Melanie turned six, he decided it was time to cash out and give her the childhood he had only dreamed of. The money was in place. He and Sharon quit their jobs, and the family moved to Maine's northeastern coast.

"Guys, we made it," David said with an ear to ear grin, "I didn't think it would ever happen myself."

Sharon was proud of their accomplishment as well. She tried not to spoil her husband's fun, but three days of hearing him go gaga over their good fortune was about as much as she could handle.

He squeezed Sharon's hand lovingly. "We did it, baby."

"Yes we did, hun," she said squeezing his hand in return.

"Daddy," Melanie asked looking over the edge of the table, "When can we explore the lighthouse??

Sharon got up to clear the table. "You've gotta get some sleep first, young lady."

* * *

Melanie sat in the clutter of cardboard boxes on the living room floor singing a wildly untamed version of *Ring Around the Rosy*. Her pigtails bobbed up and down amidst the cardboard flaps, and high pitch barks split the air from the excited Cocker Spaniel she wrestled with.

Her tune ended and she squealed, "Daisy, let me brush your hair!"

"Ok, girls." David appeared in the doorway to the living room wearing his usual fall get-up of flannel shirt, jeans, and running shoes. He was a thin man in his thirties with wavy brown hair and a neatly trimmed beard. "Your mom and I have some work to do, so why don't you two go outside and play?"

David gave her a serious look and raised his finger for emphasis. He knew exactly what was racing through his daughter's mind. "Listen-"

The brown haired girl in the blue overalls and the white top shot up like a popgun. "Come on Daisy, let's go!"

"Melanie," her father's lecturing tone drew her attention from the dog. "Stay on the grass by the house. Do you understand?" Her impish nod came to easily. "If I come out there, and you've left the area by the house you're going to be in big trouble."

In disgruntled silence the girl nodded. David smiled at her response. Only when she was mad did the word "ok" take so long to get out.

The sky wasn't exactly cloudy. It was more of a sheet of solid gray. A cool wind came off the Atlantic throwing Melanie's long hair in her face while Daisy ran in a tight circle around her human playmate. Laughing, the girl spun in place to keep up with her dog. Then the sweet rush of dizziness filled her, and she flopped onto the cool grass. In a flash, Daisy was on her, and the dog's barrage of licking brought a stream of giggles from the child.

They played for a good twenty minutes before the omnipresent specter of childhood boredom set in, and Melanie grew tired of the rough and tumble with her oldest and dearest friend. She pulled herself to her feet with a grunt, and like a nail to a magnet her eyes were drawn to the lighthouse. Wonder at what was inside promised her stimulation-seeking young mind a grand adventure on the other side of the old wooden door.

"Come on, Daisy." She skipped toward the ivory giant humming a random tune.

Breaking through a wall of cobwebs, the door opened with a rusty squeak. Stale breath came from the old structure, and Melanie wrinkled her nose as she slipped into the crack in the open door.

The skittish Cocker Spaniel hung back and sniffed the air anxiously.

"Daisy, come on!" The faithful friend hated to be away from her human, but something kept the dog on edge. Melanie's voice was a Pavlov's bell promising much love and attention, and with sorrowful eyes, Daisy entered.

The floor was covered in a decades old layer of dust. Crates and barrels filled the lower level of the lighthouse, stacked along each wall. A single dust-smeared window let in a shaft of sickly light that did more to intensify the eerie feeling in the room than to dispel it. Melanie fought off a shiver from the cold air held prisoner by the stone walls. Starting next to the door, a railless staircase wound it's way higher into the tower.

A strange feeling stirred inside her. It was the same as when she felt her mother staring at her for disobeying. The uneasiness seemed to reach out and physically touch her. Daisy sensed it too and stuck close to the girl's feet. Melanie's head bobbed around searching. . . for what, she didn't know.

"Melanie." a singsong voice echoed through the cold stone building.

The child's eyes opened wide. Fear rooted her to her place on the dusty floor.

Chk! Chk! Someone was walking down the steps. "Melanie," an otherworldly voice floated through the air. "Leave here, Melanie, or you will suffer"

Winding into view from the upper floors of the lighthouse, Melanie could see the flowing hemline of a dress coming down the stairs. The underskirt rustled against the dark fabric.

Chk! Chk! The figure was mostly in the room. Melanie's mouth rounded to cast out a scream, but the hand of fright stayed the sound. The dress was a dark blue, cinched tight around the waist, giving the body a curvaceous form.

Another step brought the slender arms into view. The skin of the hands was soft and pale like driven snow.

Chk! Chk!

Long midnight locks came into view. The hair was thick, perfectly straight.

"Melanie. . ." the eerie voice made the child's name sound perverse and unholy. "Leave this place or die."

Chk! Chk!

The figure was in full view. A woman stood on the staircase, arms at her side, and the gloom of the lighthouse interior wrapped around her blue dress. Melanie could see it was old and torn. Long black hair hung around the hideous remains of a human face. The skin of the left half of the woman's face was scraped to the bone. Jaw, cheak, and forehead were exposed. A thin film of bloody fluid glistened and dripped down her neck.

Melanie quivered. Daisy's hair bristled, and she bared fangs, barking wildly.

The woman pointed a finger at the terrified girl. "Leave this place!"

*　*　*

The shrill scream cut into Sharon's daydreaming mind like a rusty knife. Maternal dread awakened inside her, and her body went numb at the sound of her daughter's peril.

Bolting across the box-strewn floor, she almost tripped over a stack of dishes. Sharon ran into the gray morning. "Melanie" she called frantically.

David was close on his wife's heals, voice reflecting a similar dread. "Melanie, Melanie, where are you?"

The child's terrified sound came again like a feverish cry for help from a nightmare. Helplessly, David looked around the bluff, Melanie was nowhere in sight.

"The lighthouse," Sharon said in a state of panic as she pointed her trembling finger at the slightly open door.

"Oh God!" David gasped.

They found her lying on the dusty floor. Daisy stood over defiantly, barking at the empty air. All the color was gone from the girl's features, and she quaked as if death had patted her on the back.

Sharon fell to the floor and scooped up her baby. "She needs a doctor!' The panicked mother fought the urge to scream and put on a false face of calmness.

*　*　*

"Shock!" David's face mimicked the word he spoke. "Why would she have gone into shock?"

The woman in the lab coat as white as the little room they were in clutched her clipboard to her chest casually. "Mr. Blayloch, I really don't know what to tell you.

Shock is the body's response to a trauma of some kind. Most often we hear of it in terms of some physical injury, but a serious fright has been known to elicit a similar reaction."

David was skeptical. "Are you trying to tell me something scared her? I don't think so. You didn't see how pale she was."

"Like I said," the doctor defended herself, "I don't know what else to tell you."

"Do you think it'll happen again?"

"What we do know is you found her in the lighthouse. My guess is she got herself worked up when she saw a shadow or something. I'd start by keeping her out of there."

After a few minutes of dealing with paperwork, David left the Urgent Care Clinic. His faith in the medial field was now a little worse for the wear.

Melanie slept comfortably on the back seat of the Ford Explorer. Dr. Harston's sedative had effectively assisted her into a peaceful state of slumber. Curled up at her feet, Daisy trained a watchful eye on Sharon looking over her shoulder at her resting daughter. "So the doctor said she's fine?"

David started the engine. "She thinks something in the lighthouse scared her."

Sharon shook her head, and her face fell into her hands. Her nervous system was finally slowing down after the morning madness. All the worry surfaced as a loving mother's tears. "We should have made sure the door was locked."

She looked to David for something. He thought it was reassurance, but he couldn't be certain. Her soft face and red lips bordered by a bouncy spiral perm showed the horrible thought that plagued her mind. "If anything happened to Melanie. . .I"

She broke down into silent sobs.

David reached over and embraced Sharon lovingly. "It's ok, baby. . .It's ok." For a long moment he just held her. "We'll go by a hardware store on the way home, and I'll get a padlock."

* * *

Sharon sat down on the couch next to David, exhausted from another day of unpacking. Reaching over, he gave her shoulder a gentle tug. Responding to the ritual that had been established when they were dating, she lay down using David's lap for a pillow and immediately snuggled into the couch's cushions.

The room was bathed in the warm light of a small blaze flickering in the fireplace. Silence was a welcome companion after the day's labor.

"She asleep?" David broke the silence.

She responded with a tired murmur. "Her response was a tired murmur. "Out like a light."

A log in the fire popped killing the deep silence before it could settle over the room again.

"You know when I got the padlock the other day? The clerk gave me a weird look when I told him we were living out here?"

Sharon patted his leg. "You sound like the doctor now. There are no scary things in the lighthouse." She yawned. "He was probably just getting a look at who the new owner was."

"I know."

"You read too much King." She concluded. Sharon climbed off the couch groggily and headed down the hall. "Let's go to bed."

* * *

David blinked. Something had lifted him from the folds of sleep. Not only was he no longer asleep, but he was wide awake like he'd never been to bed at all. Sitting up on the edge of the bed, he snatched his jeans from the floor and pulled them on.

The room was silent except for Sharon's restful breathing. Crisp air entered the bedroom through the open window across from the bed, and midnight's breath filled the house with darkness.

David slid into a sweatshirt he grabbed from the bed stand and quietly stood up so as not to disturb Sharon. The wooden floor was cold beneath his feet as he walked to the window.

A thin opaque curtain waved in the night wind, but even through the gray veil, the lighthouse was unmistakable. By the pale glow of moonlight, it showed its age. The white paint was faded in spots revealing the true color of the stone beneath. The few windows up the side of the tower were dark, and the pains were broken.

An unexplained feeling stirred within the man. His mind reeled with the morbid curiosity of a child staring at a corpse.

On his way to the door, he looked in on Melanie. She slept peacefully with Daisy beside her.

The padlock was frigid to the touch. David hesitated after he withdrew the key from his pocket. A moaning wind cut into him, chilling him to the bone. Whitecaps curled on the dark water, then crashed on the rocks in front of the lighthouse. He rubbed the key between thumb and index finger. David was certain he wanted to go in, but. Melanie's episode and the odd look from the man behind the counter at the hardware store had shaken him.

The key slid in. He felt the muscles in his forearm tighten. This was his last chance to forget it and go back to bed.

David startled. Voices came from behind the weathered door. A man and woman were in a heated argument.

"Nathan, you've got to light the lamp! They'll hit Widow's Rock for certain if they can't see it!"

"Woman, they're pirates, and I'm not going to help them get ashore!"

"But they'll drown in that sea tonight!"

Then there was silence.

David felt like a voyeur, but some strange fear in him stayed his hand. He couldn't force himself to open the door.

"If you won't light it, I will!"

It sounded like someone was moving higher in the lighthouse.

"Get back here, woman!"

David listened in shock at the drama that should not be happening. The door was locked, and he had the only key. The windows were too small for anyone to climb through. There was no way anyone could have gotten in there.

"Woman, don't make me come get you!"

The woman screamed, and then a second set of feet overtook the first. . .Smack. . . "By Jesus woman, you will learn your place!"

Someone ran up the stairs again.

David stepped back from the door to see if he could make out anyone through the glass of the light room. A lurid silhouette moved behind the dusty glass.

One of the large panels exploded, and mingled with the razor shards was a woman in a blue dress plunging toward the earth. Her body hit hard, and she lay limp on the ground, then vanished.

* * *

"We're leaving Sharon." David exclaimed as he poured himself a cup of coffee.

"What!' She had been reading a paperback at the kitchen table. Closing it she looked up at her husband. "What do you mean we're leaving?"

By the tension in her voice he knew this was going to be a touchy situation. "I don't know how to explain it, but something's not right here." Crossing his arms, David leaned against the counter. "I think we should move back to New York."

"What are you talking about? We've saved years for this! All the long hours and sacrifices! What about that! Now you just want to throw all that away!"

His response was little more than a whisper. "Something's just not right. I think we should go."

Disgust turned to anger, and Sharon raised her voice. "Ok, David, let's go! But tell me this! Who do you think is going to buy this place! It's a dump!"

"Sharon, will you relax please."

She glared at him. "I've given up everything for sixteen years, so you could have this place. I'm not doing it anymore. If you go back to New York, Melanie and I won't be going with you."

"Sharon-" His protest was cut short. She turned and stalked out of the room.

The day dragged slowly by. David and Sharon avoided each other, but when they were in the same room, not a glance or a word was exchanged.

He knew his reasons for wanting to leave were irrational, Melanie's episode, the look at the hardware store, and his hallucinations. How could he tell Sharon he wanted to leave because he was afraid of ghosts? It hardly made sense to him. She certainly wouldn't buy it.

There was no visible sign of the sun. The sky still held the same cottony gray clouds that had been there for a month. His watch indicated sunset had been twenty minutes ago, but all he could make out was the darkening sky out the window of the small study.

He slapped his left pocket, keys were there. It was time for a drive. The isolation in his own home was making him crazy.

The night air was brisk, and the repetitive sloshing of waves against the coast soothed him. David climbed into the Explorer and started off into the wall of trees.

The gravel road wound unevenly into a thick tangle of trees. Beyond the border of the headlights' glow was darkness laced with the occasional moon shadow. Potholes and dead wood repeatedly tested the stylish four-wheel-drive.

An unexpected dip in the road caused the SUV to swerve toward a massive tree trunk. Spinning the wheel, David corrected the vehicle's course just in time. Terror surged in him, and he stomped on the brake pedal.

In the farthest reaches of the headlight beam he saw a pale woman in a dark dress approaching. The left half of her face was badly lacerated. Blood trickled down her white skin. Her pace was slow, and her sad eyes seemed to look right into David's soul.

He felt violated.

David finally breathed and felt like his heart resumed beating. What the hell's going on? Am I losing my mind? He leaned into the windshield looking for any sign of the woman.

She was gone.

"D. . .A. . .V. . .I. . .D."

If it weren't for his seatbelt the sudden jolt that climbed him would have thrown him through the windshield. The creepy voice that crawled from the backseat caused the back of his neck to prickle. He spun around.

Nothing.

"D. . .A. . .V. . .I. . .D." He didn't as much hear it this time as he experienced it. His skin went cold and clammy as if he were submerged in glacial waters. David felt vulnerable in a way he'd never known. There was no question that he was at the mercy of something greater than himself.

He had to know the source of his terror. It was closing in on his mind, scraping at his sanity. He whipped around searching desperately for the evil that threatened him.

The woman he had seen at the end of the road was now four inches from the glass of the driver's side window. David screamed and recoiled with fright. Her face was motionless. The woman's hair was long and smooth, black as the unluckiest of cats. The high cheekbones and the crow's feet at the corners of her eyes gave her the appearance of a distinguished Victorian woman.

At the close distance, David could see her badly sliced face was peppered with shards of glass. A section of skin on the left side of the woman's angular jaw was peeled away. He could see bone covered by a thin layer of mucus, and the borders of the torn skin gleamed with thick crimson clots.

"Leave, David, the damned have awakened." Sad eyes stared at the man from the mutilated face, soft and begging. It looked like she would burst into tears at any moment.

Then she vanished.

* * *

I did not see a ghost.

The lighthouse is not haunted, and I'm being irrational. Sharon's right. We've worked too hard to give all this up.

He rolled over on his back. Sleep was not coming easily on the November night. The air was cold, and warmth had not yet returned to his and Sharon's relationship. She was practically sleeping on the edge of the bed.

This is stupid, but what the hell did I see. And Melanie? God, am I losing my mind?

Shit. . .He rolled onto his side.

* * *

Ominous thunderheads rolled across the sky like an army gathering strength. As day passed the dreary heavens darkened. Poseidon thrust his fork from the ocean depths causing the seas to boil and spew sheets of frigid mist.

The day wore on, the weather intensified. Cold gusts from forgotten storm gods gnawed at the lighthouse like hungry wolves trying to strip a carcass. Gradually the pale daylight surrendered to the veil of night, and the heavens grumbled violently. Sudden flashes of lightning illuminated the lighthouse in an eerie glow, but the dominance of night could not be toppled for long.

David and Sharon sat at the kitchen table sipping hot coffee. Daisy and Melanie slept soundly on the couch nestled comfortably in the Raggedy Anne Quilt. Outside claps of thunder dragged on like sliding slabs of granite that finally crumbled at the bottom of a deep quarry. Ghostly tones sang through the old Cape Cod home as the wind blew through the boards.

The bad weather had brought a temporary truce to their war. Both David and Sharon were now more concerned with keeping their daughter and themselves safe.

"I think we better stay awake in case we need to leave quickly. We'll just let Melanie sleep on the couch."

Sharon added. "Yeah, I feel better being able to see her."

The dark Atlantic churned like a caldron under a witch's spell. On the shore the lighthouse jutted up from the earth, a single black fang in a mouth of darkness. Carried by the howling wind, rain fell to the earth.

A clap of thunder shook the small house from window pains to floorboards. Rain fell in buckets, loudly crashing on the roof. Sharon did her best to hold her cup as if she was composed, but her skin went white with fear. This was the worst storm she had ever been in, yet neither the TV nor the radio had made any mention of it.

David stood up and walked to a closet across the room. "I'm going out to check the tide," he said pulling on his yellow slicker. "We're not staying if this gets much worse."

Sharon sat alone at the table. Maybe she had been too hard on David. He wouldn't have just up and wanted to leave unless he really thought something was wrong. She had trusted his judgment before, that's how they afforded this place. Seeing him walk out into the harsh weather to protect his family reminded Sharon of all the reasons why she married him in the first place. In that instant her mind changed. If he said go when this weather cleared, they'd go.

* * *

The raindrops exploding on the hood of his raincoat were like gunfire. Bitter wind pelted him angrily with wet fists. With head bowed to protect his face, David staggered forward against the elements. Out of the corner of his vision he saw a strange glow radiating in the night.

His water-streaked face turned upward, and a gasp of disbelief passed his trembling lips. The lamp chamber of the lighthouse burned brightly with a weird glow. A red fog within the glow of the chamber swirled chaotically tempering the brightness.

David was assaulted by a haunting gust that nearly took him off his feet. Two staggering steps into a massive puddle allowed him to regain his footing.

Crashing waves shrapnelized against the shoreline thrusting sheets of cold spray into the night air. The Atlantic's fury kicked up a notch as wind and rain whipped the water into a maelstrom. David stared in terror as pale bloated corpses clad in seaweed marched forth from the ocean. A shudder of panic ran through him as he imagined their hands groping his sleeping daughter. This couldn't be happening; he threw back his hood hoping that would dispel the storm's trick before him.

Knee-deep in the Atlantic, they had bleached mops of hair over vacant eyes in pasty features. Green slime gurgled from bluish lips. Flesh dangled from the walking dead where creatures of the deep had obviously feasted well. Their progress was slow, but David noticed each pair of white lifeless eyes were locked on him, arms draped in rags lifted, moans sounded in harmony with the haunting wind.

Dozens of the zombies stumbled onto the rocks and clawed their way toward the dry earth. At their back, something was coming out of the murky waters. The massive object pushed waves over the undead causing several to be thrown against the rocks. Unaffected by their falls, the zombies staggered toward the frightened man. With their arms up and mouth's wide they were a perverse parody of natives worshipping a strange idol.

David realized what had pierced the water was the gutted husk of a ship. The mast remained intact, but decayed sails hung from the rigging like deflated ghosts. Seaweed and ocean debris clung to the ship's railing, and blowing in the wind, an unidentifiable flag flapped from the crow's nest. Defying the laws of science the ship was afloat in the raging ocean tide even though there was a jagged opening in the hull just below the bow.

All regard for himself was gone, but David had to save Sharon and Melanie. This whole situation made zero sense to him, but the time for second-guessing was over. He had to get them off the point no matter what it took. With water streaking his face, David raced toward the house.

Ten feet from the door, he saw it open and Sharon was silhouetted against the fire inside. "Get Melanie, now!" Not slowing the slightest, David almost bowled his wife over, and then slammed the door behind him.

"You've got to get Melanie and drive down the road! Wait ten minutes for me! If I don't show, you go for town! " Slinging his coat to the floor, David moved straight for the closet door he had left open. Pawing around on the top shelf, he pulled out two revolvers. Neither gun was full, but the few rounds he had left would have to do.

"Go get Melanie!"

"David, what's going on?" Her voice trembled. "You're scaring me."

He placed his guns on the table and grabbed Sharon by the shoulders. Eyes, a mixture of fear and resolve, cut into his wife with such intensity that she looked away. "You're going to get Melanie and get in the car! When you get outside I don't want you looking around, just run for the Explorer, got it!" She didn't know how to respond. "Got it! Tell me you understand!" His cold hands shook her firmly.

"Mommy, Daddy, what's wrong."

Both heads turned toward their daughter. It was David who ran over and scooped the girl up in his arms. Forcing the excitement in him to take a backseat to his paternal drive to keep Melanie from experiencing the horror outside, he smiled tentatively. "Baby, you and your mom and Daisy are going to take a ride, ok. Daddy will meat up with you in a little while."

"How come?' She asked, tugging her ear innocently.

He kissed her forehead. "Tell you later, sweetie. Now you mind your mommy, ok."

"I will." She looked over her shoulder and called, "Daisy, come on."

Amidst the clamor of paws on the wood floor, David handed their daughter to Sharon. "Remember, get in the car and don't stop."

She nodded. "Ok."

David kissed her. "I love you, Sharon. No matter what happens, you've got to keep Melanie safe."

Thud. . .thud. . .something was banging on the outside of the door. David picked up the pistols. "I'm going first and when I call you run for the car."

"Let me get the keys," Sharon answered shakily. Keeping his eyes fixed on the door David heard his wife fumbling around behind him.

Thud. . .thud. . .thud. . .the blows were getting stronger.

"Ok. Got 'em."

David raised the pistols and fired two shots through the door. As he kicked the remains of wood open, he heard and regretted the shrill cry of his daughter.

It took a second for his eyes to adjust to the absence of light. Six of the creatures had made it to the cottage, but twenty yards ahead through the sheets of rain, he could see two-dozen more headed his way. Two gaping holes leaked gore from the chest of one of bloated beasts in front of him. His bullets had done nothing to stop it. He fired again, this time square in the center of the corpse's forehead. A shower of bone fragments and gray matter exited the back of its head, and it fell to the ground, still.

The others were closing fast, arms outstretched. One of them grabbed David by the arm, and its touch was like ice. Their skin was in contact for the briefest of moments before David fired into the creature's forehead, killing it, but in that time, the man felt his energy drain. Suddenly his body stiffened; it was as if he were sore from a long day of physical labor.

The others encircled the man, grunting with dead eyes rolled back in their heads. He fired, again, and again. Two of the zombies staggered backwards, one fell to the ground, motionless. The next fruitless squeeze of the trigger told him the gun was empty, and he threw it to the ground.

A sharp pain dug in the center of his back, like a twisting blade. He felt his body growing weaker. Using his remaining gun he dropped the two corpses before him.

He turned. The final of his adversaries was staring him straight in the face. After its long touch, David noticed he was moving slower, and his skin was freezing. The last bullet in his gun threw the corpse against the side of the house, and a smear of brains was left on the white siding when it slid to the wet ground.

He had to act fast or Sharon and Melanie would never make it to the Explorer. The remainder of the beasts were plodding onto the shore. All his energy was required to get the words out. "Sharon, now, run to the car!" Then he fell up against the wall of the house.

As she stepped outside holding their daughter, Sharon was overcome with confusion when she saw all the bodies on the ground. "David what's going on," she screamed frantically over the howl of the wind and rain.

The dead neared.

"Get to the car," he forced himself to speak. David was so tired and cold.

Sharon shook her head in disbelief. "David what are they!"

He raised his pistol in the air, and his voice was almost a growl as he spoke, "Sharon, leave now or you won't make it."

Corpses were closing fast in a crescent formation

She turned and bolted for the car. David realized he had but one chance since his gun was empty; he could distract them. The gun slid from his stiff fingers, and he ran in the opposite direction of the Explorer. Each step took more and more of his endurance. Soon he couldn't walk.

His heart lightened when the sound of the engine cut the windy night. The glow of headlights washed over him, swaying, barely able to keep his feet under him.

Sharon watched in horror as the ranks of the dead closed in on her husband, arms reaching out towards him. Slowly he was engulfed by the approaching mob. The touch of their cold dead hands sent chilling pain through David. Frenzied cries climbed upward from his chest, but he was too weak to even attempt to fight them off.

The army of the bloated dead turned and moved back in the direction of the ocean. Fear filled David as he realized he was helpless to resist. He could not will himself to move, he was paralyzed. They carried him into the frigid water, slowly moving toward the ship.

His senses began to fade, vision blurred. The sounds of the groaning dead were distorted in his ears.

Raising him into the air, the dead arms pressed his limp body against the side of the ship. Splintered wood pierced him, bringing forth a sputtering cry of agony. He felt his flesh sundering like hands were pulling him apart. Then the zombies stepped away from him and started climbing the sides of the old ship. In silence they pulled themselves aboard.

David's skin and bones spread out, covering the hole in the hull.

From the comfort of the Explorer Sharon sobbed bitterly. The windshield wipers slapped water away from the glass, and she watched the ship move out into the Atlantic.

Waves lapped against David. Pain raced through him, but he was powerless to do anything.

The dead ship sailed into the dark horizon.

WINDOWED EYES OF HOME

BY JASON HUGHES

She looked out of the window, into the front yard. She witnessed it. The dark secret that no one else had known. He never knew she was there. He could not see her, but could feel her presence. Her eyes, glaring down upon him from the window to the bedroom on the top right. A subtle, pulsating light was burning inside, illuminating the room with a hellish crimson glow of a dim and morbid radiance. She saw what he did to her, when not a living soul was watching. She was his wife, Jenny Hill, the one whom he buried in a shallow grave beneath the soil in the front yard that night.

His name was William Hill. He swore one day she would drive him stark raving mad. It finally happened. "Where are you going?," Jenny screamed with a howling shriek.

"I'm going to the fuckin' store! Is that aright wit' you! Shit, woman!," William barked in retaliation.

"Are you getting cigarettes?!," Jenny asked in the same ear bleeding blast of verbal vengeance.

"Yes!! Leave me the fuck alone!, God damn it! I'll get back when I get back!," William yelled as his voice was muffled by the car windows and the slamming door. The above mentioned did not include the fact that he lowered his voice in a cold sense of callus silence as he entered the vehicle.

William had just finished a long day in the field, tackling massive bushels of sharp, dirty hay. Needles stuck to his overalls dropped to the floor as he made sudden moves throughout the rest of the night. He knew he would have to go home to her when he left the store. He dreaded it. He could not bear the thought or keep it locked in his gray matter for more than five minutes before struggling for decent thought patterns. *I could leave. I could take the car and never return*, he thought to himself on a regular basis. These phantasmal wishes were no more than illusions at a constant pace, throughout the night and day. Almost dreams too good to ever become a reality. This dark, black pit of a hole that was known as his reality was always there. He could not dig himself out... No matter how hard he tried or wished to do so. The thick pressure of everyday life with a spouse suffocated him immensely. He could never seem to breathe.

As he passed the kitchen appliances and silverware in the store, his mind started to drift into darker realms of an overactive imagination. Rationality was starting to become a blinded speck in the distance of his brain. William was descending to the depths of unkind reason and blissful to his burial of rotted benevolence. Reflections in the sharp cutting tools of kitchenware became progressively sinister with each passing blade. Something was taking over William's mind. Someone else... Someone with a violently angry time bomb inside was taking shape with each step down the long isle of shining tile and several surrounding meat (and veggie) dicing provisions. He soon saw the enclosing super mart as a super center of torture, mutilation and murder. This place had everything.

His passing face started to fall from grace and morph into her tearing lace at a murderous pace. He could see spatters of Jenny's blood splatter on the shining metal before him. This cephalic regurgitation was almost all too real for imagination. He could literally smell the blood and see each drop run down the myriad shapes of reflective blades to their angled and cloned wooden handles as each hung in clear individually cased plastic display packages. Each stainless segment of passing metal was a morbidly shaped mirror image of William's inner being, waking and becoming enhanced as he walked alone down the empty isle in a drone styled trance. Fragments of fearful self reflections fractured William's cracking self perception. He could hear their silently echoing footsteps on all four sides of him. They were always beside him. He was slowly, but steadily following them ahead. They were right there, trailing in a walking corpse stagger behind him. He could see her missing gravestone within the shining chrome. Jenny's angry screams were all around him, swarming through William's ears and aching skull. They would sometimes fade to screams of crying and pain. To William, her anguish drenched suffering was his dying strain. Straight from a brain that was dry and insane, these feelings of foul play became disturbingly mundane. A motivating melody of malevolent morbidity was mind mellowing music to his morbidly mental (pre)meditation. The rumbles of rage mumbled numbly within his murderous memory and granted a grim gratification of gratuitous ungratefulness. Even though not a breathing soul would know this fatal bestow beneath the dusk's afterglow... Someone's eyes were gazing below. She sewed the secrets that were never told. She silently witnessed the grim facts as he thought no one else would notice the act. She was there, standing above him the whole time. She was alone as she accompanied William, but not by his side. She was spying from inside... Hiding behind the flame glared glass in which he and his wife once resided, but never confided with an undying and selfish pride which always shined through their empty eyes. *It's time for that bitch to die,* William thought to himself as he reached the end of the stainless steel rack. The thoughts were behind him, yet still lingered within as he did not look back.

William walked around the store in a zombie like daze for quite some time. He did not know where he was going, as long as it was not home. Not yet. He still had to think and take his time doing it. Despite the random drifts into a dark pit of void reasoning, his mind was on a one way track. He could think straight for the most part and he knew what he had to do. He knew how he was going to do it. He had it all figured out and documented by systematic subliminal replay in the back of his mind. Serial killer, Gordon Drake, was never found. He remains at large today (he could be outside the window...). William thought he could surely pull it off as well. He could maybe even copycat the killings and get off clean. No blood would stain his hands of deadly sharp steel, so to say.

He could hear Jenny complaining, bitching, fussing, cussing and moaning the whole car ride home. He was trying to mentally stride and prepare for what he would be in for as he arrived. The dreadful music he would have to eventually face. It was morbidly mandatory... It was a small taste of malignant, cancerous suicide that was destine to happen with every nagging word that was about to bellow forth from her. He could hear it as it rang through his ears and left a bad, foul taste in his mouth. Her prior nagging was stabbing and numbing his now staggering senses. He was driven defenseless and nothing less than relentless consequences should follow in his senseless mechanism of maniacal malediction. This began to make since to him. His rhyme had a dark reasoning beneath the harsh, brutal surface of metaphorical ways to dispose of his verbal headaches. *Kill her. Bury the body. No one would know but me,* he thought to himself as he pulled into the driveway of the house. His unloving and mutually hated wife was waiting for him inside.

"What in the fuck took you so long!," she screamed at the top of her bleeding lungs and semi-cracking throat.

"I looked around fer a bit. Couldn't find anything. I'll be damned. That some fucked up shit 'er what," William said as he sat on the couch with a plopping thud. Jenny was far from impressed wit his blatant act of stubbornness. Insubordination was a well practiced craft within the home by the couple. Any skill honed to fray the other's nerves was always held in the highest regard by the both of them. They found a sadistic pleasure in probing at each opposing mind. Almost as if it were a game, the prize to be won was driving a so called loved one insane. Love and respect were two emotions and feelings that were vowed to be kept, but lost long ago... the night after the vows were read. After the ceremonial night of bliss had ended, so did the cherished honor in which they promised to hold so dear. It only got worse and worse from there.

"You better have gotten the cigarettes! That's the only reason you went to the store in the first place! Where in the hell are they!? If you forgot them, you're fucking going back!," Jennifer scolded at maximum volume. William could feel the anger boiling inside as he reached in his pocket. He knew all along that he was not going anywhere. Not if he could help it. She would soon find out."Here are yer God damn cigarettes! Choke on 'em! Better yet... Go out to the field behind the house, douse yerself from head to toe in gasoline and light up! Have a blast, honey! Just leave me the hell alone! I'm sick and tired of your nagging! That's all you ever do! It's the only thing yer fuckin' good at, nagging me slowly to an untimely grave! Nag, nag, nag, nag, *nag*!! It's like you started yer period and can't get off or somethin'! I swear, sometimes I wish I could make you a paid fer..."

"If you feel this way, then what in God's green hell did you marry me for?! You knew the way I was on the night we unfortunately met! I told you! I warned you! You..."

"I was wrong! I made a mistake! Are you happy now! I fucked up! I screwed my life up by wanting to be with you! There's nothin' we can do to fix that now! Filing for a divorce will take to long! We... are stuck... here, together! Forever! Get over it! You have nowhere to go!," William screamed bloody murder as the act began to seep into his brain once more. *No one will hear you scream. No one will see you descend beyond the flowerbed in the front yard. We're out here in the middle of nowhere. No one will smell your body as it mummifies below the moist surface. Most of all your constant, habitual, ritualistic sacrifice of my fuckin' sanity will be dead and buried fer good. No one will see me, no one will care, no one will know... and no one will MISS you,* William thought to himself as his breathing got heavier. His eyes drew beady, his brows sunk to a downward slant and his head dipped in a sulking position, obscuring the true horror that he possessed inside... preparing to put into a brutal fruition.

Jennifer could feel the aura of retribution that rose from him, like smoke on an ocean of fire. He had been this way before. Sometimes she saw it as a challenge... A mission. It was almost a recurring occasion and eternal cycle that threw a wrench in the spokes of William's well being. Being well was a far cry from William's present and past states of mind. He could feel the stability inside, withering with time. If one more word came out of her pie hole, it could set him off. It may very well bring him to the edge of sanity, the brink of mental corruption. The shortest straw could very well be the final of them all to push him over the..."William! What did you just have the nerve to say to me!? Get over it!? *Get... over it!??* We are together almost twenty four seven! We live together! Oh, we may not sleep together, and fuck knows I haven't been fucked in a century! It's okay though, William, because we swore ourselves to each other, right?! Through all of the unhealthy sickness we could fucking muster up for each other! This is what we both wanted, William! Look at us now! We're living happily ever after! Just as we always wanted! You and me, baby, God forbid... *FOR ALL FUCKING ETERNITY!*"

William stood in silence after the smothering assault of suffocating words and viscous verbal violence. *I could get this all over with in a few minutes. We got our own kitchenware here too. I got a shovel in the backyerd by the shed. You'd shut up fer good. Ferever, you bloody poor excuse for a human,* William thought to himself as he uttered..."I'm goin' to go lay down upstairs. My head is killing me."

"You do that then, William. Don't ask for any fucking supper. Starve to death for all I care. You deserve it." Every last quenching drop of starvation was savored in her mind. She relished the taste of his mental demise. Her eyes visualized in lies and deceitful cries of wishful good-byes. She thought of poison a few times, but the vindictive act of subliminally force fed toxins slipped her mind.

William, on the other hand, had something else in store for Jenny that night. Something much more than she would have liked. He was calculating a conscience state of guiltless innocence, just in case of an ambush questioning by the local authorities. If he could, he would murder her with his bare and bloody hands... and indeed come up with a quick and effective get-away plan. This was only if he needed it, of course. In his mind he was certain that not a soul would find her corpse. He would make sure of it. He had to. It was the only way he could get away with it with the deed without the entire small town that surrounded finding out about it. The execution had to be perfect and flawless. Anything less could cost William his only freedom left. A fate much worse than a nagging wife that drained his sight of decency and rationality. Twenty five to life was surely worse than a wife which induced mounds of strife that dimmed the lights of reason... Yet, it was all that William believed in. It was his only way to a brand new start. A new beginning of peace and tranquility that was soon to be if he fulfilled his darkened destiny. This would mean his other half would have to be eliminated. He lied on the bed and plotted it all in his head. He jotted down the reasons for his soul mate to be dead. A dreadful fate would soon await and he could live in peace, as his wife's short life was taken by him and lowered among the deceased. His judgment was diseased. The boundaries of right and wrong had been blurred and broken long ago. William could see no wrong or harm in such a criminal choice of acts which shattered the lines of decency. His mind's eyes faded from blurred, to fuzzy, to double visioned, to a coal and void black beyond a cold impurity. It was almost time. Time for jenny to die. A rhyme within a line that never grew bitter with time. The invocation of intolerance was approaching as William starred at the ceiling with a gaping mouth and wide eyes. The snail paced fan blades spun a reflection in his irises from above, which shunned all emotions of a once dying love. They were nothing to him now. He had lost them all somehow.

As he lied alone in a pool of hesitation devouring anticipation, perspiration began to pour... To waste away the heartache and cursing betrayal of this useless, pathetic whore. The one he could never adore. She was immensely becoming a bore. This abyss of agony, he could accept no more. A caress of deception would soon be the blessing that buried her terminally. The infection that rested was a result of rejection and molested patience within the collective minds of the two. One stood alone in following through with the ghastly crime. The secret would be taken to his tomb. He would never tell a soul. Only the worms and the maggots of hell would know what happened on that night... as no one else would remain in sight.

William did not look up behind him. He could not see the light. The shadow was there, starring as he buried her beneath the surface of the earth, in front of the house... and below the right bedroom window. Someone was in the dimly illuminated room. They were watching through sectioned glass as she secretly entered the earthly doom. They had arrived a few moments prior to the improper entombment within the dirt. They were looking down on him with every thought.

His wife, Jenny, was alive and well and in the kitchen. She was fixing herself something to eat. A midnight snack at that. He was dreaming lucidly. No one else could have ever known. His eyes were layered in stone. Little did he know, someone would watch from home. His clandestine revealed was the least of his worries of what was soon to come. She had seen what he had done. Was it all a dream or a prediction of summoned punishment, the web that he had spun. William was coming undone.

The footsteps traveled closer with every stomp on the wooden floor. He was awake and the living nightmare was headed his way. Down the hall and to the door of the room, in which he lied awake. He could made no mistake in delivering this terminal fate. If he fucked this up, he'd be shit out of luck and it would be too late. To procrastinate would resonate and lead to the elimination of William's desired extermination... The suicide of this chosen salvation. He wanted her to die and she was the reason why. The genesis of a madman was spawned from a bed full of lies. This is where the egg met the cell, to birth a monster conceived in Hell. A relationship that would burn to shit was crawling from the deep, blackened well. He could hear her breathing at the door. His heart started to race and suddenly skipped a beat as she began to pound on the closed entrance with all of her might."William! Let me in! What are you doing in there!? You can't turn me on, why bother with yourself! You suck and that's not a fucking compliment! Take it as an insult to you pathetic, weak-willed manhood!," Jenny screamed as she rattled the locked door with a furious vengeance.

"Go away or I'm goin'...!" William began to scream as he drew back and swallowed his words. He would choke on them with pride this time. It was the difference between sparing his wife's life... and living his own. "If you don't open this door, I'm going to kick it the fuck down! I mean it, William! Open the God damn door!," Jenny wailed as she did the same with her balled fists on the bedroom door. She was determined to never let him rest. "Can't I just be alone for five fuckin' minutes, woman? Just five minutes? That's all I ask of you! I need rest or I'm... I'm goin' ta snap!," William backfired from his verbal canon once more. He almost had a hard time holding the verbal action of premeditation in for the most part. It almost slipped. He almost spat it out. It could have been a venomous call on his part. One that would have come back and bitten him. He could never let her know. Not a single soul would or could know. His eyes drifted in a constant scan around and across the room. Paranoia was starting to nest within. Jenny continued to pound on the door with a demonic fury of anger that would not seem to cease. It seemed never ending. The appending decline of descending sanity was easy for William to see. He noticed these traits, indeed... yet not a phase was issued.

He knew what he was going to commit and did not care. William had finally been pushed over the limit and he was determined to follow through. No matter what. His eyes scanned the room faster and in rapid jerking motions. The room almost began to spin. He spotted tools of interest and walked through a scenario with each object. He cited the pros and cons. He re-examined and re-played them mentally, over and over as the beating continued. It was almost as if her death was flashing before is eyes. With each vision, the reality of the calculated matter drew closer and closer and *closer*. He could hear temptation's bells tolling from somewhere down below. The tone was low and cold. Their icy fingers reached into William's heart where no one had touched before. They came in the human form of Jenny, his wife. She possessed his soul, life and household. He had to exorcise her out forever. The time was drawing near. Something had to give and soon. He still had the guidance at night by the light of the full moon.

His palms began to sweat. He knew this would be best decision in the long run. Even if he had to run long and hard from home to save the omened destiny of incarceration. A fifty-fifty chance in reality's eyes. He began to shake nervously. It was almost a quaking quiver as if the temperature steadily dropped at an unholy rate. His sweat turned cold... ice cold, but William kept sweating as he shivered with almost a convulsing motion. He crossed his arms as if he were trying to warm himself while drenched in a cold sweat. His soul's temperature drastically dropped as his body temperature rose. The plan was starting to unfold.

It was all coming together. The shovel was in the back by the shed. He could lure her into the same room, commit the act or distract her for a moment before doing so and bury her in the front yard. It was getting too late for anyone to be awake and besides, no one resided for miles. William recollected every thought within his head. It had to be perfect. He was sure it had to be. He had already made for sure that is would be that way. Full proof. Flawless. The master plan. He just needed the subject matter. Opportunity was not only knocking, it was wrapping viscously on the bedroom door and blasting obscenities on top of that. He ad to answer. This was his calling. This was his final chance screaming out to him. His eyes slowed down and came to a halt as they fixed on the old cycle that was hanging on the wall.

His grandfather had given him the cycle for a gift. He had it since the first World War. It was a small, hand held handle made of wood and a curved blade, which had been rusted to a fine weathering by now. He slowly wiped the sweat on his overall pants legs and stood up, clenching his fists tightly. He walked over to the cycle and removed it from the wall. At the same time he reached out his hand and began to proceed toward the bedroom door. He unlocked it and the beating bled over by at least six or so violent pounds. His heart was next to take off in a blasting fury. He saw the doorknob start to turn as he gripped the cycle handle in his clenched fist. The door flew open."William, I... Want in the fuck are you doing with...," was all Jenny could muster before the cycle met the flesh of her neck. Her throat had been cut in the bedroom Where she would forever lie. Jenny's life was slipping away as she glared at her draining blood, which began to form a crimson staining pool in the carpet. She began to choke and gargle on her own vocal chords with each gasping breath, grasping for fresh air. Her sharp tongue went numb as heartbeats leaped to thuds, and the blood recolored her hair. She strained for air and restrained the despair as her vision began to fade. Not a tactic she tried would give back her life. In this room she met her fate... It was already too late. She died on the floor in ponds of gore galore and met a gruesome demise. He kissed her head and said farewell to the whore that provided the lies. He gave his good-byes as he gazed into her dying eyes and parted his ways with despise.

William then had to plot the plan for getting the body to its final place of rest. The earth would be the best. He picked up Jenny's lifeless corpse and carried it down the stairs over his shoulders. He had another six hours before the sun arose for the day. He had enough time to uncover a shallow grave, place her body beneath the earth's surface and cover it up before the roosters started to crow by the first light of the dawn.

William reached into his pocket and pulled out the un-opened pack of smokes from the trip to the store before. He flipped over the box, tapped the top and packed the tobacco against the rough side of his palm. He tore open the pack, then walked around to the back to grab the burial shovel. He lit up the smoke and inhaled the first gulp with a relieving sigh of visible breath. His wife was no more, William knew this for sure, for he had laid her to death. He heard her last gags and gasps and hacks, as she was struggling for air. She came to for a split second and he completed the job in a swift swoop. He thought about burying her alive. That would have been a challenge. She was as dead as a doornail and as silent as a rock on a pond. He lit the cigarette and began to dig. He could still hear her complaining as he buried her. Even in death, she would not shut up. He dug and dug. As he dug the hole and sifted through the blackened soil, his mind began to drift and his blood began to boil. It was sightless inner turmoil. His mind began to wander into a frozen state of wonder. A place he could not ponder.

William began to think of all of the good times they had (which very few there were), that soon became the bad. He knew they were few and far between, but acknowledged their presence at least ten percent of the time they shared as well. Some of the good times lingered with him as he dug her shallow grave in front of the house at the end of Mapes Street. William Hill buried his murdered wife, when he thought no one else could see. She was witnessing it through her own two eyes. She was watching his every move. Every pile of scooped and shoveled dirt from the earth was seen from the eyes of the buried.

Her soul exited the now hollow shell formerly known as a body. She had crossed over moments after her murder. She was trapped inside the top bedroom on the right forever, even though her body was buried in the front yard. Jenny was watching William the entire duration of her own burial. She watched as her body was carelessly nudged with a booted foot, three and a half feet into the worm filled dirt. She witnessed as he buried her clothed, casketless body in the front yard... In a hole, beneath the ground, near a tree, by the house at the end of Mapes Street. She knows who put here there when no one else was around, beneath the cold ground. Her husband slaughtered her in the bedroom in which they once made hateful love. She silently watched him and sewed a thick, sickening curse from the window up above.

A year passed and all seemed to get better for William. There was no more nagging. There was no more pestering or false accusations. One year later, on that very night... Strange things started to happen. Jenny had seen what William had done that night. She watched... and she waited. It had been a year and she was ready to resurface and come home to show her husband William, that he was not alone. Jenny died a painful death and her spirit could never rest. She was resurrected from the grave a year to the date, to haunt William as he slept. She knows where he lies. She can see it through her eyes, in the room in which she had died. She looks down upon William and can still see her body, lifeless and still as well. She watches as he sleeps, and as her jugular bleeds. As William lied there silently with his new interest, his dead ex-wife, Jenny was standing at the foot of the bed. She was looking down on the sleeping couple. This was once the pillow, in which she rested her head. Her hollow soul has now returned to burn the guilty heart instead. Jenny's entity has come back from the dead...

The End

Lucidity

By Matthew Burgess

As I watched the inmate ram his head over and over against the wall, all my mind would think was: "I wonder if human heads are as similar to chicken eggs as they look".

As it turned out, once the inmate had finally broken his neck and lay twitching on the floor, twice as much "yolk" covered the wall and floor than I expected.

I took a step back from the window partition that separated myself from the body on the tiled floor and tried very hard to focus on the fact it was human being dead in that cell. A living soul. A person just as lost as I was.

But I couldn't. The medicine made everything so...

Foggy.

I shook my head and looked back at my open cell door, swaying on its upper hinge. The middle and bottom hinges dangled freely where they had been ripped from the frame. I could have starred at the shadowy opening forever. What I saw wasn't the darkness leading into the prison cell I had spent so many years in, locked away, but the gapping mouth of a giant fish that lie dying on its side. The inch wide claw marks that ran along the hall made for excellent gills.

I followed those marks, my fingers trailing their jagged surface. The light in the hallway began to flicker and somewhere in the distance I heard a bulb explode. The lighting, for some reason, made me think of a garage. The dozens of cell doors that lined both sides of the hallway had been torn away similar to mine, their residents already scurried off to cause mayhem somewhere else in the prison.

As I took each step slowly, only lightly touching the claw marks but feeling as though that touch was the only thing allowing me to keep my balance, I saw myself walking down the hall of the house I had built. My house. The place I had raised my family.

...in my house...

No! Not my house. Not anymore.

That was a long time ago. Another time. Another life. I was here now, this is where I belonged. I knew that. But why? I tried to remember, but the medicine...the medicine —

Someone screamed. The voice echoed down the hall and seemed to wrap itself around me, drawing me forward. The scream made me feel sick, nauseated, but I couldn't stop moving towards it.

The claw marks ended when the hallway opened into a round multiwindowed and multidoored room. I lost my footing and spilled into the room. This was where we inmates were searched. Every day. Both before and after our sessions with the doctors. For a second the image of me being probed, not so gently, by the guards flashed before my eyes, but it quickly dissolved into the smiling face of my wife.

...in my house, my wife smiles at me...

I tried to grab the image of my wife's face and hold it inside my head, but it faded almost as quickly as it had appeared. This was the first time since being locked up that my mind had been clear enough to even recall those light blue eyes. I wanted the image back!

I tried to pull myself to a standing position using the railing the inmates were forced to lean on while another man jammed his ringed fingers inside of us. I heard someone laugh inside my head. I couldn't tell if it was the laugh of the guards or that of my daughters giggling from the second floor.

...in my house, my wife smiles at me. I can hear the girls giggling overhead...

My daughters...I had forgotten them too. The medicine had made sure of that. But the medicine was fading now. There was more to my life than that prison cell where I had drawn ovals all over the walls because I couldn't remember what a smile was.

I stepped over the shredded body of a guard on my way to the exit. I passed a shattered window where a doctor had always looked on, stone faced, as the searches progressed.

"This is for your own good," one of the doctors had said. "We don't want you sneaking anything into your room that you could use to hurt yourself. Now do we?"

Another hallway. This one I knew nothing about. If I had ever passed this way it was long before my blood had been diluted by three shots in the ass a day and a cup full of pills. There were claw marks here, but they were along the ceiling where I couldn't reach. I had to concentrate on my destination, another door at the end of the hall, to keep myself from falling.

Again I remembered the hallway of that long ago house that I had once called my own. It was nighttime in this memory, I knew because I could hear the crickets outside. There hung picture frames at eye level, but the faces inside were nothing but a blurred mess. I remembered the wall paper in more detail. My wife had picked it out. It was patterned with yellow triangles.

...in my house, my wife smiles at me. I can hear the girls giggling overhead. I follow the sounds of their voices...

I was back in the prison, almost to the next door. Why was I here? Why did I feel that I belonged trapped behind lock and key?

The door swung easily open. In a flash like lightning, I saw the door to my little girls' bedroom.

This was some kind of cafeteria, but if it was for the inmates, I had never seen it. Stainless steel seemed to have overgrown everything like a ravenous vine. My reflection starred back at me from the tables, columns, trays, and counters. I tried not to look at myself. The medicine made me see things in the steel that couldn't possibly be. Eyes that weren't my own. A grin that I'd never grinned.

"Hey man, wait up," someone shouted from behind the serving window. An inmate dressed in dirty white pajamas (same as me) came charging out, puffy red hair flopping on his head. His eyes were bugging out of his skull like that of an owl. He knocked over a stack of trays as he pulled to a stop in front of me.

"Hey man, where you going? Can I come?" He said, looking both frightened and excited at the same time.

I said nothing. My tongue felt far too swollen to speak.

"Those things are still here...you know?" He turned around to show me the back of his pajamas where there were two long tears from shoulder blade to hip. Only a light trickle of red marked the edges. He chuckled loudly. "Think we need to get out while we can."

I wasn't entirely sure if this redhead was something I was really seeing or a cross between the fading medicine and a jumbled memory, so I tried to ignore him and I continued on.

"We can escape...you know?" the inmate said, obviously taking my silence as an invitation to follow. "Most of the guards are dead. Any that aren't have too many other things on their minds to worry about us...right?" He gave a pitiful roar and clawed the air. He started into a chilling laugh that made the dull silence vibrate.

I had been working; the memory hit me like a punch to the gut. I had been working late and I was angry about it, but was glad to be home to my family. I had come home and my wife had left the garage light on and it was flickering.

I am angry because of the garage light being left on once again. In my house my wife smiles at me. I can hear the girls giggling overhead. I follow the sounds of their voices...

The next room was littered with bodies, two dozen guards in riot gear. Blood and gore lay under a mound of shields and batons.

It almost looked as if a bomb had exploded in their midst's, but the spray of red and claw marks told another story.

The redhead laughed hysterically after picking up the decapitated head of one of the guards. He showed me the head which was frozen in a grimace of fear and pain. I'd seen that look before.

Something slammed into the door to my right. A door I hadn't even noticed because of the blood rolling down the seam blending wall and frame.

The inmate dropped the head and retreated to the far side of the piled butchery. My reaction time was much slower. I could still feel the medicine clogging my veins. I didn't even look up until the door bowed outward like an inflating balloon. There was an exhale of breath from the other side. It was deep and primal and I felt it roll up my legs and settle into my stomach.

"We gotta go...you know?" the redhead said.

I couldn't move until he grabbed my arm and jerked me in the direction of the exit. I turned just in time to miss (by the sound of it) the door crashing into the far wall.

I hadn't realized how much concentration walking had required until I started to run. My legs weren't listening to my brain. They were weak and wobbly and each time I landed a step I was convinced they would fly out from under me. The redhead was far ahead, beckoning in between his bellowing laughter. Behind me I could feel a presence. It was close sending a prickle along my neck line. I knew it was galloping, I could hear each long nail as it clang against the floor. The next door was so far ahead it looked impossible to reach before whatever was behind drew one of those elongated nails down my spine.

The only thought that came to mind was that I couldn't believe how many hallways this place had.

I looked over my shoulder, hoping that seeing whatever was hot on our heels would spark just enough fear into my body that I could run straight. The medicine! The Goddamn medicine would not let me see anything but a blurred shadow filling the dim hallway behind me.

I am angry because of the garage light being left on once again. In my house my wife smiles at me. I can hear the girls giggling overhead. I follow the sounds of their voices. My wife is behind me. She wants to know what I am doing...

I slipped through the door—I see my daughters' bedroom door—just seconds after the redhead. There was something in front of me. Something dangling from the ceiling.

I tried to stop. I tried to steer around it. But there was nothing I could do. I collided headfirst into the hanging body and cartwheeled to the ground. The body dropping a second later.

The redhead's laughter was punctuated by the sound of a slamming door. Then a second sound; nails on metal.

I pushed the body off me. It was heavy for a dead man. I almost found this funny, but there was a long enough gap in my foggy mind to repulse me. I saw the other bodies hanging from the ceiling, but they did not register. I was concerned only with the door I had just made it through. It was shut and locked. I waited for it to burst off its hinges as if a wrecking ball were entering a party unannounced.

Nothing. The door remained still and peaceful. The redhead was on his knees cackling.

"You see that?" he said, between gasps. "Damn thing nearly took your head off."

Inside my head, my little girls' bedroom was dark, but I knew they were laying down pretending to sleep. I could feel their presence. And what was once unconditional love was slowly becoming uncontrollable rage.

It was then that I felt fear. The fear might have been a little slow on the uptake. But it was there as I looked towards the ceiling expecting the clawed beast to crash down upon us. It was also then that I noticed what the hanging bodies were attached to the ceiling with. Their own entrails were wrapped around their necks and the ends tied to the air conditioning piping.

I scuttled like a crab against the wall to get out from under the lab coat covered bodies. The blood drenched coats were made even more red by the only light in the room; a glowing red exit sign. I recognized some of them, although I couldn't remember their names. They were doctors. The very same doctors that had interrogated me. Drugged me. And allowed me to be searched both inside and out. Not even if every last drop of that god forsaken medicine had worked its way out of my system would I have felt sorry for the horrific sight before me.

"What the hell was that thing?" I said, finding my voice slurred but coherent. When was the last time I'd spoken? I knew the answer and for some reason it broke my heart.

I am angry because of the garage light being left on once again. In my house my wife smiles at me. I can hear the girls giggling overhead. I follow the sounds of their voices. My wife is behind me. She wants to know what I am doing. I tell her to leave the room...

"That thing?" the redhead said. "You know what it is...right?"

I shook my head. I felt as though I was swimming upwards. I knew I was far from the surface, but it was within my grasp. The fog thinned a little more.

"Ah, you must be one of the violent ones."

Violent? Me? I tried to say no, but I heard a clacking echoing from below.

"They keep you doped up?" the redhead inmate said, his eyes narrowed then widened. Narrowed then widened. "Economic counseling. Dope up a patient instead of helping him...you know?"

I didn't know, but I said I did because I knew medicine. I felt the medicine weakening.

"As for that thing; you can't confine so much evil in one place without there being consequences. It always finds a way to seep into everything."

"Evil," I said, tasting the word and trying to remember what it meant. "What evil?"

"You...me...the rest of them," the redhead said, his laughter had subsided, but it look just on the edge of reappearing. "This is an insane aslyum. A house of the mad. What kind of people do you think they store here?"

"I'm not evil," I said. I remembered getting so mad at my wife for being in the same room as me I couldn't stop my hands from balling into fists.

"Sure you are," the redhead said. "I raped three people." He bent down to where I sat, resting his hands on his knees. "But I also peeled their faces off."

I could feel movement below the floor.

"What'd you do?" the redhead said. "You wouldn't be here if you hadn't done something."

"I didn't do anything," I said. I saw my smiling wife. I saw the hallway leading to my girls' room. I felt my anger. My possessive uncontrollable anger. The doctors had told me later that I had a tumor suppressing a portion of my brain. They claimed this had been the cause of my "outburst". I had refused to believe them. I hadn't even allowed my lawyer to use it in my defense. I was innocent. I couldn't have done...

"Sure you did."

I am angry because of the garage light being left on once again. In my house my wife smiles at me. I can hear the girls giggling overhead. I follow the sounds of their voices. My wife is behind me. She wants to know what I am doing. I tell her to leave the room. When she doesn't, I grab her by the throat and squeezed...

"No," I said.

"We're all crazy here...right?" the redhead said. "You kill someone? Probably, that seems to be a big trend around this part. Evil? You see?"

"No. I..." Suddenly I wanted my medicine. I wanted to pour it down my throat. Pump it into my veins. I remembered my trial. I remembered the verdict. I swore I was innocent, they said I was insane. Insane and innocent are two words that could never be paired together.

"This place is our cocoon...don't you see?" the redhead said. "Trapped we crawl into our cells only to be transformed. Evil evolves." He stood and spread his arms like a mock crucifix. From below the floor the movement became a rumble. The redhead looked down and for the first time did not wear a grin. A black, oily shaped burst through the tile. The shape was not blurred like it was in the hall. I caught every rippling detail as it clamped its massive jaws around the redhead's lower body. Dust, wood, concrete, and blood filled the room along with the redhead's deafening laughter.

The last bit of fog burned off as adrenaline sped up my blood flow. I tried to push myself to my feet using my hands, but all I could feel between my fingers was my wife's delicate neck. I hadn't done it. It couldn't be me. I would never hurt her.

As I crawled away from the demonic figure, I knew the truth. Even though I hadn't killed my wife and girls, they had still died by my hands. I was evil. Maybe not all of me. Maybe only a tumor that slowly ate its way through my gray matter. But it was enough.

I ran for the first door I could find and discovered open crisp air. I kept running. The line of chain link fencing became a solid wall of silver, the razor wire shimmering blue from the moonlight. I passed inmates wrestling guards to the floor. I saw men running around waving bloody masses above their heads. The smell of smoke was everywhere. The sound of gunfire became thunder from the sky. I saw carnage and chaos. I saw evil.

I ran down the driveway I only vaguely remembered from inside a police cruiser years ago. So many years ago. How old would my daughters be now? I had no way of knowing, the medicine had stolen time. But it had also stolen my rage and my guilt.

As I passed below the gate that should have been closed, I stopped to catch my breath. Even this far away I could hear shouts and laughter over my shoulder.

I am angry because of the garage light being left on once again. In my house my wife smiles at me. I can hear the girls giggling overhead. I follow the sounds of their voices. My wife is behind me. She wants to know what I am doing. I tell her to leave the room. When she doesn't, I grab her by the throat and squeezed. Her neck breaks with the ease of a hand with strength far superior to my own. I am not myself. I know this, but I cannot stop myself. I have been taken over. My girls trust me too much to even cry.

I cried for them. At the end of a dirt road, I cried great breath stealing sobs until I felt light headed and thought...no, hoped...that the medicine has kicked back in.

I looked down at my hands and wondered when they would become claws.

THE EVE OF ALL SHADOWS

BY DAHLIA WOLFFE

Very few people know the truth about Halloween. Some people argue that it was a day created solely for the entertainment of children. Others believe that it is Satan's birthday, while many others disregard this day altogether. All three ideas are terribly wrong.

Halloween was the Finnish name for this day, in laymen's terms it was the name for this day translated into a historically Wiccan language, a language used by witches. The name that stretched back centuries beyond our spiritual conception, our creation, was All Hallows Eve. The word hallow referred to any spirit, good or bad, though more often than not, it referred to the bad. This day gained its fame by being recognized by occult scholars, spiritual mediums, and psychics as a night in which such activity was at its height. As far as all childlike things were concerned, it was the night when the spirits came out to play.

But just because the masses were blind did not mean everyone was.

It may seem as though the explanation of the language of this day fit with nothing else about it. As the presence of myself in this story should prove, this notion is false. October was the festival of Samhain, and for us witches, this was a month long holiday. Like many of our other festivals (Imbolc, December, Beltane, March) it was revered due to the fact that nature seemed to shine in favor of our practice, with frequent full moons. On Samhain, however, it is full nearly every night, more often than any other time. Full moons are the best times for spells to be conjured and rituals done, putting the desired spell in motion. This often conjures the image of Satanic witches (there is a big difference) doing human sacrifices. I cannot deny the fact that it happens, but I can say that I am not among them. I have been alone in my practice, as well as socially for as long as I can remember, since the death of the one who taught me. That said, I was never active in celebrating these days. The most notable night of Samhain was Halloween, and this was the only night of this celebration that I was ever active with my craft.

How fitting too, that my name is Eve. To start, I know I am nothing like what you would expect from her. Most people, myself included have this mental image of some pale beauty with red or brown hair, snake charming as she ate her apple and batted her eyelashes at Adam, feigning innocence.

Unfortunately, I am quite pale, but my hair is long and black, with naturally ocher eyes. It's quite strange; my hair always seemed to change color with the seasons. In the spring and summer, I was a golden blonde. Towards fall and winter, my hair changed from red to black. It changed early this year, never stopping for that striking, bold crimson shade. That was how I knew something was wrong.

I suppose it's because I am tied too closely to nature. After all, I was born and raised Wiccan, a pantheon that thrived in, worshipped, and took its energy in symbiosis with nature. I was a part of the oldest living line of Celtics; for all my talk of witches, I am one. It seemed everything about this heritage always followed me, as I lived in a town named Greenwich. I was arguably the most modern of my legacy, a true American of 22 years and living in the year 2010. I had seemingly only one person in my life who cared for me, my Aunt Elizabeth. When I began dabbling in matters of the occult I was thirteen and from then on, my parents became wary of me. When I refused to stop, despite the fact that nothing strange or terrifying had befallen the family in these years, they kicked me out of their home and disowned me at seventeen. Thankfully, my beloved Aunt had set up a trust fund in my name, foreseeing this, as this had happened to her in her own adolescence and I made my own life from that point forward. Because of my family's hatred of me, I do not claim their surname; I am known simply as Eve. For my age, I must apologize for my pattern of speech. This is the effect of reading only the Necronomicon (The Chronicle of Death) and the Holy Bible. What a combination.

Never mind to me; once again I was always the one who was part of some sort of preternatural happenings, confused as a central figure when I was no more than a mere pawn in the grand scheme of things. This is about what was happening in this town, the day and the night of this holiday (or should I say, hallow day).

August was another person like me. He wasn't involved in witchcraft, no; it was that he was spiritually minded. He knew there were things in this world that we couldn't or shouldn't see, or that shouldn't be there. As with anyone so like minded, he thought about the application of the spiritual world to this one, with angels, demons, ghosts active in this world—as it truly is—and was burdened by it. He thought of it as if there was something he could do about it, sometimes as though it was his fault, that his mind had brought these things to life.

Like me, he lived independently, twenty four to my twenty two, with short brownish red hair that was bone straight. His eyes were a strange chameleon shade, appearing blue and green only to become a greenish yellow when he turned, to become a gray blue in the light.

He was affected by the spiritual world as well. Every house he had lived in since his childhood was haunted. He always remembered nightmares, sometimes waking to find his whole house rearranged, everything placed upside down or at obtuse angles. Other times shadows followed him, shadows not his own. His parents had both died when he came of age. His mother had been committed to an asylum for admitting to seeing demons, and upon her release committed suicide. His father was discovered on his bed, bloody and as if he had been murdered, though no one had been in the house but the spirits believed to haunt it. Considering all that happened to them, and that in the six years there had been no justice, August knew the murderer was not one of flesh and blood. He knew the one who had killed his father was just one of many evil spirits that had surrounded them for so many years.

They hadn't quite stopped, his nightmares and these hauntings, but it seemed narrowed to only one now, and though he shouldn't have to live with that, it was much easier than dealing with several. His little sister stayed with him too, as she had been left behind in all of this. Legally he was her father and guardian, but he did not want, nor could he quite enforce such power over her. Instead he remained her brother, as he always was, and she seemed to take to him more for that. She was so lucky, nine years old now, with nothing haunting her. He intended to keep it that way, looking at her and smiling as they shared breakfast that morning.

It was the morning of Halloween, and his sister was dressed in her costume, a black and red dress styled after medieval ages with a long, red wig that seemed a bit upstaged by her blonde hair that peeked from it in places and hazel eyes. She was nine now but seemed as messy as a toddler, eating a strawberry pop tart and smiling back at her brother.

"So, when people ask you what you are, what are you gonna say?" he asked, keeping his spoon motionless in his cereal and looking up at her.

"I'm a vampire princess," she said, stopping to hiss, strawberry jelly around her mouth. They both laughed, and knowing it, she took a napkin to her face, wiping it all off. August looked at his watch and her.

"Time to get going," he said. She nodded, grabbing her other pop tart and her backpack, August behind her as she walked out the door.

In minutes, they arrived at her school, through streets that though modern still held an old air about it, as one of many places known to be run and lived in by "old money". The trees all had red and yellow leaves on them, and both of them looked at it, how beautiful all the color was as leaves fell around them during the drive. He drove a white mustang, possibly his only pride and joy despite a broken fender that needed to be fixed. She opened the door, unbuckling her seatbelt and getting out. August watched as she walked along, as other kids greeted her, wearing costumes too.

"Bye Elise! Love you!" he called from her window.

"Love you too," she shouted back, turning around to wave. He waved again with a smile, and after watching her for a beat pulled away. He drove home slow, now that the only thing keeping him happy there—Elise—was gone. It was lucky that it was daytime. He had many things to pick up now, in preparation for this day. He had no decorations up, let alone candy. If nothing else, he needed to get out, and after only a few minutes at home, he did.

That was something I needed to do, get things to prepare for this day. Who would think that someone like me wouldn't be prepared? I only had one thing to get, and it was neither candy nor decoration, nothing so superficial. It was something I had to have, and it couldn't wait. It had to be tonight.

Despite how I talk, my history, my legacy, I was fully assimilated to this time and place. I dressed the same as anyone, in jeans, screen tees, tank tops — everything. Unfortunately though it seemed I had nothing but time on my hands, time had gotten away from me, and my entire wardrobe was dirty laundry — except for one thing. My black robe, yes, the traditional, archetypal black velvet robe that dragged the floor with long flowing bell sleeves and a hood.

I kept it only for ceremonial purposes, and it was more of a necessary part of my closet than anything. I didn't have to wear it, didn't want to wear it, but I very well couldn't step out as I was, in a tube bra and shorts that barely qualified as any sort of covering. With a hesitant breath, I pulled it from my closet and pulled it on.

There were two things I wore at all times, my talisman and my pentacle. My talisman was more like a charm, a golden crescent moon less than an inch around on a thin, silver chain. I also wore my pentacle, five point star in a gold that had an uncanny black sheen, an inch and a half around on a thicker gold chain. Together they brought me tangible power when needed, and though with any other outfit they might be taken as normal jewelry, in combination and with my robe it would make what I was — a witch — obvious. Despite the world's new fangled acceptance of various belief systems, including my own, I wanted it private. Just because witchcraft was legal now, it was linked in with other things (Nazism, drugs, Satanism, ect.) that were merely accepted by law and not the people, and more misunderstood because of that. I wanted it secret anyway, as if it became known, every person to show me favor, every boyfriend, every friend, every acquaintance, would somehow apply this to me and our relationship, however long or short, in whichever course it took. I would naturally become a pariah, perhaps executed by those masses with no understanding of the general realm of the unknown, (and let me tell you, the unknown becomes interesting and full of wonder once you pass the point of fear).

In my favor, however, today was a day of costumes, and I knew it wouldn't be taken as literal as anyone who truly knew this secret about me. As it stood, the only ones who did were spirits, relatives and coven mates, the living of which were states or countries away. I didn't want to hide my charms, as I wasn't ashamed near as much as I was protective, and thus I did better with them showing, and I did.

When I left my house, closing and locking the door behind me, I could tell my outfit was shocking. I raised my brows at a pack of children about to leave, next door neighbors of mine. There were four of them; one was a boy dressed as a pirate, two girls dressed as princesses in matching costumes, and one as a witch, with a dress and a hat. I couldn't help grinning as I muttered, "Nice try."

I should've taken off on a broom for effects sake, but instead I got inside my car, a 1975 Buick Riviera, all black with a chrome grill, chrome rims, and a black snakeskin interior. Though I had never been one for cars, even retro ones, I liked it, saw the need to have it as if to counterbalance all the severity in my life and mind, the ability to take a calming drive in a low-rider. It may have looked as though I had customized it myself, but in reality I had only gotten lucky at an impound auction. I pulled off as they all carpooled, taking a final look at them as I headed to the store, the same one August headed to.

The store was as big as a Wal-Mart, and the heading was "All Things Halloween". I found it almost shameful, that such a large store was open for only one month, pertaining to only one day of it, only to close again and be useless until the next year came. As I went inside, I saw it live up to its name, with everything from jack-o-lantern candy buckets to costumes, to horror stories, make- up kits, Halloween cookies, and other endless decorations rivaling those made for Christmas. I shook my head at it all, bored of the day already. The lines were full, mainly adults with children. I simply headed to the side that seemed to be more of autumn decorations, with small scarecrow plushes, toys and pumpkins. I pulled one out of a heap of pumpkins in a large box, with others looking at me as I was the only adult there, costumed and without children, single mindedly headed there and nowhere else. I simply gave a split second grin as I replaced it and found another, a large one that was bigger than all the rest and carried it away with me.

Searching through lines was a pain, and rather than try to sift through which looked shorter I settled for the express line, with only two people ahead of me, each with no more than five items although the sign allowed ten. I closed my eyes and hummed silently to myself, feeling as though I was trapped in a cage in here, as if everyone's eyes were on me and refusing to speak to anyone until I was gone.

I opened my eyes instinctively as the woman in front of me headed on, now finished. I set my pumpkin on the table now, only one left in front of me. I was about to close my eyes again when I felt my talisman glow with energy for a spurt, telling me something I couldn't quite understand. I looked behind me a moment and that was the first time I saw August, wearing a white tee shirt, torn jeans and a brown leather jacket, hair a mess and yet still stylish. I gave him the same as the others, an artificial, momentary grin before turning away. That was when he spoke.

"So you're a witch."

"Yes," I said, rolling my eyes and seeming to rub my eyebrows but merely using this motion as a ploy to hide my face, embarrassed and yet fighting to hide it. "That is my costume."

"It's — very realistic," he added.

I gave another smile that seemed even more fake as I turned away. I felt like asking him if he was dressed as some drop out slacker, but that would have been uncalled for. "Thanks", I slowly gave, covering my face as I spoke through my teeth, smiling again for the cashier. If that was his way of flirting in some manner, he was failing horribly and would surely fall behind a grade or two.

She didn't even swipe my pumpkin, which had no tag anyhow, just typed in some numbers as I reached for my wallet. He reached for his in that moment, in the time it took for me to pay and pick up this large fruit. He got it, lifting up to ask, "So, are you chaperon—"

He looked up to realize I was long gone.

When I got home, the first thing I did was put my pumpkin beside my bed and sort my laundry. I tried to wait through the loads that were running, turning on my TV. As I flipped, it was nearly impossible to find something that wasn't some Halloween special, and I quickly turned it off. It got to me, that not only was this day so over celebrated, it was made through culture into a complete satire of the truth. As I waited impatiently and in silence for my loads to run through, my eyes were instinctively brought to my pumpkin. I shouldn't be wasting time like this, and so I moved for it.

I know it was a wonder, why I needed one. It was a similar reason that others in my neighborhood did so. I grabbed it and moved to my kitchen, setting it on the counter. I took a small sized knife from my drawer, pulling up a chair and carving into it. The scraps fell freely to the floor and Miles—my cat —began eating them. I smiled at him and he meowed back, licking at the pieces. He was all black, not much bigger than a kitten though he was fully grown, with yellow-green eyes. He was always like this, appearing only when he wanted as though hiding away in my house rather than being a resident.

I carved a face into it, but not in a normal way, chanting as I did. The eyes and mouth were oblong, shaped by words rather than made into intentional shapes. The true reason why jack-o-lantern's were made and placed around houses was to ward off demons, namely the great pumpkin, who was the worst one to appear on this night. His most memorable feature by those to ever sight him was his oblong shape: a large, oddly shaped head and a thin body that resembled tree limbs. It pleased and warded off because mimicry was a sort of flattery, a way of being revered and it served as a form of protection by witches and even merely the superstitious in earlier times, that seeing a form that was as terrifying as their own would ward them off. It was a tradition that was unquestioned and practiced through time with no knowledge of this fact. My lantern, however, would have a different effect. The candle I put inside of it was carved with this name, as his true demonic name was now lost from recording. This was also one of many candles I had made myself, a combination of yarrow and sage (yarrow to wage war against the spirit, sage to ward the evil spirit off) and lit the wick, igniting this combination and setting their effects in motion.

The words I had inscribed in it were Latin, a dead language that seemed to likewise only be understood and known by these sorts of beings. In combination with my chant and this candle, it would bring a curse on him if he indeed came near my house, just by looking upon it, just by coming close. I needed the largest one so that it would be easily spotted and send him and his minions away.

As with those who didn't know the truth about these lanterns, I did this every Halloween, like the others merely for the motion's sake, though mine had always been in fore thinking the worst case scenarios this night could bring. It had never seemed to be necessary before, nor did it have any effect, as all the other Hallows Eve's to pass were uneventful.

I sat it on my porch, only to realize how quick the day had gone by. It was about five o clock but looked to be nine, a dark sky. I watched kids run down the street, others gawking at me and my lantern. I just smiled at them as Miles brushed against my feet, purring.

That was when violent winds began, taking the leaves of entire trees as they blew. Miles hissed at the sky, pulling away from me and as I looked at the sky a white mist came from it, my talisman glowing red.

Of course, the color was to alert me of a spiritual presence nearby, though it never did distinguish good from bad. That was when I went inside, Miles behind me and running to my room. He stood on my bed, meowing at my mirror and coaxing me to follow.

The mirror seemed to be doing the same thing the sky had done, this white, cloudy mass moving on it, slowly forming a shape. When the image came into full clarity Miles ran off, and I stood looking at it in shock.

"Aunt Elizabeth," I breathed, unbelieving. The form of her that I saw was even more perfect than how I had remembered her, with long brown hair and blue eyes, maybe thirty years old, dressed the same as I was. She had been a solitary witch (one who practiced without a coven) like me, considered to be the black sheep of the family and yet the one I was closest to. She took me in as a protégé, teaching me everything I had come to know about the craft. She died in a train derailment ten years ago now, and though the others who died in this accident had died by injury, she seemed to have died in her sleep, so tuned with her soul that she released herself into the afterlife, or at least, that was how I imagined it. Seeing her reflection then, knowing she had transposed herself and had done this for me only confirmed my imaginations. I smiled as my eyes watered, trying to fight my emotion as I stared at her. Despite my shock I knew it was her, as we were too close for me to be fooled by some evil spirit's interpretation of her.

"I know you've missed me, I've missed you too," she said, smiling back at me as her own eyes watered.

"What is it like, where you are?" I asked.

"Peaceful," she started. "No fears, no worries, nothing negative," she finished, smiling again before taking on a serious expression. "I can't stay with you for long. I came here to warn you. As I'm sure you know, this Halloween is not going to pass as normally as the others have. This time, all the spirits are coming out from the shadows, more bad than good. You've been looking for a chance to use your gifts. Tonight is your chance."

"But why this time?" I had to ask. Why on this Halloween and none of the others.

"They come and go like this," she answered. "Some places have spiritual protection, others have none. Though you yourself may have this protection, your town does not, and by the nature of this day, the spirits can impose their will. This time, the balance has been broken, evil spirits unleashed. You have to do something Eve, and I have full faith in you."

Even though her explanation was short, I caught her meaning. There was an endless list of possible reasons why such spirits could break free from the borders of the spirit realm and this night had historically happened this way, with terror and paranormal activity at its height. The reasons for these portals opening were truly inexplicable and too depthless to describe or tell. The most that could be said was that on this night, the final night of Samhain, the gates of both heaven and hell were opened. It happened every Halloween, however the effect of the dead and demons being seen and unleashed didn't take effect in every place or on every Halloween because some places had angels to protect them, others light witches or past spells that had been cast, any number of mystical happenings to protect these places, or at these times, keeping its horrors unknown and its people safe. Greenwich had no such protection, and therefore we would feel this night's full effect. I was possibly the only thing standing between this town and utter chaos.

"Am I alone in this?" I asked. Were there no others like me, would I have to fight by myself?

"No. Your protector is coming soon, before it escalates. Don't be afraid. Though it may not look like it, you have me and other good souls on your side." I knew this, too, but the aid of good spirits did no good. They had no more power than whatever would cross through, no aid in any supposed battles that I imagined would take place.

That was when the image of her faded, into a white fog that dissipated almost instantly. Only a moment later though, I felt a warming presence around me, and I knew it was her. It felt like comfort, beyond a hug or loving words, bringing tears to my eyes until it left.

I sighed and wiped my eyes, getting up and knowing my role to play. My first concern was all the children who were out on this night.

Maybe a few minutes before all this happened, August sent Elise on her way trick or treating. He was hesitant, feeling something odd about this night himself and moving rather slow as he put her coat on her. She could see the worried look in his eyes and said something.

"August, what's wrong?"

"I'm just—worried—that's all."

"It's only Halloween", she began, sounding both shocked and exhausted, as though he might tell her no from his own fear.

"Crazy things happen on Halloween night", he began, kneeling down and smiling. "Even if they aren't ghosts", he finished, tickling her. She laughed and he stood up, handing her an empty jack-o-lantern shaped candy bucket.

"So you're gonna be back home by no later than eight, right?"

"But the other kids are out until nine thir—" she stopped, sighing as she looked at his stern expression, with a brow raised and in this way telling her he apparently didn't care about what the other kids were allowed to do. "Yes", she answered, sounding annoyed.

"Don't take that tone Elise," he said, giving her a look of his own. "I just want to make sure you're safe. Me, you, and Miss Blake go over this every year", he started, referring to the chaperone that appeared at the door, eavesdropping innocently and wearing a gentle smile. "When I ask for your candy, it's not so I can take some," he added. This was just another truth about Halloween, all the vile people putting poison and knives into children's candy. All the missing children, not to mention murders. He hadn't told her all of this, of course, but he had explained some of it, many times before.

"I know", Elise gave with a partial smile.

He smiled back, holding her a moment and reaching inside his pocket. He produced his cell phone, an iphone, and handed it to her.

"I know I don't usually do this, but I want you to keep this with you tonight. It's not like I don't know you've played with it before," he added.

"Okay," she said, taking it and putting it into her pocket. "Have fun," he added, smiling at his sister as she walked away, Ms. Blake holding her hand. He closed the door as they left, locking it and watching her for a moment through the peephole. He looked away and sat at the table, head in hands until he heard them pull away.

He walked to his liquor cabinet with a sigh, taking a bottle of Hennessey from it, a cup from the cabinet, closing them as he moved to the freezer, putting three ice cubes into his glass and kicking the door shut as he poured the liquor into his glass. He left the alcohol sitting on the countertop, drinking as he walked to the table and leaned into his chair, staring at the cup a moment. By the nature of this day most people were watching television, at least listening to music, but instead August sat in silence. One might say it was an effect of the demonic oppression—a feel of gloom and helplessness, fear—resounding in his house, but it was mainly him knowing that nothing would drown out the spirits following him, the tormenting poltergeists he'd dealt with for many years. He had gone to a demonologist at one point, and he told him of the many foul spirits that wandered in his house, told him that now he had to only one left. This spirit had been silent, unlike the others, and had he not been told he may never have known. However, despite the silence of this ghostly devil, he was indeed that, one that was infinitely more powerful than the others.

August put the cup to his lips again, getting up only to grab the bottle on the table, pouring and drinking another one dry. As he finished it, he heard a deep, menacing laugh.

"You know you can't drink your way out of being haunted, right?" it faded in, a voice that had only a semblance of a human one, sounding as if it were burned, a deep thunder behind it. August didn't even question the voice, just shook his head, facing it.

"Know that too damn well by now," he continued, pouring another glass.

"It's a good thing you're sitting down. About time I revealed myself," it continued. August looked away from his drink to see a black mist seemed to pile and form together, ashes and rags materializing into one. It slowly formed the dark spirit he knew had been watching him. He had brown and green skin, hollow black eyes and worn torn, black rags, sharp nails that were inches long and sharp teeth.

In all the time that August had been haunted, he had never seen one in the flesh. Never looked into ones eyes, never spoke to them, nor had he been spoken to. He stood, dropping his drink and closing his eyes. He faced the image of this demon, taking a deep breath. He didn't know what to say or feel in this moment, and it seemed as though the fear lifted, turning to anger. Still he knew it wasn't best to fight with this creature, knowing its capabilities and looked entirely calm, despite the fact that his heart was flipping in his chest.

"I didn't figure you'd scare easy, not after all the things you've seen, but I guess I was wrong," he continued, changing his form slowly with a glance at his arm. He became human now, giving himself fair tone skin, long brown hair and green eyes, his rags now a perfect robe now, looking to be Augusts own age. It all took a mere blink of time, and August took him in warily.

"Is this better?" The spirit asked.

"Why—are you—"

"I'll explain," the spirit began, waving his hand. August ran a hand over his face, cutting his eyes at it.

"You weren't one of the ones—that killed-"August began, only to be interrupted.

"I wasn't around then," the spirit knowingly answered. "And though I am far from innocent, I drove them out. Evil had done enough to you and your family," he added, looking somber now.

"And why would you even appear to me?"

"Something—strange—is going to happen tonight. All hallows eve will live up to its name, and you have to survive it. I enjoy your company too much."

"And you're going to help me?" He gave with a grunt, unbelieving and shocked at once. In retrospect, neither him nor I could believe he could even process or understand what this demon was saying to him, beyond the fear that made his skin crawl, the anger behind it.

"Yes. You have no say," He said, moving to August and holding him until he felt bound, until he couldn't move and the true demon flickered back for a moment. "Don't worry August, if I were going to kill you, I had decades."

He pulled August forward, hand on his head as he stared into August's eyes. It was like looking into the soul inside, and August could feel it too, this cold feeling. It wasn't until he met the demons eyes, fighting the urge to look away did he see this spirit too, a spirit of fire and darkness that was both chilling and marvelous. Soon the flames spread into August, inside and out, the darkness too. It felt like hot and cold at the same time, surging over and through him, until the spirit finally pulled away, a shell now. They both knew what this was, a power transference. He felt changed now, predatory, seeing and hearing everything with superior clarity.

"Don't fight this, August. It will be with you for a while. You need it. You can see me now, what I really am, can't you?"

He looked at the spirit, and it had reverted to its earlier form, though now it was without color, from giving his power. August nodded.

"You need this, if only for tonight. They're coming," he said, giving no more away and running from the house, moving in quick lines out of the house. Though he did not tell August what he meant by that, he knew, having this creatures power now. He could sense them, evil spirits coming. He could hear the spirits whisper in his mind, echoing. *Find the witch, August. She is the only one who can help you. Remember, your sister…*

His mind instantly brought up the image of me, and he knew it was what I was, the power of their minds communal now. He saw his sister, remembering the image of her as she left. He stepped into his lawn, listening to powerful thunder break free, lightning scorching the sky as winds moved roof shingles, trees bent by its strength. Rain fell heavy and hard, pouring from angry skies. He had no choice but to brave this all, and with a deep breath he cut his eyes at the town, to find us both. The fact that he had been haunted by and seen evil spirits before had only hardened him against fear he may have felt for them, making the terror of this night nothing new for him, and able to brave it without any fear.

The kids who were out at this hour were the trick-or-treaters, trick-or-treating being one more thing misunderstood by the masses. There were two origins of this practice. The first, most popular theory as also the most frightening, the idea that ghosts and demons initiated the practice, acting as poltergeists on this night, crying for either food, blood, or souls. Others also offered food to the spirits of passed loved ones. Costumes were worn to blend in with these spirits and therefore be safe. Of course, as time progressed the people poked fun at these traditions, thereby turning it into a more unholy day than it was to begin with. I'd known all these things, all these years, but it all came rushing back to the forefront of my mind this time, as these myths were brought into reality and application.

I rushed from my house to the children across the street as the storm worsened, now no trees held anymore leaves on their branches, as thunder, rain and wind continued to torment the townside. Entire roofs and some cars were being pushed now by this all. My hair blew all over as I rushed to the herd of children, whose chaperone called for them to come inside. As I moved closer so did she, until lightning struck a tree beside the house and it caught fire, falling near them.

Clear crystal in hand, I aimed it at this tree, which formed a shield of light that held the heavy thing up until I could get to them, holding them tight as I let the tree fall, away from it now. I released the children and a spirit followed, to them a black mist with a wicked, widening smile.

"Back!" I commanded, using my crystal again. Another hand and a short chant and its form began to burn inside and out, and it blew away.

I took a deep breath as the lady looked at me, giving both a shocked and thankful look.

"Get them inside," I answered and she nodded, eager to get them to safety. I handed her my crystal just as she began to leave. She looked at me, then the crystal.

"It will protect you. Put it on your door," I shouted over the rain, handing it to her as the winds continued to blow. She took it, running with the children inside, placing this trinket on the door mailbox. I sensed and watched more spirits move, looking around for others. I couldn't count the ones I found and helped, but the most important ones slipped away.

Elise was riding with her chaperone and the others back home when all of this began. It was determinism at work, as the lightning struck a branch and it fell on the road, driven over by Ms. Blake in her white Tahoe, six children in tow. The handling now seemed to be loose, out of control for only an instant as she quickly slowed down. The children screamed, all but Elise. Elise looked at her.

"What was that?"

"Flat tire," she said, putting it in park. She turned to the others. "Everything is gonna be alright. Stay in the car."

She got out and Elise took August's phone from her small purse, dialing as Ms. Blake walked to the trunk of the car, getting a jack and rolling her tire to the tire on Elise's side. As Elise dialed home on it what looked like a black ghost, a shadow passing by the car formed like a torn cape. She saw it but ignored it, hitting call, holding it to her ear. Another passed by and that was when Ms. Blake looked up, when all the children screamed again in having seen it. Elise just coaxed the phone to ring, and though August had left he had a feeling in the few moments just before it happened, rushing back into his house. By the time he was inside the phone was on its final ring and he picked up.

"Elise?"

By the time he picked up it was just in time to recognize the number and hear Elise scream, as the phone disconnected and the dial tone blared.

Ms. Blake seemed be having a seizure standing up but in truth it was a possession, and when she stopped her eyes were hollow and black and she was pale, now with sharp teeth, forming into a wide and haunting smile. Her head bent to one side, giving a burned laugh that released black ash. Elise beat at her door — which had child lock engaged — to no avail as it watched them. Elise quickly darted to the driver side door and got out, letting out the others. They got out and ran, as a woman called for them to come inside. In all my attempts to save these children it led to a sort of community awareness, she one of those that helped, a crystal on her door as well. They ran inside as the possessed chaperone howled and attracted more of her shadowy friends. She was the last left outside, after all the others ran inside, this creature and its friends swarmed Elise, cackling as they disappeared. The phone fell, broken now, the only trace left of her.

I felt terrible for Elise but I didn't know what had happened then, otherwise I'd have acted. I couldn't save everyone on this night, as much as I might want to. That problem was one of many to be solved that night, after another crucial part of this evening took place.

Elizabeth mentioned my protector, and though she kept it vague, open for endless interpretation, I knew what she meant. Every witch had a protector, whether a person or creature, whether for one night or a lifetime. I didn't quite know mine, had never seen him, nor ever been in any situation to need one. My life had been as mundane as any other, save the ability to have luck on my side in some cases.

After only an hour of this, I was tired, Miles walking circles around me as I entered my house, walking to my room. I knew I couldn't do this alone, that I hadn't even been through half the city yet, and that more would come. It looked like some hurricane outside and I felt as though I had been hit by one in every way, sitting in a perfect circle on the floor.

I knew it wouldn't be long before I knew my protector, saw him. Things were only starting to get bad, and Elizabeth had at least warned me. I took a deep breath, holding a hand over the wick of the candle inside this circle. It lit, and with another deep breath, I began my calming chant.

It was an old Latin chant Elizabeth had taught me as a child, one I used when unsure or frightened, to keep my own calmness and draw evil away. It was said as a song, its own slow rhythm from both my voice and hers and sounded more like a Vedic prayer than what it truly was. I closed my eyes, now in a calmer state as I continued to chant. As I did it was as if my senses heightened and I could hear this gradual growl, the sounds of running. I could see a wolf with red and brown fur, with perhaps an even more vicious look than the average wolf, certainly leaner and more muscular, with color changing red eyes as it bared teeth, coming closer. I continued my chant, and despite the fact that this should obviously terrify me, the fact that it hadn't stopped told me it meant no harm. At the same time, if this was what I thought it was, I should be. Blood was on its mouth, on its paws as it ran. I just stayed, chanting, until I heard a sound in the back of my house, a sudden movement. That was when I stopped, moving my hand from the candle and the light going out. The lack of light was no reflection upon the situation — necessarily — it was caused by me, but inside I truly did not know what to expect. That was when I heard it again, this hiss meshed with a growl, deep and powerful. I heard Miles as he hissed and ran off, and suddenly this figure moved closely, and I was too stunned by the sight to keep my eyes on it.

"Cute kitty," I heard her say with a soft Russian accent, giving a laugh and a smile as she moved towards the light. In my moment of shock she had transformed her shape, now a human as opposed to the wolf she once was. She had shoulder length red and brown hair, which seemed both wavy and curly, in a sensual, naturally voluminous style. She had a defined jaw line, sanguine with full lips, dark blue eyes and an olive skin tone, maybe a few inches taller than me. Her complexion left her ethnicity in question though I knew it to be her natural tone, when combined with her accent. She wore a red tinted leather outfit, fitting but not as if to cling to her figure, with fingerless gloves to match. She came to me, smiling and showing her fangs. She was wolf like in every way it seemed, playful and dangerous.

"I'm Idara, your protector", she gave with an inflection at the finish, mocking my surprise in this way. "I know, you were expecting a male", she said, moving even closer, slinking around me. "One who could be your savior, sweep you off your feet, woo you with strength," she teased. "I can do that as well as any male can," she said, running a finger under my chin and grinning as she rubbed against me. I sneered a moment, moving away.

"I'm not interested."

"I'm fucking with you, Eve", she began with a laugh, now clapping her hands as she laughed, holding her hand over her mouth a moment and taking a deep breath. "You are too serious. You wonder why I never come around", she sneered, touching one of my books. I couldn't help looking at her still red lips, her hands.

"Why are you — "

"Oh, I'm sorry," she gave, licking her lips and her hand now, smiling after deviously. "No need to get up in arms. The man I fed on was one of your worst killers, no match for me," she added, lifting her brow a moment. I didn't need to ask what she was; she was one of the wolven. They were wolves in the shape shifter, animalistic sense, but with a highly vampiric nature, and in their human forms easily mistaken for their counterparts, the vampires. After all, they were part of their origins, and wolves had always been predators. "Before you start to think that I came here for introductions sake, let me remind you, I had to fight my way here," she added, giving me silver eyes.

"I need time," I said, looking up at her and knowing her meaning. There was more to be done I knew, her appearance seeming to stand more as a reminder than anything. She nodded, grabbing the remote and turning the television on.

As she did I could hear the static of the television set, as it became snowy and eventually cleared. Miles returned to the room, meowing and hissing at Idara again before receiving another low hiss and becoming silent, moving away again slowly. I took out all my books of spells, every item I could think to, head in hands. It seemed like a lot was riding on me, but in truth, it was me burdening myself with it, knowing that it wasn't fair for me to have such power and never use it the right way. I couldn't let these innocent people come into terror, harm or evil when I had any power over it, but in those moments I felt so lost, feeling that I had no more power than they did.

It was then that the television screen finally came into clarity, a news channel that played as I gathered my thoughts.

"As you can see, tonight we are experiencing a tropical storm. It seemed to drop in early this afternoon, rapidly progressing within a matter of hours from Connecticut all through the east coast."

The news broke away from the weather, as another newscaster appeared on this screen.

"Breaking news, just a few hours ago in Greenwich, Connecticut, there was a murder. It was a high school sophomore, whose name is still being withheld pending further investigation. The murderer is unknown, and the witnesses had this to say…

I could hear the change in voices, as an older man spoke. "Thing I saw go in that house — it didn't look like a man. He looked all — emaciated. He looked — like a man but I know he wasn't. He looked like a ghost or something."

"Greenwich police have been on patrol tonight, and with the weather also in mind, we have been urging everyone to stay indoors, as several accidents and power outages have been reported. Eyewitness news, we'll keep you posted."

And suddenly, all the lights went out. They went out slowly, around the city as I looked out through the windows and doors of my house, knowing what was coming next. I rushed back to my room, grabbing two crystals from my dresser top and putting them into my pockets, holding my talisman close. That was when Idara got up, smiling.

"About time," she said, changing forms, becoming a wolf again. She appeared at my side in her fearsome, true form again, the transformation taking less than a blink of time, impossible to describe or see in such a vapor of time. I couldn't help admiring it a moment, her bright coat and the muscles beneath, this vicious yet magnificent creature. It was only long enough for me to open the door, feeling shock with a calm exterior as I looked upon my neighborhood.

Every house looked haunted now, some roofs gone, some homes dilapidated. It gave the town a look of a ghost town, as people ran or drove off. Idara and I weren't the only people who could see this, the town and the spirits at work there, but we perhaps the only ones to face it. The veil that kept the sight of this other world was gone now, worse for it.

These hallows floated around us. Some had wings, creatures that looked like some cross of demon and fairy, some beautiful, others grotesque. Their appearance only solidified the tales of fallen angels as demons. But these weren't the only things we saw. The dead were there too, one I passed that had an eye missing, the other a cataract with only one leg, half of his body and clothes burned. He could see us too, lanky and decrepit, and howled at me before walking on. Idara growled, wanting to attack, but I reached for her, brushing against her fur. He meant no harm and sadly, he was just one of the damned that had come into our world. He wasn't the only one. Another walked beside a house across the street, an old woman with a grey mist around her, looking at us both with a depressing face and floated away.

Idara growled again, standing on her pincers, baring teeth. I could hear her heart pounding away. I could hear her whisper in my mind… *They're coming.*

It was a pack of demons, howling and bringing the stench of brimstone and death. There were two hellhounds and three soldier demons. The hellhounds were mutated mastiffs, glowing red and singed with black tar, growling at us with shark like teeth. The soldier demons looked like imps, without wings, toothless and with long nails and tongue that dragged the floor, black, burned skin and bloodshot eyes. I held my talisman as I faced them, shooting a beam of light at them. It failed, turning to darkness as they headed for me just as Idara acted. She pounced them, one after another, clawing at ones throat and cutting his head free, biting into another's chest and spitting out his heart. The hellhounds she fought, seeming to glide over one, to bite one's underbelly and fling him into a nearby house and into a fire. The other tried to pounce her in that time but she switched forms again to become human in what seemed like less than a split second, flipping under the other hellhound, and suddenly holding a knife to his throat, holding him immobile with another and in a ripping motion tore it apart.

All their ashes began to pile together, blowing away like ash and dirt. I should perhaps be more terrified by the actions of my counterpart, but I was thankful to have her.

"They call me and my kind demons," she began, scoffing and twirling her blades. It was just as she said that we both sensed it, more of them coming, attracted by our battle. She threw two blades in that moment, hitting two dead on and causing them to become ash, bringing out two more as she glared at them, shifting again. I reached into my pockets, a crystal in each hand now as I took a deep breath, whispering the final bit of my earlier song as I looked up at them, all around us.

It was then that the crystals began to glow through my robe, turning it white now. The energy moved from them into my hands, from my talisman too.

"Back," I barely muttered, holding my hands out, palms flat against the invisible wall I willed into creation, which became a blinding light around us in a perfect circle, burning the others instantly. They hissed from beyond the bounds of my power, and Idara growled her approval, seeming to smile despite her wolf form. I did too, moving forward and reflecting the light into an even wider circle, burning more. In anger and in challenge of this power they moved forward and I released my shield.

"Get them," I whispered, and without another word Idara ran ahead into the crowd of them. I stood there as the storm reached its peak, but I paused, a light coming out of my eyes as the rain paused a moment only to start again slowly, thunder following.

They began to shriek, as the rain caused them to burn as Idara ran through them. They were weaker now, in this pure rain as it stripped their power and their energy, causing them to slowly run part from the two of us, eventually running. Idara looked at me a moment, as my eyes returned to normal. Though it seemed like she was expressionless, it was one of feeling calm. I looked at the skies, how soaked we both were, taking another slow and deep inhale. Both me and Idara looked up to see a stranger approaching us.

We could both sense something in him, and as he walked to me Idara shifted once again, standing in front of me and meeting his eyes in her human form. He didn't look like one of them at all, neither the dead nor a demon, but he wasn't quite human. His eyes were a perfect, translucent emerald that became red with a change of expression in his face.

"You're one of them," Idara breathed, moving closer. "You smell of demon." She paused a moment, looking back at me and drawing her blades.

"No," I said, moving forward and studying him for myself.

"You're Eve."

"Yes, I am. Who are you?" I posed, raising an eyebrow.

"I'm August," He returned, in the same biting tone that I had given him. "I was told you could help me."

"Sure," I answered, walking back into my house. I didn't ask him anything then; I would give him an interrogation once we got inside. Luckily we hadn't moved more than a block away from my home, and when we got inside I shut the door with a wide smile. As the three of us made our way in, I lit more candles, same as the ones inside my pumpkin. I lit one and moved it to the main room of my house at a window, pulling the blinds on the demons calling my name in haunting voices and growls, so as not to have my attention diverted. Scare tactics were no match for me, the fact that I had dealt with such things before. Apparently the same principle was at work in August as well, and went without saying for Idara. I lit several, posting them different places before moving into my bedroom. August followed and took a seat on the chair in my room. Idara leaned against the wall beside me, glaring at him.

"What do you need from me?" I asked, looking into his ever changing eyes.

"I need to find my sister," he said, looking back.

"What's her name?" I asked, getting up and heading into my room. He somehow knew to follow, Idara behind him.

"Her name is Elise."

"Elise — ?" I gave, standing and facing my mirror, needing the last name.

"Merove," he hesitantly finished.

"I looked into it, closing my eyes and meditating. Mirrors were multipurpose: sometimes they projected the image of spirits, such as it did with my aunt, other times to conjure images of people, ghosts, places. Slowly it became black, filling with what looked like smoke, only to become white and blue, still giving nothing back.

"Elise Merove," I chanted, continuing to seemingly mumble this name into the mirror. It was as if all the images moved at heightened speed as I carried on, repeating her name over and over. Both August and Idara seemed shock by what they saw, images of old women, dead women, young women and children passed by the second. It was as if a part of my mind continued chanting, these words echoing seemingly through both the mirror and the house. I broke away and my voice somehow continued in this reverb, opening my eyes a split second.

"What does she look like?" I seemed to shout, not losing focus on what I was looking at. I was so sucked inside that for a moment everything in this world seemed to slow, and as he answered it became a whisper in my mind...*Blonde hair, hazel eyes, four seven, pale, freckles...*

And then I saw her. The mist around the mirror grew at this moment, as if not only was the other side pulled into our world, we were pulled into the other side. The image that I knew was only on the mirror was now superimposed into my room. We all three saw her, walking door to door, saw shadows slowly move behind her. It quickly moved to the flat tire, to Elise trying to call home. You could even hear the phone ring, her panicked breaths, and Ms. Blake becoming possessed. It moved in slow motion as the spirits gathered around her, taking her away, and this vision stopped as the phone dropped from her hands, breaking.

The trance of all this power fell from me and my room was normal again. I looked behind me to see August both shocked and angry, looking back at me. I moved away from the mirror slowly, still standing near it a moment.

"Where did they take her?"

I couldn't even look at him. I had to close my eyes myself, knowing how I would feel. Though at the time I was unaware of what their relation to each other was, I could see enough of her in him to know. I didn't need to ask, knowing that he felt such emotion for her.

"To the underworld," I answered with glazed eyes, looking into his eyes for only a second. "I'm sorry," I added, sighing.

"How do we get to her?" He asked.

"You want to battle your way through hell", I began, shocked. "Really?" I asked him, looking in his eyes.

"We both know she does not belong there. And how do I know I can trust you, or that you had nothing to do with it?"

Idara moved for him, but I gave her a gentle glance, shaking my head. "Easy," I said, causing her to look away. I looked at him then, leaning towards him, holding the arms of the chair.

"If you were told I could help you and now you suddenly believe I am a culprit in all this, in your shoes, I would question the one who gave you such advice. While I may be a witch, you possess the power and quality of a demon. If we can't trust each other, there will be absolutely no peace tonight, no solution, and the powers that took Elise away will win."

He took a deep breath, running a hand over his face. I moved away then, to sit on my bed.

"We can help each other. We don't have to go to the underworld to find her; the underworld is here now. We simply have to find our way to her," I finished.

"And to do that means more fighting," Idara added, eyeing him but deciding to give him her trust too.

"I'm game," he answered, meeting both our eyes. By now the rain had stopped, and I knew it would make it harder for me to fight. I could manipulate the rain, but I couldn't cause it. Still, I had plenty of tricks up my sleeves, not to mention Idara, who looked at me as she sensed my doubt. I gave a nod, moving out of my room, through the front door. Idara and August followed. We opened the door in time to watch the spirit of what was only known as the great pumpkin, looking upon us both and the lantern, burning inside and out, screaming and seeming to separate as he did. It reminded me once again of the power I held and I smiled, leaving now.

I don't think it would be fair to say there were more hallows out and about than before, I was just more aware of them all. The damned that roamed aimlessly seemed to remind me of all the ways there were to die. One was only a torso, moving on its hands along the road. Another was headless, holding his head in his arms as he walked along. A third looked like a tragic burn victim, a woman that was barely recognizable as such and could easily be mistaken as a demon, muttering to herself. Yet another had an open chest wound, showing his literal heartlessness. While many of these I saw were streets or houses away, a woman passed us by. She looked normal until she passed and we saw the opening in the back of her head, brains blood and worms oozing from the wound. A younger man, walking along the sidewalk had been scalped, looking as though dried blood served for hair. One farther away looked as though he had been whipped to death, bloody lashes over every inch of his body, a chain dragging from his leg as he walked.

"Are you sure we shouldn't attack them?" Idara asked, growling her question through her teeth.

"Leave them be," I answered, though I couldn't help being unsure myself, as a feral looking corpse of a woman dragged on slowly behind me, with a face that looked to have been scraped off. As I watched her she watched us too, seeming to react to our conversation, moving her neck in a snakelike motion and giving a low howl as the others moved away, her as well.

That was when another soldier demon appeared, larger than the others and with burned wings. I met his eyes and he howled in a deeper and yet shrill voice that brought more demons of all shapes and sizes, at least a dozen more. It seemed to laugh at the three of us, moving towards me.

I held out my hand, shooting light through him that coursed its way through him slowly. Idara attacked just as it began to work its way through him, cutting his head free as August took out a sword. My eyes had passed it over earlier, worn on his belt and he was dressed nearly the same as the first day I saw him but with a longer black coat.

As the others moved closer Idara became a wolf again, advancing on them with August following her with uncanny speed that left a trail of darkness behind him as the two battled these forces. Lighting struck two trees at once, causing a fire to start around us. Though I was worried for the town catching fire, I was more worried about its ultimate fate. That was when I looked at them in the fray and stepped forward.

The burning light was building up inside me with every breath but I didn't release it yet, continuing my walk to the center of the crowd, August and Idara now fighting around me.

What are you doing? Idara growled in my mind, still battling.

"So long as I know what I'm doing, you don't need to worry", I answered, cutting my eyes at the ghouls around us.

I outstretched my hands, forming a perfect line of light that cut through them. I clapped my hands together and the ripple effect of this power caused a transparent mushroom, the light and darkness coming together and exploding, causing them to implode instantly. We all took a deep breath in that moment, as we watched them blow away and others run closer.

It was then that I heard this crackled howl mixed with a shrill, behind it a thunderous sound that likewise affected the storm around us. It was then that the demon parted seven ways, from this voice that rivaled all the rest. Spiders and serpents came with them this time, two more hellhounds, seeming to part from the orange horizon, given a dark blue backdrop by the night sky.

The spiders looked to be crossed with scarabs and scorpions. The hellhounds looked twice the size of the others we'd seen. The serpents looked even exotic, despite the fact that they looked decayed and had no eyes. There were cobras and mambas, even a few boas. All of these moved around the center of this spectacle, a sight that caused August to drop his sword, his heart seeming to stop to a dead halt.

In the center of all these creatures was Elise. She wasn't herself though, the image of the demon so strong that Idara moved forward and I had to use all of my energy to hold her back. Elise was in full possession, eyes now entirely red and lined in black, long nails, long, pointed teeth and decayed skin. Whichever of the demons that was inside of her seemed to be leading these creatures along.

Just as many demons, this one surely took pleasure in human pain, fear, and emotion. It seemed to tell us that, playing a truly wicked game by taking her form and using her against us. Tears welled both August and my eyes but we stood our ground.

That was when the spiders came to us, climbing over us. August and Idara fought them off, as I did. I picked them away, and though they seemed to be leaving my two comrades alone they continued crawling over me, a snake finally working its way up my leg and around my neck. When Idara came for me it pulled on my throat harder and finally stopped, Elise meeting eyes with us.

"Is this the child you're looking for?" It teased, meeting both our eyes. It was a corrupted version of Elise's voice, a hoarseness to it. It laughed, pulling the snake from my neck and meeting my eyes, projecting flames inside me. It had an effect, burning me, the spiders pinching at me as they climbed over me again. Idara moved forward and I couldn't hold her back from her attempted attack, shifting forms in midair to strike him with her talons.

"No," August breathed, jumping in front of her and managing to toss her aside. She shifted human again and gave him silver eyes as she seemed to advance on him, taking out her blades and bearing her teeth in reminder, looking again towards Elise.

The spirit smiled, holding my face now, moving it as easily as it willed and laughing.

"I can see I'm causing dissent," it began, looking at them as it held me. "I will give her back, but I need one thing in return."

"What?" August asked, moving closer to her. the demon smiled at his willingness and gave him an answer quickly, smiling even as it talked.

"I will leave your beloved sister, for the price of the witch's heart."

The witch's heart... a chant came from behind them from the other demons that were nearby. *The witch's heart, a witch's heart, Eve's heart...*

There were a million reasons for him to want my heart. The first, most prominent and obvious was that he was a demon, and irrevocably, ruthlessly evil. The second, which seemed just as obvious as the first was that I was stopping the madness he and what one might call his friends—the other demons—had caused. Third was because, of course, I was a witch. Though our history and rituals, and usage of our powers varied, the craft was originally intended for use against his kind, all to control spiritual elements for a greater purpose. What he might do with my heart—eat it, bleed it—use it to harness the power of my soul, to torture me, seemed not to matter in the face of the idea of me dying and it being removed from its rightful place in keeping me alive. It was a lose-lose situation either way, as because he was a demon, demons were known as tricksters, and I knew he had no intent to do as he promised.

Both Idara and August seemed befuddled in that moment and Idara focused entirely on August, what he might do. August struggled for the moment, the concept of killing me and giving this devil my heart for his sister, despite the fact that she was his sister. However, at that moment I was willing to give this of myself. The demon holding me projected images of my worst fears the entire time, an early death, a possession, a fire, any and every terror one could imagine. Though it may seem a hyperbole, these images were burned into me for those moments. I felt like maybe death was better than being here, maybe being in hell would make hell less terrifying. August inched closer to me, sword in hand, and I took a deep breath. Idara shifted her form again, moving closer to him. It was in this moment that I realized that without me, all this was a stalemate. It wasn't with a sense of conceit, it was knowing I could do something, and something had to be done. There was always a loophole, and I found one that thwarted having to go through his promise, and without harming Elise.

I pulled away just slightly, looking at Idara and telling her mentally what my plan was, in the blink of time it took for her to move him away from me.

My hands turned white again, as the spiders formed whole demons and the snakes as well, the hellhounds into a wolf that rivaled Idara. This was because they sensed what was coming, though there seemed a Mexican standoff for a moment, all of us facing our enemies. Elise's demon manipulated her neck, causing her to look at me fearfully as I lifted my hands from hers, light running in them.

"Fight fire with fire," I muttered, holding its head as though to meet its eyes, as the white energy took the form of blue and white flames against the red ones all around the creature. I held her, and I could hear Elise scream from inside this creature for help, only for the demon to try and attack, using her again. As I strained to hold her still as the others began battles with the spirits around them, beginning my chant.

"Separate, penetrate, fire for fire. Light for dark, dark for light, make it right, make it right. Separate, penetrate, fire for fire. Light for dark, dark for light, make it right, make it right..." I don't know how many times I said it before it all seemed to run together, as a bloody, hellish battle happened behind me, even as the wildfire spread all around us, circling us. My spell indeed had an effect, causing what seemed the reverse effect of what happened to August, the demon now assuming an angelic form through Elise. It seemed like pain and terror for him, and it was, as just as vile as they were to heaven, heavenly things were vile to them. It shrieked at me, and I met his eyes.

"Just as you hurt good, good hurts you. I can make this your true form, Kafziel!" I shouted, knowing his name now. With all the energy flowing through me, a psychic link had seemed to click on, allowing me this knowledge. It was easy for me to ignore and continue, having felt this before, and I shouted, without pause, "Release the child!"

It gave some sort of bellowing howl and the fight seemed to get more vicious behind me, the other spirits acting to help this demon. I chanted again, holding his eyes and he held its head, crying out in a demons voice in agonizing pain from the pure flames against him. "Release the child!" I shouted, breaking my chant again.

It reacted violently now, shaking and seizing, black ectoplasm oozing from its mouth downwards. Its head shook faster, coming against me and turning demon through Elise somehow. This demon had to be seven feet tall, a cross between the great pumpkin and one of the fallen, shrieking and shaking only to come back to her size. I continued my chant in this time, watching this and knowing it to merely be resistance to my power, but certainly hurting him until he did bend. Just as he reached to rip her hair I aimed a hand over hers, then over the other, seeming to hold him in a force field of light.

"Release the child!" I called, the white flames now coming out of my mouth. In that moment, his flames seemed to mix with the darkness, all cut through by my light and coming out through her mouth in its full form, burning and screeching at us as he fled.

When Elise fell limp August caught her, holding her close, pressing his face to hers. She was breathing slowly, holding him. She was in such shock that she was nearly stiff, clinging to him, shivering and crying. I could hear him mumble sweet words to her as he rubbed her back. "It's okay, I'm here. This is all a bad dream, but I am here..."

"Thank you," he said, looking up at me. I just nodded, without enough energy now to say anything, dizzy myself. All my power was now gone, my eyes their natural color again. I was no longer glowing, and my gown returned to black when the spirit had lifted. Idara moved to me, touching me in her human form again, looking at me with a worried expression. My hands were shaking, I was sweating, and my nose was bleeding, dripping on the ground as I stood.

"You need rest," she said, and I could barely make it out over my headache.

"We both do," I said, wiping my nose with a pathetic motion as I looked down at Elise. He stood, still holding her, and the three of us moved back into my house, the damned screeching at us a moment.

She looked back at them as we did, growling. She held the door for the both of us, locking it as I sat at the table in my kitchen, holding my head in my hand, taking slow and deep breaths.

"Too much, you've done too much—"

"I know," I replied as I glared at her, my nerves on edge in all of this. I didn't need her to tell me, I knew. People believed that the powers a witch held were from sacrifice, but it wasn't always so literal. Power required power, and all the energy I had exuded was a piece of mine, energy I couldn't physically expend in a year. It was my energy that I gave up in return for the kind that was spiritual, now weakening me to a point of near uselessness. I looked over at August as he held his sister, rocking her in his arms and looking more like a father than an older brother. I gave a brief smile at the image, getting up and going into my cabinets. I took out a jar of ground lavender, with the look of a purple spice. I grabbed a plate, pouring some into a plate, holding my countertop. "Lay her on the couch," I advised, picking it up and following them. He laid her there, and I grabbed a match, lighting it like a pile of incense. "It will give her good dreams, relax her," I said, looking at August and moving back into the kitchen. In the same cabinet was a jar of what looked like ground cinnamon, another with that looked like green cinnamon, another filled with green leaves. I took a cup, filling it with hot water, running through my remedy. I put a spoonful of each of these into her cup, stirring it until everything inside disappeared, taking it to August, who was still beside his sister.

"Sit her up, she needs to drink it," I said, sitting on the couch adjacent them with a lazy movement. "It will help her sleep, make her forget everything," I explained, knowing he had paused for this without looking, without the energy to move. As she drank it in a trancelike state, I looked out of my window with a deep breath, face into my crossed arms.

"You know she's not the only one, right?" I asked, facing August again. He looked up at me as Idara shook her head with a sarcastic look, knowing it too. "There's dozens, maybe hundreds of children like her, women like her, men... everyone maybe. Others have been murdered by the dead. Have you seen *this* side of Greenwich?" I asked, bringing the gravity of this all to both of their attentions. Idara understood it better, but neither would have truly understood the devastation of what was happening without this inflection. Even as it may have been happening here, there was no count to the other places it could be happening as well. Sadly, I could only help the place that I was in of the many places this mess could all be possibly taking an effect on, and it frustrated me to no end. My bold, harsh voice and my statement weren't in anger at them, though they seemed to be. It was anger at the spirits, at the demons, at this damned night. Without all the pomp and circumstance that had been created in the beginning, about what really happened on All Hallows, I knew there would come a time when I would have to face it, and I hated it worse than I could have hated anything.

"So what are you going to do?" Idara asked, giving me golden eyes. I knew what she was getting at, daring me to find a solution. There was only one thing I could do at this point, and holding eyes with her I stood, moving into my kitchen again and taking a knife from the drawer, moving into my backyard and opening the patio doors only to instantly slam them shut once outside. I know I looked like an absolute madwoman then, moving with passion to the center of the yard and carving a circle in it, lined with a star. My hair was an absolute wet, tangled mess, my robe now singed, bloodstained and torn. I blew the hair hanging in my face away once finished, holding the blade where the moon was in the sky. "As above..." I stuck the blade into the ground, "So below."

Thunder crackled then, and I faced the north side of the winds. The call I made tonight wouldn't be like normal ones, praising the spirits, considering at the moment I wanted to damn them all for allowing this to happen. I held my composure, closing my eyes.

"Guardian of the north, spirit of the earth, you have shut your eyes to tonight. You owe me for saving you from total erosion," I began, with a glare, moving so that I was facing the south. "Guardian of the south, joy and fire, you have looked away too," I continued, quickly pivoting to the west. "Guardian of the west," I began, then facing east suddenly, "And Guardian of the east, you have also failed in the protection of creation," I began, bellowing. Even Idara looked at me in shock as I challenged my own gods. They were guardians, just as their name entailed, angelic beings. They had not guarded, and though they only worked their work in witches, like myself who called on them, if they were intended to protect, they should have protected regardless. Though to my knowledge Idara had only seen me once, I figured she had before, and she also knew that I had missed important pauses. Normally I would address each being once and with praising names, joyful, giving each their own span of time. Not only was I rushing through this ritual I had done it immensely different than any witch had done it. No matter whether or not I called on them happily or to the qualifications of a written ritual, they heard me. They gave me thunder for my anger but I did not stir, boiling in my skin. The sky was red now with a gray cloaking it, dark blue clouds filling the heavens, no stars and yet a full moon.

"That's right, you heard me. You have all *failed* tonight," I began through my teeth, lightning seeming to crackle through every inch of the sky, the damned now running as I pointed at the earth in my rage though looking up at the skies, where they were. "And you owe me, for still revering you, for taking up in what you didn't. You will give me what I ask, if you want me and your earth in one piece."

Thunder came and gave the effect of a vacuum with wind too, every element seeming to respond. There was an earthquake a moment—the north, fire swarming—the south. East and west came as wind and rain, until I heard all their voices as one in a booming voice.

"What do you want?" They questioned. "Ask."

"All the children, all the people, free from the chains of evil," I said, envisioning all the people who had been possessed. I could also see a white flash move over them. It moved then to three voices. "Yes."

I could tell I had been harsh in my approach, that they needed me to act, but at least my anger proved good. The quick pace seemed to make up for the fact that we didn't have much time to waste. I understood later that they understood my anger was with good intentions, wanting it fixed so badly. I answered, opening my eyes only a moment.

"All the damned and the demons, back to hell," I breathed.

Back to hell, back to hell, it whispered, and I envisioned the guardian of the south, a being made of fire that wore a robe, dragging the demons and the dead on chains and back through the gates.

"The fires...stop the fire." I said breathlessly. A being of rain obeyed and I watched him, seeming to fly through the city side and beyond, all fires waning. *Stop the fire, stop the fire...*

"Go on", the final asked.

"Everything as it was, all this mess undone and forgotten. Protect this with an unbreakable shield, and never shall these things happen in Greenwich again", I said, trying to remember anything I had left out. I saw a white mist move over the city now, like a line of snow hanging in midair, over all the houses as they slowly returned as they were before. I slumped to my knees now, and I could hear them whisper... *Not here, never again, forgotten and undone.* The storm stopped, wind, thunder and lightning, and I took a deep breath.

"Anything else?" one asked.

"Energy", I barely began with a laugh. "So I don't pass out."

I went inside and as I did the power returned through the city. I gave a smile at it, taking a deep breath, and looking back at the two who had gone through all this hell with me. Elise was snoring softly now, and as I closed the doors it seemed known by all that all this mess was done with. That in mind I could tell by August's expression that he felt out of place, picking up his sister.

"I'll take you home," I answered, still with a weak voice. I grabbed the keys from my wall and got into my car as he followed, sister in tow. Idara didn't follow and I didn't call her to my side. Once we were all in I situated my mirror, pulling out of the driveway. In attempt to thwart a feeling of dead silence, any remaining sense of horror in the aftermath of all this, I turned on my radio. It played the song, *Low Rider*, and though I couldn't help feeling that it was inappropriate to play, I let it. The feeling of joy and calm was one that we needed, both he and I mouthing the words low, smiling as I drove the streets. The homes were all normal now, the people in them sleeping regardless, us the only traffic. When I pulled to his driveway, he opened the door but stopped, looking at me.

"Something happened to me... one of them, changed me."

I sighed, not looking away from the windshield. "It's permanent," I said, turning to him. "But *you* have control of it. It helped save *souls* tonight," I added, looking into his eyes. "And the spirit who gave you this power will never come back, none of them," I added, giving a half hearted smile. He gave one back as he got out, going into his house. I got out of my car and stood, as I couldn't help feeling a bit on edge, sensing a slightly disheartening quality about this place as I read all the horrid things that had happened here as I looked on it, but they were all gone now. He placed her on the couch, moving outside. Just as I moved for my keys he was outside again, walking towards me.

"I know, we don't know each other, but everything —"

"August, I—"

Before I could finish he moved in and kissed me, and I kissed back. In everything that had transpired romance should have been the farthest thing from our minds, but we had indeed needed each other on that night. I had helped him, but the appearance he made reminded me of all the emotions I had lost in my years alone, all my disassociation nullified by empathy. He pulled away and so did I, smiling as I looked away.

"So, I guess, I'll see you around."

"Yeah, I guess so", I answered, moving away. He watched for a moment as I pulled off, all the weather slowly stopping now. He went inside and attended to Elise as I went back home, inside. I tossed my keys on my couch and laid on it lazily, holding my arm over my head.

"So, he gets a kiss and I get, what?" Idara challenged, moving from the shadows. I gave a short laugh and smile.

"Well you're stuck with me," I answered with a devious grin, relaxed now. "You've seen me naked", I joked.

She licked her fangs and laughed, moving to give me a hug. We needed each other too, I needed her protection, and she needed me to give her purpose. It should have maybe been a more romantic ideal than anything I felt for August, but of course, I saw her as she was, a guardian and a confidante. She released me, moving away.

"Get your rest. When daytime breaks, even the good guys will be gone", she finished, leaving me.

Though I lay on my bed, I did not rest until I saw this. Though perhaps I should have called for all the spirits to be returned to their rightful places, the righteous dead were different. At midnight they all moved, these glowing white spirits through the streets. These were the ones the people watched, as these angelic, loving spirits moved to comfort their loved ones, others simply smiling as they looked upon it all, as the bells for the vespers—evening church bells—rang behind them, giving this all only more of an effect. I fell asleep watching them pass through, as I saw Elizabeth smiling down at me.

The three of us were the unsung heroes of the night, the only three who would remember what happened. I knew Idara hadn't abandoned me, not by the comforting, low growls I heard as I tossed in my sleep. She would be there when I needed her, invisible in all other times of my life. The next morning it had snowed, and when I woke I danced in it, though it came early. Snow was a sign of purity and it formed perfect, quilted sheets in my yard, the rest falling slowly. This was sadly, my last day there, as I thought upon what the truth was.

Was all our fighting truly necessary? Would this power, these things only have happened on the evening of Halloween, to affect no other night? I knew it wasn't all a dream, and though I may have asked for this all to have been forgotten, it certainly couldn't be wiped from the minds of us three. Evil had left virtually no print on the town, life returning to normal as though nothing had ever happened. I knew it had though, and though it would never happen in Greenwich again, thanks to my spell, it could anywhere else.

If not only to leave the memory of this all behind I moved to Sacramento, California. August had moved there too, it seemed coincidentally around the same time, as though drawn by me. A year passed quickly, until it was Halloween again. Going through the same motions as I had dozens of times before, I stood at a checkout line with a large pumpkin. I had taken back to my lax attitude about Halloween, determined not to let it terrify or control me, as I had controlled it once already. I was dressed normal too, jeans and a tank top, hair red now. As the cashier punched in my total and told me, I quickly paid. As I returned my wallet to my pocket, she greeted…

"Happy Halloween."

"Halloween is never happy," I muttered, my hair becoming black again.

°About The Editor°

Nickolaus Pacione is the author of a number of short stories for two decades he's been writing horror fiction and in recent years Science fiction. Since 2004 he found his short story, Bite of the Spider, published in an anthology called Reality Check: An Anthology Of Horror, then he got published left in right in different horror magazines appearing on table of contents with authors Paul Melniczek, Terry Vinson, and Ken Goldman, then working with a host of authors in the small press on his anthology series, Tabloid Purposes, which he started his imprint on Lake Fossil Press with. In turn he got a novella published with Naked Snake Press, which was co-written by Canadian action novelist, Barbara Shenouda.

Pacione edits and publishes the magazine, The Ethereal Gazette, which he also publishes horror, science fiction, literary fiction and dark creative non-fiction. He got published in Diabolic Tales II, though he never got a copy of that book and did signings at Gothicfest, a festival in the Midwest which he will do from the time to time. In magazines he got published in the stories he wrote ranged from horror fiction to non-fiction with dark subject matter. He currently lives in the Joliet area with his cousin and uncle on his mother's side. When he's not writing he's also doing photography which he used a lot of his photography on the cover for Tabloid Purposes IV and the layout of the series itself.

More about his photography can be found on the website, located on this web address, http://nickolaus.deviantart.com and he edited six anthologies up this point then authored two short story collections, one novella, and one non-fiction book.

Pacione accumilated 30 credits in print and they're still growing. His appearences came from Withersin Magazine which gave him wider exposer in western Cook County then saw his work on specficworld.com with his Science Fiction. He's edited and copyedited all the anthologies he produced. He got his publishing history in print by publishing other writers and trade his manuscripts with them. If you, the reader wants to learn more about this triple threat author and publisher go to http://npacione.ulmb.com.